Airtight

AIRTIGHT

J. P. Smith

The characters and events portrayed in this book are fictitious. Any similarity to real persons, living or dead, is coincidental and not intended by the author.

Published by Thomas & Mercer
P.O. Box 400818
Las Vegas, NV 89140

ISBN-13: 9781612185668
ISBN-10: 1612185665

For Cheryl and Sophie, who matter most of all.

October 16, 1970

I T BEGAN AS A RIVER OF ELECTRICITY WORKING ITS WAY UP his legs, into the pit of his stomach, through his heart and settling in his head, where it would cook and bubble for the next eight hours, wreaking havoc with the primordial life that clung to the corners and corridors of a subconscious that had eluded parents, teachers, counselors, and physicians for all of his eighteen years. In time he would come to pinpoint it on the map of his life: it was sometime between "To a Skylark" and "Ode on a Grecian Urn" that he went quietly out of his mind.

Outside, the wind wove through the leaves and branches like fingers of bright tin, twitching toward a sky so azure that it became a line from a familiar song or a photo he'd seen a million times before. Messages were being sent to him from the trees, rumors from another world, telegrams in unfamiliar languages. Climbing the venerable old oak outside the window, a squirrel with a cigarette butt in its mouth turned to him and said, "Bird lives, man."

All the pointless details of his surroundings oozed with consequence, begged for interpretation: the chalk in the professor's hand, the brushed-chrome knob on the door, the tortoiseshell clip in the girl's hair in the seat in front of him. He drew nearer until he could see the individual brown hairs emerging from her scalp, a flake or two of dead skin, and wondered, if he looked any closer, whether he might see her skull and beneath it her brain throbbing with dreams of escape as vivid as his. For a moment he nearly put his hands on her to reach inside and take hold of what she was thinking, seize her thoughts and confront her fantasies in all of their wriggling, frantic glory.

Like soup left too long on the stove, the air in the room simmered up a texture, rippling as though thick with ghosts and lost souls, the echoes of those who had passed into some other world long ago. Sounds took on a hollow, uncertain quality; words lost their meaning. The faces of those around him faded into something he could only call the uneasy past: They were not where he was, nor would they ever be. They were a moment or two behind, then a minute, then five, ten, until, like passengers waiting on a railroad platform, they passed as a blur while he glided to his destination.

Man, he said to himself, who *made* this stuff?

The acid came by way of a friend back in the city who got it from a cousin in Long Branch, who in turn bought it from a guy he knew in Morningside Heights who imported the mixture from Greece, where a draft dodger ran a lab in a suburb of Athens; rumor had it that it was a mutated form of LSD-25 and thus unstable, unpredictable, longer lasting and a lot more interesting. Earlier trips—for he took these every Friday like clockwork, dropping his tablet just before his Romantic Poetry lecture—had been courtesy of Augustus Owsley Stanley III, whose purple pills etched with the caped crusader known to some as Mr. Man, first name Bat, could almost be considered dependable. Like ex-lax, they took effect when expected and achieved the desirable results without surprise or detour. You dropped it at two, by a quarter to three you were in Neverland, and when ten o'clock rolled around that night your feet were back on the ground and you were ready for whatever else you had stashed under your bed in the dorm—a little weed, a little speed, a puff of opium or two to get you into a mood of delicious despair. An Owsley experience was a trip in the way a subway ride to Coney Island might be to someone from the Bronx: a few hours away from home in a familiar place that flourished with a pleasing kind of decrepit madness.

This, though, was the Tahiti of acid trips. This actually took you places, and the rides were, well, *amazing*.

"In the summer," he said aloud, and the professor glanced up from his notes.

"Yes, Mr. Copeland?"

"I didn't say anything." Great: now he was narrating his own life.

The professor pushed his glasses up to the bridge of his nose. "Now let me see. If I'm correct, this is English 103, also known as Romantic Poetry. And you are Nicholas Copeland, who elected to take this course. With me so far?"

Many in the class, who were not, like Nick, in some other, higher dimension, had a nice little laugh at his expense. He nodded vigorously, as though deeply invested in the professor's every thought, and watched his world blink green and pink and yellow, traffic lights in a land of tangerine trees and marmalade skies.

"And we were just about to move on to Keats's 'Ode on a Grecian Urn' when you began to speak."

"No," Nick began to protest, when the girl with the clip in her hair turned and snappily said, "Don't you lie." Nick knew she was from Kentucky and expected not a lot more from her than a sassy mouth and a sneer. Now he was glad he hadn't probed her brain after all. God knows what he might have found in her bluegrass wonderland.

"Did you want to comment on the poem on page two hundred and fifty-six?"

"Oh no, I don't think so."

"Still with us?"

The professor, much beloved throughout the campus because he was a soft B-plus verging on an A-minus—especially if you were a basketball player, which Nick most definitely was not—despised Nick. He despised Nick because Nick was everything the professor, a failed writer of road novels, a castaway on the desert island of backwoods tenure, would have liked to be: cool, far out, most definitely hip. Nick wore Landlubber bell-bottoms, while this dude was sketched out in chinos and a short-sleeved shirt. At least the prof had a goatee, which was about as far as one could go on the campus of a Baptist college. To some it indicated a rebellious nature, a latent bohemian streak, while to Nick, who had a good read on this man, he was nothing more than a poseur. Because if he weren't, he'd be out on the road, eating peyote buds and drinking beer on his way to Mexico, wouldn't he? What may have stood in the way was the prof's wife, Margaret, sometimes seen waiting for him after his last lecture of the day, a fidgety, bug-eyed woman with a white handbag and nurse's shoes to match.

In the summer, Nick began again, this time without moving his lips, in the East Village mostly, and over the past few years, he spent his time like a bedouin, shifting from one apartment to another, picking up odd jobs along the way as he occupied spare mattresses belonging to his more settled friends, and being asked to leave when he'd overstayed his welcome, sometimes as soon as two hours later. He waited tables at the Eatery on Second Avenue until, stupefied by a pill someone had handed him by way of a tip, he slept through his shift two nights in a row and they hired another freak to take his place. He swept floors three mornings a week at Warhol's Electric Circus where, at odd times, Andy himself would stop by, usually in the company of one of the Factory kids, nod slowly to himself, and slip away quietly and unobtrusively back to the haunted blank sheet of his life.

The Owsley tabs came via Railway Express all the way from San Francisco. Trading on the street for twenty bucks a pop, they were bought by dealers in the Village wholesale and by the gross for a nickel apiece from a dealer known only as Superspade, who lived somewhere in the Bay Area. People took turns going to Grand Central to claim duffel bags filled with acid, handing in their ticket and hefting the bags onto their shoulders for the long, tense walk past the cops that always seemed to be hanging inside the Vanderbilt Avenue entrance where, especially in the winter, the heating vents were most active. Deliveries ended when Superspade was found stabbed, shot, and left dangling in a sleeping bag from the top of an oceanside cliff in Marin; though there was also a rumor back east that his torso was found floating in San Francisco Bay, and that every few weeks another essential element of Superspade—a Superhand, a Superleg—would bob up to be retrieved.

Nick's connection in Brooklyn, an Italian of Neapolitan vintage who had gone to college with him a year earlier and who, gently nudged out for being what the college called "socially unacceptable" (it was the machete he kept strapped to his Honda 350 that might have tipped things out of his favor), had returned to the havoc of Bensonhurst, would send a powdered version of the stuff in undetectable tinfoil packets, flattened and packed inside birthday cards designed for children, all doggies and ducks and bears and cowpokes. "Happy Birthday to a Special 4 Year Old!" Inside would be the speed or the acid and a handwritten note: *Say hi to the boys from me.*

He looked around the classroom and watched in wonder the professor's hand moving through the air, leaving behind it the shuddering contrails known to anyone who had ever taken

LSD or its equivalent. Class was over for the day, for the week. Ding-dong: magic hour had arrived.

"Mr. Copeland? Nick? A moment?"

Nick floated to the man's desk. He felt as if it had taken him an hour to reach it.

"You seem oh, I don't know, kind of…out of it?"

"I'm kinda tired," Nick said. "And I've got a…head cold, you know."

Everyone on campus was a narc, Nick knew, and though his friends told him this was the standard attitude of the paranoid drug user, he also knew that getting kicked out of college was one thing; getting kicked out of college and then ending up in the hands of the Allenville, Pennsylvania, sheriff's department would be the kiss of death.

The professor eyed him warily. Undoubtedly he noted Nick's dilated pupils, which always looked so much better on people like Robert Plant and Roger Daltry, a little stardusted as they stepped off their tour planes in photos published in *Rolling Stone* and *Tiger Beat*. But Nick didn't look as if he were about to spend a blissful three days in the arms of half a dozen groupies; he looked hunted, as if he knew even then that his days, if not his hours and minutes, were numbered.

"Maybe you should see the nurse," the professor said, and Nick just laughed, because, well, the nurse, that was Margaret, and she'd bust him but good after one glance at his face.

He drifted back to his cinder-block dorm room, with its Tensor lamp, KLH stereo and poster of Allen Ginsberg in an Uncle Sam hat, put Jimi Hendrix's first LP on the turntable, and lay down on his bed to settle in for the remainder of his trip. He held a hand out in front of his face, and though it was numb, though when he touched it with his other hand it was like something made of rubber, it shimmered like a bulb about to burn out, then—*zzzzip*—disappeared. He made a fist and it reappeared. *"Groovy, man,"* he would have commented under other circumstances, but something was different. He sat up and looked at the spinning record and it was no longer black; it was flesh colored and soft and the needle seemed to be carving canyons into it. He reached over and pulled the plug and Jimi sang, *"Manic de…press…ion…is…"*

"OK," he said to himself as he sat up. "Be calm. Be cool. Relax." He put his hands on his thighs and they seemed to sink into them.

Deep breaths. Nice thoughts: pretty girls, good music. Happy, happy.

Nick stood in front of the mirror mounted over his desk. His first twenty trips or so had been guided by one friend or another who knew what they were doing. But Nick was a pro by now, and this time, when things were starting to tilt into the Very Weird and Abnormal he had no one to count on; at least no one any closer than a specialist in freak-outs known as Magic Dan, who lived on Thirteenth Street and Avenue A, which required a toll call and a bus ticket. He lit a Camel and when he went to take a drag his hand blended in with his face and his cigarette fell to the floor.

He bent down to pick it up and when he stood he was gone. He had no reflection. He had disappeared. It was a completely finished hallucination, something brilliant and ingenious that he would have admired had he not been the object of it: All three dimensions were covered. In the mirror he could even see *through* himself to the furnishings behind him: the Jimi Hendrix record as it melted into the turntable; his bed, last made, oh, some three weeks ago. He was the haunter and the haunted, all at the same time. And then it came to him: He'd opened a metaphysical door and was standing on the threshold of his own death. He was both in a dorm room in Allenville, Pennsylvania, and in a place that was beyond time. One step and he would be gone forever.

This was the big one, he thought, the thing bands from San Francisco to London had sung about, that sacred texts had so reverently spoken of as something attainable only after a life—or many lives—of contemplation and abstinence; the state of grace that would change his life forever: the Clear White Light itself. At least one of the Beatles had been there (he could never see Ringo or Paul communing with the Great Divine, and as for John, well, that was anybody's guess); David Crosby had a permanent round-trip ticket to it, as though he had access to a shuttle between Times Square and Grand Central Nirvana; and the Velvet Underground, who wrote a song with nearly the same name, had achieved it through different means. But now he had joined the pantheon of the Enlightened; he had been ambushed by the One Magnificent Truth. It was staring him in the face, and his fate was sealed. He knew the meaning of life. He understood what people tried to say when they spoke of God. Kubrick's *2001* now made perfect, impeccable sense to him. All that was left was for him to step up to the window, crack it open, and let himself drop. He wouldn't die; only his body would be crushed and mutilated, but he sensed—no, he *knew*—he would live on somehow, and in that state, whatever it may be, he would be a force in the universe: a shadow in an afternoon world; a breeze that breaks the stillness of evening. He pressed his forehead against the cool glass and peered down to see not a monolith standing in a lunar crater but a red Firebird, a black VW Beetle, and the housemother's shit-colored Buick. One of them might be in for a big surprise.

But there was a choice. There was a choice, there was a choice, there was a choice, there is a choice, and the words kept running through his head as he paced the room and caught glimpses in the mirror of his not being there. He could live through this. He'd be damaged in some obscure way, he knew that much; he might end up in a vegetative state in an institution outside Buffalo for the rest of his days, dutifully visited by his aging parents each week until they ran out of money, time, and patience for the eight-hour bus ride from Jersey, or he might turn out to be a valuable member of society, brilliant and blazing beyond anyone's expectations, a kind of savior or prophet, a man whose eyes glowed with intelligence and insight. Women would flock to him, chauffeurs would open doors for him, he would walk on water, and, when he wasn't walking on water, he'd be counting his millions. The choice was his to make. And with that, death was off the table.

There was nowhere else to go but back to the beginning. He had to start all over again, this time from scratch. He was a baby in a bubble, rising up over Jupiter, far, far away from home. Cue the music. Bring on the awe.

But first he had to bang like hell on the wall and get some help.

A minute later, tears rolling down his cheeks, he heard pounding at his door. "What?" a voice shouted.

Nick opened his mouth but nothing came out, and when his door flew open and the guy from the room next door pushed his way in, Nick looked up from where he was crouching in the corner and said, "I think I'm losing my mind. I'm going to die."

All Nick knew about this guy was that he kept to himself, but that he was definitely not like the others, which made him more like Nick. He had hair down to his shoulders and his musical tastes, Nick could tell from the chaos coming through the wall at times, ran more to Three Dog Night and Iron Butterfly than the music Nick favored. This time he'd let it go.

"You overdose or something?" the guy said.

When Nick looked up he could see something radiating in the middle of the guy's forehead, a swirling mandala that branched off to connect with the mandala in his own head. Things—molecules, atoms, whatever—flowed through the air between them. "Whoa," Nick said. "Look at that. We're all connected. We're all one."

"Yeah, well, I wouldn't tell Stumper that."

Gary Stumper was a linebacker on the Eden College football team who had been kicked out of his fraternity and was now living in solitary squalor at the end of the hall, sneaking in six-packs of Pabst Blue Ribbon under his jacket when not submitting to prolonged sessions of self-abuse, heard nightly through the thin wood of his door.

"I mean it—we're all one, we're all joined up. I'm seeing it and it's like this great, I don't know, this great...thing, this big idea that holds us all together, I mean, I'm dead, man, I've seen it all, I've seen the light." A tear rolled down Nick's cheek.

"You are either definitely very fucked up or you're messing with *my* head, which is exceptionally uncool of you. I mean, you don't even know who I am."

"Just," and Nick slapped the floor a few times, "sit with me, OK? I've got to be watched. I might do something crazy. Don't let me out of the room. Or near the window."

There are three stages in a typical acid trip: the buildup, which is like the red carpet before an awards ceremony, when everyone looks pretty and you think you're God's gift to mankind because being high makes you, well, higher than everyone else; the ego death, typically a period of angst when you rail against your father and cry at the sight of family photos and realize you're not worth the paper your birth certificate is printed on; and the mellow period, when you can listen to music and feel the ice cream go down hot and skip in the park and make garlands out of wildflowers. Nick was obviously having the ego death to beat all ego deaths. His ego had died, his body along with it, and all that was left was the merest imprint of a life once lived—eighteen lousy years—which he was about to leave far behind him.

"You cool?"

"Did you just ask me if I was cool?"

The other guy nodded.

"Good. That's what I thought." Funny acid: this was a quick intense trip and it was already starting to wear off. "How long have I been here?"

"You mean since I came in?" He looked at his watch. "Five hours maybe? You got any food in here?"

Nick looked around. Where the window had previously framed a sunny afternoon it was now pitch black. Someone had switched on the lamps. "Five hours? Are you serious?"

"I've been sitting here working the whole time." He showed Nick a constitutional law textbook.

"Did I do anything...weird? Like take my clothes off or tell you things that if you tell anyone I will have to kill you?"

The other guy laughed. "My lips are sealed, my good man."

They sat in silence for a little longer. The guy said, "Where are you from?"

"Jersey, Morristown," Nick said.

"I'm from Montclair. Not too far, right?"

"Are you just telling me this to keep me from losing it?"

"Something like that," the guy said.

"Good. Keep doing it, because I think it's working."

Things were still radiating in the middle of the other guy's head, sending out a steady stream of whatever they were toward Nick. It was after eleven when they decided to head down to the student union for a cheeseburger. Nick promised he'd pay, recompense for the other's presence in his time of need.

"So what's going to happen now? You going to get all spiritual and stuff and give up dope and start walking around in robes like the Maharishi? Because I've seen you around sometimes and always thought you were kind of hip. Just hip in a different way. Not the robes kind of hip."

Nick hadn't thought that far ahead.

"Because I've got this big deal coming down in Cincinnati and I could use a partner. I'm talking about big money, man, once we sell the stuff. Like maybe even two thousand bucks?"

"I don't know," Nick said.

"Only cost you two hundred up front."

"Even split?"

"Hey," his neighbor said, "we're all one, right?" He put out his hand and Nick grasped it.

"What's your name again?"

"I never told you in the first place. Rob Johnson."

"I'm Nick. Nick Copeland."

Peace, said Rob's two fingers, as the two of them stepped forth into the future.

Thirty Years Later

1

WHEN HE WOKE THAT MORNING, IT WAS ABRUPTLY AND out of a dream he'd sometimes had over the years. He was sitting in a college lecture hall, and a man with a goatee and black-rimmed glasses was looking expectantly up at him from his lectern, as though waiting for an answer. Others, at desks identical to his, had turned to him, familiar faces with forgotten names.

Mr. Copeland?

Beyond the window the wind rose and rattled the leaves before everything fell still. He parted his lips, blinked his eyes…

And then it vanished: professor, students, desks, classroom, the view from the window. Something had gone very wrong between then and now. He tried to cast himself back to that room, that building, that now-nameless professor and the campus that had faded so much from memory. He had been there for only two years before being euphemized out of matriculation by being asked to withdraw, the same way people leaving government under a cloud always claimed they were retiring to spend more time with their family. Only some of it remained with him: the names of friends he'd lost touch with long ago; the bile-colored cinder block walls of his dorm room; the local restaurants that catered to the hungry young men and women of his college—Mother Hubbard's Pizza with its sad pepperoni specials and acne-ridden delivery boys; the twenty-four-hour Waffle House on the corner of Walnut and Franklin with the cherry pie that so magnificently sated three-a.m. munchies.

He sensed that something had happened there that had led him to this place, that had formed the soul contained within the body of a man for whom turning fifty was a mere two years away. Only a splash of dignified gray at the temples and a body passably fit from a sporadic regimen of racquetball, bench presses, and crunches stood between him and the past: years of struggle, success, and now failure—the exquisite bell curve of the twenty-first-century executive in a failing economy. Where might he be today had he taken another route? That was the question he always woke with, and, as in the dream, no answer to it could be found. All he had now were new questions. He had failed. He had lost his nerve, and he was paying for it with his life.

In digits big and bright enough to discern without his reading glasses, the sleek black Bose that Joanne had given him in the palmy days of his forty-fifth year told him that it was now a minute past nine. In a few seconds Carl Kasell would gently beckon him awake.

Silently, he counted three, two, one…

"And some say the Tate-LaBianca murders in Los Angeles and the Rolling Stones concert at Altamont brought the love-in known as the sixties to an abrupt and bloody end. We're reminded of this as Charles Manson, now sixty-six, enters his latest parole hearing today in—"

He hit the off button, rolled onto his back, and put his hand on the sheet beside him: neither Joanne nor the residual heat of her body remained, and when he held his breath and listened he could hear that the house was absolutely silent, save for the whispering waves of radon radiating up from the granite ledge beneath the cellar. The kids had gone off to school; Joanne had left for work. And on his desk in the little office he kept in the basement with its pool table and a wet bar that had shed all its novelty were the final notices from the gas, electric, and phone companies, a literate though unmistakable letter of threat from the head of the board of trustees at his kids' school, and worst of all a sinister, black-bordered notice from the people to whom his mortgage payments were now dangerously overdue.

He stood under the shower and thought that Charles Manson didn't have to pay for a roof over his head or the food that was served him three times a day. Charles Manson was never in debt and never would be in debt, except to society, who'd mostly forgotten he was still alive. Charles Manson had a private armed escort wherever he went. Charles Manson received fan mail from women who wanted to marry him and have his babies. Charles Manson was a crazy fucker, tipsy with demons, which placed him a degree higher than Nick Copeland, because Nick Copeland had had everything to live for, had put his family first (well, in a way, so had Manson), and had failed without even a hint of notoriety. There wasn't a speck of helter-skelter in this man's life. He had gone down quietly, unobtrusively, bloodlessly. Which of them, he wondered, was the truly free man?

2

"**I**'VE HAD THE CHANCE TO LOOK OVER ALL THE MATE-
rial you sent me, Nick."

Jeff Spence gestured toward a stack of documents on his
desk. He squared them up, then sat back to swivel, like a boat
bobbing in a gentle wake, this way and that in his leather desk
chair. A photo of his thirty-five-foot schooner christened *La Vie
en Rose* hung on the wall behind him. When he wasn't sailing it
he was treading the polished wood floors of what he referred to
as a bungalow and others might call a waterfront principality in
Mamaroneck. "I don't want to mince words."

"OK," Nick said.

"I'm going to be brutally honest."

"Good," Nick lied.

He swept his hand through the air over his desk. "Control
has been lost here, my friend. Something's gone seriously awry."

"I know, I know."

"How aware are Joanne and the kids of all this?"

"Joanne knows everything. The kids, well, they must
hear us."

"Fighting?"

"I need solutions, Jeff."

Jeff took off his glasses. He rubbed the bridge of his nose and stretched his arms over his head. Nick had known him since college. In fact, he had sold Jeff three ounces of fairly low-grade marijuana he and Rob had scored on the big deal in Cincinnati back in '70. No, that wasn't right. It demanded capital letters, as if this were the title of a film shot on the mean streets of New York. It was more than a big deal, it was a Big *Fucking* Deal—at least in those days—and even now, when in the odd moment of distraction he looked back on it, he recognized it as something out of the ordinary, especially for a couple of suburban college kids with nothing better to do. They'd made what they calculated to be a 300 percent profit on that transaction and the ten others they'd successfully negotiated in a student body more keen on drinking beer and reading *Playboy* than in expanding its consciousnesses. Jeff was a novice smoker, a pretender to the toke, a Doors fan who secretly yearned to be an accountant; somehow it felt like some sort of cosmic justice that he was now Nick's.

"And how are you holding up?"

"I have my moments," Nick said. "But I always clean up afterwards."

"Ready to declare bankruptcy?"

Nick just gazed at him with that look that Joanne liked to call "flinty," though in fact it was more of a way of detaching himself from the unpleasant side of life. He would move into a zone that put him beyond the reach of earthly concerns, and sometimes he wondered if it were a side effect of his momentous last acid trip, as if the reflection that vanished from his dorm room mirror lingered in some other dimension, and at times of stress he'd catch a glimpse of this double through a shimmer in the air.

"Nick?"

"Yes. Sorry. I was just thinking."

"You looked a little lost there," Jeff said. "So tell me." His grin gave it away even before he voiced it. "You still get high?"

Nick laughed. "Why, are you looking to buy something?" These days it wasn't too tough. You walked up Eighth Avenue and every third person was offering you something to smoke, shoot, or take to bed.

Jeff laughed. "We're all a little past that, aren't we?"

"I like a drink now and then. But I haven't touched any of the other stuff since college."

"Guess you'd had enough to tide you over for a few more decades. That last acid trip of yours?" He sat forward for emphasis. "You were a *legend*, my friend."

"Anyway, I got laid a lot." Amazing how eight hours of cosmic bliss could put a shine on your sexual charisma.

"Before then, no, right?"

"Before then never."

Jeff stopped bouncing with laughter. "You mean you were a virgin?"

"Weren't you? Oh no, that's right, you told me you'd lost yours when you were, what? Thirteen? How old was she? Twenty-three or something? Some sort of flight attendant?"

"I was exaggerating."

"And you did it in the plane's bathroom."

"It was a joke."

"I would say so."

"But you believed it, right?"

"Actually, none of us did," Nick said.

Jeff's smile fell. Happy accountant; sad clown.

"But we humored you, Jeff. Just as you humored us." Nick's story was that he'd lost his virginity while on vacation in Spain. The girl's name was Conchita Madero. She was twenty-two, Nick was fifteen, and they'd spent the night in a barn in

Ciudad Real, when he'd supposedly gone on a teen tour through Europe one summer. He had seen the name on a map and it sounded a lot more credible than Madrid or Barcelona. In reality, the closest he'd ever been to Spain was a great little tapas bar on Second Avenue.

Jeff sat back and swiveled a bit more. "Well. Those were the days, right?"

Nick had continued to have flashbacks to his legendary acid trip as recently as five years ago. At first they simply came upon him without warning. He'd be walking down Park Avenue, or raking leaves in his yard, or, years earlier, changing one of his kid's diapers—once even during a presentation before a team of clients, which he found, well, *interesting*, especially as they were from one of the big pharma companies—and, wham, he'd be in a whole other place and time, in a full-blown hallucination, fading after a few minutes and leaving him exhausted and vertiginous and more than a little scared. Eventually, he learned to control it, or at least disguise it. People assumed he was merely pondering things; what they didn't know was what he was seeing and hearing—the sweating walls, the bending sky, the melting flesh, the murky thump of an unseen bass guitar. Once he'd even caught sight of Syd Barrett's living face in a beam of sunlight striking a bottle of Evian. Joanne knew nothing about it. Each time it happened he felt himself vanish, or if not exactly vanish, somehow not *matter* very much anymore, as if all his substance had been removed from him. Now he'd lost these occasional glimpses into this other world where newspaper taxis appeared on the shore, waiting to take you away.

"How can I avoid it, Jeff?"

"There's no shame in bankruptcy, you know. Happens every day to some of the best people."

"Just not you."

"Well," Jeff mumbled, all modesty. "I've been prudent."

"I still don't want it. I want to get through this, I want to save my family, I just want us to land on our feet. And soon."

"So let me lay this all out for you. One," he said, holding up a finger. "Joanne needs to get a job—"

"She started work last month. A new daycare opened in the neighborhood. It's called Li'l Rascals." Nick spelled it out, apostrophe included. He was still a little bewildered by it. "But she really wanted to work for the Dead End Kids."

Jeff's accountant's body shook like jellied laughter. "That's good, Nick. You always were a funny guy."

"She hadn't had a job since Eric was born."

"She doesn't mind?"

"Actually, she minds a lot. But for right now it brings in a little money."

"Puts food on the table."

"Let me remind you that my wife has a master's in history from Columbia."

"Big step down, then."

"I'd say."

"Minimum wage?"

"Barely."

A second finger. "The kids need to go to public schools."

Nick had dreaded that one. "That's going to be difficult."

"Everyone has to take a hit. You, Joanne, the kids. You all have to make the sacrifice."

"Jen got the lead role in *Hair.*"

Jeff gazed at him. "They take their clothes off?"

"What do you think, Jeff?"

"What's that song? 'The Age of Aquarius'?" He started to grope for the words while trying to catch hold of the melody. Nick was sick and tired of the thing. Jen had played the original cast album over and over again until she'd memorized the words, and at odd moments he'd find that he was singing it himself while mowing the lawn or driving to the train station to go to work. It reminded Nick, painfully, that once upon a time he had hair to his shoulders and didn't give a shit about anything except for music and dope and girls. Sometimes he wondered if, like Chad Bakeman, president of the college's Young Republican Club and the only human being on campus under the age of thirty who wore a tie and jacket each and every day, he had taken everything more seriously he would not be sitting here, facing ruin opposite a millionaire. But then again he wasn't in prison, as Chad now was. It was one thing being an upright and loyal member of your party, quite another when you'd been caught in your White House staff office having chatroom sex with a detective pretending to be a twelve-year-old girl named Tonya.

"How about your son?" Jeff said.

"Cocaptain of the lacrosse team. So they tell me."

"So taking them out—"

"Won't be easy."

"Tuition's almost..." He sifted through the sheets on his desk till he found the right one. "Christ, it's forty grand for the two of them."

Nick was amazed the man's hair didn't stand on end. So far Jeff was doing his best to raise the whole sordid situation to the level of melodrama.

"At that kind of price they should be housing the kids, feeding them three times a day, and giving them preferred tee times at the club. Speaking of which..." He shuffled the papers until he found another.

"It's the right school for these kids," Nick said. "They have friends, they have great teachers. A beautiful campus. And they're motivated. At least Jen is."

"Look, if your kids are that good they'll do well anywhere. But that kind of money? You don't have it, my friend. Not anymore."

"I know. I know."

"The club," Jeff said. "Have you applied for a deferral?"

"Of annual fees? No. I canceled our membership."

"You're joking, right?"

"Jeff, I can't afford it, remember? Anyway, we rarely go there. Jen went to the pool maybe three times last summer. Eric hasn't been there since he was fourteen, and since I don't swim or play golf there isn't much for me to do, is there? I'm just as happy going to a local gym a couple of times a week. What's so damned funny, huh?"

"I was remembering your boy—he was, what? Five or six? He'd stand by the first tee by the little scrubby machine, asking everyone if he could wash their balls."

"He didn't know," Nick said, still embarrassed for his son, who meant well but couldn't for the life of him understand why all these fat, bald executives in their plaid pants were laughing at him.

Jeff made hands in the air. "Sorry. Sorry. But you know what this means. If you ever want in again, you'll have to go through the process from the word go. That means another review and initiation fee."

"But they already know us."

"Uh-uh, doesn't work that way. You're withdrawing for financial reasons. That means they'll look extra closely at your tax returns and financial records."

"Then we'll stay out for good. I never liked the food there, anyway." He also disliked most of the people, who in a vague way reminded him of Chad Bakeman.

Jeff sat back, signifying time was running out. By his own admission he lived a threshold life: people coming, people going, the endless busyness of a man who had no other world than the screen on his computer and the *Wall Street Journal*, especially the pages with all the numbers and charts. "And how about you? Looking for work like you're supposed to be?"

"I signed up with a headhunter."

"Which?"

"Brewster and Scott."

"Good people. What else?"

"I look at the papers." He glanced at his Rolex, a gift from his old company after an especially profitable year. "I'm heading off for the Javits in a little while."

"The big job fair? Wait till you see how crowded it is. Lots of others like you, Nick. You're not alone in this world."

Jeff stole a glance at his own fine timepiece that cost him upward of thirty grand. Nick's twenty minutes were up. Jeff rose and held out a hand.

"Good seeing you, as always."

"Likewise. Send a bill."

"Not until you guys get back on your feet. Now get out there and find something, OK?"

3

A FEW PEOPLE LINGERED OUTSIDE THE JAVITS CENTER, smoking and staring at their résumés. Some had a look of borderline despair on their faces, others, of simple resignation, as though they were waiting outside a penitentiary for the doors to open for visiting hour. Jeff was right: There were others just like Nick; in fact there were many thousands, from what he could see as he walked into the place. There were reception tables for those who had preregistered and others for those who had just strolled in, and there were banks of computers where one could browse through lists of other registrants and the companies participating in the fair, along with contact names, e-mail addresses, and phone numbers.

"Nick Copeland," he told the man at the registration desk. The man found him on his computer.

"Is that cash, check, or did you pay by credit card over the phone?"

He rarely used a credit card, whipping it out only when he'd had a few too many drinks and needed to pay for them, or if the pocket in which he carried his cash, as was usually the case these days, proved to be empty. He handed over the fee in real money, tens and twenties—flip, flip, flip—counting them out into the man's palm like a character in a Jean-Pierre

Melville film. The man handed him a receipt "for tax purposes," he explained, as if to rub Nick's face in his own misery. He waited for Nick to give way to the next person.

"What do I do?" Nick said.

The man spoke as if to a child, lifting slightly from his chair to point. "You go to one of those computers, OK? You put in your search requirements and find the companies that are the best match for you, all right? You can enter your name with each one and set up an appointment right there. Did you bring copies of your résumé?"

"I've got everything right here." Nick tapped his pocket.

"On the main floor," the man said, aiming a finger at the ceiling, "there are HR people from nearly six hundred companies."

"Oh good."

"Plus we have seminars," he said, handing Nick a slick little trifold in four colors, "in résumé writing, in the art of the interview, and in…" But Nick's attention had drifted, not to anything specific, but just away from this embodiment of everything he had begun to dislike in his life.

"OK, sir? Sir?"

Nick looked at him.

"Now you need to let the next person have his turn, OK, sir?"

Did you go pee-pee? Did you wash your hands?

Since losing his job Nick had feared a total breakdown and only hoped it wouldn't happen in public. It was one thing being a teenager and freaking out on an acid trip—these things happened, and back in the day it was more or less the expected thing to see someone staggering down First Avenue tearing his eyeballs out—but now that he at least looked like a respectable human being, anything less than modest and respectable behavior would be considered criminal or insane. He had already told Joanne—in fact had told her more than once—that it was unlikely he would come away from this place with even a lead on a new position.

"The longer I'm unemployed the less interested people will be in me," he explained to her. "It's like food in a super-market. Eventually it gets stale and they stick it on a rack for poor people to buy at discount. And then when it goes green and putrid they throw it in the Dumpster out back, where the homeless can have it for nothing. I'm almost at that stage."

"Then you have to stress your unique qualities," Joanne said. "You have to think about what makes you so good at your work. What makes you shine. What made you such a success while you were at Stevens Breakstone Leary. And don't ever forget that you weren't fired because of some, I don't know, some personal failing, or some crime you'd committed. You were just—"

"We were bought out and I was phased out. A younger advertising genius took my place. Someone with a nice smile and the brains of a baked bean. That doesn't make me feel any better."

"What matters is that it wasn't your fault."

"I could have saved myself, though. I could have sold my soul to Baker Burton Hofstader. The offer was on the table from the start. Jeff Hofstader told me personally he wanted me to get onboard with them."

"But you didn't, Nick."

"He courted me, for God's sake."

"It's ancient history. So it's not even worth thinking about. At the time it seemed the right decision. You can't go back and change things."

Three decades earlier he'd been this far from opening his dorm room window and leaping to his death. That would have solved several problems at once: the remainder of his education, the onset of middle age, the responsibilities that came with being a husband and father, the time the police had come knocking at three in the morning when a thirteen-year-old Eric and his friends decided to break into the local skateboard shop. But then again he would have missed out on all the joys: the birth of the young criminal himself, and two years later the arrival of Jen, who these days shed money as quickly as her parents gave it to her. Joanne would have married someone else and would probably not be cleaning up baby puke at Li'l Rascals.

Instead he'd banged on the wall like an idiot and met Rob Johnson. But then of course he'd never have gotten laid to the extent that he had. The idea that he had touched some other dimension, that he'd engaged with the mystical, had lent him an aura of desirability he only later realized he could have achieved simply by lying. He didn't have to take acid to get that far; he didn't have to toy with the edge of his own sanity to bed half a dozen of the best-looking girls on campus, including Melanie Spector, who was president of the student council, on the dean's list for six semesters running, an older woman—she was twenty-one—in fact you couldn't call her a girl at all. She was definitely a woman and even dressed like one (while Nick dressed like he'd just wandered out of the back forty of Wavy Gravy's Hog Farm, in buckskin moccasins, his trusty Landlubbers, and a French sailor's shirt with holes in the seams), in nice blouses and stockings and what he discovered was spectacularly expensive underwear bought not at Hoagie's Army & Navy in downtown Pittsburgh but at Bloomingdale's.

He wondered why, while Joanne was trying to boost his confidence, he thought of Melanie. In fact he thought of her at least once a year. He suspected that this was what life would eventually become for him: a continual looking back at lost opportunities; an endless rephrasing of memories as if they were snippets of poetry whose meaning might radically change with the simple shifting of a single word. All of these people who'd been in his life represented another road not taken: Spector Avenue, Christopher Alley, Normandy Street. Yet part of him knew that had he married Melanie Spector he would no longer be married to Melanie Spector. Though great to look at and amazing to talk to—she was well read, well bred, and clearly destined to marry someone with more ambition, wit, and family money than he had—she began to lose her appeal once he found that she would not only talk to him but also go to the trouble of sleeping with him. It was fortunate, he thought then as now, that the excitement of the concept quickly faded, as a brownout occurs when the juice fizzles in the main power plant.

But it was more than just words. He was told on more than one occasion that his eyes looked different after his encounter with the Clear White Light. In fact they did: darker, more sinister, useful during a meeting when you were trying to convince—i.e., hypnotize—a potential client into buying your pitch. He remembered Melanie looking into them and saying something like, "They're great deep pits of knowledge that I could see myself drowning in..."

Damn, he really liked that woman.

"If you'll let me, that is."

"Nick?"

"Hmmm?"

Joanne smiled at him. "Thought I lost you there for a moment. I was just saying that maybe Jeff Hofstader will keep you in mind."

"He won't. He has a reputation. Once you turn him down he pulls your card from his Rolodex, dunks it into the wastebasket, gives himself two points, and refuses to return your phone calls. As far as he's concerned, you're dead and buried."

It was taking a pay cut that had scared him off the position at Baker Burton Hofstader, though he'd been promised a good deal more creative latitude. He'd gambled that he would find something elsewhere, something that included both better money and a certain amount of freedom, when a day or two later he was walking through Grand Central and saw on the front page of the *Post* a photo of Alan Greenspan looking like an undertaker at an airplane crash. There was no shade of irony, no subtlety: this was the bad news written all over the man's face. He didn't have to buy the paper to read the story. It was all around him, on the faces of other commuters, in the very air he was breathing. He had become redundant. There was no point in anyone writing clever ads anymore. Smart people, successful individuals, those who could afford to buy anything they liked, didn't actually buy things, they were given them, everything from tickets to the Liza Minnelli show at the Palace to invitations to gallery openings to goody bags filled with TAG Heuer watches and weeklong passes to Canyon Ranch. That was why a potbellied man with hairy shoulders was selling crappy furniture on TV dressed in a bra and bikini bottoms. He was there to remind Nick that if he weren't careful he, too, might end up hawking his talents dressed like Joanne's stepmother.

"Advertising's a tough business these days," she said, but all he could think about was how, since she seemed to have lost all interest in being intimate with him, she was going about fulfilling her desires, assuming he hadn't killed those off as well. She put her hand on his and looked into his eyes. Here it was, then: the thing that had lived with them for six months now, the ruffian on the stair that would tear down the door and finish him off for good.

"Is there something you want to tell me?" he said.

She paused a moment to let the light in her eyes dim. "Just that I'm behind you one hundred percent, Nick. We'll get through this together."

He gave her hand a little squeeze, the discussion was over, and the light came back into her eyes, as if someone had given her a jump start. OK, he thought: Who the fuck is it?

As he waited in line for a computer—just as he'd waited for a train earlier that morning and as he'd waited for sleep the night before—he ran through all the possible candidates for Joanne's lover. And because none took the lead, he realized it was undoubtedly someone he didn't know, someone like the proverbial postman or the UPS guy, or maybe even—here was the *Aha!* moment—her personal trainer at the gym, except that Joanne's trainer, now that he thought of it, was named Ariel and was married to Harve the racquetball coach. He knew that had he dared ask Joanne it would have been the beginning of the end. She would have turned his suspicion around and driven it through his heart. Some things, he thought, were best left undiscovered.

When it was his turn and he went to type in the key-words—"advertising," "creative," "team leader," "self-starter," thinking he might as well add "tough motherfucker"—he realized he was instead at a screen showing all the registrants for the job fair. He wondered if any of his other colleagues who'd been phased out were here, in which case they'd all be competing for the same position. He scrolled down: Julie Alter, Barry Bartlett, Amy Fuller, Alan Beckett—Jesus, it was the whole top echelon of the creative wing at Stevens Breakstone Leary, except that they were anywhere from five to ten years younger than he was. Now he was sorry he'd wasted the trip into the city and the cost of walking into this place. Put him next to Barry Bartlett, who looked like he'd started shaving only five months earlier, and the contest was over before he even opened his mouth. He continued browsing through the names, stopping when he saw Charlie Ingersoll and Kevin Jergens, the latter two having been top men at Sternberg Eisner Glassner, his company's stiffest competitors and the bastards who stole the Lexus account out from under their nose the year before. And then he stopped scrolling. Just like that. His lips were moving, but he was deaf to what he was saying.

"Were you talking to me?" the man standing at the next terminal over asked.

Not unless your name is Holy Shit, he thought.

4

THEY WERE ALREADY ON THEIR SECOND BOURBON WHEN Rob looked at his watch. Nick gave him a questioning glance. The idea that the same guy who came into his dorm room to save him from the jaws of a guaranteed acid death was the same loser sitting across from him was still sinking in.

"Habit," Rob said. "This is when Janet used to come home. We'd always have a drink together and debrief."

Nick gazed at him. "She was in the military?"

"You know. Talk about the day. Get things off your chest."

"What did she do?"

"She works for Condé Nast." He seemed to cringe at the thought of it.

"No kidding. *Vogue*, that kind of thing?"

"The free stuff she used to get. Man oh man. Cell phones and wristwatches and underwear—you know, French lacy stuff. CDs of boy bands, as if we'd sit around listening to that kind of thing. And the parties we went to..." He shook his head, as if trying to rid himself of the memories that seemed to stick to him like old spills in the freezer compartment. "Eight months ago, something like that, we were at the Met. A thing for Gloria Vanderbilt. Birthday shindig." He made a sour face.

"No good?"

"No, it was great. Good food, lots to drink. Interesting people. Mike Nichols. George Clooney. Julia fucking *Roberts*, for Christ's sake. It's just that I didn't realize Janet's…"—he waved his hand vaguely in the air—"thing would be there."

Nick stared at him. "Thing?"

"Damn, this is really painful. I mean, I think I'd rather have my toenails pulled out."

"Come on, Rob."

"At least they'd grow back. Unlike my balls."

Nick shook the ice in his empty glass and the waiter, ever alert, brought him a fresh one. He wondered if Rob's admitted castration had been to blame for the weight gain.

"And can we get some more nuts, maybe?" Rob asked the waiter. "I haven't eaten all day."

"I'm kind of lost here, Rob. Your wife's *thing*?"

"Her, you know…"

Rob's face told it all. Lover, paramour, sweetheart: fuck buddy. That covered the second question as well. "I don't even want to talk about it."

It occurred to Nick: "How did you know it was him?"

"She broke the news to me a week later. It was like someone had flown a plane into my eye and smashed open my brain."

The image was striking. He pictured various of Rob's hopes and dreams leaping to their deaths.

"I mean, the thing is, he was at this Vanderbilt party and I'd even been talking to him. For what, something like fifteen minutes? Now I know why he seemed so interested in what I was saying." Rob shook his head and looked away. His face, until then as pale as any committed resident of the Upper East Side, turned a faint purple. "Guy must've been thinking, Jesus, this is my lover's husband, what a loser. He's a little chunky, he's going gray, he's nothing to look at."

"Was *he*?"

"What?"

The waiter brought Nick his drink and Rob some pretzel nuggets. He clutched and came away with half the bowl in his fist.

"Anything to look at?"

Rob took his time, as if to let the pain subside a bit. "He's twenty years younger than Janet. Well, maybe not twenty, but ten or twelve. Eight, I don't know. He's tall and he's got all his hair and he looks like he goes to the gym every day. He looks a little like Keanu Reeves. But with a smile, and muscles. OK, now can we change the subject? Because in a minute I'm throwing up."

Nick didn't think Keanu Reeves would be much competition even for Rob Johnson, since he hadn't made a really good film in a while.

"Don't beat yourself up, Rob."

Sensing a long evening ahead of them, his gaze shifted outside, beyond the humming neon glow of the window of Murphy's Tavern, a saloon that he knew in two or three years would be replaced with something named Trump or McDonald's. It was times like this that made him miss his work the most. The boundless potential to say something smart, to grab the public by its lapels and drag them into an imaginative zone that would lead them through the doors of whatever palace might be standing there—this is what was now behind him. Now he was just another bewildered schmuck wondering how the world had passed him by.

The day was drawing to an end, dragging with it the threads and tatters of a long, pleasant summer he'd barely had the heart to enjoy. Autumn was the way people held their coats against their chests and struggled against the stiff winds and stale attitudes of Eighth Avenue. Autumn was the color of the sky, the leaves that drifted over from Bryant Park to scutter down the sidewalk like crabs on a dry, sandy beach; it was the look on the faces of those who still had jobs and were looking forward to Christmas, the New Year, more wealth, more happiness, more gimme.

"What does he do?"

"What?"

"Your wife's thing? What does he do?"

"He's a lawyer."

"Like you."

"No, not like me. He's with Laycock Sherborn."

Nick opened his hands. "Am I supposed to know who they are?"

"Yeah, like only the top law firm in the city. One of the top five in the country. Remember the guys who defended O. J.?"

"That's *them*?"

"No. These guys are a million times better, trust me. They could've gotten the Unabomber off, for Christ's sake."

"Ah," was all Nick could say.

"And I'm an unemployed attorney," Rob reminded him. "Which these days is like being a leper. I should walk around ringing a bell to warn people off."

"Why don't you set up shop for yourself?"

"Takes money, man. And what am I going to use for my office, my living room?"

"It's got to be tough."

"It hurts, man. It really fucking hurts." Rob sat back. Now that he'd had a few, in fact two more drinks than Nick, he took a moment to bring Nick into focus. "That was really weird running into you there. Who would've thought that of all the people in all the world *you* would've walked into the Javits."

"I counted about eighteen people on the roster I personally know. There'll probably be a lot more tomorrow."

"You thinking of going back?"

"I don't see the point. You?"

"I mean, I touched base with, I don't know, four firms today. I also spoke to a couple of corporate guys who were looking to buff up their legal departments. I guess they're expecting a slew of lawsuits. Bad meat, bad drugs—what the hell do I know."

The universe of the unemployed was like a house of mirrors, Nick thought. Once he stopped running into himself he'd start seeing the same faces over and over as they all competed for the same lousy position. They were like contract players at a movie studio. Shuffle them every now and again and the good guy would be playing the bad guy and the bad guy the pope. Was this what life was really all about? Or was it just a matter of being in the right place at the right time?

"Think about it," Rob said. "Back in the day we would've looked on it as some kind of, I don't know, synchronicity or something. All of those hundreds—"

"A couple of thousand maybe—"

"I mean, I'm coming down the escalator at the same moment you're going up. Who saw who first?"

"Let's both take credit," Nick said with a nice big forgiving grin. After all, he thought, we're all one.

Rob took an appraising look at Nick. "You didn't do so badly, you know. You look good. Together, you know. Like someone who has a life. I mean, look at what you're wearing. It's good stuff. It's a suit my clients might wear. Me, I don't work out, I don't jog—c'mon, I don't even walk. I'm surprised you even recognized me. I'm shocked you stopped to talk to me. You want to hear something really funny? Three years ago we went up to Boston to visit her parents."

"This is your wife?"

"Janet, yeah, my ex. Anyway, so we're walking down Commonwealth Avenue and I run into Kacey Christopher's roommate. You remember her, Lori Streeter?"

Nick felt his heart come to a dead stop before it quickly thumped back into life. "Really."

"I had to laugh, because I remembered how you used to sneak Kacey up to your dorm room. Right under Ma Jones's eyes."

Ma Jones was their housemother, a secret drinker at sixty-eight, widowed and living in the basement of a boys' dorm, a fact that alone would have left any human embittered for her remaining days. Her duties were to provide moral support—always in scant evidence—sort the mail, and call security should Nick or any of his type step out of line. Football players such as Stumper could stagger in stinking drunk with their pants around their ankles and she'd smile to herself, because, well, boys would be boys, especially if they were linebackers or tight ends. But had she detected Nick floating by reeking of Panama Red, she would've had Eliot Ness on the phone within minutes. Sometimes, when he was tripping and in a particularly good mood, he'd stop down and poke his head in her sitting room and rouse her from her nap, spent daily in front of some soap opera or game show. It was amazing how when you were on acid, real people living their real lives always seemed somehow less than real. She could barely bring herself to smile when he appeared. "Oh hello, Nick. I hope there's not a problem." Because if there were, she undoubtedly suspected, it would somehow be beyond her abilities to imagine it.

He'd always wanted to tell her he was on LSD and that she was glowing yellow and would soon die, because on acid you felt invincible and would say anything to freak people out. Or else take her at her word—which from the start was always that she was there for the boys, her door always open, a kind word and a mother's shoulder to cry on—and ask for a quiet chat, just the two of them, and ask her weird things like: "Anal sex. What's your take on it, Ma?"

"Just passing through, Ma. Thought I'd say howdy."

Ma. On his first day on campus he was informed this was what she was meant to be called, as if he were expected to be endlessly homesick and desirous of seeing his mother (or any reasonable substitute) as often as possible, while in truth Nick's mother was a blowsy alcoholic divorcée living in the Barbizon. Once every six weeks he'd call for a money fix and be told she was shopping at Saks or dining at 21 or was sleeping out, meaning with his parents' old friend Oscar Seamans, who was a big shot in commercial real estate. Years later, when Nick was on his honeymoon with Joanne in Greece, his mother literally slipped out of this life after leaving a party on the Upper West Side and falling headfirst down a flight of subway stairs. Someone had forgotten to clue him in to this until a week after they'd returned, and then only when he received a letter from her attorneys regarding the disbursement of her remaining assets, the majority of which—her jewels and the two paintings she'd once hung on to for dear life: a small Picasso dating from the late fifties that had once belonged to Nick's father and was part of their divorce settlement, and a Larry Rivers given her during a difficult ten-day affair with the artist—had either been sold for cash or somehow mislaid during the meandering course of her final fifteen years on earth.

Mostly the thing he liked about Ma was that his mail passed through her mail-sorting fingers—not just the meth and acid sent on a weekly basis by his Brooklyn connection, but his subscriptions to the *East Village Other*, *Ramparts*, *The Realist*, *Evergreen Review*, *Creem*, and *Rolling Stone*, any of which must have raised an eyebrow or two every now and again.

Part of the thrill of being stoned all the time was knowing that others weren't.

"Kacey Christopher," Nick said aloud and once more she popped into his mind with all the vividness of a memory that had never faded, only been tucked away for some rainy day.

"She had the most amazing black hair," Rob rhapsodized. "And a killer body. And those eyes. I gotta tell you, but you lucked out with her."

"Yes," Nick said; that killer body, those eyes. And as if it were true that the past really was contained in the present, she was before him, sitting on the edge of his dorm room bed, asking him to please lock the door. Her sleek, shiny hair hung down over her perfect little breasts, her nervous hands rested on her bare knees, and she couldn't look him in the eye until he kissed her. She tasted like Juicy Fruit gum. He wondered if he bought a pack today whether he might summon her in all her youthful glory, like some spirit from a magic lamp.

She had lost her virginity to him that lazy spring afternoon while Joni Mitchell's *Blue* spun out its sweet, honest melancholy on his stereo. It was quick and clumsy, but boy did it feel great. And it wasn't just the sex itself; it was the fact that for five minutes they were the perfect couple, united in mutual desire, perfectly coupling. When they met up again an hour later outside her dorm and walked in the sunshine and the breeze on which their feet rested, he felt somehow eternal. Although sleeping with Melanie Spector had been tremendous, and his time with Diane Normandy not shabby in the least, this was the first time in his life he felt like a million bucks, and every succeeding time he felt that way, wealthy and without worry—on his wedding day, and the days the kids were born, not to mention the morning he was hired by the same company that would eventually let him go—could be counted on the fingers of one hand.

These days he felt like thirteen cents. Soon he'd have to take his sorry ass back to Grand Central and get on the train with the commuters who were gainfully employed and return with the news to Joanne. His future in advertising was not going to happen unless he radically reinvented himself. Stevens Breakstone Leary wanted to inject a younger outlook into the company, as Larry Stevens told him the day he gave him the bad news. They were going to hire a whole new team, apart from his replacement a few of them fresh out of college, still reeking of bongs and cheap beer. And he was too old to change professions. This was even a feature at the job fair, a whole corner of the first floor devoted to learning diverse skills, finding fresh paths, setting different goals, and unearthing new metaphors for killing time on your way to the grave. Smiling counselors offered to probe your psyche and see what undiscovered talents you possessed, and as he'd walked by them to the escalator and grabbed one of their brochures, he'd wondered what they would have come up with for him.

Page three: Might he become a children's entertainer, for instance, doing simple magic tricks at birthday parties, folding balloons into llamas? See the old man taking a quarter from a child's ear. See the boys and girls laughing and jumping with glee. Page five: Being a Realtor was a terrific career, and the commissions were out of this world, exclamation point. It allowed you to exercise all your selling skills in the relaxed setting of someone else's home, though the accompanying photos showed a silver-haired ex-CEO showing a thirty-year-old knockout around a condo, which implied there were perks to be had, my man, there were joys to be savored. Or maybe he could become a trucker, proud owner of a sixteen-wheeler, traversing the country, seeing America anew, listening to cowboy music and picking up hookers at roadside rest areas when not voting Republican and trying to run Jap cars off the road.

"You're never too old to change your life," an attractive woman on the cusp of fifty said to him as he placed the booklet back on the table. Her smile caught him like a net. It exuded confidence, inner happiness, strength. This was a woman who could do whatever she liked, he thought, and here she was reeling in all the walking dead of the economic bust.

"Been phased out?" She said it so quietly, in the intimate twilight space between his shoulder and ear, that had he not been paying attention he would have heard it as, "Looking for a good time, sailor?"

"I'm afraid so," Nick said. Not only attractive but trim and rather shapely. Good face, nice smile. Too good, too nice. "What's the catch?"

"I'm sorry?"

"How much?"

Here came that smile again. "Well, of course nothing worthwhile is free, is it?" She waited a moment or two.

"I don't believe that," he said.

"Really. Can you name something that is?"

"My family. I don't pay to have them nearby, and they're worth a lot more than anything I've ever seen in my life."

She had an answer for everything. "Be selfish for two minutes." She looked at his chest. "Oh. You've lost your name."

"Oh great," he said. "First my job, then my identity."

"I meant your name tag."

"They didn't give me one."

"Then why don't I?"

She took a blank label off her table and, peeling the backing off, smoothed it firmly against his breast pocket as he spelled his name. Then she took her felt-tip pen (in green, of course, for *Go!*) and slowly tickled his nipple as she finished with a nice flourish at the end of the *k*. "Nick," she said. "Neat.

Nice and easy. Nick at night." She looked him in the eye. "A name to reckon with. There's potential there, you know."

"I do know."

"You have confidence, then."

"You can't imagine."

"All you need to do is let him out."

What the hell was she talking about now?

"We all have another person inside us," she explained.

"Now *that's* a scary notion," he said, and she laughed, though he suspected she'd heard it often enough before.

"So tell me. Who *is* the other person inside Nick's body?"

"Charles Manson." It was the first thing that came to mind.

"I beg your pardon?"

And then he discovered that the person she had inside *her* body was Houdini, because in two seconds flat she had vanished.

Rob was still talking about Kacey's roommate. "So we're on Commonwealth Avenue and guess who I see coming toward me but Lori Streeter. A little heavier, not a lot, just a little. Her hair's shorter and streaked with gray, and—catch this—she's visiting colleges with her daughter."

"Frankly, I can't see Lori as anything but really slim."

"Well, you know. Gravity and that kind of thing. But she still looked great."

"Did she…say anything about Kacey?" When he thought of Kacey he could hear her voice bubbling in his ear: *"Don't stop, Nicky, oh God don't stop."*

"The whole point of the story is that she didn't recognize me. Or I recognized her first, whatever. So I stop her and introduce her to, you know—"

"Janet—"

"And we trade a little small talk—how are you? What are you doing these days?—that kind of thing. She says, 'You've been sick?' and I say, 'No, I haven't,' and she says, 'I didn't recognize you.' And here's the kicker. She says, 'You look like you've been on cortisone.' Why is that so funny all of a sudden?"

Nick held his stomach as tears came to his eyes and his laughter diminished into chuckles. "I don't know. It just—it just seems a weird thing for her to say. No, that's wrong, it's perfect Lori. It's just what she would say," and he realized that throughout all of this he was making the assumption that if Lori were alive and well then Kacey must also be. Through all of the others he had dated, through his courtship of, cohabitation with, and marriage to Joanne, through the birth of two children, Kacey hadn't really faded at all. She was still there, he saw now, sitting on a stone wall, waiting for him to stop by and smile. Would she be precisely the same? Good advertising man that he was, one who understood all too well the difference between expectation and reality, he knew that the Kacey trapped in memory's glistening amber would be nothing like the living, breathing Kacey of today. He knew, too, that when he looked in the mirror and saw a twentysomething guy in terrific shape, he was seeing nothing more than the blinding, overwaxed state of his mind, not the dull truth of honest evaluation.

"You know what that means?" Rob anguished. "That I looked puffy. Like I was sick and on medications. And I looked at myself in the mirror in the hotel that night and you know what? I really did look like shit. Like sick shit. No wonder Janet left me. Now may I have another drink? Because frankly I need it." He held up his glass. Nick had lost count of which one they were on, but he was feeling pretty mellow, and somehow, possibly circuitously, he would make it back home. Already he was working on a story for Joanne, sensing it was going to be a good one. A much better one than the one he'd been intending to make up in the train on the way home.

"You still haven't told me," he said. "Why were you laid off?"

The waiter brought Rob another drink and whipped away his empty glass.

"I really liked where I was. I'd moved from criminal to civil and was bringing in some serious money. I was handling suits against some pretty major companies." He shrugged. "They needed new blood, they said. Wanted to have a more," and he hooked the air with two pairs of fingers, "youthful profile. Young and forward looking. You hear that and what do you think? You go to the bathroom and stare at yourself in the mirror for a long time. All this time you looked and you saw the kid you used to be way back when. Now all of a sudden you look and you see death in the eyes, despair in the wrinkles. Erectile dysfunction."

"Don't," Nick said, because these were the very thoughts he worked so hard to deny.

"Then came the Janet thing."

"Jesus," Nick said. "You've really had it rough. But why was the...attorney at the Vanderbilt party?"

"Because he went to Dalton with Anderson Cooper. I mean, she thinks it's going to be an amicable divorce." He shook his head sadly. "And we always thought life would turn out great."

"So money must be tight," Nick remarked. Now he felt sorry for Rob. No woman, no job. It was like a reggae song.

"It wasn't supposed to be like this, Nick. Back in college, we thought we had it all. Remember? You always told people you were going to be a rock star. Not a great musician. A *rock star*. That takes balls."

Nick had owned a Gibson Thunderbird bass that had fallen off the back of a truck somewhere near Bay Parkway and Cropsy Avenue in Brooklyn. He could play the bass line to every song on the Paul Butterfield Blues Band's first two albums, which meant that he was fairly proficient in playing blues changes, useful in a pinch. Back then he would sometimes entertain the thought of moving to Chicago, taking a cold-water flat on the South Side, hanging with the old-timers in some juke joint, drinking bourbon, and smoking himself to death while he watched Buddy Guy count his millions. Well, thousands, maybe.

"It just takes being young," Nick said. "That's the time to take risks. Get crazy."

"Are your kids like that?"

"I try not to think about it. If I can't imagine it then they're not doing anything as insane as I did."

He didn't like the direction the conversation was taking; it reminded him of all those years earlier, before the Clear White Light visitation and the Great Disappointment of recent memory.

"We had it all. High hopes. Big dreams." Rob let his expression drift off into some darker territory. "I mean, we'd get excited, you know? We'd plan things, we'd start schemes, everything was big and bright and bold. We took risks, man, risks we'd never think about even going near today." Rob smiled, mostly to himself, as memory kicked in. "Remember how we used to rob the business office?"

The memory was as fresh and exciting to Nick as when they'd first decided to jimmy open the window in the administration building and relieve the place of its payroll machines, all two of them. Disguised as armored typewriters, heavy as refrigerators, each had to be carried by a working team of thieves—one in front, the other behind—as if heading toward Calvary. They'd walked across campus unnoticed by campus security, loitering professor, or Chad Bakeman, dropping them off in Denis Whidbey's blue Volvo PV544, customized for racing and guaranteed to outrun cops and townies alike. Unimpressed by their assertion that these two guys with long hair and bell-bottoms were updating their office, the guy at the Son of Pittsburgh pawnshop gave them thirty bucks for the two machines and promised not to call the police.

"And you," Rob said, "you were screwing Kacey. Living the life I should've been living."

"Kacey wasn't a risk. She was my reward for being alive."

"But you were the only one who had the guts to walk up to her and ask her out. I saw you do it, Nick, I was there. The whole thing took, what? Five minutes? I saw how she smiled. What did you say to her anyway?"

Nick sat back and let the memory—until now lost in the fog of years—wash over him like sunshine on an August afternoon. "I told her that I'd help her get high."

"You bribed her?"

"No. I tempted her." He'd shyly told her that she was the most beautiful woman—not *girl*—on campus and that it would be his privilege to share some of his pot with her. And he meant every word of it. She'd found his approach both charming and novel and two days later was sitting naked on his bed reminding him to lock the door.

Rob just stared at him. "You had that much grass stashed away so you could just give it away? Where'd you get it, because I didn't have access to anything near a cornucopia of dope back then."

Now it came to Nick. "Think, Rob."

It took Rob a full ten seconds before it came to him. *"Cincinnati!"*

"Yes!" said Nick, more *Sssssss* than affirmation.

"Holy shit."

"Yes indeed. Cincinnnnnnnati," Nick repeated, stretching out the word so that it told a whole story.

"Mama loves mambo!" Rob cried, playing the table like a bongo drum.

"Guys," the bartender counseled.

"Cincinnati." Even whispered it possessed a certain ripeness, suggesting that the city had provided Rob with pleasures hitherto unimagined. "Jesus, wasn't that something, huh?"

"Yes it was," said Nick.

Rob put up his palm for a high five. "And we set that all up by ourselves, remember?"

"Well, you did, anyway."

"Every dealer in the city knew about it. But we were there *first*."

From the start Rob had been vague about the details. He'd set up the purchase not of some agreed-upon amount, but just six hundred dollars' worth of pot and hash, domestic stuff that could be shifted quickly to those not of the aficionado class. It was like going into a restaurant, throwing a twenty-dollar bill at the waiter and simply asking for "food." The arrangement was that they'd take an early bus into Cincinnati and meet at Love's coffee house on Calhoun Street. Neither Rob nor Nick had ever been to Cincinnati in their lives. They'd never heard of Love's. They didn't know that a local band known as the Lemon Pipers sat in there ten hours a day in varying poses of lassitude, caught in the funk of ennui and caffeine poisoning, feeding the jukebox and repeatedly playing their one hit, "My Green Tambourine," until someone would come over and say, "Would you stop playing that shit?" or, more hopefully, "Hey, you're the Lemon Pipers, right?"

"I wonder where this Calhoun Street is," Nick said in the Greyhound that morning. Only a handful of other passengers had come to fill the void: a few soldiers on leave; one or two other freaks huddling in the back; a few old fugitive types with haunted Dick-and-Perry looks in their dead eyes and thoughts in their heads that would be left unexamined until the advent—many years later, and to young Eric Copeland's unnatural delight—of serial-killer movies.

"We'll ask at the bus station. You ever do this before? I mean buy from someone you don't know?"

"How the hell did you set this up, anyway?" Nick asked.

"Friend of a friend, guy from prep school. He goes to the university there. He knows this guy who's trying to dump the shit."

"Any idea who we're going to sell it to? I mean, Eden isn't exactly Bleecker Street."

Rob smiled. "Maybe we can do something about that, then."

"You thinking about a full conversion, or just working on a rolling crusade?"

"Hey. You're the guy who's seen the light, right? Have a little faith, why don't you?"

Nick sighed and watched out the window as they passed down the anonymous lanes of Interstate 70. It was going to be a long trip, almost the whole width of Ohio, with a ten-minute stop in Columbus, there to discharge the ex-cons and pillheads and replace them with a whole new load of bad news.

"What kind of money are we looking at?" Nick asked. He realized it was a question that should have been posed the moment Rob had first invited him in on the deal.

"Well, as I see it, we can process the stuff next week—"

"Process meaning what?"

Rob looked at him. "Look, this isn't the highest grade shit. It's going to have stems and seeds and if we just grind it all together, we'll have even more to sell."

"So you're going to push some pretty crappy stuff."

Rob touched the side of his head. "Psychological, man. It's all in the mind. You'll take a toke and your eyes will roll up inside your head and you'll sort of go limp, and the customers'll think, shit, this is dynamite stuff."

It was an early version of a celebrity endorsement, he now realized. That final acid trip had really given him the edge.

"Doesn't matter who does it. As long as they *think* this is the best pot going."

"So we're talking about what in terms of profit?"

Rob lit a cigarette. "I figure we'll end up with at minimum two grand."

"Wow."

"Maybe even three if we dump it all."

"That's amazing," Nick said, and he balled up his hand into a fist and gave Rob a light tap on his arm.

"The whole take'll be split three ways."

Nick looked at him. "What do you mean?"

"I forgot to mention it. Jerry Bruno also kicked in two hundred."

"Jerry Bruno."

Nick did some quick computing: Jerry was the guy with the perennial five o'clock shadow and the car no one was allowed to touch—a red Firebird with New York plates he washed every Sunday in the parking lot behind the dorm. Herbie Hechinger, a few too many beers in him and minding no one's business but his own, once leaned back on it and a minute later was writhing on the ground with three broken ribs. Jerry's father was in the haulage business in Great Neck, which said a lot about the kid's genes. Jerry was also the guy who, when you played poker with him, always ended up the winner. Guy sat down, got his cards and started raking in the dough. You couldn't accuse him of cheating—which of course he was—because he always had a friendly smile and treated the other players as if they were long-lost cousins. It was thought that Jerry would eventually either end up on death row or at the bottom of the East River.

"Let me tell you something," Rob said. "Jerry doesn't ante up unless there's something in it for him."

"So that two thousand isn't for all of us—"

"No, no, man, that's for *each* of us."

"You didn't say that."

"I was saving it." Why Jerry wasn't with them, sharing in the risks of the operation, was a question left unpondered.

So as Nick saw it, they only made that kind of profit if they sold every last nickel bag of the stuff. They were going to have to work hard and fast to hit their goal. The word "pusher" would have to take on a whole new meaning. No more the gentle urgings of "Wanna get high?" Now they would have to rely on something a bit more compelling, such as: "If you don't buy at least a dime bag I'm going to burn down your parents' house."

The bus pulled into the station in Columbus. It was like every other bus station in America: a slum, only with diesel fumes. Nick needed a quick pee and a Dr. Pepper. He stood and got ready to leave.

"Wait," Rob said. "Let's be clear from the start. Are you carrying?"

"Me? No, man, I'm clean."

"Because I'm worried that if we're carrying and we get stopped—"

"Wait a minute, we're about to score a ton of dope and you're worried about carrying a joint?"

Rob looked deflated. He dug around in his pocket and, taking out a red pill, tossed it in his mouth. "Guess I'd might as well get rid of this now."

By the time they were on the last leg to Cincinnati, Rob was seeing bats flying around in the bus.

"This doesn't sound like acid," Nick whispered to him.

"It's something Jerry Bruno gave me. For the trip. You know, to tide me over."

Nick looked at him. "And you don't know what it is?"

"Not a clue, man. Not a clue."

Nick lowered his eyes into a squint and tried to send himself back in time to that bus, that moment, that potential. They had the whole world before them. And now here they were, three decades later, on the wrong end of success.

5

THERE ARE NO POTHOLES ON MEMORY LANE. NO RUTS, NO broken bottles, no dead squirrels, no speed traps, nothing but green trees and pretty flowers and a road bathed in sunlight. It's a well-kept place, the past, for even the bad neighborhoods seem in retrospect to have had that little bit of charm which you'd somehow forgotten. School hallways, once the province of bully and beggar alike—"Can I hold a dollar? No? Then I'm gonna kill you"—lose their grim associations; the headmaster's office, redolent of pipe tobacco and reeking of punishment, now seems quaint and harmless. The gingerbread cottages of lost loves and broken hearts, the humble bungalows of misplaced affections, the hills and dales of jobs gracefully offered and just as easily taken away—once they're behind you they lose their weight and value. They become picture postcards, tinted by loving hands, hidden in the back of a drawer, waiting to be rescued by nostalgia.

And so, when Nick once again said "Cincinnati," Rob's face brightened for the first time that evening. The memory of it took them both back to a time when the simple release of a new album—by Hendrix or Dylan, Beatles or Stones—would bear the weight of a presidential proclamation at a time of crisis and war. But Nick knew also that it carried them back to when life and its risks were not so much frightening as tantalizing, when the seductions of dodging the law and loitering in the lower depths carried its own kind of allure, and Desolation Row seemed a prime patch of real estate. Had Nick been compelled to reveal to a prospective employer exactly what he had done in his life, he knew that he would leave the questioner slack-jawed and bug-eyed, as though, instead of sitting across from Nick Copeland, advertising genius, he were in the presence of Hunter S. Thompson, madman and renegade.

"You know what I'm thinking?" Nick prompted.

"Maybe."

"Remember what we did?"

"Say it."

"No, Rob," Nick said calmly, "*you* say it."

It's not that the weekend had gone badly in Cincinnati. In fact, the whole deal had gone down almost suspiciously well, the kind of well that often stops going well and gets bad very quickly before it turns dangerous, followed by tragic, with fatal fast on its heels. They hung around at Love's, drinking one coffee after another and becoming well acquainted with the tiny bathroom over by the jukebox and the Lemon Pipers, who barely acknowledged their presence, though they, like everyone else, must have known what was coming down.

No sooner had they taken a table than the waitress—cute, redheaded, single braid down the back and with lots of beads around her neck—came over and said, "You guys must be here for the big deal."

Nick and Rob shared a look. "What are you talking about?" Nick said.

"They said a couple of guys from out of town were coming." She shrugged and smiled prettily, from dimple to shining dimple. "Can only be you, right?"

"Sit down," Rob said.

"I gotta work."

"Sit. Down."

"My Green Tambourine" was playing for the third time since they walked in. Nick looked over his shoulder at the band, already a blur on their fast ride down the ladder of oblivion.

"What deal? What guys? What do you know?"

She looked from Rob to Nick. "You're scaring me."

"Good," Rob said, "because you may end up being the cause of a lot of unnecessary suffering if you keep talking like that."

Nick sensed that in a moment she would start to cry. Even her lip began trembling. He put a hand on hers. "Hey. It's all right, it's OK, babe."

"OK," she blubbed.

"No one's going to get hurt. As long as no one says anything. All right?"

Nice and calm, nice and quiet. Good cop, bad cop.

"Because," Nick went on, bringing his lips very close to her remarkably lovely ear, "if someone did, things could get very, very scary. Understood?"

A single tear rolled down her cheek. All she could do was nod. "Now can I go back to work?"

Rob shot him a look as if all of a sudden he'd found himself sitting across from a whole new Nick Copeland. She was heading back to the counter when Nick grabbed her arm, but gently. "One more thing. I think you're very pretty."

She smiled through her tears and went off to serve the Lemon Pipers' bass player a prune Danish.

"Whoa," Rob said. "That was slick."

"Had to be done."

"You didn't tell her what we'd do if she did talk."

"I hadn't thought that far ahead. But it won't be pretty."

Rob laughed. "You wouldn't hurt a chick like that."

"I'd just break her heart." It was kind of fun living inside a B picture for a weekend.

He looked up to see someone hanging around outside the coffeehouse. Long hair. Mustache and a little patch of goatee, like Jimmy Carl Black, the Indian of the group. The guy had maybe ten years on them. He looked at his watch once, then again a second or two later. Then he took another look. He was like the lunatic who does the same thing over and over again, expecting something new. He was definitely a lousy advertisement for the stuff he was about to sell them.

Rob said, "Showtime, Nick. Man's here."

In fact they returned to college unmolested, unstopped, and unbusted that night, a little dazzled by their luck, a little rattled from the bus ride, considering that all of Cincinnati knew why they'd been there. Over the following three days they proceeded to process (meaning pour small batches of seeds, stems and leaves into a hand-crank coffee grinder and turn the stuff in it into something that at least *smelled* illicit) before unloading six ounces, four dime and seventeen nickel bags of the lowest-grade marijuana ever harvested on any continent in the world. Fraternity boys with Chad Mitchell Trio records handed over their money; a couple of outriders in their social quarter, art majors and the sociology teacher who lived in a trailer out in the woods with one of his female students happily made purchases. Though people called grass "shit" because it was a handy euphemism, like "tea" and "boo" and "reefer," this time the name seemed appropriate. Nobody seemed to care, though; like a placebo administered by a serious man in a white coat, it was assumed to be dynamite stuff, especially as one of its purveyors was now famous for having seen the Clear White Light, very much a *Good Housekeeping* Seal of Approval; customers puffed away and seemed to get high as a kite. By the end of the week, the show was over and the business had folded. There were no more buyers, no more happy repeat customers, no lines at the door. Even Stumper, whom they talked into buying a joint for two bucks, never returned for a taste of their brand of slumland euphoria.

The only problem was what was left over: three pounds of processed seeds, stems, and leaves that smelled a lot better than they actually were. Had it been halfway decent they might have been looking at some serious money, but the best they could hope for was merely "smokeable," as one tastes a nine-dollar Cabernet and sniffily calls it "amusing." Certainly, if you had enough of it—a couple of joints would do the trick—you'd feel high enough, though it was a lot better, Rob discovered, taken as a tea with lots of sugar; the experience left him lying unconscious on his dorm room floor for the better part of eighteen hours in a puddle of what he was amazed to discover was his own sperm.

Rob and Nick and Jerry Bruno convened at the Hungry Steer up on the highway, where the sign outside displayed a horned bovine creature with Xs for eyes. As with the Mob, who tended to meet not in their hidden dens or distant hideaways but in spaghetti joints in the Bronx or Little Italy, the Hungry Steer was both the most dangerous place they could be in and also the safest. The most dangerous, because local boys turned mean from too much Coors and Robo would cruise the place in their Trans Ams and Chevy pickups looking for girls to screw or hippies to kill, or sometimes both, and the safest because the place was always loaded with law. State troopers and officers from neighboring towns tended to be drawn there, more by the looks of the waitresses—girls in hot pants and tight sleeveless blouses and cowboy hats—than by the quality of the cuisine, though they did provide free coffee refills. So confident were these lawmen that people would be intimidated by uniform and firearm that for them it was a time of rest and recuperation, with a chance to set up a little nookie for later. So, surrounded by the heat, you could discuss a whole range of subjects, from dope to murder, and be assured that none of these men in uniform would ever suspect you of anything more than immoral thoughts and youthful indiscretions.

"What we do," Jerry was saying, and his manner was always smooth as gravy, "is let me get it back to my neighborhood. I can shift the stuff in a week and at least get us our investment back."

"Minus what?" Rob prodded.

When Jerry grinned he looked like he was forty-five years old, carried a .38 and called women *dames*. "I gotta give my people a little something for their time and effort, right? I mean, I don't do that, I'm the one they come after one night."

"We want profits, man," Rob whined, and Jerry's eyes signaled that a stranger had arrived. Rob looked up to find the waitress hovering in her white straw Stetson. "Hi," he said. "I'll have the cherry waffles. And coffee, please."

"You want a side of sausage with that?"

"No thanks, just the waffles and the coffee'll do me great. Oh, and a glass of ice water, OK?"

Nick watched the waitress write it down. Her big blue eyes shifted to him. If he didn't think about it too long he could easily find himself falling in love with this woman—barely even a woman, maybe no older than eighteen—whose name was unknown to him, and whom he'd seen for the first time only now. It happened, as it usually did with him back then, in a matter of five seconds: upon further reflection he saw the first time in bed, he saw the visit to her parents, he saw her in her wedding gown, and then he saw himself living in a trailer park outside McKeesport for the rest of his natural life.

We're all one, he continued to remind himself.

"Hm?"

"Oh, I'll have a Big Buffalo on—can you do it on rye?"

"What is that, whimsy?" Rob said. He was finding Nick more and more amusing.

"No, I'm serious."

"So is that rye *bread* you mean?" she said, wondering what kind of human being Nick precisely was.

"Lightly toasted, OK? With a side of Russian." He added, "That's ketchup and mayonnaise," making whipping motions with his hands. He didn't realize exactly how stoned he was. Following his death and disappearance that famous Acid Friday, he had given up drugs cold—renouncing all illicit substances. There honestly seemed no point in going back: He'd seen it all. What else was left for him to see, to hear, to experience? It lasted the weekend before he fell into his old habits, a prodigal son returned to home and hearth and better living through chemistry.

"And how do you like your burger?"

Edible was already an old joke thereabouts. What Nick in his highness wondered was why something made out of cow was called a Big Buffalo. He wondered why they didn't call a tuna sandwich a Monster Sperm Whale and was about to ask when Jerry shot him a look. Clearly there were cops paying attention.

"Rare, please," he said.

She raised one heavily penciled eyebrow. People out here ate their meat gray.

"Not eating?" Rob said to Bruno.

He shook his head and lit a Pall Mall.

The reason why Jerry Bruno wasn't eating was that, unlike Rob and Nick, he wasn't stoned and in fact never touched drugs, unless he was selling them. He looked at Nick and Rob in turn. "Let's get one thing straight. I don't give a rat's ass if you guys are zonked out of your brains. This is business, so I expect you to be serious about it. And no goofing on the locals. You know what happened last time you did that."

Someone had summoned a deputy sheriff, and it wasn't pretty.

"So what do we do?" Rob said.

"I say we hang on to the stuff," Nick suggested. "Wait till the opportunity comes."

Jerry sniggered. "Opportunity. Yeah, right."

"Listen, we put a lot of bread into this deal," Nick said.

"Opportunity isn't something you wait for," Jerry said. "It's something you make on your own."

Rob dropped a quarter in the jukebox at the end of the table. He smiled in that way he always did when he'd smoked too much dope. Everything was fair game, everything a laugh. Life's a cabaret, old chum.

"Jesus, man, what a lame-o you are. I mean, what am I doing here, anyway?" Jerry said, and Nick had to concur: Rob was a lame-o of the first order, considering that his hard-earned cash had just bought them Tommy James and the Shondells singing their old hit "Hanky Panky" at the little table jukebox.

"I'm just goofing. I know it's a shitty song."

"You could've chosen something we all like instead of something we're all embarrassed to have at the table with us," Jerry said, and he flipped violently through the selection cards, *whackawhackawhack*. "Look. Here's the Doors. Here's Marvin Gaye. Here's Santana. Here's the Who. *Them* we invite. Now, what were your other two selections?"

"Look," Rob said, "why don't we just move tables?" Already they'd begun to attract attention. Either it was the length of their hair or their East Coast accents, or the possibility, noted by others, that these boys might be on wacky weed, but they were definitely being eyeballed.

"Can we get back to business, please?" Jerry said.

"I already told you," Rob said. "I don't like it. I'm not crazy about this getting into the hands of a third party."

"You never said that," Jerry said.

"I thought I had."

"Look," Nick said. "Let's see what we can do with the stuff. Just…us. Keep it in the family. We've got a ton of this crap left. We'll go into Pittsburgh and see if we can move it on the streets. Whatever happens, it's still a three-way cut."

"You're going to stand around and sell to strangers," Jerry said. "Like the Good Humor man sells Creamsicles?"

"That's life, that's what all the people say," Sinatra began with fabulous bravado. *"You're riding high in April, shot down in May. But I know I'm gonna change that tune, when I'm back on top, back on top in June."*

"What is this?" Nick said.

Rob just sat there, grinning and blushing. Jerry looked like he was going to pull a stiletto on him. He shook his head slowly. "Jesus, man. I'm wondering how I got mixed up in this shit of yours. What's your third song, something by Asshole and Garfunkel?"

"You got mixed up in this because there's money in it," Nick stated flatly and seriously, and he was right; it was the only reason why Jerry Bruno would have dipped his foot in the pond of the young and the drugged. "I mean, you have a better idea?"

What happened for the rest of that evening didn't matter. He was here, now, in another time, another place, at another table. Older, wiser, more desperate, in a forgettable bar just off Eighth Avenue.

"Gentlemen," the waitress said. "Get you another couple of those?"

Rob shrugged. "Why not. I have two half-furnished rooms on the Upper East Side and a roach problem. And no one waiting there for me."

Nick said, "Sure," and smiled at the waitress. When they were alone he leaned across the table. "Remember what we did with the stuff?"

"Wait a minute." He looked at his watch. "You have a wife and kids. You're going to come staggering in—"

"Everyone will be asleep. The kids have school and Joanne teaches children."

"What, like big kids or infantile kids? I mean, what does she teach?"

"Preschoolers. You've never had any, obviously."

"Janet couldn't. I mean, we went through the motions and all, but..." He shrugged. "You know..."

"It's a big deal having kids. When they're small it's gimme this, gimme that. Feed me, change me, play with me."

"I'm not good at that stuff," Rob said.

"They get older, they expect you to read their minds. You end up with a room full of scorn and tragically bad second guesses." He thought of Eric, who in his early days showed some real musical prowess. A framed photo of him with a stratospherically rare, hence out-of-this-world expensive, Gibson Les Paul, shot at Manny's on West Forty-Eighth beneath the nervous gaze of the employees and Jeff Beck—somewhat older than when Nick last saw him play with a rail-thin Rod Stewart and who'd happened to wander in at the same time—held pride of place in what had once been known as the Den and was now referred to as simply the Basement. After Eric had displayed his licks, such as they were, Jeff was kind enough to nod and mumble, "Put your finger 'ere, lad," pointing to the note Eric had left out in his little Led Zeppelin display.

Now the kid couldn't even find the notes for an E chord, showing all the outward signs of someone who did more than dabble in soft drugs. A few years ago, Nick had taken Eric and Jen aside and gave them a lecture about the evil of, as he called it, substances, but somehow it came off as unconvincing, as if Bogart had been called upon to do an antismoking commercial.

Rob said, "I'm still stuck in Cincinnati. Just remind me, OK? We scored the stuff, we took it back to Eden, we didn't sell enough and then—what?—a week, two, whatever, we did what? Refresh my memory?"

Nick sat back and put his palms flat on the table. "We went to Pittsburgh."

"Pittsburgh, right, right, right. I called that guy in Cincinnati—"

"Guy who sold us the stuff—"

"And he gave me the number of some other guy in Pittsburgh."

All of this came back in stunning detail to Nick. Whoever said that if you remembered the sixties you weren't there was a liar; even Nick, who had smoked or swallowed anything that wasn't superglued to the table, could return to those times with great and perfect clarity. Perhaps seeing the Light had also in some obscure way tightened the focus on his memory.

"Because we didn't want Jerry to take it off our hands."

"We took a chance—"

"And I think we did OK."

Rob cast his mind back. "We met the guy at some bar, right?"

"Black guy—"

"Definitely black. Army surplus coat."

"And a big Afro," Nick said. "With a comb stuck in it. And a veneer of paranoia a foot thick."

"Sweating like he wanted to be anywhere but in his skin."

"Remember the music? Sly and the Family Stone?"

Rob laughed. "Man, you have an amazing memory. And did we go outside with the guy or am I just imagining that?"

Nick could still see snowflakes as big as dollar bills falling from the sky, passing through the cool glow of the streetlights.

But now it was all coming back to Rob: "Right. He said he'd buy the stuff from us, but right now he was in some kind of trouble."

"He was holding."

Rob's face glowed with the memory of it. "Because he was trying to sell some of his own stuff and was freaking out."

Nick nodded. "He had an arrest record. He'd already been convicted on a possession charge. Remember he told us that? He was going nuts. He was scared."

Rob sat up. "He was supposed to sell it for some other dealer, right?"

"Something like that."

"All this smack, speed, whatever it was. He knew it'd take longer, and he'd be holding for a few days, a week. If he'd got caught with the hard stuff he'd have ended up serving a mandatory sentence. He wanted a quick cash return, even if it meant taking a big loss."

"*Huge* loss. It was crazy, we couldn't believe it, right? So he traded."

"Because he could shift the pot in no time. Up at Carnegie, at Pitt—the stuff would have been gone in an hour. Make some quick cash for him and he'd be home free. We gave him altogether maybe eight hundred bucks' worth of pot. And we got what?"

Rob just looked at him. "I don't know." And then he started to laugh. "Know what else? We never told Jerry. He just wrote the whole thing off as a loss, remember? Thought we were a couple of losers."

"Dude," Nick said, "we still are." They both laughed. Nick sat back and enjoyed the moment. "Being young is vastly underrated, you know that?"

"It was fun, wasn't it?"

"That guy could've burned us. Handed us nothing but Coffee-mate or something. We never tested it, did we?"

Rob laughed a little. "We weren't that crazy."

"But his sweat was definitely real."

"You think?"

"And where were we going to sell it? If it was the real thing, who was going to buy hard stuff like that? This was one very straight campus."

"I mean, if we'd been at Berkeley or NYU, no problem, the shit would've been gone in an hour."

Nick lowered his voice. "But—listen—what if the guy was genuine? What if he really was trying to put the hard stuff on us so he could sell the grass?" He leaned in to press his point.

"What are you saying?" Rob could hardly sit still. He was moving constantly on the seat, and finally Nick grabbed his wrist.

"Shhh-shhh… Listen to me." He said it so quietly that his lips barely moved. "Remember what we did with it?"

"Why is it important?"

"Because you and I are both out of work. Because we have found ourselves in serious debt." His voice was nothing but a hiss in a world of noise. A Knicks game played on the TV over the bar. Traffic slid by outside the window. Ice clinked in glasses against the *fsst* of beer bottles popping open. "I just want you to clear your head and remember."

The sun was setting over Buckeye Hall in a hazy winter sky, "Under My Thumb" did its sinister job from an open window in one of the dorms… Nick and Rob were walking across a campus dusted with day-old snow in the week before Thanksgiving… No one else was around. The sound of the wind… The cold against his face…

"I remember," Rob said decisively. "We buried it. Because we couldn't keep it in the dorm. Stuff like that, class-A substance, if that's what it really was, would've earned us serious prison time. I remember we went into town and bought a couple of those things you put preserves in."

"Mason jars," Nick clarified.

"Filled to the top. That's a lot of dope. You could bury a jar of pickles and they'd still be good when you turned seventy. As long as the thing was airtight. So chances are whatever's in it is still good. It's still got its…integrity." He rubbed his fingers together as though speaking of diamonds. "The question is," he said, leaning forward, "the real nub of the matter is, what was the stuff the guy gave us?"

"Speak hypothetically," Nick suggested.

"Let's assume this is heroin—"

"Why not cocaine?"

"In 1970? No one we knew used the stuff back then."

"OK, so for argument's sake, let's call it…" He lowered his voice even more. "Smack."

"If it's quality stuff, which is not guaranteed by any means—a professional cuts this, puts it on the streets—it could be worth hundreds of thousands in this market, right?"

"I haven't been following the narcotics trade," Nick said quietly.

"It could even be a couple of million."

"That's a lot of money."

"Just lying there, waiting to be dug up."

"Because we forgot about it."

"Yes, yes, yes," Rob said, barely containing himself.

"Remember where it was?"

"We're talking thirty years ago, Nick."

"Long time."

"Water under the bridge."

"Yeah, well… You know what they say."

"Easy come—"

"You got it."

Nick smiled and lifted his drink. For a few golden minutes he'd forgotten about the fat, hairy monkey called Debt that clung to his back, not to mention the parrot known as Failure perched on his shoulder whispering sweet nothings in his ear.

"I gotta go," he said. He looked at his watch. "The last train's in thirty-five minutes. Otherwise I end up in a hotel that I can't afford."

He drained his glass and put down a couple of twenties. Rob, the cheapest man in the known universe, who even back in college after a meal at Mother Hubbard's or the Waffle House would announce that, whoops, he'd forgotten his wallet again, put down a ten and counted out three measly singles.

Rob gave Nick a hug at the doorway. "It's been fun. We had great times back then, didn't we?"

"We always gave it our best," Nick said.

"So," Rob said, and Nick looked his friend over one last time.

"You look all right, you know? Even if you are a lawyer."

Rob threw a fake punch at him, and they sparred playfully for a few seconds until the barman suspected it might turn into a bloody brawl.

"Time to take it outside, fellas," he called as he polished a glass.

"Call me," Nick said. "Let's have lunch one of these days." He shrugged. "I don't have anything else to do." He took the initiative and stepped out into the brisk evening air. The wind had turned and, skimming the top off the Hudson, it caused the temperature to plunge. Nick turned up the collar of his coat as he crossed Sixth Avenue, and it was only when he reached the sidewalk that he heard the sound of running feet. Two hands seized him from behind.

"I just remembered..." It was Rob, painfully out of breath, his face red in the buzzy glow of a Duane Reade. "I know," he panted, "exactly where we buried the stuff."

Part Two

1

WINTER WAS COMING; LIKE THE SCENT OF MINT, IT WAS bright and alert, and Ray Garland was glad he'd put on the camel hair coat after all. If anything, it impressed the clients, and that was half the game right there. He settled into the soft leather seat in the back, the black leather case beside him. When he shut the door all the air was sucked out of the car and replaced by the soft fizz of recycling warmth. Driver was listening to a radio station out of Newark. A tenor player on a roll confidently sketched out the chorus of an old show tune, "Old Devil Moon." He toyed with the rhythm as if he'd paid cold, hard cash for it.

Two eyes in the rearview: "Know who that is?"

"Rollins. The Vanguard. Fifty-seven."

Charles Driver grinned. "I bet you even know what time of day he was playing that thing."

"Ten to nine. Sunday night."

"You're like a—I don't know—like an automaton or something."

"Call it an educated guess."

Ray stroked his goatee and gazed out through the darkened windows, where the city was like an old movie, passing lights and silhouettes.

"Tell you what I like about you, Ray. All the street's been wrung out of you. All the wise shit's been drained away. You're a man of distinction now. You even *look* like you read a lot."

"I do read a lot."

"Yeah, but how many *look* like it, huh?" Driver caught his reflected eye once again. "We're going uptown. Man on Central Park West is in dire need."

Ray caught the glint of Driver's shades. Like a pimp, he thought. But then again, he was wearing a pair, too. Not dark enough so you couldn't see his eyes, but tinted enough—a pale yellow bleeding into gray—to mute his mood. "Anyone we know?"

"Nope. Word got out, our boy made the call, we got the job."

"How much does he know about me?"

"Only that you're Mr. Garland. Same as all our other clients know."

"How much we talking about?"

"All I know is it's a lot. Which is why you're here."

Ray considered it for a few minutes. "What's the setup?"

"We have exactly zero intelligence on the guy or his people beyond the cold, hard fact that he's something to do with the movies."

"That worry you?"

Driver pulled a Glock 19 from its holster and waved it in the air. "Not much." Ray had never once seen him use it. According to Driver, simply taking the thing out for a walk was enough to scare away even the meanest motherfucker. Ray sighed and settled back, crossing one leg over the other. The night was quiet, the traffic sparse even on Broadway. Something by Keith Jarrett was now on the radio.

"Turn it off, will you?" Ray said without further comment, and Driver hit a button. He knew better than to ask Ray why he didn't like something. Music to Driver was just something in the air, something you nodded your head to, something that made life just a little easier, like WD-40 made the gate go back and forth.

He cut a right and picked up speed till he reached the corner of Ninetieth and Central Park West, his headlights briefly picking up the edge of the park. He pulled into a tow zone and tossed a placard on the dash. "Showtime," he said, and Ray grabbed the case and stepped out into the cold. The building looked like any other on the avenue, the doorman just another pair of impassive eyes under a peaked cap. Driver put a hand on Ray's shoulder.

"You ready for this?"

"Aren't I always, Mr. Driver?"

"Always a gentleman. You can call me mister till the day I die."

Driver walked up to the reception desk. A young, clean-cut Hispanic man in a maroon jacket with brass buttons glanced up from his *Daily News*. His eyes narrowed when he saw the two black men.

Driver had the first word. "We have an appointment with Mr. Burns." In the light and on his feet Driver was more imposing than behind the wheel of the Town Car, where he seemed just another fat man looking for joy. He had an easy six inches and a good eighty, eighty-five pounds on Ray, and if Ray was a snappy dresser Driver went one better. He wore Armani suits, hand-sewn shoes, always at a high polish, and a long, black leather overcoat, his only concession to gangsterism, apart from the Glock, of course.

"I'll announce you, OK?"

Driver slid a crisp fifty across to him. "Don't trouble yourself."

Driver pressed the button for fourteen. When the elevator settled to a halt, Ray picked up the leather case from the floor. They stepped out into the carpeted hallway and followed it until they reached apartment 14F.

Driver lifted a hand to knock when the door opened to reveal a white man in a terry-cloth bathrobe with a Hollywood tan and damp hair too long for someone his age. Obviously, the goon at reception had gone ahead and alerted the guy.

"Gentlemen," Burns said. "C'mon in."

A woman probably half Burns's age sat on a sofa, drink in hand. She had long, curly blond hair and some obvious cosmetic surgery, leaving her smile fixed in place. She wore a silk dressing gown, and one slender waxed leg was hooked over the other, rocking up and down. She leafed through a copy of *Vogue*, casually turning one page after another, then looked Ray up and down and shifted her eyes to Driver. Menace and good times, baby.

Burns said to her, "Why don't you go in the bedroom. Watch a little TV, OK?"

Without a word she took her drink and strolled into the world of elsewhere. It was clear to Ray that beneath the robe she wore absolutely nothing. She shut the door and left them alone while Ray checked out the room. A few framed movie posters hung here and there. A group of mounted photos of a smiling Burns and various movie stars occupied half of one wall. Jack Nicholson. Sean Penn. Russell Crowe. Over the fireplace, under the soft glow of a picture light and nearly the width of the mantel, was a Motherwell from the early sixties.

"She the only other person here?" Driver said.

"I gave up threesomes long ago." Burns couldn't suppress a smile. "That was a joke."

Ray set his leather case down on the coffee table.

"Whoa," Burns said. "That piece of furniture cost me plenty."

"I guarantee the case cost more," Ray said. "And if you don't want to do business my way, then we'll just take our things and leave. That suit you, Mr. Burns? The city is filled with desperate people tonight."

"No, it's OK, just… Look, it's fine."

"Now I assume you're a man of your word, that your money's clean and that this transaction is and will henceforth be known only to us. Am I being accurate?"

Burns looked blankly at him, then at Driver. "Are you talking to me?"

"A simple yes or no will suffice," Ray said.

"Yes. I mean no, no one knows about this. I mean, we wouldn't have gotten this far unless you knew you could trust me."

"I don't trust anyone," Ray said. "Not even Mr. Driver here."

"Now answer the man's question," Driver said. "Does anyone else know about this?"

"Just…us."

"And Pussy Galore there makes three," Driver said.

"Who? What—?"

Driver nodded toward the bedroom. Burns laughed. "She thinks this is movie business. That you guys are investors or producers. For my next project."

"You a director or something?" Driver asked.

"More like Or Something," Burns said as he poured some Johnny Walker Blue into a Waterford tumbler. He disliked having to say *producer* too often, as though the word made his breath stink.

He looked over at them and held up his glass. "Drink?"

"Not when I'm driving," Driver said.

"What's your next project?" Ray asked. "If you don't mind my asking." Burns held the glass out to him so Ray could continue to ignore it.

"Oh, it's just this…thriller thing. It's not really something I can discuss. I mean, I have to protect the story." He took the glass back and set it on the bar.

"I know how you feel," Ray said. "I got a few I keep locked up, too. Murder stories, mostly. Lots of blood, lots of suffering. You know, it's terrible what a body can endure. I even got a love story of sorts, but I'm not going to give that one away so easily. I'm still not sure how it's going to end. All of a sudden you don't seem so interested."

"No, I'm…I'm always interested in a good pitch. I mean, if you have an agent I can—"

"I don't work with agents," Ray said. "I don't trust middlemen. Which is why I'm here and you're here and Mr. Driver is in the room with us, as he looks after my best interests. There are no middlemen this evening. This is all face to face, man to man, cash and carry. You dig?"

"I think I understand."

"And since you're a man who doesn't walk around town telling everyone your business, which in this case also happens to be ours, I think we can proceed. First, the ground rules," Ray said. "I don't nickel-and-dime. These are strictly all-in-one purchases that involve serious money. I don't do return visits because of mistakes the buyer might make. A moment of indecision, a lapse of judgment… And if you don't buy all of what's on offer, you understand, I walk out of here and I'm *carrying*, I'm twenty-five to life waiting to happen. Am I right, Mr. Driver?"

"No doubt whatsoever," the big man said.

"That has some bearing on my price this evening, should you choose not to buy the entire contents of my case. As you're not objecting to these terms, we may proceed without further discussion."

Ray unlatched the leather case and opened the lid to reveal four plastic bags filled with white powder, each nestled against the other. Ray had decided on a price the moment he'd entered the apartment. "For the whole box, two hundred and eighty. For one item…" He took out a bag and held it before Burns's face.

"Seventy thousand," Burns said.

"Whoa, ho," Driver exclaimed. "What'd you just do, reinvent long division or something?"

"Remember what I said?" Ray went on. "The *risk* surcharge. I walk out of here, *I'm* the one who could be picked up, and my friend Mr. Driver here does time for being an accessory. Mr. Driver dislikes prison life, isn't that right, Mr. Driver?"

"Never agreed with me," Driver said.

"So you don't buy it all, you pay the insurance against my going to a very unpleasant place for a very long time. One item will cost you a grand total of eighty thousand dollars. And that would be, as I understand you have already been informed, in bills no larger than a hundred. Any indiscretions on your part, such as counterfeit currency or underpayment, will be answered within twenty-four hours. It will come as a surprise, and not entirely a welcome one. So now you understand the benefit to you in making a bulk purchase." He turned to Driver. "What's the name of that place where you do that?"

"My mother likes that Costco place when she's able to get onto her feet."

"Pretend you're stocking up on household necessities," Ray said. "Buy in quantity to catch a good deal before prices go sky-high."

"It's a bargain, I'll say that," Burns agreed. "Is it any good?"

Ray started packing the bags back in the case.

"What the hell?" Burns said. "I thought we were doing business here."

"Then don't ask me if what I'm offering you is good or not. I don't ask if your movies are any good, now do I? Because I'm guessing with your name on them they are first-rate products that could stand alongside such classics as *Lawrence of Arabia* and *The Godfather*."

"OK, OK, sorry."

Ray sat.

"Can I at least have a taste?"

"That goes without saying," Ray said, and when he unsealed one of the bags, Burns started to dip a finger in it. Driver slapped him lightly on the wrist. He took a leather case from his pocket, resembling a carrier for fine cigars, and removing the lid shook it a little to shift the fifty or sixty thin wooden sticks into graspable space. Burns slid one free and scooped a taste onto the end. He felt a little between his fingers before putting it on his tongue. The man clearly knew what he was doing. He smiled, as by rights he should have under the circumstances.

Ray sealed up the bag and put it back in the case. "As with all transactions that get this far, we're now past the fail-safe stage. I don't leave without cash in hand."

"So you don't take checks?" Burns said, giving them his best Bel Air smile, all sparkly teeth and bright overworked gums.

"You Rodney Dangerfield?" Driver said. "Then stop making jokes, OK?"

"How much do you want?" Ray said quietly.

"Just one."

"And that will cost you?"

"Eighty thousand dollars," Burns said.

"You're proving to be a fast learner, Mr. Burns." He could see the man's hands were trembling, either out of excitement for another fix or out of fear, the crowbar of all blind deals.

"Now please get the cash."

"Just a moment," Driver said, pressing a hand against the producer's rising shoulder. "And where might it be?"

"In the bedroom."

"Exactly where?" Driver asked.

"In a drawer in the bedside table on the right side. Leather bag."

"Like a guy's toiletries bag?" Driver asked. "What's that called, doppo or dumbo or…" He shrugged.

"But bigger. Really, I can get it."

"Don't trouble yourself," Driver said, and without waiting for a word of objection he walked to the door and pushed it open to find Pussy Galore lying naked on the bed, pleasuring herself with an alarmingly large, black rubber penis slathered with what looked like Crisco. She screamed and rolled over onto her stomach. Driver ignored her and returned with the bag. "Your lady," he said, "she's a fine woman." He patted his voluminous belly. "Outstanding abs." He tossed the bag to Burns.

"Now count it out," Ray said.

Burns turned the bag upside down and packets of bills, each secured by a paper band, tumbled out. Ray estimated at least a hundred and twenty grand. They watched as the man laid out the money in a series of individual stacks. The four stacks left over went back into the bag. "That's eighty even."

"Now hand it to me," Ray said.

"You want me to hand it to you."

"That's what I said. Put it in my hand. I like to feel my money now and again."

Burns gathered the bills into one pile, squared them up the best he could, and handed it to Ray, who passed him his purchased goods in return. Ray packed the money in the bag he'd brought with him, buttoned his coat, and, without another word, left the apartment. Driver took his shield from his pocket and held it up before him.

"I regret to inform you, Mr. Burns, that you are under arrest for the solicitation and purchase of a substantial amount of a class-A narcotic. You have the right to remain silent. Anything you say can and will be used against you in a court of law. You have the right to speak to an attorney and to have an attorney present during any questioning. If you cannot afford a lawyer, one will be provided for you at government expense. Though something tells me you can and will afford the best that money can buy. Did I make myself understood, Mr. Burns?"

Burns just sat staring into the dark void that had become his future. When the door to the bedroom opened, Driver immediately pulled his Glock from its holster and because Ms. Galore was carrying a weapon, he put a bullet in her face, leaving him as surprised as she was. Especially as she was only holding her big black dildo.

2

"THE GUY'S NAME IS LEROY IVES."

"All those years ago and you still remember?"
Nick said. The drive from the airport in Pittsburgh to the college usually took just over an hour, longer, if, like most students at the college returning from one vacation or another, you stopped at Pam's Pancake Parlor in Gowerstown, where Pam, in her apron, with a head of loose red curls and a snarly Alice's Restaurant attitude, would either treat you like one of her own or show you the door if she didn't like your face, and where you could fuel up before the downhill journey to the dorm and the malign presence of Ma Jones, with her pitcher of freshly made hot chocolate straight out of the foil packet.

But Pam had sold her property to the Wendy's people and retired on her profits to Sedona. The head shop just around the corner was now a NAPA auto-parts store, and the only decent record shop in the region, known as Uncle Meat's and run by a middle-aged alopecic kvetch from Brooklyn, had become a Starbucks.

Everything seemed different: What had once been service roads and long stretches of nothing but farmland and hamlet had given way to shopping malls and prefab suburban developments; and though before the area was bland and monotonous, now it was simply anonymous. One glance out the window and you could be just about anywhere in this great big country.

"I liked Leroy," Rob went on. "He was a model client. Respectful, cooperative. But guilty as hell. I mean, the first time I saw him coming down the hall in cuffs and leg-irons, I thought, whoa, here comes trouble. Like something out of, you know, *Shaft*. I'm thinking this guy couldn't be mistaken for anything but a drug dealer. He's street, he's going to jail no matter what."

"And was he? Did he?"

"He had a record going back to when he was fourteen and dealing in the projects. I mean, this guy was tough. But quiet tough. Simmering tough. And he had this habit—man, it was spooky. He'd just sit there, hiding behind his eyes, you know what I mean? You could *see* the guy thinking, you could almost hear the gears clicking. You know, like he'd reached some kind of Zen place where nothing could touch him."

"And you lost the case."

"We made a deal. As long as I left his brother Sonny out of the trial I could put him up as a small-time pusher who'd maybe get the mandatory fifteen."

"He'd take it?"

"Absolutely. He figured with good behavior he could be out in seven or eight. I mean, I could have put Sonny on the stand to sway the jury a little. You know, just as a character witness. He could talk about growing up with Leroy, how Leroy looked out for him, how Leroy was such a good father and husband and brother. The usual stuff. It's completely unreliable, putting a family member up there, but you know how it is. You do what you can."

"So why didn't you just go ahead and do it?"

"Sonny had just gotten married to a girl he'd known since they were kids. Leroy wanted Sonny left alone so he could have a decent life. He wanted to protect him. Shield him. Figured he owed it to his little brother." He shrugged. "Only afterwards I found out that Sonny knew all about Leroy's business. Every detail, every name."

"He was a dealer, too?"

"A user, never a seller. But he knew enough so that under cross-examination he would have blown his brother's operation sky-high. What Leroy was protecting was a much bigger background operation that most people didn't know about. Leroy was a major, major dealer. He ended up with twenty-five years. You want to hear the weird part of it? When the sentence came down, he just turned to me and smiled."

"And the point of this story is?"

"We find the stuff and we need to move it, right? We call Sonny. As far as I know the guy's still walking around. I figure he owes me big-time for keeping him off the stand." He looked at Nick. "So the time has come to call in one very big favor."

Rob pulled into the parking lot of a Home Depot. He turned off the engine and for a moment they just sat there. Contractors in work clothes humped lumber or band saws and loaded them into their pickups.

Rob looked at him. "What'd you tell your wife?"

"That I ran into you at the Javits and that you had a lead on a one-off job with an old college friend. I'm doing the marketing campaign, you're running the legal end of things."

"And I bet you said it was for Jerry Bruno."

"As a matter of fact I did."

Rob beamed. Neither of them had ever been to a college homecoming before, not Nick, who hadn't even graduated from the place, nor Rob, who rightly suspected such events were simply excuses for extracting money from alums. Driving up the main road that cut through the freshly mown lawns of the campus, past the Kennison Memorial (a bronze plaque mounted on a slab of granite, honoring the memory of a past trustee who'd left the place a few million in his will), they watched with a kind of wonder as the campus unfolded before them.

"I don't recognize it," Rob said.

"Jesus… We never had all these buildings."

A smiling, well-groomed boy in an Eden College sweatshirt signaled them to stop and came to the window. "Preregistered?"

"Yes we are," Rob said.

"Parking lot six, just over there."

"Parking lot *six*? In my day you just left your car on the crabgrass behind the security shack."

The kid laughed and turned his attention to the car behind them. A welcome banner over the main building flapped furiously beneath a cloudless sky. Alums, many with children, some of them crying, waited on line to check in. A pretty blond coed caught Nick's eye as she took her place behind the registration table.

"Where are you going?" Rob said.

"She's waiting for us."

He was like an iron filing in the presence of a strong magnet. Nick wondered what had happened to him since losing his job. Normally he was a dedicated family man, a loyal and loving husband. He had no reason to stray; Joanne was everything he could want in a mate. She had aged so gracefully that even younger men would eye her when they were in stores or restaurants. When she sat by the pool at their club—what had once been their club, anyway—she would be the center of attention, with her long slim legs and sleek body, and the way she held her glass with the ends of her slender fingers. So what the hell was going on?

"Hi, welcome back," the blonde said. "Can I get your graduation year, please?"

"Actually, I didn't graduate," he said. "They said I was socially unacceptable."

"I did," Rob said. "Rob Johnson, class of '72. I called last week and prepaid." He turned to Nick. "Which reminds me."

"I told you I'd pay you back," Nick said.

She checked their names against a list. Nick watched her perfectly manicured finger as it moved smoothly down the column of names. She wore a white blouse and a blue cardigan, and for a moment he imagined her not wearing a white blouse and a blue cardigan, and felt something stir within him.

"Can I ask you a question, please?"

She raised her eyes to him. This time there was no smile; she'd been around the block more than once. "Is there a Kacey Christopher coming to this thing?"

"Oh for Christ's sake," Rob said.

"I wouldn't know, sir," the young woman said.

"Please check. Class of '73, I think. A year behind us."

She ran her magic finger down another list. "I don't see it."

"OK," Nick said. "It doesn't matter."

She handed them each a peel-off name tag, like the one he'd been given by that woman at the job fair. "There are pens at that table. Write your name and your graduating year—or not," she said with a glance—was it withering?—at Nick. "And have a great time."

They recognized no one, and similarly no one came up to them, hand extended, seeking recognition. "Do you remember where we parked the car?" Nick asked. "Because we're going to have to go back and get the shovel and the flashlight."

"It's over there." Rob waved in a general direction. "Somewhere." He pulled open the door to the student union. Thirty years earlier it was where the radio station was housed, in a tiny room adjacent to a snack bar that Nick and Denis Whidbey had learned to pilfer after Mrs. Burt, the snack-bar manager with a permanent scowl and a profoundly overweight son with Sex Offender written all over his face, had locked up for the night and gone home. Because back then, when security was nothing more than a Korean War vet with a two-by-four and a walkie-talkie, they had the run of the place, grilling hamburgers, making milkshakes, and frenching fries. A quick cleanup and no one ever suspected that anyone had been there. Now that he was back on campus, Nick began to tote up the litany of crimes he'd committed there: the Great Snack-bar Heist(s); the Business Office Thefts; the Bomb Scare, in which he took the hometown newspaper Jeff Felder subscribed to and, hands in gloves, cut out the letters:

THƐREISABOMBOℕCℿMPꙮ

(the last two being the "US" in an ad for the Army—a nice anti-war touch, Nick thought at the time), pasted them on a piece of paper, slid it into an envelope and casually slipped it under the president's office door when everyone had gone home. Because he'd not specified which building the explosive device was in, or a date and time for its expected detonation, they'd have to lock down and search every structure on campus. Which they did, for a full twenty-four hours, giving the facility over to guys in space suits with German shepherds pretending they were in *Stalag 17*, thus leaving Nick and his friends the time to get as stoned as possible while they listened to Hendrix's latest album, bought the night before at Uncle Meat's. When the FBI was called in and they gathered the entire student body in the chapel and explained how the crime, though no bomb actually turned up, would (not "could") result in "significant jail time" and "a blot on your record for the rest of your life," Nick kept his cool, thanks to the Quaaludes he'd taken an hour earlier. And yet what remained within him was an uneasy pain, dull and unfocused: the FBI was serious business; eventually they would hook him up to a lie detector and he'd spill it all—the bomb, the burgers, the payroll machines, the dope. His natural paranoia increased fourfold. He checked his room for bugs and found it clean; he disassembled his stereo speakers and found nothing that looked out of the ordinary. Now, thirty years later, he wondered when the statute of limitations would run out, because—and he glanced around in his old paranoid way—there was every chance the Feds were there at that moment, waiting to bust him once and for all. Maybe the whole thing—the reunion, the registration tables, the banner, the promised alcoholic beverages—was nothing more than a ploy to set up the perpetrator for a spectacular arrest.

"This place has really changed," Rob said. There was an ATM (which, had it been there back in the day, would, like the machines in the business office, have ended up in Nick's possession as well), and there were computers and printers set up at various places in the building.

The young woman in the white blouse and blue cardigan was heading their way. Nick gave his best smile and she gave it right back. Clearly rejection had just been a passing nightmare. "Hey," he said, because it was how his own children often addressed him, when not using the all-purpose "dude."

"You guys know about the films they're running? They're from way back from when you were here. In the theater."

"Oh great, let's go," Rob said.

"I'll catch up with you." He said to the young woman, "So you must be, what? A senior? Junior?"

"This is my last year."

"Sorority? Wait—let me guess. Tri-Delt?"

"Hey, you're good!" She reached out and touched his arm—briefly, meaninglessly—but it was enough; it was enough. She blushed and laughed a little. She knew her effect on men.

He knew that she knew. He also knew that Delta Delta Delta was where all the beautiful blondes pledged and actually got in, simply because on this campus it was an unwritten rule, he assumed still in force, that if you were anything but blond and blue-eyed and beautiful you belonged in a less ethnically pure sorority or even locked out altogether, as though Josef Mengele were the gatekeeper of the school's Greek system.

She started to turn away.

"Wait," he said. "What's your name?"

"Cassandra."

"I'm Nick."

"I know," she said. "I read your breast." And with a look he could only categorize as very grown-up, she turned and walked the length of the room. He thought: if she turns and looks at me I've scored. He saw the scenario like a montage in a film: girl/car/motel/morning.

She didn't turn. She had played him for a fool, and he felt like the idiot in a country song, left to sit at a bar with a bunch of long-haul truckers, drinking his dreams away.

He wandered off to the theater and found Rob in the doorway. Half the seats were filled, and most of the people there were pointing at the screen and laughing, as football players—Stumper among them—were scrimmaging in frilly pink tutus and bras.

"Amazing," Rob said. "We couldn't raise a smile while we were here and cross-dressing athletes bring the house down? Oh wait—here are some cheerleaders."

"We didn't know any, remember?" Nick said. "They were all sorority girls. They weren't allowed to talk to the freaks."

Rob laughed. "Right," he whispered. "I forgot. Look at us now. And look at them." He gestured to a cabal of middle-aged women in a corner of the auditorium, looking like people you wait on line with at the supermarket, fishing for the odd six cents in the depths of their bags.

"We're just like them, Rob. Married. Or divorced. Growing older by the minute and terrified of dying. The difference is that we're going to sell some drugs this week."

Nick looked over his shoulder, hoping that Cassandra would be standing there, waiting for more attention from this notorious social outcast and rebel without a cause. But there was no one. Rob elbowed him. "Check it out."

The footage now turned to general scenes of campus life. Fleetingly, Kacey Christopher was in her miniskirt and tank top sitting on the lawn in front of the administration building, reading *The Stranger*, smoking a Virginia Slim and looking a lot more sophisticated than she really was—and that was half her charm right there. It was still there: the old tug, the old heartache. She looked dynamite, Nick thought. With her, at least, he knew exactly what she looked like beneath those clothes, and he wanted to cry. She brushed away a lock of hair from her cheek, and spotting the camera, smiled. Oh God, he thought, and felt his stomach flip over.

"Holy shit, look at this."

People in the audience started to laugh at the screen as Nick, in a blood-red Che Guevara T-shirt, slouched in a booth in the student union, dark and brooding and desperately needing a shave, his thick black hair to his shoulders, while beside him Rob was somewhat less threatening in his ponytail and "Clapton is God" T-shirt. The table was littered with paper plates, Styrofoam cups, and a pile of smoldering butts in an ashtray. Nick slowly uncurled his middle finger at the camera. Chad Bakeman, the college's resident reactionary, in his usual short-sleeved shirt and skinny tie, walked up to them with a wise-guy neocon sneer and a microphone. He said, "And here are Eden's resident hippies, Rob and Nick. Everything groovy up where you are?"

Nick finished lighting a cigarette and gazed up at him, his dilated pupils full of dreary wonder. "Yeah... I just saw your grandmother crawling across the ceiling with a carrot up her—" And the film abruptly ended. Unrecognized, Nick and Rob rose from their seats and headed toward the exit just as footage came on of a 1969 production of *Finian's Rainbow*. Diane Normandy, in a gingham dress, sang, "How Are Things in Glocca Morra?" Nick had had a brief fling with Diane around that time, though "fling" wouldn't have been the word chosen by him back then, the term belonging more to his mother's generation and implying martinis and a suite at the Pierre rather than room four at the Puritan Motel in Beaver Falls. It went well for three weeks or so, at least until he caught a glimpse of Kacey Christopher.

As they stepped out of the theater, some guy neither of them knew walked up to them. He said, "It's Pete Hill."

Nick squinted and brought him into focus. "Jesus. Pete. Sorry I didn't recognize you. How've you been?" In fact, Pete Hill looked exactly the same; it was Nick's perception that had altered since then. He was beginning to realize the world he once inhabited was like another planet requiring periodic rediscovery.

"Pretty well, thanks. You?"

"Just great," Nick said.

"Hear about Jerry Bruno?"

Jerry's potential to step out of nowhere and instigate mayhem just when they were about to make a killing on the narcotics market had been in the back of Nick's mind ever since Rob reminded him of his involvement in the deal. He'd seen it happen before: the people you'd conveniently forgotten always returned at the worst of times.

"He died eight months ago," Pete said.

"That's great," Rob blurted, and Nick glared at him. "I mean, God, that's awful."

"Prostate cancer. Guess it was pretty rough for a while. Listen, gotta go find my family. Catch you later, maybe?"

"You really are out of your mind," Nick told Rob.

"Don't you see? It means it's all ours. Unless you want to send a hundred thou to Jerry's family as a magnanimous gesture on our part... Yeah, I didn't think so."

That evening, after cocktails were served in what had always been known as the Alumni Room but which was on more ordinary days a world of stale doughnuts and cold coffee known as the faculty lounge, and everyone had drifted into the field house for dinner and speeches, Nick and Rob made their way in the chill evening toward their rental. The air was clear, the earth at rest, and the last crickets of the year were singing their sweet valedictory tune somewhere in the great rural distance.

"I don't think I ever want to come back here again," Nick said.

"I know what you mean."

"I keep thinking of the things I shouldn't have done."

"I keep thinking of the things I didn't do."

"There's something you don't know," Nick said, and Rob slowed down and looked at him. "Kacey was pregnant."

"Are you joking me?"

"It was the end of the school year. I don't know, April or May, something like that. She was already a few months late."

"How did you manage to do this, Nick?"

Nick just looked at him. "You want the details or should I just start with the birds and bees?"

"I didn't mean that."

"It was an accident, we got carried away. We tried going to a local doctor, but he kept lecturing her about keeping the kid. So we…went into Pittsburgh and had it done by this guy. And it cost me five hundred bucks. He put this tube inside her."

He could still hear her sobbing as she knelt on the bathroom floor, the blood running down her thighs.

"Jesus. I never knew."

"I don't want to talk about it anymore."

They resumed walking. After a minute Rob said, "Did you ever tell your wife?"

"Some things you just don't talk about. Even if they happened a long time ago."

"In another life."

"Exactly."

Nick gazed at the horizon, at the distant glow from some other town. He felt an overwhelming need to shed tears—for Kacey, for what she'd been through, and, more bitterly, for how little he understood her back then, when crying wasn't an option for him. Kacey never returned to the college. Her life veered off in another direction, another point of the compass. When he tried calling her at home she was never in, or so he was told, whether it was nine in the morning or eleven at night. He realized something he had always vaguely suspected: that he'd never really stopped loving Kacey. But it had never gotten in the way for his love for Joanne, for his love for Kacey belonged to another version of him that predated his marriage. Should he feel guilty? Could one person contain so many secrets, so many and various stories, so many passions? And how many lives could one conceivably live? Could they survive all at the same time, just as, here at Eden, he'd been English major, drug dealer, junkie, freak, thief, anarchist, lover, loser? Wasn't he doing it right now, while he was supposed to be putting together a legitimate business deal and in reality was digging up jars of dope? Making things up was his line of work, wasn't it? Making things up and selling them? All it took, he thought, was a straight face, a rock-solid alibi, and a powerful instinct for survival.

Rob dug around for the keys. "Once I get in touch with Sonny Ives we'll get hooked up with someone who can take the stuff off our hands. We'll be holding for like a week, tops, and the next thing we know we'll have the cash. Best-case scenario, we make a few hundred thousand profit—don't forget Sonny's going to take a cut for his time and trouble."

And the worst-case scenario? Both of them knew it, or knew a whole array of them: *numero uno*, they'd be searched and arrested. Nick wondered how Joanne would manage to scrape together the bail money. He could see the photo in the *New York Post*: I DID IT FOR MY FAMILY, EX–AD EXEC SAYS. Second and third scenarios: that the jars were no longer there, or what they contained was not dope but something found in every household kitchen.

Rob unlocked the trunk. Lying next to the spare were the spade and a black Maglite they'd bought at Home Depot. Trapped by the handle of the shovel, the credit card receipt fluttered in the breeze, pulled itself free, flew crazily into the air and at the last moment was snatched back by Nick, the smoking gun crumpled and now stuffed into his pocket.

"You ready for this?" Rob said, slamming the trunk shut.

"As long as we turn up something. Otherwise—"

"Otherwise you go home, you tell Judy that—"

"Joanne—"

"You tell your wife that you met with me and Jerry, that you didn't think the deal was worth the time and effort, and you're back to where you started."

The practice field on the outskirts of the campus was deserted. Rob twisted the flashlight into action. "Somewhere between here and up there"—he played his beam around the distant goalpost—"lies our future."

As the wind picked up and shifted direction, they could hear a voice distantly leading the alums in song: "*We love the woods, the brook, the sky of azure blue… Our beloved E-e-den…here's to you…*"

Rob could only laugh. "Hey. Just remember. Back then they were going to pep rallies while we were listening to Jefferson Airplane and puking rainbows." His smile diminished as he surveyed what was starting to look like a much larger expanse than they remembered.

"You don't know, do you?" Nick said. "You don't remember where we buried it."

"I'm just trying to be precise. So we don't leave holes all over the place." He rested his arm on the top of the shovel and scanned the field again. "I'm trying to put myself back thirty years." He turned to Nick: "You know, you could be helping me. You were there. Look around, see anything familiar?"

"Not really."

Rob started walking. "I have a hunch," he said, and he headed off, his arm outstretched. "I remember now." He turned and waited till Nick caught up with him. "That tree. There." He pointed at a hill overlooking the field. "That was the landmark. We wanted it under that tree, and do you know why?"

Nick felt something surge in his heart. Rob was right. The tree had been planted by the retired first president of the college, a shrunken ninety-year-old in a sweater-vest and flannel trousers who'd been taken out of storage for a Founders' Day ceremony their first year there. He'd driven his spade into the ground and turned over an inch of dirt before the president of the board of trustees, a corporate type in a green blazer and khakis, relieved him of the thing, sparing him a fifth heart attack.

No one would ever allow the tree to be cut down. It would be like murdering the old man in cold blood. Unless, of course, some benefactor donated enough millions to erect some other structure in its place. In the darkness it was impossible to know what kind of tree it was. Leafless, its branches shuddering in the moonlit wind, it was undoubtedly impressive in the fullness of spring, magnificent come the boldness of summer. Now it was just another haunted bit of memory.

Rob put his hand on Nick's shoulder. "If it's not here someone got to it before we did. Simple as that." And he drove the shovel straight down into the soil and lifted out a wedge of sod and dirt.

"How far down did we bury it?"

"We must have had to move fast. Maybe a foot, maybe a little less?" He sent the shovel down again, this time more cautiously, and gently urged it in deeper with his heel. Nick aimed the beam at the hole. "One more and we should be there." This time Rob dislodged a good eight inches of soil. A few worms twisted in the dirt. He stood back and looked at Nick. "Thirty years ago we were standing right here, doing this same thing. It's like all that time has just…disappeared. Spooky, huh?"

Nick just nodded. He couldn't get Kacey Christopher out of his mind. He wished he could go back and listen to her a little better, just try to understand how she was feeling. He wondered if late at night she lay awake and thought about what happened back then. She'd only been a kid, really, all of, what, eighteen? He wondered if she'd finished her degree at another college, or ended up taking menial jobs, waitressing or flipping burgers someplace. He pictured her in her middle age, living on the fringe of society, scrounging for her next meal, like in the song. What did she tell him she wanted to do? Write a book or become a theater designer—something like that; she'd change her mind twice a week. For a while it was modern dance, then sculpture. But that was the point, wasn't it? Kacey wanted to do *everything*, to try everything, to *be* everything—how could one *not* fall for someone like that?

Yet things had gone awry. Their quarter hour of passion had turned into something sordid, curdling her youth, splashing the memory with blood and mucus, while he would leave this life in twenty or thirty or, if he were lucky, forty years, having resolved exactly nothing, having paid no price, settled no debts, saved no lives. Sometimes he would lie awake and wonder with astonishment at how much he had squandered: the life of Nick Copeland, from beginning to end, columns of numbers adding up to something close to the national debt. He could say it all he liked—yes, selling the buried drugs would help Joanne and the kids—but at that moment it felt downright *selfish*, something you did for the sheer hell of it, too much akin to stealing payroll machines or sending out bomb threats. Yet he had to admit that for the first time in years he felt utterly and completely alive. Even if they found nothing, even if the trip turned out to be a waste of time, he would take something away with him. Maybe something he'd left behind here one warm afternoon when a smile had caught his heart.

"Nick?" Rob was staring at him. "You OK?"

"Yeah, I'm fine. I'm really, really great." And he meant it. The cold, dry air worked on him like a shot of icy vodka, and his mind felt alert, sparkling, on the edge of some astonishing breakthrough.

"You want to give it a try?"

Nick placed the shovel six inches west of the first hole and pushed it slowly, cautiously, through the deep, dense autumn soil. Until he stopped.

"What?" Rob looked at him.

"Hold the light."

"Talk to me here."

"Just…just hold the light."

Nick fell to his knees and started scrabbling at the dirt with his hands. He pulled out gobs of earth that held the soul of last summer in its moist, loamy warmth. He loosened some dirt and bits of root and with both hands took hold of a pint jar. Slowly, he extracted it and set it on the grass beside the hole. Neither of them said a word. Nick pulled some more soil away until he had firm hold of the second jar. Both were intact. Rob carefully wiped away the dirt from the sides. He held one up in the moonlight. It was filled to the brim.

"Thirty years," Rob solemnly announced. "We were here then. We're here now. Seems like nothing. Now let's go rob the business office."

Nick sat back on the cold ground and laughed. At that moment he loved Rob more than anyone else in the world. It would pass, he knew, in three seconds, but Rob understood exactly how he was feeling. Nick picked up a jar and held it with both hands at eye level.

"Still think it's OK?" he said.

"My grandmother used to preserve fruit like this. Twenty years after she died we found a case of damson plums in the cellar."

"Any good?"

"I'm alive, aren't I?"

3

R OB SWITCHED ON THE IGNITION OF THE MIDSIZE VOMIT-
colored Buick they'd been forced to rent at Pittsburgh
International. He'd wanted at least a Sebring, preferably in a
nice shade of gray, but those were all gone, and Nick feared they
might end up wandering the car rental counters at the airport
until Rob could find the right fit for his personality.

"Wait," Nick said. "Just a second. I just realized. We'll
never make it past airport security with that stuff."

"Oh shit, you're right."

"It's OK. We'll just keep driving—"

"To New York—?"

"Seven hours, tops. We'll take shifts, stop to eat, gas up,
whatever. Return the car at La Guardia, pick up our cars, go
home." He shrugged.

Rob pulled slowly out of the spot, crested the hill of the
main road leading out of the campus past the woods and the
brook and, had it been daytime, beneath a sky of azure blue,
then kicked it roaring past a sign that—because someone had
crossed out the word "college," famously read:

YOU ARE NOW LEAVING
THE GATES OF EDEN

They began to laugh: a shared memory popping into the here and now.

"Was it you who wrote Dylan's name on the sign?" Rob asked.

Nick just grinned at him.

"Oh yeah," Rob said. "I forgot. I did that. Oh. Wait." He slid a CD he'd brought into the player in the dash.

"What is this?"

"Just listen."

Just the opening notes played by Keith Richards sent him back three decades. There was something ineffably sad about this moment, as if his life hereafter depended on something so simple as burying two jars of an unknown substance. What had once been a scary trip into someone else's vortex of fear was now just another tune on a band's song list, a chestnut off a Scorsese soundtrack. And yet, with the air streaming through the windows, with the silent darkness of the night hanging over them, it seemed just right. Rob offered a high five, Nick smacked it hard, and they whooped in triumph, shaking their fists out the open windows.

Until Nick glimpsed a flickering red and blue glow in the far distance. "Turn it off," he said.

"What?"

"I said, turn the fucking music off!" He reached over and hit the stop button and put an end to Merry Clayton's almighty wail.

The state police roadblock came into view, a patriotic light show featuring men in serious uniforms stopping cars.

"Oh my God," Rob said, and the Buick crawled to a stop a hundred yards away from it. There was no one behind or in front of them. The silence of the night was broken by the faraway squawk of a trooper's radio. "We're fucked."

"Get out and dump it in the woods—now!"

"Are you nuts, Nick? It's in the trunk, for Christ's sake." Rob was on the verge of throwing the kind of tantrum Eric and Jen specialized in when younger, especially in aisle three of a crowded supermarket.

"We're looking at serious jail time, Rob. I mean, you're a lawyer, figure it out."

A trooper strode out of the darkness toward their car.

"Oh boy," Rob whispered.

"Just move up slowly to meet him."

"Just remember, he's not a cop kind of cop. Don't call him officer, call him—"

Because Rob was not to be trusted in dealing with authority, Nick leaned over toward Rob's window. "What's up, officer?"

Well over six feet in his storm trooper boots, the man shone his flashlight into the car, landing the beam squarely on Nick's face. Then it shifted to Rob. "Pop the trunk, get out nice and easy, put your hands on your head and step away from the vehicle."

The trooper walked around to the back of the car. With some searching Rob found the latch for the trunk and they both got out. When they joined the trooper, Rob tried to sound casual. "What're you looking for?"

The trooper pretended he hadn't heard that.

The trunk held only the two gym bags they'd brought with them. In one, ties and jackets for cocktail hour—everything they'd changed out of before they went digging—and in the other, two unearthed Mason jars full of what looked like high-grade heroin.

"This your car?" the trooper said to Rob.

Nick said, "No, it's a—"

"It's a what?"

"It's a rental."

The trooper plunged his hand inside one of the bags. Rob's glance intersected with Nick's. In a moment, he knew, Rob would lose it. He'd either blurt out his confession or simply run away as fast as his little legs could take him. But when the trooper turned his light on Rob, he seemed remarkably composed.

"See your license, please?"

"It's in my back pocket. So I'm going to reach there, OK, trooper?"

The trooper was clearly losing patience. "Just take it out. Now, all right?"

Rob handed him the license.

"Mr. Johnson? Is that you?"

"Yes. I'm…him."

"You rented this car under your name?"

"My friend here and I were attending a college reunion," Nick said. "That's why we're here. Why we rented the car."

"Under his name."

"I have the receipt for it, if you want to look at it," Rob said, a little too eagerly.

The trooper turned to the second bag in the trunk. It seemed to glow from within with obscure meaning, like the MacGuffin in a Hitchcock movie. Then, without laying hands on it, he swung slowly around and snapped off his flashlight. "OK, you can go. There was a robbery with assault in Wilkinsburg. Couple of guys involved. A lot younger than you two. We're checking every vehicle heading away from there. Thanks for your cooperation."

Five minutes later, when they were a few miles away from the roadblock, and Nick was behind the wheel, Rob broke the heavy silence. "Pull over."

"What? Why?"

"Just stop the fucking ca—"

Before Nick could come to a full stop, Rob had his door open and was spewing everything he had eaten that day—a bagel for breakfast with low-fat veggie cream cheese, the pretzels he'd munched on in the plane, some olives, pigs in a blanket, and various unidentifiable items from the hors d'oeuvres buffet at the homecoming cocktail party—onto a deserted Pennsylvania road. The air immediately began to reek of decay and acid reflux.

"OK," he said, shutting the door. "Let's blow this town."

4

AFTER THE POLICE PHOTOGRAPHER DID HIS BUSINESS, AND Pussy Galore was carted off in an ambulance for a routine postmortem over at St. Luke's, the ride back was mostly conducted in silence, save for the low murmur of nonstop news on the radio. Word of the death of the aspiring actress and model, twenty-four-year-old Jessica Milo, shot in the Central Park West apartment rented by film producer Rick Burns, was just breaking. His name alone guaranteed speculation and continuous news coverage, especially as he'd been arrested for the purchase and possession of narcotics. Ray reckoned that whatever career the man now had would be history by dawn.

"There'll be an internal investigation." Driver shrugged. "You'll be asked to say a few words."

"As you know I will," Ray said.

"Otherwise, as far as anyone's concerned, you cut a deal, made yourself scarce, then I came in all on my own and took the man down."

"Same as always, Mr. Driver."

Ray looked at his watch. Half past bedtime. He was no longer the young man who would hit the pavement refreshed and alert before midnight and spend the next seven hours bopping between street and bar and, if someone he liked were playing, maybe take in the last set at the Vanguard or Slug's on East Third. Back then he knew everybody; back then, at least, they were all alive, and that included a dozen or so musicians he dealt with on a regular basis. Ray didn't need a dog for a friend or protection; he had his reputation, teeth bared, pulling him along from one block to the next. Once someone mouthed off to him, and the guy walked around Sugar Hill with a wired jaw for the next four months.

Too old, he thought. Too old for all that.

He put his head back and shut his eyes. Already he'd missed the late news and his cup of mint tea. A little music, a few minutes with a book, and he would be dead to the world, another aging black body sprawled out on white sheets. And then, with a glimpse at a passing taxi, he was out.

Driver must have glanced at him in the rearview, because a few minutes later he said, "You must have dozed off, my man."

"Long day, long day," Ray said, blinking himself back into life with a yawn.

"That Mr. Burns, huh?"

"Yeah."

"I tell you," Driver went on, "you turn fifty, fifty-five, whatever, and man but does your engine start to run down early."

"You seem to be managing."

"I have a good metabolism, that's why. Didn't wear myself down on hard shit and time served like some I know. When I was training as a fighter I learned the hard way. One day I comes to the gym after drinking a little too much the night before, and my trainer—I told you about him, right?"

Ray nodded. It was a dusty old story.

"He says to me, 'Put on your gloves and get in the ring,' and without letting me warm up, you know, a few minutes on the speed bag or jump rope, he puts me in with this big guy from the Heights, big brown Dominican, you know? The guy nearly killed me, and my trainer, he waited till my face was all bloody and my head dangling by a thread…"

Ray laughed. Now he was feeling better.

"You like that story, don't you," Driver said.

"I do indeed," he said, and he put his head back against the soft hand-stitched leather. Two more hours, he thought. We grab something to eat, toss down some coffee, take care of the paperwork and then home to catch a few hours of sleep. One day, he thought, he'd hit the jackpot and find a way out. And never stop running.

"You say something?" Driver said.

"Just thinking out loud," Ray said.

5

SAVE FOR THE OCCASIONAL GREYHOUND OR EIGHTEEN-wheeler making time in the passing lane, the road unraveled before them dark and empty. What seemed to be a few scattered flurries falling from a clear and starlit sky suddenly became a night full of white moths, sailing through the air, clustering around the sodium glow that frosted the darkness at intervals, occasionally hitting the windshield hard enough to become splats of red and green.

"Whoa," Rob said, as Nick dropped his speed way down. The moths danced and fluttered in the beams of their headlights—colliding, careening, a few collapsing and dying, as though from too much life.

Nick had seen this once before, the night Kacey Christopher told him she was pregnant. They had driven up to the Hungry Steer and taken a table as far as possible from anyone else. Neither of them had much of an appetite. Nick thought she was about to break up with him. He'd sensed it in her recent silences, the way her attention drifted, the way she kept her eyes open when they were in bed, as if looking for some future other than this boy whose long hair brushed her cheeks. It followed an age-old pattern of disengagement, and he was as keen to get it over with as she clearly was. Going to a public place to stage the finale was, well, also an old ploy. You couldn't make a scene at the Hungry Steer, my man, else you'd get the townies or the law doing the Bristol Stomp on your head.

"Let's get to the point," he said, and immediately tears came to her eyes.

"You don't know," she said. What was meant to be a question sounded like a condemnation.

"Do you want me to guess?"

More tears, more guesses. His mind riffled through them like a deck of playing cards. She'd fallen in love with Denis Whidbey, Kenny Gustafson, Bill Seether, Rob Johnson (Christ, not that, please not that)—his mind raced through a dozen names, any of them eligible to steal her away from him and break his heart forever. Oh, and he'd nearly forgotten that cute new studio art teacher she'd been talking about, the one who looked like Peter Fonda. Extra help, my ass. Saturday office hours? Please.

"I'm going to have a baby."

He just stared at her.

"It's yours, there was never anyone else, not before you or during you or…" Singsong, a secondhand line.

"Uh-huh." What else could a nineteen-year-old say?

"What are we going to do, Nick?"

The waitress approached and smiled. "Just coffee," Kacey said without looking up, and Nick said he'd have the same. "No, tea," she amended, and Nick said, "I'll still have coffee."

"Milk and sugar? Lemon?"

He shook his head and then she shook her head and the waitress in the cowboy hat sauntered off to the door labeled Chuck Wagon, letters burned into a plank of old wood.

"I'm scared," she said, and so was he, but he didn't say so. "My parents will absolutely kill me." She made herself as small as she could against the blue vinyl seat.

Nick's mind began to race. He saw the two of them married, living in a dead-end apartment with a crying baby, the TV playing reruns of *Dragnet* and *Gomer Pyle, U.S.M.C.*

"You'll have to have an abortion."

She seemed to be nodding, though it was no more than a gesture of acknowledgment. Those with a lot of money, it was believed, could have one done legally in Britain, where a car would be waiting for you at Heathrow and then, when it was over, you'd be driven back to your plane the next morning, with a quick peek into the duty-free shops. "I know," she said. "I mean, I don't know. It's dangerous."

He imagined Kacey being dropped off at some motel room on the fringes of Pittsburgh, her body discovered hours later in a frenzy of blood and viscera.

She sat back and looked away. "Do you love me?"

"Yes," he said, without thinking about it. When you're nineteen and it's 1971, love's just a word in a song. Or the name of a band.

"Do you really? Do you understand what that means, what it…signifies, what's behind the words?"

He reminded himself that Kacey was a French major.

"I don't know," he said, and this time he was speaking the truth. "Do you?"

"Do you think we could?"

"Could what?"

"Love each other? Like forever? Be happy? Maybe have a family like normal people?"

Normal people didn't figure into his usual line of thinking. Being a stranger in a strange land was more his mode back then, and ever since he'd seen the Clear White Light he all too often felt as if he were only a visitor, someone who'd stopped in for a glimpse and was preparing to return to whatever galaxy he had recently left.

"Let's talk about…the thing, OK?" It was as if he were referring to a monster's spawn, and he began humming the theme song to *Rosemary's Baby*. She laughed and touched her belly.

"Did the little devil kick?"

She laughed again and her eyes filled with tears. He could always make her laugh, and she'd always said it was one of the things that attracted her to him. "Silly. It's not big enough." And she put her long slim fingers on his hand. "Nick, I love you. I love you so much and I don't want to leave you. I trust you so much that I know you'll do the right thing."

"But what's the right thing?"

"I don't know. But I know you'll do it. You've always been good to me. I mean, for me. I count on you, babe."

It was then the moths appeared outside the restaurant window, a blizzard of them descending on cars and whirling around lights. Everyone stopped to stare at them. People in the carport wound up their windows; the ponytailed waitresses who moved smoothly and ceaselessly from window to vehicle shrieked and ducked with their trays full of burger-and-fries platters. Nick and Kacey didn't notice the waitress hovering over them with their coffee and tea.

"They die by morning," the waitress said. "Their lives last exactly one night. My daddy told me that when I was seven years old."

"That's awful," Kacey said.

"What you don't know won't hurt you, I guess. That makes them luckier than we are, anyway. Get you anything else?"

"I'll have a cheeseburger," Kacey said.

"I thought you weren't hungry," Nick said.

"I have to feed two, don't I." And for the first time that night her eyes sparkled with laughter.

They'd eaten and driven back to campus. He kissed her at the entrance to her dorm and watched through the glass doors as she signed in and walked into the elevator. Then he pulled open the door and rushed in.

"Hey, you can't come in here!" the resident assistant on duty shouted, but he kept running, past other girls just coming home, up four flights of stairs, and though by the time he reached her room the campus fuzz with his piece of lumber was rousing himself to catch this bad boy, he stopped the door with his foot just as it was closing, reached in and grabbed Kacey by the arm. And then he kissed her again, as if capturing a last memory. "I just want you to know," he said. "I won't forget this."

She furrowed her brow. "What? What?"

"I won't forget this. This night. With the moths and you and…you know. I won't forget you. Ever."

He turned and retraced his steps until he was out of the building, the resident assistant shouting in his wake, "Now you just wait right there, you're in a heap of trouble."

The guy with the two-by-four was just getting out of his Dodge Dart. He said to Nick, "You seen some crazy guy trying to get into a girl's room?"

"Yeah," Nick said. "I think his name is Chad Bakeman." And with a melancholic little smile—he was always game, even in the worst of times, to subvert the career of Mr. Young Republican—he returned to his dorm to get as high as he possibly could.

"Tell me something," he asked Rob now, as they drove into the endless cloud of wings. "When you ran into Lori in Boston did she…ask about me, or mention Kacey, or—"

"Not a word. Any other questions? Because I gotta tell you, I need to eat."

Nick pulled off at the Somerset exit into a service area. You could stuff yourself at Roy Rogers and gas up courtesy of

Sunoco all in the same location. He switched off the engine and turned to Rob as he was about to open his door.

"I just want to get a few things clear before we get to the city. First of all, who holds the stuff? I've got a wife and two kids. You've got you."

"So I guess I'm holding, then. Works for me."

"You have people you can call, right?"

"I have a *person* I can call. Leroy's brother."

"And if he's not home?"

"I'll leave a message."

They both began to laugh. Nick's smile flattened in a second.

"What?" Rob said. "You're having second thoughts?"

"Of course I am," Nick said. "If it works out, great, we'll make some serious money and we can pay our debts." He pictured himself walking into the head's office at the kids' school with a pillowcase full of fifties and twenties. "*If* it works out," he added, and opening the door stood to stretch himself in the cool autumn night. Only a few moths remained, drunk on headlight or fluttering their last on the ground. A hell of a life, Nick thought. Here today, gone today.

"I'm getting a roast beef sandwich or something," Rob said. "Why don't you fill the tank. You want anything?"

"Coffee. Black. Biggest they've got."

He got back in and drove up to the pumps, slid *Let It Bleed* into the player, then put his foot down and headed toward the highway ramp. He had no idea what he was doing. But for the moment, at least, he was alone in the dark, deserted night.

It was around the time when the midnight gambler jumped the garden wall that Nick pulled off the highway, followed the road beneath it and picked up the highway in the other direction. When he arrived back at the Roy Rogers twenty minutes later, Rob was standing outside it, hands on hips, a tall

Styrofoam cup on the curb beside him. Nick pulled up and rolled down the window.

"Fuck you, asshole bastard."

"Ouch," Nick said.

"What the hell were you thinking?"

"I was thinking that I'd leave you here to get murdered by a psychopathic trucker."

Rob got in and handed Nick the cup. "Very funny. You know, I was starting to lose all my trust in you. All my respect, every last shred of affection."

"I just wanted to be alone. Going back to Eden got me thinking. There's a lot of unfinished business in my life, Rob. I didn't realize it till today."

"You want me to drive?"

"I'll keep going for another hour. Then I'll need to sleep."

Nick slid the CD back in and before Mick could sing a word, Rob had it out again. "Peace and quiet," he said. "That's what we need."

Nick sipped his coffee. "It's cold," he said.

Part Three

1

"**S**O YOU GOT THE JOB," JOANNE SAID THE NEXT MORN-ing, or rather afternoon, as Nick had slept until two thirty. He sat at the kitchen table, eyes shut, as she put a hot mug of coffee in front of him. That morning's Sunday *Times* lay eviscerated off to the side, pages out of order, whole sections having waltzed away with some other eager beaver. He was grateful that Joanne hadn't heard him come in at half past five. In the first moments of dawn he poured himself a large scotch and sipped it slowly as, one by one, birds began to twitter and sing, as though relating to each other the saga of two middle-aged men who were headed down the highway to hell. But at that moment, suspended between past and present, between memory and desire, he felt as good as he ever had.

He rinsed out the glass and placed it in the dishwasher, then slipped off his shoes and tiptoed up to his room. When he reached the landing, the bathroom door swung open and Jen, in underpants and what she called a "wifebeater," stepped out, saw her father and shrieked before racing back to her room and slamming the door.

Joanne was still asleep, undoubtedly the result of the pills she'd been taking most nights kicking in around the ten-minute mark in *Charlie Rose*, or, on Saturdays, sometime during the first skit on *SNL*. While she watched TV, he read, and though by rights he should have been reading the classifieds in the *Times* or a book on how to find employment in one's golden, or rather silver, years, he was currently on a Graham Greene kick, reading all of the major novels, identifying himself with the haunted protagonists who lived on the twitching point between salvation and hell. He liked the way Greene displayed a true and lasting empathy for them, even when they were falling off the bitter end for all eternity. There was comfort to be had there, he thought, cold as it may be.

He and Rob had arrived at the rental lot at La Guardia a few minutes past four, and on the way to Rob's place on the East Side they talked not about their plans moving forward, as Rob kept putting it—as though it were he and not Nick who had fallen into the lazy verbal tics of the adman—but about the past. Rob kept returning to the few hours they'd spent at the college.

"I mean, the weird thing is that we saw nobody we knew."

"Except for Pete Hill."

"But he doesn't count, because he didn't count back then, either."

"Not one of ours."

"The epitome of uncool."

"At least the guy went off to get his MBA at Harvard."

"And where are they all today? Same place we are. Walking around with a tin cup."

"And half a million in dope in the trunk," Nick said, and Rob laughed.

Yet the whole mission had about it an existential haze, as though revisiting the past were an exercise in futility, like running backward from death: an illusion at best, a chance to drink and reminisce, at worst a reminder that all of the fun of those times when you thought you were immortal was long behind you. He still couldn't get Kacey Christopher out of his mind. Once, maybe a year earlier, after waking from an especially erotic dream that he only realized in retrospect was about her, he'd tried searching for her on the Internet and came up with nothing.

"Maybe," he told Rob, "we're looking at it the wrong way around. Maybe we knew most of the people who were there. Maybe they just changed so much that we didn't recognize them."

"Then why didn't anyone other than Pete come up to us?"

Nick had to break the news. "Maybe because we don't look like those cool guys of eighteen anymore."

Over breakfast Nick explained to Joanne that he and Rob had decided to spend a little more time with old friends at the college, skip the flight and drive back.

"Did you see *her*? You know who I'm talking about."

"No, she wasn't there."

She put a toasted bagel before him. *Thrust* might have more accurately described it. "So you looked."

"Jo, sweetheart, we've been through this a hundred times before. It was all over when you and I met. God, I'm still tired." He rubbed his eyes, shutting them tightly and squeezing out a single tear.

"But you couldn't stop talking about her."

"That was, what? Twenty-five years ago?"

"And that Polaroid of her in that bathing suit."

"It was a leotard, for God's sake. She was into dance at the time."

"Stuck between the pages of that copy of *The Wings of the Dove* you'd lent me. I mean, Jesus..."

"So I forgot to throw it away. That was a whole other life. Is this all the cream cheese we have left?"

"Eric ate most of it this morning."

"He hates bagels."

"With his finger."

"Jesus. Our son Caliban."

"People don't forget that easily."

"Look. We saw one person we know. Pete Hill."

"You said a few."

He grasped for names. "Greg Downs. Tom Spitz." He shrugged. Who the hell were these people? "Joey Scapulo. And that was it. It was boring, the food was lousy, and all Rob and I did was walk around and reminisce."

Now he knew who they were. People he'd never given a second thought to; guys who lived in his dorm and had willingly adopted such nicknames as "Animal," "Gutbag," and "Frogspawn."

"And you did business with that guy you mentioned, Jerry something?"

"Right. Right. Jerry Bruno. Bingo, yes."

"And you got the job?"

"We'll know in a day or two."

"And then we can go to the school and at least promise we'll be able to pay the rest of the tuition?" The phone rang and she answered it.

"Your friend Rob," she said, handing it to him.

"I'll take it downstairs." Juggling bagel and mug, he made his way down to the basement. "I've got it, Jo." He heard the click.

Rob said, "Your wife sounds nice."

"Thanks."

"You never told me what she looks like."

"Does it really matter?"

"I like to know what goes along with a voice."

"If you squint a little she looks like Françoise Dorléac. If she'd hadn't been killed, I mean."

"Who the hell is that?"

"Catherine Deneuve's sister."

"Wow. I'll have to look her up."

"Did you make the connection?"

"Hear my voice? Detect the tone? I just got off the phone with him. Sonny Ives can definitely help us out. He knows people we can do business with. Reliable people. Just remember we give him a cut of the take."

"How much?"

"Twenty."

"Dollars?"

"Jesus, Nick. Percent."

Nick did a quick calculation. If it ended up being a million, that would leave him and Rob to split a cool eight hundred grand. Not bad at all.

"Hey. It's a lot easier than having us go out trying to sell the stuff, right?"

"I guess so," Nick said.

"What, you're having doubts again?"

"I'm finding this all falling into place a little too easily. And what if we're trying to sell isn't what we say it is?"

"Do we look like hardened drug dealers? They'll test it, and if it doesn't turn out to be smack they'll peg us for a couple of amateurs and let us walk. Look. I'm just trying to make it work for us, that's all. I've lost my job, my wife, half of everything I own. I've lost my pride, Nick. You know what that's like? No, probably not. Because look at you. You're tall, you're great looking, you dress like a mensch and even if you were spending your nights sodomizing goats and setting fire to homeless guys you'd still pass for someone on the up-and-up.

Plus, you're married to whatever-she-looks-like. I look in the mirror and all I want to do is disappear. I have nothing to fall back on. I don't even dream anymore. I mean, what's the point? So day after tomorrow we're going to take the subway up to Harlem to see Sonny. That's the first step. We see Sonny, he sets us up with a buyer, and we're in."

Nick couldn't believe it. "So soon?"

"I can't just keep holding this stuff, Nick. We've got to shift it, take the money, get the thing over with."

"Good," Nick said. "That's good."

"Which is not to say that we're bringing the stuff with us the first time. Guy's clean and doesn't want to take any risks. He just wants to get paid. And—ready for it?—he'll test the stuff for us. Should be a done deal by the end of the week."

Nick set the phone gently down and shoved the last bite of bagel in his mouth. He slowly chewed it and considered where he was: four bedrooms; two full and two half bathrooms; an unused and expensively renovated attic; a top-of-the-line kitchen with Viking stove and Sub-Zero fridge; nearly half an acre of lavishly landscaped yard with all of his neighbors discreetly tucked out of view behind a fence that cost him nearly as much as his Audi; a basement that was meant to be a playroom for young and old alike, and that, after he and Joanne had hosted a few get-togethers around the wet bar, fell into neglect, save for the time he caught Eric and a friend down there smoking Kools and leafing through a copy of *Penthouse*. Now he considered it his office, as if he were someone low down in the Cosa Nostra hierarchy.

He finished his coffee and turned to go upstairs. Joanne was sitting on the bottom step in her jeans and white blouse. Her hair was streaked with silver but she wore it to her shoulders just as she had when they'd first met some three decades earlier. A quick first glance would have told you she was maybe thirty-five or forty while in fact she was the same age as Nick. She wore the lingering remnants of her youth with a studied indifference that came off as completely natural. "So that was Rob, huh."

"How long have you been sitting there?"

"Do I know this guy?"

"We lost touch after college. I lost touch with everyone," he said pointedly, for her sake meaning Kacey Christopher.

"He sounds like a schmuck," she said, and he laughed. "For the first Sunday in a long time we have the place to ourselves," she said.

"Let's burn the place down and collect the insurance."

"I hope you're joking."

"We can move to a trailer park. It's a lot cheaper. I'll take up taxidermy. Change my name to Billy Bob. You can be Raylene."

"Be serious."

"Where's Jen?"

"At school. Rehearsing for *Hair*, remember? Eric's gone to the movies with Kenny Siegel. You feeling all right after that drive?" The sentence carried a certain familiar look.

Years ago her favorite word was "frisky"—"You feeling frisky, maybe?"—and even if he weren't, just hearing her say it got him instantly in the mood. "Frisky" had been retired years ago for a kind of silence. Now and again the silence would have a little weight to it, and her look would say it all. They'd go through the motions, ten minutes of foreplay, though she'd given up going down on him or allowing him to do likewise with her, and because menopause had left her high and dry he'd have to take a break to get a lube job courtesy of K-Y, snap it open, pour some out into his hand and so forth. But once they got into the rhythm of it, it was as if they'd stripped away the years and touched—only just, like two billiard balls briefly kissing as they passed on the green baize toward a nice easy drop in the pocket—something of the passion they'd felt for one another when they first met.

Which is why a part of him believed that she was saving up the best of it for some guy he knew nothing about.

She unbuttoned her blouse, shrugged it off her shoulders and reached behind to unhook her bra. She undid the top of his trousers and pulled the zipper down. He pulled her jeans slowly off legs as long and firm as when he'd first met her all those years ago. He caught sight of her in the mirror that served as one wall of the room and for one brief moment he saw Françoise Dorléac leading him to the sofa in the corner, as though, dead all these years, she had stepped back into life to make some man not connected to the French film industry immensely happy.

What would be the point of foreplay, anyway? They were like starving people crashing a wedding banquet. He simply entered her and ten seconds later felt a jolt of electricity he had not experienced for a long time. She arched her body and the moan in the back of her throat swelled into a gasp. For twenty seconds all of their worries, financial and otherwise, all of their past disagreements, threats to leave one another, all of their private secret yearnings for others, vanished in a puff of pleasure.

He held her in his arms and for a few minutes they skimmed the surface of sleep. Rousing at the same time, they silently and quickly pulled on their clothes. Tiny beads of sweat rested on the slope of her upper lip. He tilted forward and licked it off with his tongue, savoring the salt of her. She sat back on the sofa and held out her hands to him. He felt like he might just be the luckiest man in the world.

2

WHEN NICK ARRIVED AT THE SUBWAY STATION ROB WAS perched on the edge of a bench reading the *Post*. When he caught sight of Nick, he tossed his paper in the same bin where he'd found it. "Right on time," he said.

Nick had chosen a conservative tie (not the horrible Jerry Garcia model Eric had bought him for Father's Day two years earlier, thinking his dad would consider him hip, while in reality Nick disliked the Grateful Dead as much as he did, say, chronic diarrhea), a blue blazer, gray trousers, brown lace-ups, a nice three-quarter-length coat: the casual, devil-may-care look for any respectable unemployed adman.

"How do I look?" he said as a train approached the platform.

"Like a cop. Lose the scowl, will you?"

"I'm a little nervous, that's all."

"Were you nervous when we went to that Pittsburgh bar carrying enough to put us behind bars?"

"I was eighteen, Rob. Nothing scared me then."

It was the dead end of the morning rush hour, the only people now traveling being the out-of-work, the self-employed, and the genuinely brain-fried, all trying in vain to catch Rob's or Nick's eye: *I will be your friend for ever and ever...* The train pulled into the 125th Street station and Nick, Rob, and two or three others stepped out onto the chill clarity of the open-air platform.

"The guy lives on Broadway?"

"He's supposed to meet us here," Rob informed him.

The sky was cloudless, the air dry and pleasingly cool. Nick thrust his hands in his coat pockets as they sat on an empty bench. Fleetingly, he thought of Joanne from the day before, how she'd come on to him like that, and instead of appreciating a moment of abandon that seemed to have satisfied them both, he began to parse it. Was she hiding something? Feeling guilty? Was she leading a whole other life that he wasn't seeing? Was this just a way of keeping his loyalty everlastingly blind?

"What?" Rob said, who appeared to be reading his mind.

"Did you have a look at the stuff?"

"I brought a little sample for Sonny to check out. Definitely not crystal meth. Doesn't have that, you know, funky look to it. Anyway, any hillbilly with a Bunsen burner can make speed. A couple of packs of Sudafed and you're in business with no profit worth mentioning. I'd say it was smack."

"Or else we got burned."

A train pulled in on the opposite track, dropped off its passengers and rolled away.

"Guy's late," Rob said.

The platforms on both sides were deserted, save for an African-American boy of eight or nine, sitting on a bench on the opposite side, his shoes dangling eight inches from the ground. He wore a clip-on bow tie and a hand-me-down sports jacket a few sizes too large. He kept staring at Rob and Nick. "Yo," he called across to them. "You the guys come to see my father? The downtown men?"

"You're Sonny's kid?" Rob said, and a train pulled in on his side to block the view. When it pulled away the boy was gone.

Except that he was now standing at the top of the stairs on their side of the platform. "Ready to go or what?"

The kid moved fast, weaving between taxis, dodging slowpoke senior citizens, his jacket flapping behind him like a pair of wings. They finally came to a stop outside an apartment house just off Manhattan Avenue. Something was going on, because there were cars double-parked outside the place, including a few with livery plates. Men in long leather coats stood eyeballing every car and pedestrian that paused to see what was going on. A black Lincoln Town Car with darkened windows idled across the street in a no-standing zone.

"Looks like someone's having a party," Rob said.

"My mama is," the boy said, pulling open the front door. Rob and Nick followed him up the narrow stairway to the fifth floor. People were already spilling out of the apartment into the narrow hallway, holding drinks or cups of coffee, speaking quietly to one another. They barely noticed Nick and Rob, as though the two men existed in another world.

"You wait here," the kid said, and he left the room.

Nick caught sight of a tall, slender, strikingly attractive young black woman, a glass of red wine in her hand. In her simple black dress and red cashmere shawl, she scanned the room with her melancholy eyes, her attention falling briefly on Nick and moving on as though no memory of him had been registered. An elderly man said to her, "Meredith, how've you been?" and she turned to talk to him.

When a woman stepped in holding the boy's hand, it was clear from her expression that she'd been saving up all this time to tell them how very unwelcome they were here.

"I'm Macey Ives. My boy's name is Terrell. You're the men who made an appointment to see my husband, am I right or am I wrong?" She looked them each in the eye. "Well?"

"We'd really wanted to see his brother Leroy," Rob said, and the young woman in the shawl turned to look at them. "But...he's probably not available," he added with a form of tact Nick had never encountered anywhere but in a situation comedy.

"Leroy," Macey Ives said. "You want Leroy but you also want Sonny?"

"I was Sonny's brother's attorney some years ago," Rob said.

"Oh, I know who you are. He mentioned you after you called. Sonny's been waiting to see you."

"We don't want to take up too much of his time," Rob said.

"Don't you worry about my husband. He's got all the time in the world."

They followed her down a hallway. An elderly black woman sat on a chair outside a room, dabbing at her eyes with a Kleenex. A man and a woman stepped past, grim faced and silent. In the bedroom an African-American man in a dark suit and crisp white shirt, his hands neatly folded across his chest, lay on the bed. An empty coffin was propped against the wall, waiting to fulfill its role.

"Oh Jesus," Rob whispered.

"Let me introduce you to my husband. Tell him how sorry you are about what's happened here. Tell him how heartbroken you are that you've taken him away from his little boy. Explain that after you called him you didn't know he'd go for a little stroll to find you a dealer and instead took three bullets to his body. Because without that phone call there would have been no bullets, and this man here would right now be shooting hoops around the corner with his son. Terrell?" The boy came running into the room. "Keep these gentlemen company while I see everyone off. Take them into your room, OK?"

They followed the boy into a small bedroom, where a portable TV stood on a folding chair. Nick and Rob sat on the edge of his bed while the boy switched on a cartoon. Outside, a hearse from Strivers Row Funeral Home pulled up and two men stepped out, impeccably dressed in dark suits and neutral expressions.

"We're really sorry about your dad," Nick said.

"Uh-huh."

On the television a red race car whipped down a country lane, past tweety birds and steepled churches, while a scowling pterodactyl with machine guns attached to its wings flew menacingly overhead, occasionally sending out streams of bullets.

"Do you know your uncle Leroy?" Rob asked, and Nick shot him a look.

"Nuh-uh."

The cartoon car came to a halt in an underground garage. Trying to show some interest Nick said, "So it's a squirrel driving, right?"

Terrell looked at him as if he were insane. "He's a Japanese guy, mister." He shook his head sadly as he turned back to the screen.

Macey stepped in and said to her son, "I want you to— I'm talking to you, son." She switched off the TV. "Go spend some time with your grandma while I talk to these men, OK?"

"But I…"

Her look silenced him. He scowled and left the room. Macey shut the door and put her hands on her hips. "You have a family?"

Rob gave her a quizzical look, so she turned to Nick.

"A wife, two kids," he said.

"So if this has anything to do with drugs, and my little boy gets tangled up in your shit, I'm personally going to hunt you down and make your woman a widow before her time."

Rob said, "I only called because I wanted to get in touch with—"

"Yeah, and an hour later the street's full of noise that he's been shot dead. This man has been clean of narcotics for going on eighteen years. You call and now he's going to be put in the ground. You want to start adding up the numbers, or do I have to lay it all out for you?"

"I'm sure there was no connection—" Nick began.

"Who's going to take care of my little boy? Who's going to be his daddy now? You cut the heart right out of this family, you know that?"

There was nothing to do but offer a few last words of condolence. Nick thought of the little boy on the bench, calling across to them.

Some of the people who'd been up in the apartment were now on the sidewalk, sharing stories and making plans. Many would undoubtedly go on to the church and then the cemetery.

From the back of the Town Car parked across the street, Ray watched the people come out.

Driver checked his watch and said, "We've been here twenty minutes. Had your fill?"

"I guess so."

Driver put the car in gear when Ray said, "Hold it."

Their eyes met when she stepped out into the street to hail a taxi, pulling her red shawl a little more snugly around her. How long had it been since they last saw each other? Back then she was just a chubby little girl, but that face was unmistakable—those eyes still bright and amused, that smile still sly, like she was trying to get away with something. One grows up, while the other just grows old. His eyes locked with hers. Her lips parted, and was it his imagination, or could he read the exact word she was saying: "Pops"? She seemed about to cross over to the car. He shook his head once.

Now she was certain; now she knew for sure.

"Can we go now?" Driver said, and Ray quietly grunted assent. And she watched as they pulled away.

"One day," Driver said, as they headed down 125th Street, "I'll take you to the cemetery so you can pay your respects." He looked in the rearview. "Hey, you with me here?"

Tears had welled up in his eyes. He slipped on his shades and took a deep breath. "I'd like that," he said. "When the moment comes."

Ray was remembering when he'd last seen her, when her mother brought her on Father's Day. He hadn't wanted Merry to see him like this, not with a pane of Plexiglas between them. She'd made a little crayon picture for him, a brown man and a little girl with pigtails in a yellow dress, holding it against the divider so he could see it. And so he could hide behind it. He glanced back at a guard.

"Can I keep that?"

"After we check it out, yeah."

"It's just a drawing."

"You're wasting visiting time. Better get to it."

Driver hit one red light after another. He shook his head at his bad luck. "Not my day," he said.

"Any idea how it happened?"

"Your brother, you mean? Couple of bullets. It's all I know."

If Meredith was still in the city, then where was she living? What was she doing? How much did she know about him? At least now she knew he wasn't locked up or dead. Ray sitting in the back of a Town Car could only mean that he was back in business. The same business that had killed her mother and got him locked up.

"Stop at the park," Ray said.

"Say what?"

"I want a little fresh air."

"Not going to try anything funny, right?"

"As if I could."

When they reached the park at 110th Street, Driver pulled into a tow zone, tossed the police placard on the dash and opened his door.

Ray hitched up the collar of his coat. Though it was a brisk day, the sun was still warm, the northern edge of the park busy with dog walkers and couples. Driver found an empty bench and, spreading his arms along the back, seemed to own every available inch of it. Ray stood in the bright sunshine, gloved hands behind his back, his face tilted to the blazing star.

"Ain't going to get any easier," Driver said.

Ray turned away from the light.

"Choice you made a long time ago," Driver went on.

"Where does she live?"

"As if I knew."

"I think you do."

"Feeling fatherly all of a sudden? Because I don't have to remind you this was all laid down as law when you was released. Contacting your relatives is out of the question. You do that and you go straight back to Attica and serve out the rest of your sentence. You just play your role, bring down people like that smartass producer Burns and you get to have some nice threads, a few extra bucks to spend on your jazz records and your books, and a roof over your head. Until you've paid your debt to society, the only prison you got right now is the one you made for yourself."

"I want to petition for visitation rights."

Driver's laugh turned into a cough that betrayed his fondness for cigars, cheap whiskey, and too many hours in front of network TV. "Your daughter's no longer a baby girl. You don't have no visitation rights. She was raised by other folks who legally adopted her. You try to track her down and besides breaking the rules of our agreement with you, there's no knowing what could happen. I mean, you do remember what happened to Oscar Fernandez, right?"

Ray had only seen him a few times, usually climbing into his black Hummer, one of the first available on the retail market. Oscar was a little guy, barely five-six, but once he was behind the wheel of that monster he could be anyone he liked. Someone told him that Oscar was the big man in cocaine, so that Ray could forget about him as they weren't in competition. And then Oscar disappeared from the streets and off the tongues of those who talked about such matters. Driver later told him that Oscar had been busted, sent to do his time, and was civilianed-in to the narc squad, doing the same undercover work Ray was now doing. But Oscar got tired of being so alone, so he tracked down an old girlfriend who, when he was in prison, had married and had two young children.

"He stalked her," Driver told him. "Yeah, he had an ankle monitor just like you, but she was in Queens, so no one noticed it. He was good at it, too. He'd just sit for hours, watching the house, figuring out who went out when. When he saw his old sweetie's husband leave for work, and then the kids put on their school bus, he made his move. He was only looking for a little face time with his lady. He knocked, she asked who it was, he said his name, and of course as far as she knew Oscar was still behind bars. He knocked again and then kicked the door in. That's when she shot him with her husband's gun. Thought he was some kind of intruder. Got him right in the heart, too."

Driver sat forward, rested his arms on his knees and looked up at Ray. "Your daughter finds out you're in deep undercover work and right away she's on the firing line. Someone who figures out who she is could lean real hard on her. You want to take that chance, put her life out there like that?"

"But she's smarter than that—"

"You saw her, when? Like when she was a little girl playing with her Barbie dolls? Maybe she was smart then, but who knows what she's like now? She could get careless, or she could be hanging with people who'd take you down in a minute. You don't know her no more, Ray. She's not that little girl with the lollipop stuck in her mouth. And you're not the man who helped bring her into this world. You're just someone else now."

Ray sat beside him on the bench and rubbed his ankle where the bracelet that allowed him only the freedom of the five boroughs still chafed even after all these years. Halfway through the Lincoln Tunnel and alarms would be going off in half a dozen offices. It was the way things came down after fifteen years at Attica. That and how he was expected to serve out the rest of his sentence. At this point there was no room for attorneys, no more deals to cut. This was the last option. He thought of Meredith standing outside Sonny's building like that. He thought of his world without her. He stood and just started walking.

"Let's go," he said.

3

I T WAS ONE OF THOSE PERFECT AUTUMN DAYS HE RELIED ON more than once in his ad campaigns: leaves drifting from trees, sunshine aslant the verdant sweep of lawn, dad in his suede coat and gloves, mom wheeling a barrow, kids leaping into piles of multicolored foliage. They were filmed at various locations: an estate in Bedford Hills; the campus of a private school in Bucks County; and, most convincingly, a soundstage in Burbank. You could sell anything with that: cars ("Here's where you could be if you owned a Lexus"), canned soup ("Hey, what's for lunch, honey?"), erectile dysfunction meds (hubby and wife playfully tussle over a garden hose that, whoops, erupts with water), and, to some ersatz Aaron Copland, life insurance ("One day you won't be there for them..."). A summer scene—with its barbecues, skimpy clothing, the hint of beer to come and bonfires on sandy white beaches—was only good for the youth market, for kids who drove too fast without their seat belts on, who drank cheap vodka from a funnel, who took Ecstasy and fucked anything in sight. Meant to sell acne cream, it edged up to but never included all the consequences: the roadside memorials with their balloons and misspelled misery, the unwanted pregnancy, the acid trip on the dorm room floor when your mind fried and the body disappeared. It was a market that only worked if you could convince audiences that childhood never ended, that little boys grew bigger, made more money, but at heart still behaved like animals in heat, still drank too much, still played at childish games and awaited their first coronary. That was when you pitched them cholesterol medicine and gym memberships.

Rake in hand, he turned to find Joanne sitting on the front step. She was wearing a denim jacket and the Audrey Hepburn sunglasses that she'd bought for seven-fifty from a vendor on Canal Street. A coffee mug hung loosely from her forefinger. She looked amazing. That was the only word for someone who was slipping out of reach. The less available she was the more he desired her. Was that somehow built into the human psyche? Was that what life was all about, the pursuit of the eternally unobtainable? He said, "I was just thinking I don't ever want to go back into advertising."

"OK." It was what she always said when things were clearly not OK, when things were in fact dire. She used it a lot with the kids. It was always followed with something along the lines of: "So what *will* you do?" At times he even found her passive aggression a little sexy.

"Selling is one of your talents. The art of persuasion."

He was never really sure when she was mocking him. He halfheartedly pulled some leaves toward him to start a new pile. That made number eight. One day he might earn enough to call the Guatemalans with the pickup and leaf blower he'd suffered without all this time.

"Nick—Nick, look at me. Can we once and for all wrap it all up and tie a ribbon around it and call this your midlife crisis?"

He stopped raking and looked at her. "Midlife crisis" was just another advertising slogan. It meant selling fast cars and beer and trips to Vegas and the Canary Islands, the shiny false expectations of romance and desire; two barely dressed, blandly handsome people walking hand in hand along a moonlit shore before they raced each other back to the room for a night full of lust. It was an advertising company's pot of gold, and Nick had been the go-to guy for all the agency's campaigns at Stevens Breakstone Leary. He could turn them out at the rate of one an hour, and everyone there suspected that he was simply reporting on his own glorious life. Yet he was as devoted to Joanne as he could ever be. He felt a kind of moral certainty that in this life loyalty was possibly the last outpost of the just person, as though in and of itself it kept you honest. Unlike, say, the supposed loyalty of his former boss, Larry Stevens, which began with "I'm going to superglue your ass to that chair, Nick. This job is yours for life," and ended with "Jeez, I hate to be the bearer of bad news, Nick, but the time has come for some fresh blood." Even if he discovered that Joanne was having it off with someone else he'd remain loyal to her. Right up to the moment she shut her suitcase and walked out.

"Because, Nick, may I remind you how really good you were at your job? Remember the baby on the changing table? 'You put your life in their hands. You put your money in Bank of America. Trust the ones you know best.'"

He laughed and took a seat beside her. "I forgot about that. That was one tough sell. They wanted me to show that the guy in the suit walking into the bank was the same guy as the kid in the diaper. I suggested we show a guy carrying a briefcase full of bearer bonds and sucking on a pacifier."

"They played it the way you wrote it."

"And people still got it."

"And we have no money left. So what are you trying to tell me, that this thing you were doing at your old college fell through?"

"It's just a matter of time. Just have to see how it all pans out," Nick said with more desperation than hope.

"And if it doesn't?"

He said nothing.

"If it doesn't pan out, if there isn't any money?" She slipped her glasses down so she could peer at him over the rims.

"We have the house. A little equity at least. I mean, the house isn't really worth what we paid for it anymore. And we've borrowed a lot against it." He could see it spread out before him: the flagstones on the side that served to support the eight-hundred-dollar gas grill and the high-end Smith & Hawken outdoor furniture; the roof that had to be replaced three years before; the additional landscaping meant to keep all of his neighbors absolutely out of sight and beyond sound, as though they belonged to a warring tribe armed with blowguns and spears. He turned to her and his smile was about as insincere as a smile could be. "But if it goes through—if it works—it could mean… It could mean a lot."

"What are we talking about? Look at me, Nick, tell me the truth. Twenty thousand? A hundred thousand?"

At that moment the magic word "insurance" popped into his head. Years ago he'd bought a policy on his life from Dave Lasker, an old friend from high school he'd kept in touch with over the years. Dave worked for MetLife and had badgered Nick into buying a policy worth a cool two million. "I know it sounds kind of morbid," he said over the lunch he was buying Nick at Maloney & Porcelli. "But once you've signed the papers you'll realize it's the smartest thing you've ever done."

"Peace of mind, right?" Nick said. He knew just what he was expected to say. He'd done TV spots for other insurance shysters and invented scenes similar to this, save they were set in someone's living room before a roaring fire, with coffee mugs and clients portrayed by former soap opera stars. "Familiar faces," he would explain at the pitch. "Always use people they think they remember." Put on someone who reminds the audience of their venerable uncle Walter and he could sell them anything, from back massagers to black-market Kalashnikovs.

Peace of mind: it was like a response to a preacher's exhortation, the insurance man's amen. In any case, he'd had two single malts and they'd already polished off a $250 bottle of Caymus 1994 Cabernet, so at that moment he would've said whatever Dave had wanted him to say. Preparing for the kill, Dave set down his glass and let his gaze settle on Nick's face. He seemed calm and logical and altogether more intelligent than anyone who'd spent those years in school with him might have suspected.

"Think about it," Dave said. "I've seen it happen lots of times. People go into debt, they get sick, they're terrified of leaving their family with nothing." He opened his hands. "Buy this and you'll never have to worry about it." And he lifted his glass and said "*L'chaim*, Nick. To life. Because *that*'s what it's all about." *Click*: sold.

Nick pulled off his work gloves and put an arm around Jo, pulling her toward him. All of a sudden he understood the notion behind insurance. When all else fails, the thing is always there, waiting to be yanked from a drawer and expedited within twenty-four hours. "Look. I'm not going to let you or the kids down. We're going to finish this as soon as possible."

If you fell on the tracks, say three seconds before the train came roaring into the station, all you'd feel was the impact from the fall and not the engine tearing you into three unequal portions. If you drove your car very fast on the Thruway and then just drifted off from the forty Ambien you took an hour before, you'd die with a smile on your face.

The screen door screeched, "*Oil meeeee!*" as Jen sent it flying open. "Dad? Telephone. Some guy named Rob?"

He strode into the house, cupping the phone in his hand until Jen made herself scarce.

"What?"

"That's how you greet me? I fucking saved your life thirty years ago, and I get a 'what?'"

"Just tell me."

"We're all set."

"What does that mean exactly?"

"Looks like we have our connection. We're supposed to meet him tonight."

Nick looked at his watch. What he was seeing meant absolutely nothing at that moment.

"Can you drive here and then we can go straight down to the place?"

"Place. What place?"

Now Joanne was in the kitchen, half listening as she took out two glasses and dropped some ice in them. She poured in generous measures of Famous Grouse and handed one to him. He said goodbye and hung up.

"I have to go to a meeting."

"Tonight?"

"In the city."

"I wouldn't have a second one of those, then."

"I don't intend to."

"What's this Rob like, anyway?"

"He's just a friend."

"Can you trust him?"

"Of course."

"That's not what your face is saying. It's saying, 'I'm fucked.'"

"I'm tired, that's all."

"We're having pot roast."

"Great."

"What time is your meeting?" She hooked the air with her fingers.

The door screamed open again and Eric blew in, dropped his backpack and cell phone on the table and made a dash for the fridge.

"Eleven."

She set down her glass. "You have a business meeting at eleven on a Sunday night?"

"It's just that...these people are from out of state. They have to fit us in."

"What are they, like on a different time zone or something?" Eric asked, opening a Red Bull.

"They're from Cincinnati."

"Cool," he said, and taking his crap off the table disappeared up the stairs, the tenant from hell. "He always seemed such a quiet boy," the neighbors would say when asked by the police.

Nick left early for Rob's place, moving easily with the traffic on the FDR and arriving there just before ten. As Rob's building was on East Eighty-Fourth, Nick had no problem finding a space at that time of night. Rob must have been watching for him, like a shut-in desperate for company, for just as Nick was about to press the intercom button the door buzzed to let him in. Rob's apartment door was ajar and Nick pushed it open. Apart from furniture, consisting of two plastic chairs and a small folding table, an open file folder lay on the floor, around it stacks of legal documents and transcripts, some of which had colorful little Post-its attached here and there—the kind Nick recognized from his accountant, with little hands pointing at things. There were holes in the walls where nails once held pictures. A chaotic hillock of bills and catalogs lay in a pile off to the side. Cheap blue curtains sagged from rods over the windows.

Rob stepped in dressed in black jeans, black T-shirt, and black leather jacket. A pair of Bruno Magli loafers finished the ensemble. The first word that came to Nick's mind was "pornographer."

Nick looked around. "At least she left you with something to sit on," he said. "Talk about being taken to the cleaners."

"Uh-uh. I had to go to Ikea in Jersey and pick these up. She left me with exactly nothing. Zero, zip, nada, I know what you're thinking. All I need is a Led Zeppelin poster, a Tensor lamp, and a pack of Slim Jims, and I'm back in college."

In fact it did remind Nick of a dorm room. Suck all the hope and happiness out of a space, and this is what you'd end up in. No wonder you smoked, swallowed, or injected everything offered to you when you arrived there.

"I hate to put it so bluntly, but she must have hated your guts."

"Do me a favor," Rob said. "Don't mention her, OK?"

"One question, and then I'll leave it alone."

"Just one."

"What does she look like?"

"Jesus, Nick—"

"Just so I have an idea of what kind of woman you would marry. In case I run into someone that might be right for you. Fair's fair, right? I mean, you asked me."

Rob went into the bedroom and came back out with a framed photo he obviously kept well hidden, like a handgun, carefully wrapped in a towel imprinted with the emblem of the NY Sports Club. It had undoubtedly been taken on a tropical beach—by the look on their faces, during their honeymoon. Rob was thinner and fitter then, his hair more copious and much longer and blonder. In fact, he looked like a surfer. Janet...

"Is that what she's called?" Nick said. "Janet?"

Rob nodded. He could barely bring himself to look at the photo.

Janet was gorgeous. She wore a two-piece bathing suit, had long slender legs, dark hair falling over one spectacularly swelling breast, and allowed one slim arm to drape over Rob's shoulder. The peach fuzz on her arms and belly was bleached to a brilliant blond and was stunning against her tan flesh. They appeared to be the happiest, sexiest people in the universe: hip, cool, deeply in love, their whole demeanor seemed to shout *"Bedroom!"* And all Nick could tactfully say was, "Hmmm," placing the framed photo back in the waiting towel, though he could understand how Rob must have been feeling. Losing someone as beautiful as her must have been like a kind of slow death. Losing someone so beautiful to a younger guy made it even worse.

"You know what kills? She doesn't look a day older," Rob said, driving another nail into his own coffin as he went to tuck the photo back in his underwear drawer.

Nick thought of how he and Joanne looked when they were first married. Considered by some to be a model couple, he was the successful, young advertising executive, she the bright and beautiful young woman sending out résumés (and a list of references that included the chair of Columbia's history department) to all the area colleges and universities. The reality was that it was a struggle to keep this appearance up day after day while bad news came winging its way down the phone line or through the mail slot. The positions weren't exactly opening up for Jo, and Nick had had to settle for a low-level creative assistant position at a newish firm called Stevens Breakstone Leary. When things started moving for them, when Jo had been hired at the last minute to teach at the Spence School (only to see her position phased out three years later), and Nick had risen to take over the entire creative department, not to mention a handsome corner office with a view over Park Avenue, they had begun to dislike one another. Not hate, that would be both overstating and underestimating the case. This was more like being saddled with a college roommate critically out of sync with your tastes, pace, and moods. You lived together only because someone assigned you to the same space. It poisoned their kids' key growth years, so that deep down he sensed Jen and Eric would eventually leave behind their dreams to become binge-drinkers and twice-weekly therapy patients. It was only when Nick lost his job that the heat was turned up and what appeared to be love and devotion insidiously and mysteriously returned. Which was when Nick began to suspect there was another man in the picture. Why else would she be so passionate all of a sudden if she weren't trying to recapture what went on when he wasn't around?

"Let's get back to business, all right?" Rob said.

"So who are we meeting?"

"Guy named D'Wayne. Top-echelon dealer who used to work for Leroy. Look." He stepped over to the stacks of documents. "This was my file on Leroy's case. The DA wanted to take down Leroy's whole operation, everyone he worked with, everyone who worked for him. But this was Leroy's trial and I wasn't about to turn this into a grandstand show so Mr. DA could be all over the front page of the *Daily News*. He wanted to cut a deal with Leroy. If he talked, if he named names, his sentence would be reduced. He wouldn't do it."

"So he was protecting this D'Wayne?"

"Because he knew that one day he'd walk out of jail. It's always best not to come home to your enemies. Trust me, stuff like this happens all the time."

"But this guy would probably still be locked up like Leroy."

"With no priors? He would've been out in six or seven years. Then he'd wait for Leroy to finish his stretch. Revenge is not a pretty thing, my friend."

Nick was kind of amazed, not at what he was hearing but at Rob's grasp of the narrative. Maybe he was a pretty good lawyer, after all. Lousy husband, astounding attorney. Same old story.

Nick propped himself on the edge of the flimsy little chair, a bit too close to the floor for comfort. He felt like he was paying a visit to a first-grade classroom on parents' night.

"Leroy established his base in Harlem and put together a bunch of satellite dealers to work for him." Rob grabbed a sheaf of documents from the floor. "D'Wayne was one of them. While Leroy was doing his thing they'd be all over town trying to set up new networks. A dealer got busted in the Bronx? Leroy would fill the vacancy with one of his men. Same with anywhere else. Any idea what happened in '69 in the Village? Remember what it was like before then?"

In those days you could light up a joint in front of a beat cop and he'd just smile and sniff the air a little. Narcs looked the other way most of the time, at least when they weren't checking out the hippie girls, barefoot and braless as they window-shopped on MacDougal Street. Nick had heard that when there was an impending bust, someone deep in the NYPD would tip off Abbie Hoffman; he'd alert the people who lived in the target, and the cops and TV film crew would show up and bang, bang, bang on the door of some crummy Ninth Street walk-up. They'd toss the place, find nothing, and the city would assume the police were on their toes, doing their job whether they found anything or not. Abbie was protected (and got his face on TV one more time), their asses were covered, and everyone went home happy. What looked like surprise random busts were staged events. Like a happening without the face paint and sanctimony.

"They let everyone relax, stock up, get high, right?" Rob said. "Then they came down hard, busted every downtown dealer, cleaned the place out. Boom, just like that."

Nick remembered all too well how things had changed. He walked into the Eatery one day and instead of finding the place full of people tripping or peeling themselves off the ceiling on speed, he saw a few sad faces nodding off over their vegetable soup. Heroin had come downtown, big time.

"Leroy saw his opportunity and started to move in. When he was busted twelve years later and I became his lawyer, he was responsible for something like forty percent of the city's major drug deals. The Mafia ran the rest of it, and even they didn't know who Leroy was. Except that he didn't tell me how big he was. I didn't know any more than that he was nickel-and-diming a bunch of strung-out junkies. But Leroy was running a high-class operation off the street. He never flaunted it. He didn't drive a Caddy or dress like a pimp, never drew attention to himself. People paid a premium for his smack, and he was always looking for the serious, high-quantity, top-quality buyer. He never sold to casuals—strangers just looking for a quick fix. And never to kids. So he had a better class of client—musicians, actors, people you'd know if you saw them. People who had to get onstage every night who couldn't perform without their fix." He glanced over at the open file on the floor. "If I told you who some of Leroy's clients were you'd be floored. And he was protected because they *had* to be cool about it. The last thing they wanted anyone to know was that they had a habit. Leaving him with a loyal and discreet customer base with money to spend on a regular basis. He kept his mouth shut, they said nothing, and everyone was happy." He shook his head in a kind of admiration. "The cops must've gotten him in their sights and in the end they nailed him on a possession charge. They were pissed off because they didn't know where he hid his money. He lived in a Harlem apartment. He didn't have a closet full of clothes, he didn't even own a car."

"And this guy we're meeting?"

"Once Leroy was out of the picture, D'Wayne became a dealer, took over some of Leroy's territory. Skimmed the cream right off the top."

"Movie stars and singers—"

"Lawyers and advertising execs," Rob said, laughing and slapping Nick on the arm.

"Can we trust him?"

"You have any better suggestions?"

"How do you still know this guy?"

"D'Wayne? Once Leroy was put away he kept me on call as his lawyer." Rob caught Nick's look. "What do you want me to do, run a credit check on the guy? We're in a black economy here, Nick, we're flying by the seat of our pants."

"That's what I'm worried about. I mean, if we only knew what we were trying to sell…"

Rob stepped out of the room and returned with one of the jars. He'd taken a damp cloth to it, so that it was as clean and shiny as the morning they'd bought it at Walker's General Store in what constituted downtown Allenville, all two blocks of it.

"What do you think it is?"

"Didn't you taste the sample you were bringing to Sonny?"

"I don't know what heroin tastes like. I mean, at least you've seen the real thing, right?"

"Yeah, thirty years ago. Just not this much of it."

Rob cradled the jar against him, as though preparing to nurse it. "I'm thinking that if this is the real stuff we just hit the jackpot. The purer it is, the more you can make of it. And that means we could be talking about a million or two."

"A cut is usually what? Something like two to one—"

"Three of milk powder to one of heroin. That would turn what we have into three or four pounds, whatever, of street-ready heroin. Maybe even more."

Nick looked at him curiously. "How do you know all this?"

"I saw it in a movie. 'Popeye's here!' Remember?"

"It's from a cartoon?"

They looked at the jar as if it were filled with something that had drifted down from heaven.

"We have to be very careful," Nick said. "Someone buys this, we have to stick around and make sure everything checks out. We've got to be really clear that we don't know what the hell this stuff is. We've got to play innocent but canny, know what I mean? Because we take the money and walk away and this turns out to be Babbo, we're dead men."

"What the fuck is Babbo?"

"Stuff my mother used to use. To clean bathtubs and sinks." He could've mentioned that he also remembered how a half-nuts ex-marine who used to hang around the Hip Bagel had supposedly shot up a nickel bag's worth of the stuff and was found dead in the gutter outside the Second Avenue Deli with bleeding eyes and a mouth full of foaming bathroom cleanser.

"Where exactly are you keeping the stuff?"

Nick followed him into the bedroom. A detached vent panel lay on a mattress and box spring covered with tousled sheets and a duvet. A stack of books and last Sunday's *Times* lay on the other side, topped with a pair of reading glasses.

"I just don't want to go to jail," Nick said as Rob finished replacing the jar and reattaching the vent panel to the wall.

"We're not going to jail, Nick. It's not happening, no way."

"I'm sure that put a smile on Leroy's face when you told him the same thing."

4

R OB PARKED THE SAAB NEAR THE CORNER OF NORTH
Moore and Greenwich and turned off the engine. He craned
his neck to look around. "That's the place, over there across the
street." He looked at his watch. "God, it's late. What is this guy,
a vampire?"

Back in the day the neighborhood was not much more
than abandoned buildings and boarded-up stores. In fact, Nick
almost never ventured this far, preferring instead to hang out
in the East Village, migrating west only when he was trying
to sell grass or pick up girls, not from Jersey or the Island, but
true out-of-towners from New Hampshire and Delaware and
Ohio who, adrift in the big bad city, would be most susceptible
to whatever charms he imagined he possessed. Now, if he went
into the East Village, he'd be as old as the guys in ruined shoes
pushing shopping carts and wearing the coats they called their
beds come nightfall.

He looked around. "*This* is where this D'Wayne operates?
It's a little, I don't know, bourgeois for a drug dealer, isn't it?"

"He just wanted to choose some more neutral territory.
As a courtesy to us. So we'd be comfortable."

"And how much are we paying him extra for *that* bit of
consideration?"

"Fuck you," Rob said, and he flung open his door just as a kid riding his bike was speeding by. The boy tumbled over the handlebars, went over the door and landed hard on the street. Though Nick saw the whole thing transpire, it didn't fully come into focus until he saw the guy lying flat on his back, apparently dead.

The kid was possibly twenty-two or so, lanky and long-haired. He lay with his arms outspread, one leg crooked to the side, as if it had been snapped at the hip. Beside him lay his bike, the front wheel still slowly revolving, and a messenger bag, out of which spilled some CDs and a notebook.

"What the fuck is wrong with you, huh?" another cyclist screamed at Rob as he rode by. "Are you out of your mind or something?"

Rob stared at the victim and only a second or two later registered the complaint. All he could think of to say was, "Shut up!"

Nick squatted beside the body and saw the whole situation spiraling out of control, onto the front pages of the *News* and the *Post*, to NY1's next news cycle, to reality TV, a courtroom in Lower Manhattan, possibly a hospital room, and even, as his imagination took over, a funeral home. Members of the kid's family would point at him and Rob and scream "Murderers!" Or, if the kid was Italian, "*Vendetta*!"

Instinctively, meaning that he'd seen it on TV and in movies so many times that it had become part of him, he felt for a pulse, found none, then put his ear to the boy's chest. The heart was beating. The kid was alive. And now he imagined this young man spending the remainder of his life as a quadriplegic, which created a whole new set of problems for them. For wouldn't Rob be sued and have to hand over an unspecified few million dollars toward the kid's care? And wouldn't it be in Rob's nature to expect Nick to share the costs?

Rob reached down to touch the boy's arm, and Nick said, "Don't move him. He might have a concussion."

Rob looked over at him with a look bordering on homicidal. "Thank you, doctor."

"Are you a doctor?" someone asked, and when Nick looked around he saw a dozen people watching. One of them, a young black woman, looked familiar. She tilted her head, and that slight gesture carried both recognition and question.

"I'm in advertising," Nick said, without knowing quite why.

"I'll call 911," the woman calmly offered, taking out her cell phone. Even in the cold unreality of the streetlamp she had an unmistakable beauty: he'd seen her before but didn't know where. His life sometimes seemed an endless intersection with the desired and unreachable, and she was clearly yet another member of that highly elite group, all of whom from time to time merged into one generic though enigmatic face. But she wasn't, and he was about to find her in time and in place, as in his memory he was going up the stairs in an apartment house and walking down a hallway, when the boy on the ground opened his eyes. "Shit," he said, wincing slightly and blinking himself back into life.

"You OK?" Rob asked, another stupid question uttered billions of times before to people who lay crushed to death.

"Yeah. Maybe. I don't know."

"Because you really should have been looking where you were going," Rob said, and Nick, yet again, had an excuse to kill his erstwhile friend, at least once the bike boy had reduced him to a pointless pulp.

"Fuck you, dude."

"Hey, I'm here. Do I look like I'm running away from the scene of the whatever?" The word "crime," on the very edge of his lips, died before it escaped. Once a lawyer, always a lawyer, Nick thought.

Now the police were there, all flashing lights and grim looks. One towering uniform looked down at Rob and asked what had happened.

"It was an accident," Nick said before Rob could spout any more inanities. "My friend here looked in his mirror, thought the street was clear, opened the door and the young man collided with it. He must have been coming around the corner."

"Is that true?" the cop asked the kid.

He sat up and started to look around. "Fuck, where's my bike?"

"Whoa, whoa, whoa, just lie back, OK? We'll need to get you braced and in the ambulance."

"My bike's gone," the kid shouted, and in fact someone had wandered off with the thing. "Fuck me, dude. I mean, fuck *me!*"

"Watch your language," an officer said.

"I gotta go," the kid said. "There's this after party." He pulled his messenger bag toward him and started gathering the contents that lay scattered in the street.

"You're not going anywhere. And you," the cop said to Rob, "you need to show me your license and registration. And give me a number where you can be reached."

Rob fumbled to find his wallet. "I'm a lawyer," he said.

"So was my father," the cop laughed. "Doesn't make him any less dead."

Two EMTs were already on their knees and preparing the kid to be shipped off to St. Vincent's, where, chased by every other unemployed attorney in town, he could at least die halfway to drawing up a lawsuit. The kid sprang to his feet and began looking frantically around. "My bike," he said pathetically. "I can't fucking believe this."

"See?" Rob said. "He's fine."

"I gotta find my bike," the kid said, gathering his stuff. "My mom's gonna fucking kill me." The woman who'd called the ambulance lingered nearby. Nick was about to say something to her when a black guy grabbed Rob's arm and reached to shake his hand.

"Hey, man, how you doin'? Jeez, it's been like years!" He smiled at the cop and opening his palm to him said, "I know this guy, he's my attorney, you know? So are we cool here and everything?"

The cop looked him up and down. "I think so." He handed Rob back his documents.

The man, arm around Rob's shoulder, led him away from the already dispersing crowd.

"OK, folks, show's over," the cop said in the grand old tradition of New York's Finest. Nick followed Rob and the black guy across the street. When he turned back he saw the black woman still standing there with her Strand Bookstore bag, watching. And then in her own sweet time she followed them into the bar, sat a distance away from them, and ordered herself a Campari and soda. "With a twist," Nick heard her say.

5

F ROM FAR AWAY D'WAYNE WOULD BE JUST ANOTHER KID on the hustle in his jeans, hooded sweatshirt and jacket; across the table, though, it was evident he was somewhere in his forties and very much on top of his game, which immediately led Nick to wonder exactly what the nature of this guy's game really was. He'd led them into the bar where they'd arranged to meet, a quiet little place that had the ambience of a café rather than a beer joint. But clearly D'Wayne was not about trends or being seen; he was about making things happen and steamrolling on to the next grand event.

He smiled, and his smile was like a cop showing up just when something bad's going to happen: you loved the guy implicitly because he was about to save your ass but good. He sat back and leveled his gaze first at Nick and then Rob. "So which one of you owns that Saab? The blue nine-five that almost took out that boy? Can tell a lot about a man by his drive. So, what, you own the thing outright or is it a lease?"

"It's Banknorth's when I stop making payments on it. Which may happen very soon," Rob said.

Nick noticed that D'Wayne was only drinking ginger ale, a clue that he was smart enough to keep his head clear. That made two of them, because he was drinking club soda.

Rob, of course, was slurping down a double Dewar's and was on the rocky road to getting sloppy. "OK," D'Wayne said, "you got five minutes. Starting now. Ticktock, time's running out."

Rob said, "Like I told you on the phone, I was really hoping to reconnect with Leroy Ives. But of course that's not possible, and I thought you might be able to help us."

When Nick noticed the black woman sitting at the bar, he was all of a sudden back at Sonny Ives's place, the day of his funeral, seeing her for the first time. It was like a game of connect-the-dots. If you drew lines between enough of them you might end up with someone's portrait. Or what might turn out to be a trap. And right now, with D'Wayne sitting across from them and sucking all the energy out of the meeting, it wasn't looking like the first option.

"What's in it for me?"

Rob was about to open his mouth when Nick leaned forward and said, "Exactly what're you looking for?"

D'Wayne spread his hands on the tabletop. "In this great big city? I mean, why me? Why not..." He shrugged. "Joe Blow?"

"Because I once—" Rob began.

"Joe Blow's dead," Nick said. Now he had everyone's attention. "Joe took a bullet in the heart a few days ago. Mrs. Blow's still crying her eyes out. Baby Blow's not doing too great, either. Now talk to us about Leroy."

D'Wayne took it in for half a second before he lowered his voice and came in close: "What are we talking about here? I'm looking for how *much* you're trying to shift. On the phone you said two. Two what? Two ounces—?"

"Pounds." Rob held up two fingers.

He was obviously impressed, though only his eyes betrayed him. "So a key?"

Nick hadn't heard the expression in thirty years. Rarely had he ever sold a kilo of anything, especially with the crap they'd picked up in Cincinnati.

"No," Nick said. "Like he said, exactly two."

"Call it a key. Everyone else does." But D'Wayne's eyebrows remained way up. "And what exactly are we talking about?"

"C'mon," Rob said. "I thought I was pretty clear on the phone."

"All I know is it's some sort of shit you think is smack, right? I mean, I'm gonna be straight with you, but you gonna get bargain-basement prices."

"Depends on the house," Nick said. "Some basements are dirt and an old boiler. Others are finished, furnished, well lit, and full of expensive things." Such as the Olhausen pool table that had cost him five grand and was now collecting dust.

"And if I can only get you to one with all the dirt and rats and shit?"

"We'll just find someone from a better neighborhood to work with us."

Although Rob continued to stare at him, Nick refused to look at anyone but D'Wayne.

"All right, listen," D'Wayne finally said. "Can you get it to me tomorrow?"

"Tonight," Nick said.

"So, what, you got it with you or something?"

"I didn't say that. I want to close the deal tonight. We just need to pick it up and bring it someplace"—he looked around—"a little less public, maybe?"

D'Wayne's eyes momentarily flashed what Nick took to be indecision. What the hell was going on here?

D'Wayne considered it. "OK. I'm down with that. Be at this address." He patted his pockets for a pen until Rob handed him, with great reluctance, a Montblanc Meisterstück 146.

"Careful. My wife gave me that for our tenth anniversary."

D'Wayne unscrewed the top and admired the nib. "Gold, huh?"

"Just be careful."

He held the top between his teeth and scratched out an address on the back of a napkin, screwed the top back on and started to slip the pen in his pocket. He smiled when he saw the look on Rob's face. "Just fucking with you, man." He handed it back. "Be there in half an hour."

Nick considered it. "Castle Hill Avenue. This is where? Way up in the Bronx someplace? We've got to shoot all the way over to the East Side first to pick up the items. Cut us some slack, will you? Or else you can find yourself another lawyer."

"One hour, then, tops."

Ten minutes later they were sitting in the parked car with Nick behind the wheel. A little numb, staring at nothing. Rob had no idea who that man sitting in the bar had been, using Nick's name, wearing his clothes, speaking words that rightfully belonged in a Scorsese movie. All he'd failed to do was take a hammer to the other guy's fingers and drill a hole in his skull.

Rob broke the silence: "What was that?"

Nick turned and stared at him.

"That thing you did in there. That was amazing. All this time I thought you were the one who wasn't so sure about this deal."

Nick fired up the engine and looked at Rob. "I am now."

It being late and the Sunday night streets empty, he hit green lights all the way up Tenth Avenue to Forty-Eighth Street and got extra lucky heading east, picking up the FDR by the UN in an easy fifteen minutes. Traffic—mostly taxis, liveries, and a few SUVs—was light and nimble, the cars hugging the practiced curves with grace and ease.

Rob sat back and looked at Nick. "So. What're we doing here? I mean, what's the plan?"

"We're going to your place to pick up the stuff and leave it in the trunk. When we see what the setup is, and we think it's OK, we'll get the stuff and—"

"What's wrong?"

Nick had spotted the headlights a minute after they got on the Drive, estimating that the car was moving at something more than eighty miles an hour. When it began passing others and locked itself into place right behind him, he knew this was what his life was going to be from now on: like Dillinger or Jesse James, he'd be forever on the run, endlessly pursued by both villain and heat, down interstate or heading west on some tragic rural road, like something out of an old song. And oddly, deep down inside, it felt really, tremendously, good.

"What?" Rob said.

"There's a car following us. Don't turn around."

In the bright lights of the highway he could see it was a maroon BMW, an old model, tight on their tail. "Nick, listen, don't push the transmission, I just had a rebuilt put in—"

The engine roared in complaint as Nick floored it. He slid the window all the way down and let the wind play in his still-thick hair. "Hold on. This could get a little hairy."

Without signaling, he cut into the left lane, back into the right, then back into the left, and the BMW eased into his slipstream each time. He shifted to the right once again, nearly scraping the barrier, and while nearby cars began to hang back, their drivers terrified of the madman in the Saab, the BMW stuck with him, this time with flashing brights and beeping horn.

"Is it D'Wayne?" Rob said, as Nick put his foot down and put some distance between his car and the BMW. It was only then he tried to imagine how Joanne and the kids would deal with the news that he had been turned into a smear on a guardrail in a high-speed chase normally seen on the big screen at a Saturday matinee.

"He's fucking going to kill us!" Rob screamed as they broke a hundred.

"Shut up and close your eyes!"

Nick followed the familiar bends and curves, veering off at the Harlem River Drive exit, brakes squealing, hanging a quick left onto 125th Street, coming to an abrupt stop and turning off the key. People on the sidewalks stopped to watch the show. Others came out of their apartment houses. A few corner boys made themselves scarce. Things were clearly going to get interesting. Someone on the pavement said, "White man inna big hurry."

A small crowd had begun to gather on the corner, as though to witness a death that minutes later, when the cops arrived, flashers ablaze, would have conveniently been submerged in the *I Didn't See Anything, Officer* book of excuses. If Nick wasn't having second thoughts earlier, he was now. The drowning pool of debt was nothing compared to this; at least when you owed money you more or less understood what your demise would be—a slow suffocation in a miasma of phone calls, faxes, bills, and the sad advent of the foreclosure sign and the wilderness of an abandoned front lawn. This, though, was beyond predictability. Here, anything could happen. He calmly stepped out of the car and found that his legs were actually shaking, as in a cartoon. He pounded his fist repeatedly on the car's roof. Rob got out on his side.

"Know what I think?" Nick said, his voice rising. "It's going to end really badly. Then we won't be alive to need the fucking money. Asshole!"

"Fine, fine," Rob said. "I'll take care of the thing myself."

"Shithead!"

"Tell him, brother," some old guy on the sidewalk said. "Kick his sorry fat white ass. He ain't worth nobody's time."

"You'll still get half, OK?" Rob was saying. "What, you don't trust me all of a sudden?"

The BMW came tearing into the street, halting a foot away from Rob's Saab, the headlights blinding them.

"Looks like it doesn't matter anymore," Nick said. He hoped Jo would remember his insurance policy. He had failed only himself. The family was saved.

The driver took her time getting her long legs out of the car. Hands on hips, she stood and took them in.

"So I understand you've been looking for my father."

6

THE COFFEE SHOP ON LENOX AVENUE WAS CALLED DIXIE'S, though the legendary Dixie had been dead and buried in her best Sunday dress since 1957. Something of a fixture in the community, it had had its share of famous customers, some of whose photos, signed and framed, hung on the wall nearest the register: Sugar Ray Leonard, Dizzy Gillespie, Redd Foxx, Al Sharpton. A pair of dusty boxing gloves, dating back over forty years and autographed in Magic Marker by Cassius Clay, dangled from a hook in the ceiling.

Apart from a few solitary customers brooding over their cups and newspapers, the only others in there were a couple of beat cops on their way out. The air smelled like a comfortable old memory: bacon and eggs and hash browns. Like an eternal Sunday morning, breakfast anytime of the day or night was the house specialty, which made it a favorite of those who lived to a different timetable, meaning musicians and cops.

The three of them sat at a table by the window. A woman in her sixties brought them laminated menus. "How're you doing, Merry?"

"Not too bad, Mrs. T. Thanks for asking."

"What can I get you?" the waitress said to Nick and Rob. "Coffee?"

"Sure."

She said to the young woman, "I never see you up here anymore. What'd you do, move downtown or something?"

"I did. I'm in Tribeca now."

"Well, I never," the woman said and, laughing, walked back to the kitchen.

"So you were just in the neighborhood," Nick said. "Because I saw you at Sonny's. And afterwards in the bar."

"I was picking up a prescription on Greenwich Street. You looked familiar. You also looked like you were in trouble."

"Yeah, well, that wasn't my fault, I'll tell you," Rob said.

"I'm Meredith Hunter. Leroy's daughter."

"But Leroy's name is—"

"I was adopted by Roy and Doris Hunter. In Philly. It's where I grew up."

That was six weeks after her father was convicted and sent away, just after she'd found her mother lying on the bathroom floor, naked, the needle still in her arm. There was no other family save for Sonny, and he and Macey, recently married, could never have afforded to care for her. She'd moved back to New York when she started college at Barnard, and would come up to Dixie's now and again just to reconnect with her old neighborhood. Maybe even to see if anyone had news of her father. All she knew was that he was in for a long time, and no one she ran into, not even her aunt and uncle, would say anything more about it. As if simply by uttering his name they might put themselves at risk with those who felt Leroy owed them something.

"It's funny," Rob said, "but I sort of remember Leroy mentioning a daughter." He shrugged apologetically. "I was his lawyer. He didn't have a lot to say about his family."

"Yeah, well, he kept quiet about me. Sonny said that my dad wanted to protect me. Keep people like you away from me.

Stop me from having to say anything at the trial. Try to give me something of a future. Because you would've put me up there, wouldn't you. Little seven-year-old in knee socks and Mary Janes saying how great her daddy was."

Rob shook his head a little. "It might have made a difference."

Mrs. T brought them three mugs of coffee. "Get you anything else?"

"I'd love a couple of scrambled eggs," Meredith said.

"You want bacon, sausages, hash browns with that, sweetheart?"

"Just bacon, please." The woman again ignored Nick and Rob and just walked away. "Oh and Mrs. T? Some of that hot sauce you've got?"

"I've already eaten," Rob said for no particular reason.

"And you haven't talked to him since?" Nick asked.

"Guess you hadn't heard. I took a Corky's bus up to Attica five years ago when I was at Barnard, waited in line, signed in, and when they checked my father's name on the computer, the assistant warden made me sit down with him in his office. He said my father had died of natural causes six months before."

Rob spent a pale moment considering this. Then the lawyer in him took over. "Did he show you a death certificate?"

She shook her head.

"Did he say where your father was buried?"

"Nope."

"You mean you were never told?" Nick asked.

"That's what I said. The guy just said there was no next of kin listed." She shrugged. "Guess they figure adopted kids just move on." She looked at Rob. "Now maybe you can tell me why they sent him to Attica. I mean, that's maximum security, isn't it? He kill someone? Look. I'm a big grown-up girl now. You can tell me."

Rob took a breath. "It was his third conviction. The first two were years earlier when he was a juvenile. Possession and selling to an undercover. This time it was for holding eight ounces of cocaine. Which he swore to me he never used or sold. That's a lot of coke. Someone has that amount he's either in LA or he's a dealer. And your father was definitely not the Hollywood type."

"So someone set him up."

"But you try proving that with zero evidence. I had no choice; I put your father at the mercy of the court. Said that he had a family to support, that he was promising to go straight. The judge gave him the full count in a maximum facility. Again, I'm sorry. I liked Leroy. I thought he was a good man with a lot of potential. I sincerely thought he would turn his life around and be a valued citizen. My deepest condolences for your loss."

"Except it's a lie," she said. "I always knew it was, I knew it the minute the man in Attica told me. And I knew it when I saw my father that day I was at my aunt's apartment."

"He was *there?*" Nick said.

Rob just stared at her. "Are you sure?"

"Outside in the street. In the back of some kind of limo."

Rob looked at Nick. For once every word conceivable failed him.

"Did you try to talk to him?" Nick asked.

"It was like he didn't want me to come near him. Like it wasn't the right time or something. Then he was gone. Look, already half the city knows someone's hanging on to something. I guarantee that you will not be spared when it all comes down. The guy Sonny called is the guy who killed him, just so he could get first shot at it. Guy's been spreading the word that something big is about to come down. The guy that shot my uncle is the one who's going to want to cut the deal with you."

"D'Wayne," Rob said. "The guy in the bar. Great."

"A lot of people are going to want a piece of that. Especially as things are a little desperate right now. So whoever gets it makes the dough."

"Your uncle wasn't going to sell it," Rob said. "All he wanted was a commission. A kind of finder's fee. That's all."

"Yeah, well, if he ever went near that shit my aunt Macey would've kicked him out for good. As far as you're concerned, I'd say things are beyond your control at the moment. Unless, of course, you want to go and deal with this guy on your own." Meredith laughed. "Thought this was going to be fun, huh? Welcome to the real world, fellas. Now take a moment and thank me for having hijacked your trip north and saved your asses."

Mrs. T stopped by to top off their coffees. When she was gone, Meredith said to Nick, "Give me your hand. C'mon, c'mon, I'm not gonna bite." She took a pen from her bag and wrote a number on his palm. "Anything comes up, call me. And I mean *anything* about my father. OK?"

"What's in this for you?" Rob asked.

"I just want to see him. Face to face. If he knows you've been looking for him he'll get in touch with you. So you and I both have something to gain from this, you understand? If he knows I'm involved with this he'll play it straight with you, I promise."

Her eggs and toast were brought, along with a plastic sauce dispenser in the shape of a red devil—horns, pitchfork, and all.

"We should be going," Nick said.

She smiled to herself. "Still thinking about seeing those guys you met earlier?"

"That's more or less the plan," Nick said.

"Any idea who you'll be dealing with?"

"We have a choice?"

"We all have choices," she said. "Which is why I'm making my father the safer option here. You go try to deal with those guys and there's no knowing where they'll find you come morning. There are lots of rivers in New York City, you know. And Jersey's just a short ride away."

Rob looked at her. "We don't even know where your father is."

"Make yourself visible. Let folks know you're ready to do business." She set down her knife and fork. "He'll find you easy enough. Otherwise, you do what you want and one day you're gonna wake up, come down for breakfast, and find five black guys sitting around eating Cocoa Puffs, talking about marrying your daughter."

It made Nick laugh. He liked her style. He could use a little of her steel. He slipped on his coat and left a twenty on the table.

"You've got to be kidding me, mister."

"For your breakfast. Dinner. Whatever."

Her expression softened. "I don't have to pay for this," she said with a glance at Mrs. T, who was preparing a fresh pot of coffee. "And if I did, trust me, I can easily afford her prices." She folded the bill and pressed it into Nick's hand. "Tell you what. There's a jar over there. It's a fund some local folks have started for my little nephew, Terrell. Put the twenty in it. Give the kid something to look forward to, OK?"

Part Four

1

B Y TWELVE THIRTY A BITING WIND STREAMING IN FROM the north had wiped the streets clean of pedestrians. Nick thought of calling Joanne to tell her not to worry, but there seemed no point as he was certain she had, as usual, gone to bed with late-night TV, sinking into a sound sleep without another thought for his safety. It wasn't that she was coldhearted; it was just altogether easier for her to pretend not to care than to reveal herself as in any way weak: a matter between her and her shrink. And soon enough her shrink would become unafford-able as well, as Jo had chosen someone who didn't take insur-ance, had bonded with the woman and refused to miss a single weekly session. When that was over there was no telling how Jo would spin out of control. The supposed evolution of the human race would be revealed for the fiction it was once people had a glimpse of the Copelands: Apart from Eric, already a model of primate behavior, Joanne and Nick would be reduced to hys-terical bouts of adultery and, in his case, downright lawlessness, which had already been unleashed. Only Jen would escape this backward spiral, forever singing a medley from *Hair* as the Age of Aquarius revealed itself to be instead the Age of Caligula.

"You're not answering me," Rob said.

They were sitting in Rob's Saab. Nick's Audi was where he'd left it, across from Rob's building with a brand-new ticket under the wiper ready to be torn up and tossed to the four winds. Another good thing about bankruptcy, Nick thought.

"I asked what you thought about all that. Leroy's daughter." He shrugged.

"If she thinks he's still alive, maybe we just wait for him," Nick said.

"I can check and see if he's dead."

"You do that."

"Tomorrow."

"Fine, Rob."

"You're losing your enthusiasm for this. I can see it."

Nick turned on his seat. "Tell you what. Make me an offer for my half. Give me the front money. Sell the stuff and we're even."

"Front money. Where the hell am I supposed to find that?"

Nick opened the door. "I'll catch you in the morning."

He got out and could still hear Rob jumping around in his seat and arguing with him as he unlocked his own car and got into it. As he drove off he saw his partner in crime standing by his Saab, shoulders hunched, arms outstretched in a giant *Why?*

Forty minutes later the garage door began its ascent even before Nick approached the driveway. He pulled into the garage and sat for a moment, putting his head back and shutting his eyes as the door slowly unfurled behind him. He opened his window and breathed deeply as the garage door completed its descent and death filled the space with its seductive smoky song.

He wondered how long it would take before he drifted into unconsciousness. He'd read somewhere that a symptom of carbon monoxide poisoning was hallucinations, which would be a fitting end to the man who thirty years earlier had seen the Clear White Light and lived to die once again seeing things that weren't there. It would look like an accident—guy drove in, the door slid shut, guy fell asleep—the sequel being eternal blotto.

Sometime in the morning, maybe when Jen and Eric were setting out for school, someone would hear his car running and smell the smoke, and Joanne would open the garage door and hack and cough and call an ambulance, which also meant the arrival of the fire department, thus drawing out the neighbors who'd want to be in on the hullabaloo, but it'd be too late. Nick would be in his seat, head serenely on his shoulder, free at last from his debts, his worries, and he'd be put in a body bag and zipped up tight and taken to the morgue.

He switched off the engine and quietly let himself into the house, reentering the alarm code.

Purchased on the insistence of Joanne, the alarm system had cost him a fortune. At first they'd lived without it, but after the Hoffmans, away for the Labor Day weekend two years ago, were visited by a couple of drunk seniors from Scarsdale High who broke a window and used the dining room table and the Hoffmans' daughter's underwear drawer as toilets, and once the Fosters at number seventeen suffered a home invasion—a polite way of saying "frenzied attack"—by a former employee of Chuck Foster's whom the newspapers and TV news labeled "disgruntled" but who in reality was out of his mind on a combination of tequila, Ecstasy, and one almighty grudge, Nick and Joanne were obviously next on the karmic list. Until then they had been the golden twosome of the neighborhood: younger than the others to the tune of four or five years; immensely attractive; the guests to die for at cocktail parties (not to mention that at pool's edge, Joanne in her bathing suit, all deep cleavage and long slim legs, became the instant center of attention); both of them witty, literate, laid-back, and all-around fun to know. In fact, what they'd become over time was the object of the neighbors' adulterous fantasies: men wanted Joanne and their wives wanted Nick. It was considered only a matter of time before they got around to separating and divorcing, as though only through the dissolution of a family and all the wreckage surrounding the split could these two people truly join the social round of Westchester County.

Around the time the Fosters bought a Smith & Wesson SW1911 and a case of ammunition, and the Hoffmans put their property on the market, the ADT people came and wired the place. Fortress Copeland, Nick called it. He briefly even envisaged having a moat dug and buying a brace of Rottweilers to rip out the lymph nodes of anyone who came too close to his castle. "My home!" he wanted to roar, bare-chested, scimitar in hand.

Joanne had left a light on for him in the kitchen and another in the living room, leaving the other lamps to the inner logic of their timers. There was a handwritten note on the counter: "Cold chicken@fridge."

He examined the carcass lying on its plate, a sad husk of a formerly hale and hearty yardbird. He peeled away a last sliver of dark meat and shoved it in his mouth. He replaced the remains and pulled the bottle of scotch from its cabinet and poured himself a neat triple, tossing it down, pouring another, and, finally at his ease, leaned back and considered what had transpired. The idea that word had gotten out about the jars amazed him. It was as if the counterculture of yesteryear, with its tribal codes and crude communication system, had become supersonic, a crafty and malign jet stream of a world where two bottles of an unidentified substance could create ripples felt throughout the city's boroughs. If they held out long enough, he thought, if they simply waited for the best offers to come through, then in the end they could only win this thing, and win it big.

Unless someone like D'Wayne got to them first, that is.

When he woke the next morning, he didn't remember actually going up the stairs or getting into bed, but he was lying there, his naked body wrapped in sheet and duvet, and when he heard a toilet flush he turned to look at the clock. He had had exactly four and a half hours of sleep. Joanne walked in nude from their bathroom, her hair wrapped in a towel. Her look demanded to be interpreted.

"What," he said.

"Nothing."

She was still beautiful, still the woman with whom he'd fallen in love all those many years ago. She'd known about Kacey then—she knew that Kacey was his first real love—and she'd made accommodations for Kacey to remain with them. At first she tried to become Kacey, tried to understand what had so excited him about this girl, even attempted to replicate the brief intense life—one measured in mere months—he'd shared with her, as though performing in a variant of a Hitchcock film. But to him she was and always would be Joanne. The woman he loved; the woman he'd married. With or without Kacey Christopher's blessing.

She hooked on her bra. "Meeting run long?"

"Too long."

"Get anything done?"

"I think so. We'll know definitely this week."

"That's what you said last week."

"This week it's definite. It will absolutely happen this week. Jerry Bruno is really fired up about this."

"Good. Get up. We're going to the school. I've already told the Rascals I'd be late."

"What school?"

"Eric and Jen's. We have an appointment." She slipped on her panties and went to get a skirt from the closet. "You did say it was definitely happening, Nick. And you've always said you were a man of your word. I'll go down and make some coffee. Take a shower. You stink like a saloon."

2

THE BLACK ESCALADE HAD BEEN PARKED HALF A BLOCK
from the entrance to Rob's building since five that morning, moving to a spot across the road at seven when the street
cleaners paraded through with desultory thoroughness. The
three men inside took turns watching the entrance, polishing
off a dozen doughnuts and drinking coffee, biding their time.

At just past ten Rob stepped out of his building. He wore
a blazer and khakis and carried a leather bag over his shoulder.
In truth the bag contained nothing. Rob was going nowhere
special. This was his routine: wake up, shower, shave, dress,
walk out. Breakfast consisted of a grande caramel macchiato
at Starbucks and whatever they were peddling in the way of
muffins. If he were feeling especially hungry, he'd stop in at
McDonald's and pick up something stuffed between two halves
of an English while he leafed through a newspaper someone else
had left behind. It gave him the semblance of being someone
in a real world rather than being a no one alone at home with
no future and an apartment full of memories, most of them
so extraordinarily wonderful that it pained him like the throb
of toothache whenever he encountered one. The strange notion
that the happiness you leave behind can somehow carry you
through the best and worst of life was clearly a myth, something

out of a Paul McCartney lyric: one happy memory of Janet and he was done for the day. Because it only served to remind him that Janet was now creating happy memories with someone else.

He'd either go down to Rockefeller Center and watch the tourists and take in some sun, or spend the morning at the Met or MoMA, which he found especially therapeutic. Though he knew virtually nothing about art, simply being around these works—whether by Vermeer, Rothko, or Picasso—reminded him that there were more important things in life, and that the vision of another could lead him into something timeless and maybe even immortal. And then, as he'd come down the steps of the Met, or exit out onto Fifty-Third Street, the feeling would leave him and he'd resort to his usual fallback: a late matinee of a movie, generally something that as an employed, not to mention married, man he would have disdained: something with a lot of shooting, car chases, explosions, and, if at all possible, Nicolas Cage—whatever it took to earn an R rating. Lately, though, he'd taken a fancy to torture movies, the bloodier the better, featuring no actor he'd ever heard of. The audiences in the cinemas he frequented—people half out of their minds on crack or cheap wine or possibly on early release from the asylum—often screamed at the screen, urging more violence, more blood, more gore, and once or twice he'd caught a glimpse of some poor solitary pleasuring himself while a coed was being dismembered in the desperate glare of an overlit sound studio. This was what being alive must feel like, he'd remind himself, turning a wasted ninety minutes into something akin to a religious experience. Being alive was not being strapped to a table with a buzz saw traveling toward your balls, or laughing maniacally while a cheerleader was being slowly bled to death in the pit in your cellar; being alive was living at the edge of all these things and knowing that this would never in a million years be your fate. It was a matter of equilibrium, of simultaneously reveling in the bloodbath while anticipating the hour when it would all have been forgotten. Wasn't this what life was all about? Not tipping into one excess or the other? And hadn't Janet allowed herself to tip out of balance? And was she miserable?

Of course not. And the very thought of it once again would beat his soul into a bloody pulp.

He'd step out of the palace of pain into the sunlight and return home to watch the wall-to-wall misery of cable television over a delivered carton of shrimp lo mein and a portion of crab Rangoon—*America's Most Wanted* had become a favorite of his—just to remind himself that were he to go to prison he would not survive the first ten minutes of it.

Now, though, knowing that word had gotten out that he and Nick had something to sell, he began to show his face in places associated with Leroy in the past: restaurants in Harlem, taprooms in the Village. A beer here, a Coke there; he'd stand at the bar and make his face known to all the other customers. His files on Leroy's case, spread out across the minimally furnished stretch of his 120-square-foot living room, revealed names other than D'Wayne's that had come up more than once in his conversations with the defendant, the most memorable being a Mr. Ping, who owned a few noodle shops in Chinatown. He didn't even know if this Ping was still alive, or incarcerated, or had simply returned to his homeland, nor had he mentioned him to Nick. He needed some time alone to explore the dimensions of this enterprise, the question in the back of his mind always being: What's in it for me? What if Nick backed out before the deal was concluded? What if Nick, well, died?

On that morning, as Rob was heading toward the subway at Ninety-Sixth Street, the man behind the wheel of the Escalade, the same one who had run a check on Rob's license plate when it was parked outside the club, said, "Apartment 5D. No doorman. Schlage B360 deadbolt. I checked it out last night."

3

THE SCHOOL WAS A FIFTEEN-MINUTE DRIVE FROM THE house, situated on a former estate once owned by a couple who, before the First World War, plundered several European countries, as well as the cities of Jerusalem, Alexandria, and Damascus, returning with antiques and bits and pieces of old abbeys in France and cobbling them together to amend and furnish the main building, once the family's residence. Establishing a school was always in their plans, and just after the war they began with a kindergarten of eight children, mostly drawn from other wealthy families in the neighborhood: never firstborns (who in their parents' eyes deserved better and hence were already on the lists for Groton, Choate, St. Paul's, and St. Mark's), but usually the runts of the litter, the third or fourth child who from the start was destined to become a criminal lawyer or—God forbid—an advertising executive. Maria Montessori, whom they'd befriended on their travels, gave the school and its founders her blessing, made sure the faculty was trained in her methods, and left the place alone, so that in time it would evolve into just another ordinary private day school in a county brimming with them.

The idea of filling the place with items from the past was so that the students, being exposed to such antiquity, would have the ideals of ancient Greece and Rome and Renaissance Europe leached into their souls. The combination of antiques— bronze busts, sixteenth-century wooden benches, vases and friezes—and out-of-control students (including Eric, who was once suspended for three glorious days for playing touch football with the head of Augustus Caesar) had, once the founders were both safely dead and buried, led one of the headmasters to rescue what remained of the treasure and stash it for two hundred bucks a month in a U Store It on a service road in Armonk.

When Nick turned into the main gate at the bottom of the long, sycamore-lined drive that led to the main building, Joanne said, "What are you going to tell her?"

"I'm just going to try to buy a little time. Do you have a cigarette?"

She just stared at him. "We gave up smoking when Eric was born, remember?"

"I know, I was just—"

"Nick, are you OK?"

"I was joking," he said, though at this stage he wouldn't have refused a cigarette, stiff drink, or even a taste of the heroin Rob was keeping for them back at his apartment.

When they reached the top of the drive, the building with its majestic colonnade came into view. A few boys in blazers and khakis and sour expressions stood outside, also perhaps hoping for a smoke. They stared at the car as Nick pulled into a parking space.

"They're going to look at you," he said. "They always do."

"Boys will be boys."

"Just don't encourage them, OK?"

"You're a pig."

"I know."

"Please think, Nick. We're up against school policy—"

"And the kids have been there since kindergarten. She'll be flexible. You'll see." He took her hand, and like a fish it wriggled away.

Once the house's mudroom, Kathleen Warner's office was a square, multi-windowed space with a fireplace, above it a decent painting from the Hudson River School, shelves full of books and a desk that looked more like a prop than a work station, whereas his desk at work was—had been, rather—forever covered with Post-it notes, slips of paper, items torn from magazines or newspapers, as well as wrappers from energy bars and a framed photo of proud husband and papa with Joanne and the kids in happier days. To him it was a sign of the creative mind, one that focused on important things, such as how best to sell Brooklyn College to its alumni donors, or ways in which Charmin might be pitched as the best paper for America's assholes. Now it belonged to Fowler Benjamin, the man sucked in from the ether of the advertising workforce to replace him. Fowler Benjamin had been with Spencer Blackwell Ferguson in Los Angeles for five years, and the subject of a profile in the business section of the Sunday *Times*, telling the whole world what a great ad executive he was and would continue to be. He was twelve years younger than Nick, had two perfect children, one perfect wife, three perfect purebred dogs, and, until moving to New York lived in a perfect house in Malibu, one of the three most perfect places in the galaxy. He had friends in the film, music, and political spheres, Brian Grazer was the best man at his wedding (barefoot and on the beach), and he had famously hosted a fund-raiser for a Democratic presidential candidate during which a B-list actress drowned unnoticed in his swimming pool. The photograph in the *Times* showed that he wore perfect clothes and had a smile that would perfectly kill you. Having only met his reputation and not the living embodiment of it, Nick developed a pathological hatred of the man and began talking incessantly about him over the dinner table, saying things ranging from "I hope he's caught stealing" to "I hope he loses the Marriott account."

He took it a step further, imagining the man toppling from his office window—what had been Nick's corner office—as well as scenarios involving dismemberment via a Metro North train and a drowning in the waters off Montauk, where Perfect Man would of course keep his Perfect Boat, and though he wished no harm to the perfect man's perfect family or pets, when it came to the man himself, all bets were off. Nick had begun to understand what it was like being a Shakespearean character, consumed with vengeance, a hooded figure in the Rialto destined to fall.

"You always said hatred was a self-destructive emotion," Jen in her braces period brightly offered one evening as he went off on yet another tirade against his usurper.

Of course she was right. It was a wise reminder that while he was condemning Fowler Benjamin, what he was really doing was committing a slow form of suicide, allowing himself to rot with envy and despair from his soul outward. Bitter and pustular and loveless: That's how he would end up. The bad end of a cheap morality tale.

Nick looked at his watch. "She's keeping us because we're late with the tuition. See? It's a lesson. She's trying to make us feel just how she feels. God," he said, sighing, "I hated school." Even this office, years and miles away from his own experiences as a young scholar, contained the familiar smell of recrimination and punishment, with overtones of dry sherry and old leather and an aftertaste of bitter tears. One after another of his private schools had parted ways with difficult little Nick: the first because he refused, ever, to go to gym class (and why would he want to be subjected to a daily regimen of what, in his eyes, was plainly a form of torture, followed by the humiliation of standing in a shower with a bunch of other underdeveloped boys while the gym staff watched and called them things like "Small Change" and "Peanut"?); the second because of the tiny matter of stealing a chemistry exam key from the desk of sad, trusting old Mr. Harper; the third—well, he'd forgotten exactly what had happened; but the fourth had kept him on and let him graduate, because his English teacher, Ms. Stokes, apart from having the best legs in the known universe of the then adolescent space explorer Nick Copeland, saw his potential and made sure he lived up to it. In the end he came to like the school, respect the teachers, and, even better, it was located on a piece of property where, to relieve midday stress, he could wander off and smoke a joint when he wasn't feeling up Penny Daniels under the weeping willow by the football field.

The door opened and Kathleen Warner breezed in as if life within those hallowed walls were a whirlwind of activity, Hepburn in a Philip Barry play.

"Good morning," she said, shutting the door behind her with graceful finality. She was a solidly built woman, designed for intimidation, her hair dyed a deep copper, a color of such glow and sincerity that it dared you to suggest she had gone prematurely gray.

Nick stood and they all shook hands. "How are you, Kathleen?" Jo said, trying to be casual.

"Busy, busy. My daughter's getting married next weekend and we're preparing for the eightieth anniversary of the school." She threw up her hands and laughed. "I mean, really, who in the world gets married in November? But it's their choice."

Nick offered his congratulations and best wishes, though she was clearly seeking commiseration.

"And don't forget the annual auction. That's an important part of the festivities. Our goal this year is to get that theater of ours in absolutely magnificent condition."

The invitation was under a magnet on their fridge at home. Nick hated such events: finger food and cheap wine followed by some serious fund-raising. It was like stopping strangers on the street, telling them how nice they looked, sharing your sandwich with them, and then pulling a gun and demanding their wallets.

"So," Mrs. Warner said, now all business. "You asked to meet with me."

"It's about the tuition," Joanne began.

"Well, yes," she said, and she sat back and sighed a little. "I know that you must be under exceptional stress, both financially and otherwise. To be frank, it's not a healthy environment either for you or your children." She glimpsed down at some papers on her desk. "Although Jen has done superior work this year, Eric is barely holding his own. Looking at his last term reports, I'm seeing two D-minuses, two C-minuses, an F in chemistry, with the only decent grades a B in English and an A-minus in gym."

"What are you saying?" Nick said.

"Just giving you an honest assessment of where your son and daughter stand. I believe that both would shine in a public school environment. Jen, especially, would be at the top of her class, and Eric, well, he'd certainly be less, shall we say, challenged?"

"That's not what we want," Joanne blurted out. "We want them to be challenged, but in a safe place. Where there won't be any...outside influences. Especially for Jen. She's at that age—"

"We always want what's best for our children," Mrs. Warner said.

Nick could tell she'd grown bored. This was Kathleen Warner boilerplate, something she'd pulled out of a file somewhere. Her eyes kept drifting to the window and the panorama of the distant playing fields, the flag flapping in the wind at the top of its post, the faculty members as they walked by.

"Let's be honest," he said. "Are you kicking them out?"

As if instead of speaking his mind he'd produced a grenade and already had the pin between his gritted teeth, she became alert and tense. "Of course not," she said.

"Then what are you saying?"

"Simply that as you are no longer able to afford to pay the tuition in a timely fashion I believe it's in everyone's best interest that this be Eric and Jen's last term here. They can begin public school after the New Year, and I assure you they'll adjust very quickly. And, you know"—big smile here—"they will make friends there just as they have here."

This, Nick knew, was no different from Larry Stevens patting him on the back and telling him that he was so talented every agency in town would be calling him: encouraging words that lasted all the way down to the ground floor, Nick's smile diminishing as the numbers systematically lit up and faded on the brushed-chrome elevator panel. By the time he stepped out into the lobby, stunned and numb, he knew that no one would be calling him, that in fact in something like thirty-seven seconds every agency in town would know he'd been shoved aside because of his age. It didn't matter that his ideas were extraordinary and that his accounts had always been profitable for Stevens Breakstone Leary; no one wanted someone entering the bramble wood of middle age in an economy more geared to brain-dead fourteen-year-olds. He was, as they said in the business, yesterday's man, just another name on the tip of the tongue.

"With drug dealers and addicts," Joanne said, and Nick, waking from his reverie with a start, simply stared at her. Where had that come from?

"In our local public schools?" Mrs. Warner said. "Let's remember where we are. This is an affluent community." She passed her eye over another page, undoubtedly the Copelands' financial fact sheet. "In your case an exceptionally affluent community. I assure you there are no drug dealers living there."

When the phone buzzed she excused herself to take it. Nick whispered to Joanne, "We're finished here."

"We haven't made our case."

"She's already made it for us."

Mrs. Warner hung up. "Wedding planners," she said with a laugh and a shrug. The laugh died, the smile went belly-up. "I have to be frank with you. Because of your outstanding balance we've had to contact Citibank—the company holding your mortgage. As a matter of course they're naturally checking on all your other creditors."

"May I say something?" Nick said.

"Yes, of course, Mr. Copeland." Until now he'd been known as Nick. Now she was taking her leave by reducing him to the status of stranger.

"As I told you on the phone a few days ago, I expect to be tying up some loose ends on a new project. This will bring in all the funds we need to pay for Jen's and Eric's tuition and to secure next year's deposits as well."

"This is serious?"

"It's why we're here. To let you know."

The light in her eyes changed. "So it's now definite."

"Absolutely."

"I told Citibank that we'd arranged a payment schedule for you. Just to forestall anything going to a collection agency. Of course what I suggested is impossible under current board policies. I just—"

"So you lied to them," Nick said.

"Let me finish, please. I just wanted to give you an opportunity to find the required funds to meet your responsibilities to the school."

She'd saved their ass, in other words. Now they were her slaves. Nick and Joanne stood and shook her hand. Nick didn't let go until he said, "You'll have the money by next Friday."

4

BEFORE HE COULD PUT THE KEY IN THE IGNITION, JOANNE said, "Tell me I didn't imagine that."

He sat back and let out a breath.

"You lied to her."

"No, I speculated."

"Don't play games with me, Nick."

And yet he felt better than he had in days—a little drunk, even. He'd crossed a line; he'd made his intentions public. He promised at least the immediate future of his children and now he was committed to win. He and Rob would shift the dope, take the cash, split it, and walk away. He knew that when this was over, Rob was the last person he would ever want to see again. Although he couldn't define it with any precision, he knew there was something essentially corrupt about his old friend, and he realized that even when he was losing his mind on acid and a potential liability to anyone situated within a hundred yards of him, the guy sitting on the dorm room floor beside him had been in the service of only himself.

We're all one? In your dreams, pal.

"You have nothing more to say, then," she went on.

"I think I've said it all."

"I'm your wife."

"I know that. I've been aware of it for years."

"The least you can do is—I don't know—clue me in to whatever the hell is going on in your life."

"I just want things to work out smoothly and successfully so we can bring this whole thing to an end. I just want to live."

The road leading away from the school followed a gentle curve around the main building and playing fields. There was something blissfully timeless about the landscape, the way manicured academe artfully gave way to the gradual thickening of woods as far as one could see on either side, the fading reds and oranges and the sad yellow of the final days of autumn. Nick knew that beyond the woods were the estates with their six-stall barns, lighted tennis courts, and Olympic-standard swimming pools, forbidden areas reachable only by private road. He had always felt out of place here, as though all along he had only pretended to be a guy in a suit doing his job, living in this millionaire's paradise, treading water for too many years. It wasn't that he deserved better; he deserved honesty.

But now, as they drove down the deserted road, he remembered all the other times he had taken this route, late on autumn afternoons, when the light grew angular and the air took on a chill, and you could see the cross-country teams everywhere, hearing the crunch of dead leaves beneath their feet as they ran through the village, past the Unitarian church and the library, the Starbucks and the Jacob's Ladder health food store, the high-end Realtors and the new brick firehouse. It was a scene that reminded Nick of his own school days and of things passing him by. In a way a piece of him missed not the days of his unhappy times at school but of the times that he *might* have had, happy at school, good at sports, respected by teachers and classmates alike. It dawned on him in an odd, abstract way: this is why he became an adman, because whether he was selling

Preparation H or an inferior brand of frozen pizza he could always make people understand that through these products they might just touch the dreams that had so eluded them, the life they should have lived. The consumer existed in a universe of *might* and *may*. You kept them in this happy state of suspension, let them know what was out there and tantalized them periodically with the new and the improved and the things that could touch their hearts even more than the things that had so moved them eight months earlier. It was the most exhilarating of professions and also the most dishonest. And maybe that's why he liked it so much.

He rounded the corner just beyond the rail station and moved slowly up the south end of Main Street. This town they lived in, this drain on their hard-earned money—a place of high taxes and retail shops full of two-hundred-dollar T-shirts and handmade furniture—with its Victorian architecture and charming little shop signs, was nothing more than a movie set, a place of secondhand charm, something he could have devised in an afternoon at his desk at Stevens Breakstone Leary. If you had the means to live here, he knew, you were supposed to feel that you fucking well *deserved* it.

A group of runners from the school passed by, a tight pack of seven girls, their faces earnest, their ponytails bobbing, their smooth, muscular legs pink in the afternoon cold. He watched their firm little backsides, which barely moved as they notched up the miles. He knew that Joanne was watching him, looking for a twitch of hunger on his lips. It was time to change the subject.

"What sport is Eric playing these days? Or has he given up physical activity altogether?"

"You should know, you're his father."

"He doesn't tell me things like that. I only know Eric as the guy who lives in a room at the end of the hall and occasionally takes meals with us. Like the boarding-house killer in a Hitchcock film."

"Stop it, Nick. He's your son. You two should be communicating."

He turned right at the next street and followed the road as it wended past Time & Tide Antiques and Bronson's Garden Center, where every price was guaranteed to be inflated 400 percent, before coming into the center of town a few moments later. He had the idea of taking Joanne out to lunch, perhaps to Chez Félice or the Oak Cask, because he was in a peacemaking mood and, in fact, was dying for a drink in a setting other than the polished-granite hell of their kitchen. "Hungry?"

When she said nothing he looked over at her. "What?"

"I'm just not buying your story with this, this, this guy in Cincinnati. Usually you tell me all the details. Now all I'm getting is some vague description of some one-off job you might do. And I don't understand these late nights, and I'm still wondering about *this*."

She took his right hand off the wheel and held it palm up. Meredith's number, faded but legible, came into view. It didn't matter if it disappeared overnight; he had already keyed it into his cell phone. He pulled into a space near Chez Félice and turned off the engine. Buddy Futterman, the tennis pro from the club, stepped out of the restaurant with a woman that was definitely not his wife. "I'm not having an affair," he said.

"Obviously, because how the hell could you afford it? Are you telling me the truth about this…thing you're supposed to be doing?"

He held out his palm again. "It's a contact number for Jerry Bruno's estate attorney in New York. Rob referred Jerry to him, and I'll need to speak to him…somewhere along the way." He looked at her. "To coordinate our efforts." She was still making that crooked face, meaning she was in standard bullshit-detector mode. "Rob doesn't do estate work," he rambled on. "You need a specialist for that. And that's why Jerry hired him."

She looked him in the eye. "Don't make me start to hate you, Nick. I can distrust you, I can suspect you, but don't let it reach the point where I can't even look at you, OK?"

"All right. Fine. Great. I'll tell you the whole story." He took a deep breath. "After we finished college, Jerry Bruno joined the Weathermen." Where the hell had *that* come from? "Like the Dylan song." He shrugged.

"These people were terrorists, Nick. They blew things up, killed people. Didn't they try to murder Dustin Hoffman?"

"Jerry wasn't involved in any of the bombings. He was just a member and his name came up at the trial. Then after they blew up some army reserve building he got scared and went over the border to Canada. If he'd just been a draft dodger he would've been pardoned by Jimmy Carter with all the rest of them and come home thirty years ago. He came back over the border to see his...dying mother. Eight months ago. And now he just wants his life back. That's all."

She looked very carefully at his face. "This sounds... insane, Nick."

Insane enough, he knew, to be completely credible. "Look, let's have lunch at Félice, OK?"

"On whose money?"

"I'll put it on my AmEx. It's not maxed out. Yet."

"I was hoping to go to the gym."

"Just something quick?"

Lunch hour had already come and gone, and only the retired and wealthy and spiritually broken could afford to linger over one more martini or a second cup of coffee. Joanne glanced at the menu, then up at the specials board. "I'm just having a salad."

"Drink?"

"Before gym? Are you crazy? Tell me something. How does all this business with this guy who came back from Canada involve you?"

That was a question he hadn't anticipated. Rob's role was easy; he was the attorney. People like that had their hands in everything.

"It's kind of complicated. When his father died—this is Jerry I'm speaking of—he left his son his business."

"What business?"

"A big furniture business. A chain of stores all over Ohio. Bruno's Furniture Outlet. And it's gathered a lot of equity over the years, because his mother refused to sell to one of the big chains, and he'd like to reintroduce the brand, do a makeover, run some ads, the whole nine yards. TV ads, print ads. He feels he owes it to his family. Especially his niece, who's in a vegetative state." Oh, that was a good one. In three seconds he had a backstory for this fictional relative: cheerleader, booze, fast car, crash.

"And Rob's role is?"

"Negotiating a pardon so he can live and work here again."

He was pleased because, really, it wasn't such a bad story; far-fetched enough to be believable and actually, in a way, a little touching.

"When Jerry was in Canada he married a young widow and took her three kids as his own, and he wants to give them the life they deserve in Ohio." He was about to add, "Including the one with Down syndrome," but figured that was one too many crosses for a single lie to bear.

Jesus, he was good. This was right out of one of his ad campaigns. He'd once put together a series of commercials for a carpet company that, if you turned the sound down, looked exactly like testimonials from cancer survivors, complete with close-ups and what appeared to be misty eyes. Turn the sound up and you heard firsthand how wonderful the experience had been in dealing with the people from Proctor Flooring. When he first screened it for the people from Proctor, he was certain he even heard a tearful sniffle or two.

"It's a good story, Nick. You've almost sold me. You were Stevens Breakstone Leary's creative director. It's your job to pull the wool over people's eyes. But I'm not really buying this one." She took his hand as the waitress approached their table. Then she flipped it over to reveal once again Meredith's number. "Should I call when we get home or wait till you're asleep tonight?"

5

"I TOLD YOU, MAN, THERE WAS NOTHING," THE GUY SAID after he'd returned from searching Rob's apartment.

"Did you look everywhere?"

"A room and a half. There *is* no fucking everywhere."

The Escalade reached Scarsdale almost an hour later, due to a rollover on the Hutch. They parked just around the corner from the Copelands' house, giving themselves a clear view of the driveway. None of the men heard the cruiser come up behind them, and when D'Wayne caught a glimpse of the big white cop strolling up and checking out the plate number, all he said was, "Man's here." When the cop reached the driver's window, one hand resting on the butt of his revolver, D'Wayne already had his shield slapped up against it. The officer did the universal wind-it-down with his hand.

"Kind of out of your jurisdiction, aren't you?" he said, taking his hand off his weapon and eyeballing the driver's shield.

"Ongoing investigation," D'Wayne said. "Have gun, will travel," and they shared a laugh.

The cop noticed the other two. "This your team?"

"I get what they give me." The others in the Escalade laughed.

"Someone dropped a dime on you. That's why I'm here. I've got to be honest, fellas, but around here you stick out like a sore—"

"Nigger," D'Wayne said.

The cop paused a moment to figure out how the hell he'd gotten into this. "Well, let's just say people around here aren't accustomed to seeing a big black—"

"Dick," Lamar said. Valentine, so named by his mother and known to the ladies as Master Heartbreaker, chuckled quietly to himself from the back seat.

"How long do you think you'll be here?"

"Till we're done, no doubt."

The cop looked up at Nick's house. "We've never had any trouble at this address."

"We're just in the early stages of these things, you know how it is," D'Wayne explained. "We're just taking the temperature of the place."

"All right. Take care, guys." They waited for him to get back in his car and drive away.

"Time to roll," D'Wayne said. "Just remember. He's got an alarm system. ADT Essentials Plus."

"That's the one with the Pro 3000 panel, right?"

"Get in the door, do your thing with the code and get hustling. And don't forget to reset on your way out."

"One thing," Lamar said. "Dog or no dog?"

"Only dog there would be you," D'Wayne said, flipping open his cell phone.

6

LUNCHTIME, AND THE PLACE WAS AS PACKED AS IT ALWAYS was, with cops, plainclothesmen, a few guys from the City Hall detail, and the odd newspaperman or two looking for a story. Ray and Driver waited inside the door by the register until a table came free. Driver nodded at a familiar face or two, faces Ray didn't recognize, as their office was located not at One Police Plaza but in an anonymous office building two blocks away. In fact, Ray knew none of the other undercover officers (who in any event worked out of separate precinct houses) and had he run into D'Wayne, he would have only known him as a guy he'd worked with in a forgotten life, as a rule never giving anyone, even an old friend, a second glance. One baby step back, as Driver liked to remind him, meant one giant step straight to prison.

They watched as the waitress quickly bussed their table, wiping crumbs into her hand. When she was finished she took her pad and golf pencil from her apron pocket.

"What's good?" Driver asked as he always did, though no one had ever said to him that anything, ever, was bad.

"We have a nice open-faced turkey sandwich. Big boy like you could probably polish off a couple of 'em." Driver looked up at the woman and laughed. Just his type: all business and second helpings.

He shut his menu. "I'll have it."

"Just coffee," Ray said. After she left he said to Driver, "I'll eat later."

"All that healthy stuff. Little bits of leaves and stuff people find in the woods, huh?"

"Man's gotta keep himself together, you know," Ray observed.

"Well, you're not doing too badly. For someone your age you're looking good, Ray." He patted his wide belly. "Lot better than I am."

"Praise from you always comes with a price."

Driver's cell phone went off: the theme from *Shaft*. Without a word of greeting or identification he just listened. "You're there now? Let me know what you come up with." He clicked off and set it on the table next to his water glass.

It was none of Ray's business. He could never be allowed to forget that he was legally a prisoner of the state of New York. But he had depths that Driver, still something of a novice diver in the sea of human motivation, could never sound. Ray's deep had always been his key to success. As a dealer, as a prisoner, now as a narc: his stillness and silence took people right off their game.

"So the girl," Ray said.

"You mean that guy Burns's woman?"

Ray nodded.

"Yeah, well, it's open and shut, isn't it?"

"You're calling it self-defense? Against a naked woman with a dildo?" A few heads turned his way.

Driver opened his arms wide. "How was I supposed to know it wasn't loaded?"

Even Ray had to laugh. He'd come to learn this was how a cop got back on his feet after a day's work. Bloodshed, bodies found, signs of abuse, broken bones—if you got yourself even to crack a smile you'd buy one more day of sanity.

"Listen, got something interesting for you," Driver said. "Word's out that someone's looking for Leroy Ives."

Ray took it in. "After all this time."

"Thing is—thank you, darling." The waitress smiled as she set their coffees before them. "Thing is," Driver went on, "the people looking for him are a couple of white guys. Older guys, closer to yourself in age. Nobody knows where they got it, what they want for it."

Ray considered this for a long moment. "Anyone made the connection?"

"What, that you're really Leroy? I don't think so. We've kept you out of your old neighborhoods. All your busts have been mostly rich white guys who weren't even born when you were out doing your shit."

"And they're looking for me. By name." He sat back.

Driver nodded and hummed his assent. He waited for Ray to take it in. "You do a lot of business with white folks at all back in the day?"

He shrugged. "Far as I know most of them are dead. Musicians mostly."

"All I know is it's a big package that could mean a lot of money to everyone involved. Especially those with the intention of redistributing said stuff."

"That depends on what it is we're talking about."

Driver tilted forward and lowered his voice. "That being smack."

"Not a lot of that around these days."

"It's why people are pricking up their ears, you see."

"Any idea how much?"

Driver held up two fingers. "Pounds, possibly a key. Not serious weight, but nothing to sneeze at, either. If it's pure, well, cut it, get it out on the streets and you're looking at major money coming in at a steady pace. Question one is why are they selling it as a single lot? Assuming, that is, that there isn't any more."

Ray opened his hands. "What do we know about them?"

"That's the thing. We don't know diddly about these guys. Don't know if they're pros or civilians or what."

Ray sat back and tried to make sense of it. This was the first time anyone had stepped out of his past to do business with him. Could be a setup, he thought, someone trying to settle an old score. But since getting out he'd carefully avoided old streets and neighborhoods, and as far as he knew all of his former clients were either dead or doing time.

"Talk to me," Driver said.

"OK. Right out of the box I'm thinking these guys are fronts, say, for some European syndicate. Russian, maybe. New faces, people trying to get a foothold in the city with a taste of their product. Which could mean some serious turf wars on the horizon. Except if you want to make an impression you bring in eighty pounds, a hundred. The bigger you come in, the bigger the footprint you leave, you know that. You've got to show some serious muscle in this market. So let's say this is domestic. Homegrown dealers. I wouldn't make my move till I knew more."

Driver smiled. That's what he liked about Ray: years away from the streets, but he still had a nose for the strategy. "So these guys are what, couple of losers who took the stuff off someone else?"

"Losers usually end up dead," Ray said. "This is no game for amateurs."

"Don't I know."

"Unless they're very, very stupid."

"Maybe, maybe," Driver said.

"Or very smart and only want us to think they're stupid."

A couple of uniforms strolled in, a bad day written all over their faces and obviously in no mood to acknowledge friends or colleagues. They made their way to the counter and grabbed a couple of coffees to go. Have a nice one. Yeah, right.

"Still, it'd be a decent bust," Driver said. "Biggest in a long time. We do that, we can start looking at all kinds of rewards and perks trickling down from above. Except that this time you're going to need to put yourself front and center. Not as Ray Garland but as the man you used to be."

"Leroy Ives."

Driver nodded. "From now on that's what you'll answer to. Reintroduce yourself to the community. Let these guys know you're out of prison and back in the game. Make them come to you."

"What's my story?"

"You did ten years and scored early parole on exceptional behavior. Since then you've been keeping your head down, reestablishing connections, laying the foundations. The boss is backing us up on this."

Ray sat back and looked around the diner, though his thoughts were elsewhere, such as with his brother Sonny, who for no good reason had got himself shot. Sonny, who'd been clean for years, who'd become a figure of respect in his community and his church. He wondered if his death had something to do with this. In which case the two white men looking for him could be a lot more dangerous than he was thinking they might be.

"So I'll be working alone."

"But you still answer to us. This is our operation and—"

"I'm just the sitting duck."

Driver laughed. "Yeah, well, better than sitting in your cell upstate, right?"

"I get a weapon?"

"No way, uh-uh. And you know the rules. You even try that on the sly and you get caught with it, you'll be up on a whole new set of charges. When the time comes for the bust, just this one time you'll have a shield—a vest if you want—and I'll be coming in on it when you're ready to move them out. All I need to know is the time and the place, and I'll be on standby."

"So I'll be alone."

"They want to deal with you exclusively. Bring me in early and they might take off. And don't think you still won't be wearing your monitor. Business moves outside the boroughs? Make them come to you. Do your job just like you used to. On your terms. At your own pace. That's why you're here and not in Attica. Because you were the best."

The waitress brought Driver his turkey plate and looked at Ray. "Sure I can't get you anything?"

"Actually, I'll have a tuna sandwich. On toasted whole wheat, please."

"Got your appetite back, huh?" Driver said, not trusting for one moment Ray's self-satisfied grin. He waited for the waitress to leave. "I know what you're thinking. You're thinking you can cut a deal."

"There a chance?"

"Depends what you're looking for."

"Well, let's weigh it up, all right? This goes through, you take the credit, get yourself a step higher on the ladder, maybe even a raise in pay. But all I want is to see my daughter."

"Not happening." Driver chewed on some turkey. "Judge's ruling. No family contact."

"And this is because…?"

"So that you can act on our behalf without interference, prejudice, or potential profit. Like the man said."

Ray watched as Driver deftly and daintily cut himself another piece of turkey.

"Now let's think about this. I see Meredith for one hour. Say on a park bench not ten feet away from you. Now, really, what do you think I might get away with during that time, considering I haven't seen, spoken to, or written—not to mention received word from—my daughter since she was still in knee socks and eating a fistful of Good & Plenty?"

"Not my ruling."

"And you're the public servant who's to carry out the letter of the law."

"Yes, sir. Your gold star is my gold star."

The waitress brought Ray his sandwich. "All I want is my life. Just my life. And all that's left of it is my little girl."

"Leroy," Driver said, leaning forward and throwing a shadow over their food, "that *was* your life."

7

LAMAR LOOKED AT THE ALARM PANEL AND WONDERED IF he was missing something. He entered a cancellation code and the thing beeped, telling him it hadn't been set when the owners left earlier that day: the first and last sign of people who'd grown comfortable in their neighborhood, or else had other things on their minds. He came into the kitchen and looked around. Dirty plates in the sink, breakfast stuff on the table. Box of Honey Nut Cheerios, box of granola. A few coffee mugs, a small glass half-filled with Tropicana. He gave one of the boxes a shake and took out a few Cheerios to give himself a lift.

He checked out the stuff stuck to the fridge: a photo of what he presumed was the daughter of the house looking like a hippie in a headband, bell-bottoms, and buckskin vest; a note from a school about some auction. A few supermarket coupons, little handwritten reminders and shopping lists. He took a moment to check it out: orange juice, milk, coffee beans, toilet paper, Tampax. He walked briskly from one room to the next. There was nothing there indicating this was the headquarters of a drug dealership. In fact, the place reminded him of something you'd see in a sitcom, all sofas and easy chairs and big-screen TV. He pulled his gun and went down into the cellar, had a quick look around just to make sure there wasn't some hungry pit bull waiting for him, then headed up to the second floor just as Nick and Joanne pulled into the driveway.

D'Wayne pulled out his cell phone, hit a button and Lamar's phone shivered.

"Yeah, I see it," he said.

He stood in the master bedroom with its giant bed and Sony Trinitron and peeked out between the curtains. The Audi was there but no one seemed to be in a hurry to get out.

"You checked out the cellar?"

"Nothing. Pool table. Bottles of tequila and shit. I'll take a better look in a bit."

"Sit tight," D'Wayne said.

"This could be bad," Valentine said to D'Wayne as he gazed out the Escalade's smoky, dark window.

"Lamar'll show a shield, say they'd left the door open, he was passing by, just checking to make sure all's good. Nice big smile and everyone'll be happy."

"As if they're gonna believe that," Valentine said, rolling his eyes. "Walk in your house, big black guy roaming around. That'll go down real well around here."

"You got a better one? Huh? I didn't think so." He settled back into the leather comfort of his seat. "You want to be a good cop, you've gotta have as many alibis as the bad guys, you know? More, even. Show up at the wrong time in the wrong place and all you need is a good excuse."

"Best excuse is your best weapon," Valentine observed.

Nick and Joanne remained in the car because during the twelve-minute drive from the restaurant to the house the single glass of Pinot Noir Nick had had at Chez Félice went straight to his mouth. "I have to ask you a question."

"Can't it wait till we get inside?"

"No. I need to know now. Just tell me yes or no. Are you having an affair?"

One eye on the car in the driveway, Lamar already was searching the dresser drawers, running his hands through the lady's underwear—nice stuff, lacy stuff, 36C stuff, but no dope. The guy's bureau was no more enlightening: socks, Jockeys, T-shirts, ties rolled up in neat little ranks.

"Well?" Nick said.

After a few seconds she said, "What did you say?"

"I asked if you were seeing someone else. Look, it's OK, I won't do anything crazy. I just want to know." That was only a half truth, because the first thing he actually would do would be to find a chainsaw, drive ninety miles an hour to the guy's house, kick down his door, and with zeal attack his organs of generation.

"People's fighting," Lamar said as he stationed himself back at the window, phone pressed to his ear. "Shit, I could've used this time, searched the place better."

D'Wayne craned his neck, hoping it would provide him with a clear view of marital discord. "Fighting like what? Hands and fists?"

"No, like words, you know? 'Cause they don't look so happy all of a sudden. The missus is blowing her nose."

"Find anything?"

"They got two kids. Boy's into heavy metal. Megadeth posters and shit. Girl's still in training bras."

"Don't get funny, you hear?"

"No, man, I'm just standing here trying to figure out how I'm going to get *out*."

Joanne looked at Nick as though he were one of the crazy people you see on Eighth Avenue. "Oh I see. OK, yes, I'm seeing someone else."

"Ah," Nick said, as calmly as ever, though he could feel his blood coming to the boil—and, oddly, a tremendous sense of relief that he dismissed immediately, because it seemed irrelevant to the revelation. Having spotted the tennis pro from the club with some other woman, he naturally focused on Buddy Futterman as the Other Man. He imagined the guy with the thunderbolt serve and the man tan on top of his wife.

"OK, so…how long has it been?"

"A little under a year," she said. "Now can I go?"

"Let's finish this."

"Ho ho," Lamar said into the cell phone. "Guy's got a whole other space up above the closet. That's where I'd keep my dope, no question."

"Be quick, man," D'Wayne said.

"What does he have that I don't have?" Nick was saying.

She just looked at him. "He's good looking. He's funny."

"I'm funny."

"No, Nick, you're the Prince of Darkness. This guy's funny, he makes me laugh."

"When? When do you see him?"

"When I close my eyes. He's good looking and he's warm and terrific in bed and great with the kids. He knows how to please me in all the right ways."

This was unbelievable. "The kids know him?"

"Hm-mm. They adore him."

When she saw his face she laughed, the last thing he expected.

"Did you hear what I said, Nick? 'When I close my eyes.' Because this guy's name is Nick Copeland. He's this man I used to live with. Then he left and this imposter moved in. He lost his job and lost his will and his sense of humor and his sense of purpose and has some stranger's phone number written on his palm."

It took Nick a minute to get it. "Oh. Right. So there isn't someone else."

"Not at the moment," she said, getting out of the car. "And if you're going to the city, make sure you nail that job today, OK? Do it for the kids. Do it for us."

Lamar was still poking around the space above the closet, finding nothing but a shoebox full of canceled checks, and another with baby shoes, when the front door opened and shut. "Fuck," he whispered. "*Fuck.*" He switched off his phone and stopped at the bedroom door to listen to someone opening the mail, opening the fridge. He heard the Audi pull away, which meant only one of them was in the house. The woman would call the cops, which meant he'd have a lot of explaining to do, especially as he was undercover, and probable cause was definitely not airtight. If it was the guy he'd probably go find his gun and try to kill Lamar at some point. He imagined himself at the local police station, sitting in a plastic chair and saying, "The guy pointed his weapon at me. I shot him in self-defense," the only problem being that Lamar was in the guy's house and couldn't in any way, shape, or form be considered the injured party here, especially as Nick would be lying on a slab in the county morgue, his head like beef stew from the wondrous effects of a Speer Gold Dot hollow point. Lamar put his hand on his Glock as an answering machine broke into life downstairs.

"You have one message, received today at twelve-thirty-three pee-em." Then: "Hi, it's Doctor Shriner's office, just confirming Joanne's appointment for a cleaning on Monday morning at ten."

It's the wife, he decided. Guy wouldn't've bothered checking. Lamar always left such things up to his lady, who consistently never remembered to pass along the message to him, so that a forgotten appointment, a meeting missed, would forever be her fault.

When he heard the woman coming up the stairs, he moved swiftly and noiselessly into the daughter's room and carved a path for himself through a thicket of a few thousand dollars' worth of clothes. He leaned against the back wall of the closet and peeked out between a rack of blouses and skirts and jeans so tightly packed that he could hardly breathe.

Joanne went into her bedroom and unbuttoned her blouse and slipped off her bra. As she walked past the door to Jen's room, Lamar caught a reflected glimpse of this naked woman. He guessed the message from the dentist made her feel guilty, because now she was brushing her teeth. She returned to her bedroom, and a minute later, dressed only in sports bra and panties, stepped into her daughter's room. She was a fine woman, even if she was a little old for him, and he wondered why her husband was messing around with dope when he had her nearby.

Lamar tried to keep his breathing shallow as she sifted through the crap on her daughter's dresser—packs of chewing gum, junky jewelry, notes passed to her by friends in class. She paused for a moment to look out the window and saw a black Escalade parked just around the corner from the house.

What caught her attention was the guy leaning out it and staring right at her. Jesus, she thought, and pulled the shade down. She put up her hair and doubled one of Jen's scrunchies over it once, twice, then a third time, so it would hold securely, which is when she saw the open closet and seemed to look Lamar straight in the eye.

He rested his hand on his gun, and immediately the entire scenario was clear to him. Shooting her dead would be the only thing he could do, and the crime would go unsolved, as he'd make sure to wipe down every surface he'd touched. He'd ransack the house and make it look like a robbery gone bad, because robberies in the middle of the day usually did go bad. And then before he knew it, she shut the closet door and he was standing in darkness. He could hear her rummaging in another room, then her feet going down the stairs. After a few minutes the front door opened and then shut, the garage door opened, and she drove away.

When he returned to the Escalade, D'Wayne declared him one lucky motherfucker.

"Yeah, I know. I also got to see the old lady naked."

"Any good?"

"Man oh man."

"You look everywhere? Check the cellar? What's that like?"

"Power tools. Jars full of nails. Pool table. Like my father's cellar, only white. This guy's smart. He's leaving his dope in some other place, a safe-deposit box or his office or something. Like a real professional."

"Or else there isn't any dope. In which case these guys are fucking with us."

"So what do we do?"

"Easy," D'Wayne said, firing up the Escalade. "Check back with Driver and go get us something to eat."

8

LEROY IVES HAD BEEN ARRESTED JUST WHEN HE WAS START-
ing to establish an identity in Lower Manhattan. By bringing the owner of Lucky Eight into his profit loop, making
Mr. Ping his presence in the neighborhood, he extended his
sphere of influence all the way downtown. Until one hot August
night, as he was about to enter the Village Vanguard to catch
Joe Henderson's ten o'clock set, two men got out of a Crown Vic
parked across the street: a much younger and slimmer Charles
Driver and an Italian guy named Joe Grillo, the senior man on
the operation. The moment he saw them he knew exactly what
was about to happen.

Other people waiting to get into the club—including
Henderson's drummer, Al Foster—turned away to spare him
the shame. Too many had seen this before.

"Who talked?" Leroy asked.

"We tell you that, there's no saying what might happen if
you ever got out," Driver said. But of course Leroy understood
that only too well.

He watched the city pass him by. He wondered if he'd
ever walk these streets again.

"Here's the warrant," Driver said, displaying it over his shoulder. "We searched your place an hour ago. Your wife let us in. And, yes, we had probable cause."

Now Leroy would serve a full sentence and, if he didn't die in prison, he would emerge a broken-souled man of seventy. They continued the conversation within the confines of the precinct house.

"So here's your choice," Driver said. "You can talk—and I mean name names—and serve a reduced sentence. No more than, say, ten to twelve, guaranteed in writing, signed, sealed, and delivered."

"With option for early release on good behavior?"

"Maybe."

"Yes or no," Leroy said.

"Depends on what you mean by 'good.'" They all turned to see who'd said it. The chief of the narcotics division, Gerry Grady, was standing in the doorway of the interview room, his arms crossed, a cigarette between his fingers.

Everyone there knew Leroy would sooner serve his time than turn a handful of friends and associates into enemies. And a man like that, Driver sensed even at that early stage in his career in undercover narcotics work, was a man you could trust. All the way to the end of the line.

Once he was convicted and sent upstate, Leroy chose to work in the library, not, as others did, to learn the law in preparation for some future appeal, but to be where all these stories lived: silent, waiting, somehow bigger and more profound than anything he could imagine, as though they held the promise of some other future for Leroy.

"Got a visitor," a guard said, poking his head into the library a few years later.

When Leroy entered the interview room he stopped dead. Driver sat back, a big smile on his face. "So. How's life treating you?"

"Looks like you're not doing too badly."

Driver smiled and patted the belly that hung over his belt. "Little too much sweet potato pie. Bet they don't feed you stuff like that up here. You're looking good. Working out much?"

"Some," Leroy said.

"Keeping it real, then, right?"

"What do you want?"

"Look," Driver said, leaning in to speak more to the point. "I never had anything against you personally. In fact, I've kind of admired you in a twisted sort of way."

Leroy had been through this before: a guy with a shield and a gun blowing smoke up his ass. He'd heard it all, too: the half-baked flattery, the eye-to-eye of one professional to another. He glanced at the clock high up on the wall. After this it was back to his cell, supper, a game of cribbage with his cell mate, some reading, lights out. After that, his thoughts were his own. He could think of Meredith and her mother, the woman he should have loved better, the woman who'd grown a little too fond of the stuff he sold. He remembered when they came to tell him what had happened to her. It was Driver and another man, one he hadn't seen before. Driver held an interoffice envelope with the little length of thread that was supposed to keep it shut. Except it wasn't shut, it was open, and they kept talking about how his little girl had woken to find her mother lying on the floor like that. The crime-scene photos were in the envelope, but at least they spared him that. They just waved it around until he was convinced they were bluffing, trying to dig something else out of him: names, dates, phone numbers. "For your daughter's sake, all right? Give us something solid, and you're a free man."

"OK. Here it is. My man in Canada's named Jimmy Garrison. My man in Paris is named Gordon, first name Dexter. Guy in Philly is Kenny Clarke." Driver sat there, smug as a prince, taking it all down. It took him three whole days to discover that he'd been given the names of jazz musicians, a few of them long dead.

When he came back a week later, this time Driver took the photos out. Leroy glanced at the first one and looked away.

"That was the first thing your little girl saw that morning she woke up. Exact angle, exact light of day."

"I can't give you names."

Driver threw down another photo. "Your code of honor isn't a lot different from mine. This isn't about names. You're not gonna tell us anything, we know that. But this time I'm here to discuss an arrangement with you."

When he scattered the remaining crime-scene snaps across the table, Leroy started to pay attention. Driver told him that all the brass had signed off on it. All he had to do was slip back into his old role, cut deals, walk away. The police would take care of the rest.

"Become a dealer all over again, you mean?"

"But working for us this time."

"Why me?"

"Because you were one of the best. No, that's not right. You *were* the best. You never used, you kept yourself clean. Kept your head low and your mouth shut. You were always a class act. A true gentleman of the narcotics trade." Driver laughed, jiggling a little from chin to belly. "No way that you can even smell like police. Cut you any which way and you still bleed like a dealer. People trusted you, Leroy. And we want that trust back on the street again. That purity."

"You want me to help set people up."

"To put it crudely. To dress it up a little, this is a way to make up for what happened to your wife. A way to get at the people who made it easy for her to buy the junk off the same streets you managed to keep under your control."

"And what happens if someone from the old days spots me?"

"You'll be dealing with a whole new class of buyers and sellers. Rich white guys. Out-of-towners. People who don't know you from nothing."

"And let's say one of your busts decides to finger me? How long do you think I'd stay alive?"

Driver took some documents from another envelope and tossed them onto the table. "Welcome to the world of Raymond Garland. That's what'll save your ass."

A laminated New York State driver's license sailed across the table.

"That's my mug shot."

"Uh-huh. And here's a birth certificate attesting to your new identity. A lease on an apartment in the Bronx in the name of Ray Garland. All this other stuff you may need. Leroy Ives is no more."

"Ray Garland," Leroy said, taking a taste of his new identity. "And what happened to Leroy?"

"Leave that up to me."

"So I get to live on the outside."

"The hardest part," Driver said, "is going to be keeping yourself balanced. You're going to feel free. You'll have a place of your own, your own furniture, records, books, whatever you want. Not only that, it'll be rent-free and you'll get enough living allowance to make your life a lot better than it is up here. What you'll also have is one of these." He took an ankle monitor from his pocket. "The five boroughs and no further."

"That's not free."

"It's a hell of a lot better than what you've got here. Put all those boroughs together," Driver said, holding out five fingers and shutting them in a fast fist, "and you've got enough town to last a lifetime."

"And that's it?"

"And no contact whatsoever with any members of your family. That includes your brother Sonny and your daughter, Meredith. Who in any case now has a different last name. Lives in a whole other place altogether." He shrugged. "The kid couldn't look after herself, after all. Someone had to adopt her, right?"

"What town?"

"I couldn't tell you, Leroy."

"You don't know or you—"

"It's not a police matter."

Leroy leaned in. "How long?"

"How long what? No contact? As long as you're serving your sentence."

"That's a long way off."

"You do the crime, you do the time. Anyway, she's all grown up, you wouldn't know her if you saw her. She probably forgot all about you, too."

"You never married," Leroy guessed, and Driver shook his head. "So no kids, either, I take it?"

"Not that I know of," he offered with a raunchy laugh.

"Then you wouldn't understand."

A week later, late at night when the other inmates were sleeping, Leroy was taken from his cell on a stretcher. He was wheeled out by two prison orderlies into the infirmary and then out another door into a waiting car. Driver was behind the wheel. Another plainclothesman, holding a pump shotgun across his knees, sat beside Leroy in the back. He cuffed Leroy and with a chain secured him to a ring bolted to the floor. Driver said, "Welcome to probation. Try anything on the ride back and he makes sure you stay upstate forever. That clear?"

9

IT TOOK ROB AT LEAST FIVE SECONDS TO REGISTER THAT someone was sitting in his living room, the person's face hidden in the long shadow of day's end. He let out a prolonged horror-movie scream while Nick, his legs casually crossed, his coat folded and resting on the floor beside him, savored the moment. Few such episodes came along in life, and he waited until it had reached its natural conclusion: the tremble and sweat of a terrified man, the smell of risen adrenaline.

"Jesus, man, don't fucking do that anymore. You scared the shit out of me."

"You forgot to lock your door," Nick pointed out.

"No I didn't."

"Do you want to think about that for a moment? Because not only was it unlocked, it was off the latch. Just imagine if the guy who did it was sitting here instead of me. You'd probably be lying in a pool of blood right now."

Rob dropped his keys on the table and took off his coat. "How did you get up here?"

"Like in the movies. I buzzed half a dozen other apartments. Good thing no one looked in your bedroom vent."

Racing back to the door, Rob checked the lock. "Looks clean to me."

"At least someone knows what he's doing."

"You don't think I—"

"I didn't say anything, did I?"

"I didn't tell anyone."

"OK."

"Then how the fuck do they know I'm holding?"

"You keep your voice up like that and the whole god-damn apartment house will be lining up for a fix."

"Jesus," Rob said, more quietly this time, shaking his head and taking a seat.

"Someone's onto us," Nick said. "Onto you, anyway."

"What do you think? Maybe I should report this?"

"Good idea. Call the cops and tell them you have a hunch someone tried to rob you of two pounds of heroin. Be outraged. Demand satisfaction. Anyway, where were you?"

"Just now? Doing business. For us."

"Any luck?"

"I don't know yet."

"Because I'm telling you, we'd better move this stuff fast. I mean in the next day or two."

"I'm working on it," Rob said, and it came out like a line he'd used a million times before, a bone to toss his wife, his law partner, his accountant.

"What's that?" Nick nodded to the plastic bag Rob had brought in with him.

"Noodles. I bought them at Lucky Eight. I felt guilty. You know, going into the guy's restaurant and walking out without buying anything."

Nick looked lost.

"This is the guy I told you about," Rob said. "The one who knew Leroy."

Lucky Eight on Hester Street was run by a middle-aged man known to his customers as Mr. Ping, whose mirthless cooks were bussed in from downtown Yonkers every morning in an unmarked van.

"Show me the noodles."

"It's my dinner."

"Show me your fucking noodles, Rob." Lunch at Félice hadn't been enough to satisfy him. Rob unhinged the white carton and Nick reached in with his fingers. The whole act was hardly less than disgusting. "Garlic and, what, chilies or something? You have any beer?" He sucked the sauce off his fingertips. His mouth smeared with it, he looked like an extra from *Night of the Living Dead*.

"You're eating my noodles, Nick. You have a wife and a home and a suburban kitchen and you're eating my one decent meal of the day. Christ knows where those fingers of yours have been."

"That's for me to know and for you to find out, buddy."

"Always the asshole, always the fucking joker. Just like in college."

"Just staying young at heart, my friend."

"Yeah, well, it doesn't suit you, Nick. It doesn't work when you're almost fifty and look like a businessman."

"What am I supposed to look like? *You?*"

He regretted it the moment he said it. Rob's self-esteem was already in the toilet waiting for a second flush, and it was obvious he didn't need an extra dump on top of it.

"Sorry," Nick said. "That was unkind."

Rob looked at the toe of his shoe. "It's OK."

"No, really, that was shitty of me. You look good."

"You think so? Because I'm all of a sudden getting this vibe that you're not trusting me."

Nick threw up his hands. He was going to be there all day and night, entangled in the sad logic of Rob's brain. This was what acid was sometimes like. You plucked a subject from the air and didn't leave it until six hours later, when you found yourself sitting alone, shunned by friends, listening to "White Rabbit" for the hundredth time and thinking something profound was in the air.

"Look," he said. "If I didn't trust you the stuff wouldn't be here. Remember? You're the custodial half, right?"

"You think I'd sell this and not split it with you? That's exactly what you're thinking, because I've got to tell you, Nick, you're not very good at hiding these things."

The only way to deal with a mad person was to resort to facts.

"Let's look at how things have gone down so far. No, not even that. Let's just look at one thing. You went to see this guy Ping without me."

"Because I didn't want to crowd the guy and freak him out. This is a very delicate matter, Nick. It has to be handled with kid gloves."

"And does your relationship with Ping have any impact on the deal between just the two of us?"

"You mean his cut?"

"Exactly what I mean."

"Well, he is my contact. And I did go down there. Look, we're not talking a lot of money here, Nick. This is like a minuscule amount."

"OK. I'm going to start tossing out numbers. You stop me when we hit the jackpot, OK? Five percent? Seven? *Ten?*"

Rob said nothing.

"Twelve? Fifteen?"

"That's it. Fifteen percent."

"He wants *fifteen percent* for what?"

"For putting us in touch with Leroy."

"All because of your friendship with this prince of noodles. Plus—just wait before you lose it completely, Rob—plus, you get to hold the dope. Looks like you've got it all. Smack, connections, and five percent more of the profits, all because you have all the inside leads. There's only one problem. And maybe it takes a guy in my field to see it."

Nick dipped his fingers once more into the noodles. Rob just stared at him.

"Remember what Leroy's daughter told us," Nick went on. "People already know we've got something we need to sell—not want, need. Right away it's a buyer's market. No one ever pulls in a profit when all the need's on the vendor's side."

"And that changes anything here?"

"It changes the equation, Rob. We're no longer running the show. They know we're a couple of amateurs trying to get rid of the stash. Now they can name the price and probably get it."

"We can hold out."

Nick swiftly left his chair and in seconds had his face inches away from Rob's. "Listen to me. I made a promise today that I'd pay my kids' tuition by next Friday. We sell the stuff no matter what. Because right now you're letting these guys play us. And for this to work it's got to be the other way around."

"All right, all right, man. You don't have be so...confrontational."

Nick returned to his chair and rubbed his neck. The day was already running into overtime; the sky had grown wan, as though from fatigue and disappointment. First the drive to the school, then lunch, not to mention a glass of wine, then a drive back to the city, then the long wait here. While at Rob's he'd had a thorough look around. It was true: Rob's wife had taken everything but the basics. There wasn't any porn or stash of condoms, nothing that suggested Rob had even a solitary sex life, much less one involving women other than the Janet of recent memory. He looked at Rob and felt a kind of pleasant sorrow wash over him. The guy was a loser, full stop. What did he have, really? Two jars of a dubious white substance that for all they knew could be enough anthrax to take out the entire hemisphere. A wife having the time of her life with Gloria Vanderbilt's son's old school chum. At least he and Joanne were still a couple and had kids they loved more than life.

"All right," he said calmly. "Let's try to figure out what's happened here. In this apartment, while you were out."

"Are you thinking it was that D'Wayne guy?"

"I'm also thinking Leroy. Because we know he's no longer in prison."

"Speaking of which," Rob said, and he started going through his coat pockets until he pulled out a folded piece of paper. "I did a little checking. Called a few people I know. Just to be on the safe side. No one named Leroy Ives has died in the New York State prison system in the past twenty years."

Why tell his daughter that he was dead? Yet she'd seen him the day of Sonny's funeral. Then why hadn't he contacted her? Or was Meredith simply playing them as much as everyone else seemed to be?

"I'm just thinking," Nick mused aloud. "Whoever broke in was maybe seeing if we're the real deal. If people want what we have—what they *think* we have—they're not going to spoil their chances of getting it. We're an unknown quantity. Some guy breaking into this place? Maybe we chalk it up to routine."

"Yeah, well, you don't have to sleep here. I mean, already I'm thinking about having the lock changed."

"If someone did this, it was professional. The guy knows locks and he has tools to pick them. He just lacked the basic good manners to close and lock the door on his way out. Or maybe he wanted you to know you're being watched. If I were you I'd buy the biggest gun I could afford and keep it loaded and right next to my pillow. And if anyone tried to break in,

I'd splatter his brains all over my nice white wall. Ask questions later. Hell," Nick said, then shrugged, "it might even be your wife's new boy toy coming to haul away some more of your crappy furniture."

Rob propelled himself across the room and threw his entire body onto Nick's. His hands found his throat and exerted so much pressure on it that for a moment Nick's eyes rolled back into his head and in his brief loss of consciousness he saw Kacey Christopher sitting on a stone wall, distantly waving to him. Then Rob let go and she vanished. Nick shoved him away.

"What the fuck is wrong with you? You could've killed me."

"Maybe I should have."

"Then you get all the money off this deal."

"Fuck you."

"No, my friend, fuck *you*. We're in this together and we're going to seal the deal before Monday. Cash money split two ways. I don't give a shit what you do with it, but I have a family to support."

Rob stood, slightly trembling. "Can I ask you something?"

"As long as you keep your hands off me."

"Why don't you just get a job, Nick?"

"I could ask you the same thing. I have my pride—"

"And I don't?"

"I'm not going to flip burgers or wash dishes or whatever."

"As if they'd hire a guy like you. Your wife took a crap job, though."

"Yeah, well, that's different. She *wanted* it."

"Bullshit."

In fact it *was* bullshit. He'd sat there while she talked herself into it, waiting for him to put his foot down and say no. But he had let her do it. He'd watched as she e-mailed off her résumé, listened as she spoke on the phone to the head of the day care, waved goodbye when she went off to her interview at Li'l Rascals, while he sat at home, calling every guy he knew in the advertising business, trying to catch a lead. It was when he started to enjoy his days home alone that he knew he'd tipped over into the dark side. Waking late, watching morning TV and actually enjoying it, as though tuning in were like visiting old friends, all of them middle-aged women with expensive hair talking about breast implants and vegetarian cookery; standing with his hands in his pockets in the backyard instead of mowing the grass that had already begun to reach his ankles; driving into town and spending a pleasant thirty minutes over a specialty beverage at Starbucks.

Rob was looking pensively at the noodles trapped between the tips of his chopsticks, glancing up at Nick, who pitifully rubbed his neck where Rob had nearly strangled him to death.

"I'm sorry about that," Rob said. "It's just that…"

"I know. This whole thing's driving us crazy."

"Leroy's out there. Ping pretty much said so. It's just a matter of his getting in touch with me."

"And you trust the guy."

"Absolutely. Whether he does it himself or gets someone else to do it, we're in good hands."

Nick stood and got his coat. "So, what, you'll be in touch?"

"Definitely."

"Can I ask you one more question?"

"Shoot."

Nick walked to the door. "Did you ever thinking of killing yourself?"

10

WHEN HE ARRIVED HOME, EVERYONE HAD ALREADY
scattered to the four corners of their lives: Joanne to the
Internet, Eric to the private horror of *Grand Theft Auto*, Jen to
the cellular world of innuendo and gossip. Dinner was now just
a trace of a scent in the air—pot roast, green beans.

"Hel-lo!" he called out, feigning cheer and goodwill, real-
izing at that moment just how weary he was, how trying it was
attempting to negotiate the sale of illegal substances, especially
when his partner was a man bloated with risk. Nick had too
much to live for, far too much to lose.

When no one answered, he climbed the stairs and peered
into the bedroom. The moment she saw him, Joanne—on the
bed, fully dressed, propped up against two pillows—shut her
laptop.

Lover: the word popped into his head, and with it a whole
panorama of images, mostly soft-focus porn, all of them starring
Joanne and some beefy dude named Biff.

"Hey," he said, just to sound Eric-casual.

"Hey." But she wasn't casual, she was wound a little too
tightly. "You ate, then, right?"

"I wish. I was with Rob. Going over the plans." He
remembered that he'd wanted to call Meredith earlier that day,

but not from home, from his car and preferably out of the Joanne Copeland Zone of Influence. He shrugged. "Any leftovers?"

"No. The kids were hungry."

"Everything OK with…everyone? Have a good workout at the gym?"

"Before I forget, Jen became a woman today."

Nick just stared at her. He imagined that either in the fine tradition of the Deep South she'd run off with Jerry Lee Lewis and tied the knot in some strip-mall chapel, or she'd lost her virginity and had taken the trouble to share the news with her mother.

"She's not even fourteen, for Christ's sake."

"So? Mine began when I was twelve."

He sat on the edge of the bed. "Help me out, will you?"

"Her period, Nick. She started her period today."

"Ah."

"Just remember she's still a kid. We have to make sure she feels loved… We all know what being thirteen feels like."

He put his ear against Jen's door. Music played quietly; some woman singing about love lost. He rapped lightly with his knuckles.

"What?"

"Can I come in? Are you decent?"

Her pause indicated a need for her to shift out of her private-Jen mood into the exasperated one reserved for dear old Dad. She opened the door and went straight back to her desk, turning off her music until there was an appropriately uncomfortable silence. He sat on the side of her bed.

"So," he said.

"You left the door open."

"Want me to close it?"

She shrugged.

"Because I will. I can, I mean. If you want."

"You'll be leaving soon, anyway."

"So. How're you doing?"

When he followed her gaze it was to Joanne, monitoring the conversation.

"Hi," he said. "Just chatting with Jen."

Eric joined his mother in the doorway. "You guys getting a divorce or something? It's like you're never here, Dad."

"No, we're not getting a divorce," Nick said. "I'm involved in what I hope will be a successful business project. It just happens to keep me in the city. A lot."

"With Rob," Joanne said. "Whom I'd like to meet some day soon. Think that's possible?"

"So," he said, "school good for everyone? Happy there, Jen?"

"It's OK," she said suspiciously.

"Big day, huh." When he looked up he saw Joanne glaring at him. "Show's coming up soon. *Hair*, right?"

"Duh, Dad."

"How about you, Eric. Good year so far for you, too?"

"Sucks like usual."

"Great. Want to go to public school?"

"He's not going to public school," Joanne said decisively.

Nick rose to his feet. It was time to muffle reality with a few stiff scotches. "Well. I guess everyone and everything is all right, then."

Joanne followed him down the stairs and watched as he poured himself what in convenience store circles would be known as a Big Gulp.

"Are you going to eat anything, or is that what you call dinner?"

"It's a cocktail, Jo. It's what you have before dinner."

She opened a cupboard and took down three boxes of cereal. "This is what we eat when dinner's officially over. There's no tuna, nothing frozen, nothing hiding away in the back of the fridge. Once upon a time we could afford to phone out for a pizza."

He settled for Rice Krispies with a side of Johnnie Walker Black, polishing it off in a matter of minutes as he looked over a copy of the school newsletter that had been left to drift its way across the table on its way to the recycling bin, seeking out mention either of Jen or Eric and finding only news of sporting events and the forthcoming annual auction, which he sincerely hoped Joanne intended to miss. He brought his bowl to the sink, sucked down the last few drops of his scotch, then opened the cellar door and descended into the lower depths. The fluorescent lights flickered on, and standing there he realized how much he hated this space, this house, this neighborhood, this town. He didn't belong here; he didn't fit in here; *here* didn't even exist for him. And now that he thought about it, neither did *there*. Because *there* could only happen if you had the money to lay out for it. And so he found himself in a place between here and there, his feet firmly planted in the former, his dreams floating in the otherworldly splendor of the latter.

He turned on his laptop and watched as a day's worth of e-mails popped up. The usual dreck: Viagra, New Car Quotes!, Buy Land in Costa Rica Now! Fast! Hurry! A mass joke e-mail sent by Lenny Somers, ball-bustingly still at Stevens Breakstone Leary and ignoring all of Nick's requests to be taken off his e-mail list: "What do you get when you cross a bishop and a rooster?" Nick didn't even bother to scroll down for the punch line, and—*bing!*—it was gone.

He went to his browser and did what he should have done years ago. His preliminary Kacey Christopher search having proved fruitless, he summoned up Google and typed in "Lori Streeter" and watched as four entries popped up, three of them pointing to Lori being employed by the *Baltimore Sun*, the last being an obituary for a nonagenarian of the same name in Hooper, Oregon. He did an image search and, lo and behold, there was Lori Streeter: the usual generic headshot known to executives everywhere; another with a few other *Sun* employees. Rob was right: Nick had to stare at the headshot for some minutes until he could see the Lori Streeter he knew once upon a time, the girl who'd been Kacey's roommate, the keeper of the gate to a princess out of some extraordinary fairy tale. Amazing what three decades could do to one. As a matter of routine he looked in the mirror several times a day—not necessarily for self-assessment but rather to shave, to moisturize, or simply to catch a glimpse of himself post-pee as he washed his hands—and each time could see only a charming twentysomething on the make. He'd become blind to all the intervening years of decrepitude and decadence that must have been evident to anyone who lived with him or crossed his path. At least he hadn't descended into the hell that was Rob Johnson, who wore his misery in his upside-down smile, the melancholic droop of his once-merry eyes, the belly that pressed a little too insistently against the waistband of his Dockers.

Lori had become the health and wellness editor at the *Sun*, and a further search uncovered her e-mail address. His finger hovered over the button on his Mac. To click or not to click? He looked again at her photo. Back in the day she had been spectacular, lean and long-legged in her bell-bottoms, jiggly-bosomed in her T-shirts. If it hadn't been for Kacey, Lori would definitely have had his arm around her.

Hi Lori, maybe you won't remember me, but I was Kacey's boy-friend way back when we were at Eden.

After rereading it three times and deciding he sounded like someone far more conceited and obnoxious than he was, he erased it, backspace by backspace. Before starting all over again.

Hi Lori. I hate to step out of the past like a ghost, but after visiting Eden for homecoming weekend I was thinking wondering if you might possibly could maybe have been in touch with—

Click, click, click… All gone. Was it the triple scotch that now lay in his belly, shooting out its magic grammar-fucker into his veins and arteries? Or had recent events simply reduced him to incoherence? And this from the man who had been paid handsomely for: "Lexus… From a roar to a purr in four seconds flat." (And after the car tore away, all that was left standing—another of his ideas—was a majestic lion, watching the sedan disappear in the distance, its mane waving a little in the backdraft, as the kitten beside it looked over its shoulder at us.) *Nice one, Nick. Don't spend your bonus all in one place.*

He looked again at Lori's photo. Now he could see it: all of her youth was still there, deep in those eyes that sent him back thirty years, to when he was on the cusp of twenty and, yes, charmingly on the make.

Hi Lori. This is Nick Copeland from Eden. A quick visit back to the college has made me think about some of my old friends there, including you, of course. So I'm wondering if you've stayed in touch with Kacey Christopher? An e-mail address, home address, even a phone number would be much appreciated. Hope you and your family are well, and, of course, I'd love to hear how you've been during these three lost decades. All the best, Nick Copeland.

Click and with a whoosh it was gone. A grown-up inquiry from a grown-up man.

He shut the computer and cocked an ear at the bottom of the stairs: Joanne was on the kitchen phone, talking to her oldest friend, Ellen Forrester. He knew it would be a long call, because Ellen had a big mouth and could never seem to shut up about her favorite subject, namely herself, her second favorite being why did you marry Nick Copeland?

He took out his cell phone and found the number he had added to his directory. After four rings a machine picked up. He listened to the message, clicked off and redialed. There was something about her voice he wanted to hear again. "Hi, you've reached Meredith Hunter's answering machine. You may leave a message for it or for me. One of us'll get back to you. And that's a promise."

It was a voice that tugged at his most vulnerable point, not necessarily a location in his brain, and when he came to his senses and dialed one more time he found his words: "This is Nick Copeland. We met in the city about a—"

And then she picked up. "Who is this again?"

"Nick Copeland. The guy you—"

"Yeah, I remember you. So does my aunt Macey."

"Any chance we can meet?"

"Just tell me one thing. Have you heard from him yet?"

"Your father? No. Not yet."

"So why are we talking?"

He ran out of answers, explanations, the very words themselves. "I just need a little help." He might as well have added, "I need therapy, I need a straitjacket."

"You want me to aim you in the right place, then, right?"

"Something like that."

"Because I cannot be involved in any of this stuff of yours, you understand?"

He nodded. "Absolutely."

"You in the city?"

"No. I'm home. In Westchester."

"Poor baby. Call me when you come in tomorrow. Then we'll meet."

"How will I—" But it was too late. Like everyone else who held out some promise in his life, she was gone.

He speed-dialed Rob's number. After four rings Rob answered.

"Why are you out of breath?" Nick said. "Were you jerking off?" He immediately regretted saying it, though it was a scene easy enough to picture.

"You're a fucking asshole, you know that?"

Nick smiled, because obviously, in fact, he was not only drunk, he was ultra perceptive.

"What do you want?"

He was about to tell Rob about his meeting the next day with Meredith when something told him to keep his mouth shut. Rob wanted to go see his Chinese amigo, fine. Then *he* would go see Leroy's daughter. When he caught sight of Joanne at the bottom of the stairs, he said to Rob, "I'll call you back," and clicked off.

"News?" she said.

"Looks like things might really be coming together."

"This is Rob you've been talking to, right?"

"What? You don't believe me?"

"Well, I mean, you're out of this house every waking moment, or at least it seems that way, and of course I'm— we're—starting to think that you've become an absentee father, not to mention husband."

"You think I'm seeing someone?"

She said nothing. Her look was enough. He pressed redial on his phone. Now Rob sounded positively winded. Nick held the phone out to Joanne. "Go on, you're the one who wants to invite him."

11

LEROY'S, OR RATHER RAY GARLAND'S, APARTMENT WAS ON the fringe of the Bronx neighborhood known as University Heights. No one could remember when this was a decent place to live, but for Leroy at least it wasn't Attica, and the only bars he could glimpse through the windows were the railings of the fire escape and the Four-Leaf Clover, a saloon on the corner of Aqueduct and 181st.

He'd bought a turntable for the LPs he collected, buying them used in East Village shops and off a few people he knew back in Harlem, and had saved up enough to buy a pair of secondhand B&W speakers off eBay. He built his own shelves, patiently sanding down the rough edges and adding a coat of paint, so that he could store his music and books in some kind of order. He kept the place efficiently furnished, owning nothing that wasn't of use to him, nothing that could be construed as frivolous or wasteful. It was something he'd learned in prison: you got used to possessing very little and appreciated those few things you had. It was also easier to walk away from less than it was from too much.

His closet held the clothes bought for his work thanks to an NYPD expense account—Hugo Boss suits, Joseph Abboud topcoats—quality items that only a top-level drug dealer would wear. Over the past five years he'd dealt with French politicians, Spanish filmmakers, and a great many Russians with no profession to speak of. In a crowd, walking into a building, waiting for a table at a restaurant, he'd be taken for a successful businessman, an attorney, or someone in advertising. He even smelled like a man of vast success—good cologne he would never have worn in real life, his shoes giving off the self-satisfied scent of fine, hand-stitched leather and brought to a high polish once a week at the shine stand at Fifty-Third and Madison.

In a leather box on his bureau were his cuff links and wristwatch, courtesy of the New York City Police Department, goods confiscated over the years and held for a time as evidence, meant to be returned eventually by Leroy. Driver used to enjoy saying that the five-dollar gold-piece cuff links had once belonged to John Gotti, while his watch had been pulled from the wrist of "Sammy the Bull" Gravano at the time of his booking. It didn't matter much to Leroy: everything, he well knew, was temporary.

Stuck to the fridge under a magnet was a crayon drawing Meredith had given him when she was four. What had once been a cat, or a self-portrait, or even a picture of her father, had faded in the sunlight of years, becoming just a scribble of lines. Alongside it, also under a magnet, was a photo of Theresa and Meredith that had been on the wall by his prison bunk. Even now, when he went to open his fridge, he sometimes laughed a little bitterly. My family, he thought. My victims.

He dropped the needle onto the first side of Wayne Shorter's "Speak No Evil" and sat for a moment on the side of his bed, gathering his thoughts. He knew just what he had to do. It was only a matter of time and luck. But he would get there; he would have his life back.

He slipped off his clothes and stood under the shower, scrubbing the day from his skin, watching the residue of his job run down past his ankle monitor into the drain: the sweat of others, the thin, oily finish of fear. He dried off and went to his closet to put together his outfit for the evening—clothes fifteen or twenty years out of date: turtleneck sweater, black jeans, black ankle boots, leather jacket. He slipped on a pair of shades and an hour later he was hitting the pavement: Leroy Ives had come back to the streets.

Part Five

1

THEY'D BEEN WAITING AT LEAST TWENTY MINUTES, WHICH was definitely uncool, as everyone was at the table starving, with Rob's increasingly deteriorating reputation sitting there right among them. Nick himself was standing in the front yard in thirty-degree weather, shouting out directions into his cell phone to Rob, who for some reason had ended up taking the wrong turn off the Hutch.

"Fuck it. I'm going back to the city," Rob finally said.

"You do that and I will personally come down there in..." He checked his watch. "One hour and put my foot up your ass, you treacherous son of a bitch."

"Why do I have to do this, anyway?"

"To prove to my wife that you're not some bimbo I'm laying on the side."

"Jesus, I talked to her already, right?"

"Where are you?"

"Eastchester. I think."

"Great. At least you're in the right county."

Rob not only apologized profusely as he walked through the door fourteen minutes later, he'd also had the decency to pick up some flowers and a bottle of eleven-dollar Merlot at some First Avenue plonk shop. Nick took his coat and tossed it over a sofa. As their guest walked into the dining room the kids sized him up, like mobsters casing out a hit.

Nick made the introductions. "So. This is Rob Johnson. My daughter, Jen, son, Eric, and of course this is Joanne." He went to put a hand on her arm and she was suddenly out of reach.

Rob took his seat beside Eric. "Thank you for inviting me," he said to Joanne. "Again, forgive me for being late."

"My directions were perfect," Nick said.

Rob bared his teeth. "Nobody said they weren't."

"For a while I thought you might be a figment of my husband's imagination," Joanne said. Her smile diminished as her eyes shifted from Rob to Nick.

"Sometimes I think I am, too," he said, and everyone but Nick laughed. "I mean, he's hallucinated some really strange things in his day. Like that time you disappeared, remember?"

Jen and Eric just stared at their father. Nick understood that, had he been armed, Rob would now be nothing but a man choking on his own blood. He explained to his kids that back in the day everybody claimed they hallucinated.

"But you didn't take drugs," Jen said. "That's what you told us."

"A beer now and again but no drugs. No, no." He turned his glare on Rob the dickhead, who seemed to have shrunk from his already diminutive size.

In any event, Nick knew that his imagination was perfectly capable of coming up with better figments than this guy. Which reminded him: he'd been checking his e-mail a few minutes before Rob called and there was something from Lori

Streeter. He'd only been able to read the last line—"All I have for Kacey is her parents'"—before Joanne came down the stairs wondering where the hell Rob was, as the Moroccan chicken and couscous and broccoli (exactly what they'd had the night before) was starting to dry out. He'd been doing some mental math, calculating how old Kacey's parents might be by now, and whether they would be sound enough in mind to pass along her address and phone number. In truth he had absolutely no interest in resuming ongoing relations with her; this was something beyond the physical, something he hadn't yet defined but knew had to be done. Words only, maybe, but ones that needed to be said.

Nick opened the bottle of wine Rob brought and poured the three of them a drink.

"So that's really cool that you guys knew each other when you were, like, not a lot older than me," Eric said.

"We try not to think about it too much," Rob said.

"You really saw Hendrix? Like, live?"

"And Janis."

"Who?" Eric said.

"She's dead, too," Nick said. "In fact, everyone's dead. Except for Paul and Ringo."

"And Mick and Keith," Eric said. "And the old drummer guy, whatever he's called. Gary something."

"Charlie," Rob said.

But their time would come, Nick thought. Just as his would.

Rob ate as though he lived in a society where no other human beings existed, only wild dogs and vultures, gloating, desperate things that waited for others to die and then pounced and tore and fouled themselves with the blood and offal of their supper.

"This is wonderful," he said finally, sitting back and man-handling his glass of cheap wine. His plate wouldn't even have to be washed: Rob had devoured every last crumb of his meal.

"I'm glad you liked it," Joanne said. Nick noticed that she'd worn one of her clingy cashmere V-neck sweaters that revealed more than a little cleavage, still freckled from a long hot summer. She raised an eyebrow at bachelor Rob and very lightly touched his hand with her finger. "Why don't you tell me about your friend Jerry. Bruno, is it?"

She was in the zone, as he liked to call it, at the top of her game. She was as good an actress as he could ever hope her to be. Wasted in the classroom, she could have gone on to do great things: Hamlet's mother, Cleopatra, Lady Macbeth.

"We're still in negotiations," Nick said, trying to salvage the moment.

"Well, I'd like to hear Rob tell it. He is the lawyer, after all."

"There are some legal roadblocks we have to get through before Jerry can get his full rights back." The words just poured out of Rob's mouth. "This is the part where I'm most involved. Nick, of course, is in charge of the whole ad campaign."

"So he's going to trial?" Joanne asked.

"Actually, we're trying to avoid anything to do with the law," Rob said.

Eric laughed. "You're a lawyer, right? That's pretty funny."

"Yeah, well, part of my job is getting out of my own way."

But he wouldn't shut up. Fueled by an additional two glasses of wine, necessitating the opening of a bottle Nick had paid for with his own good money a year earlier (and at inflated Scarsdale prices, to boot), Rob began discussing the facts of the Jerry Bruno issue with what increasingly was an extraordinary, never-before-seen amount of bullshit laid on, to the point where even Nick was impressed. Rob had even come up with a name for

Jerry's make-believe wife, Brenda Flanagan Bruno. The detailed explanation of Jerry's flight to Canada, his life there, the legal entanglements of his father's business, and his desire to return home and restore the family business and name, was breathtaking and utterly boring in its detail, dovetailing perfectly with Nick's thumbnail version of it. Nick could see that Joanne's attention had begun to drift, a sure sign that she was absolutely convinced Jerry Bruno was a living, breathing human being and not a leathery thing in an overpriced box in a Long Island boneyard.

"And the company?" Joanne said, and when no one answered right away she said, "And the company? The one you said he'd inherited?"

"It's solvent," Nick said.

"Definitely," Rob echoed. "If you like"—and he took out his Montblanc—"I'll be happy to run over the figures for you. In a general way, of course."

There was a pause while Joanne considered it. Nick had forgotten that back in college Rob was a pretty good poker player.

"Just the bottom line," she said. "Nick's, to be exact."

"Well, if everything pans out as projected, I think we're looking for a minimum of a hundred to a hundred and fifty thousand for Nick. Again, there are variables to consider."

"A hundred thousand for doing the advertising? A furniture company?"

"With twelve retail stores and two outlets," Rob lied, putting his pen back in his pocket. "Necessitating different TV and print campaigns according to region."

After dessert and coffee, Nick walked Rob out to his car.

"Holy crap," Rob said. "I was sweating in there."

Nick put a hand on Rob's shoulder. "I was really impressed. Your capability for shoveling it on is amazing. So where are we at this point?"

"I've spoken to Ping. I know that if he's in touch with Leroy, he'll pass the news along that we're in the market. I told him to give Leroy my cell phone number."

"Your cell phone number. Why not mine, as well? What if you're at the movies or at a restaurant or—"

"Nick. Man. You know me. My social life is limited to takeout and basic cable."

Nick considered it. Whatever the risks, at least it was a step ahead, even if it would cost him a small premium to make Rob happy.

Rob opened the door to his Saab. "Thanks for dinner."

"Glad you enjoyed it."

"Your wife is beautiful."

"Don't I know it."

"Kids are fun."

"OK."

"It's a nice house," he said, looking at it over Nick's shoulder.

"Go home, Rob."

Rob turned the key and the engine fired up. "So I make a right at the end of the road?"

Nick shut the door and walked away. Tomorrow he would talk to Meredith. Tomorrow he would start the process.

When he returned to the house, Eric and Jen had retired to their rooms and Joanne was putting the dishes in the machine. It was so cold outside that he poured himself a very tall scotch and leaned against the counter, waiting for the heat to rise up in his veins. Joanne said nothing. She looked good this evening, even in her orange Playtex Living gloves. She pulled them off and whipped them down in the sink. Her eyes seemed glazed from too much wine.

"You call that man your friend?"

"He's a business partner. When we were in college we were friends."

"Were you as much a loser as he seems to be?"

"He did all right. I did all right."

"With that...girl. The one with the Mouseketeer name."

"Kacey wasn't responsible for naming herself."

"Still on your mind. Still there, bumping and grinding in the strip joint known as Nick's Place. Everybody goes to Nick's," she said, echoing a line from her favorite movie.

He reached out and when he took hold of her arms she folded up protectively as he drew her to him. "What's wrong?"

"I'm afraid, Nick. I'm afraid we're going to lose everything. I'm afraid I'm going to lose you."

He turned her face so she'd look at him. "We have each other. We have the kids. We're all healthy. We'll get through this."

"You think so?"

He held her against him. "Of course we will," he lied.

2

WHEN HE WOKE THE NEXT MORNING AT JUST PAST NINE thirty, the house was so quiet he could hear the birds singing in the trees, a far-off plane, a dog barking a mile away. And the constant roaring noise was only the blood coursing through his veins. It was at times such as this that he seemed to rub up against his own mortality. In ten years he would be almost sixty, which, as everyone knew, was when you faded into the background and became inconspicuous. Sixty? Go away, old man.

When he was ten he'd say that in ten years he'd be twenty, which didn't seem anything but blissful. At twenty you could drink, have girlfriends, drive like a lunatic and go to movies normally restricted to the seedy and those over eighteen. When you were twenty it didn't take much to make yourself look good; and as for brains, well, he was at least good with words. Now ten more years seemed like a death sentence. At sixty he would be getting up three times a night to wait for his urine to dribble past a swollen prostate gland.

And where would Joanne be? Just as she was now; as she had been ten years ago; as she seemed to him when he first met her, when she was barely twenty—radiant, placid, impossibly beautiful, and too smart for him by half.

He rose from his bed and walked past the nightstand, with its Bose and the Penguin paperback of *A Burnt-Out Case* he'd bought when he and Jo had gone to London five years earlier, passed through the battlefield that had been the kitchen—the remains of meals half-devoured, the residue of citric acid already souring in the carton someone had left out, the stale coffee— and went into the basement and opened his laptop. There was a second e-mail from Lori, but first he read through the earlier one: *What a surprise, Nick! You're the last person I ever thought I'd hear from, LOL. Well, yeah, I'm at the* Sun *(we call it the BS! LOL LOL!!!) and really enjoying it. I'm married and have a son (Dylan, 12) and a daughter (Suzanne, 20, yes, after the Leonard Cohen song, LOL! LOL!). Anyway, Kacey and I sort of lost touch after she left school. All I have for her is her parents' address and phone number, but it's from a long time ago. Hey! Call me sometime, ok? Let's catch up!*

He jotted down the Christophers' phone number in Bridgeport, then, silently congratulating himself for having had exactly zero romantic dealings with this cute girl of eighteen who seemed to have turned into someone who saw humor in nothing that could even crack a smile on his face, clicked to read Lori's second e-mail: *Just remembered—Kacey married Jerry Bruno—did you know him?*

Nick sat there for a long time, trying to bend his mind to the contours of this new fact. His first temptation was to pick up the phone and share this bombshell with Rob, but decided against it. Kacey a widow: it was beyond imagining. He continued to picture a slim, sexy, braless eighteen-year-old in a purple T-shirt and miniskirt and couldn't stretch that to put her in gray hair, a black dress, and orthopedic shoes. It was as if someone had come along and woken him from a wonderful dream to show him the way the world really was.

Kacey Christopher Bruno. It didn't even sound right. She was beautiful, she was fragile, she was, for Christ's sake, *his*.

With a name like that she might as well have become a professional wrestler. Killer Kacey Bruno. The pain was something he hadn't felt since he was a teenager. Someone had stolen his girl, for God's sake.

He picked up the phone anyway and woke Rob up. Why waste any time with "Hello" and "Good morning"?

"Where was Jerry Bruno living when he died?"

"What? Jesus, how the hell should I know? Pete Hill was the one who told us he was dead. Why?"

"I want to spit on his grave," he said before hanging up.

3

WHEN LEROY STROLLED INTO THE BAR OFF LENOX Avenue, eighteen pairs of eyes belonging to no one he had ever met before turned their dissatisfaction on him. This was his old territory, streets abandoned long ago. As a narc, he worked only the best addresses in town these days: the Central Park West penthouses, the Park Avenue duplexes, townhouses in the Village, and an apartment at the Dakota.

He could read it clear as day: they were waiting for the man, and these days the man was running just a little late. He knew how dry the town was; half the sales that had been made in New York this past year were through Ray Garland, and all that junk was now sitting behind the locked doors of an evidence room. As long as you weren't looking to buy big you had to drive up to White Plains or even to Connecticut to score, which meant you either had to borrow or steal someone else's ride. And when you got there you were off your own turf—you didn't know one street from the next—and as for trusting those out-of-towners? Forget about it.

Someone, he knew, was going to make a killing in this city.

"Hey." It was the bartender that took him out of his skin. For a few minutes the guy just looked at him, as though trying to find a way in. "Remember me?"

The face looked familiar enough to elicit a standard nod, but Leroy knew that he'd then be playing by the other guy's rules.

"Attica?" The bartender said it so quietly it was almost under his breath. Leroy wondered if he should just turn and walk out. The man held out a huge hand with a scar running down the back of it. "I remember you from the yard, brother."

He took the man's hand and felt himself get lost in it. He'd hang around here after all, then. His back had already been had.

"Yeah, I remember you," Leroy said.

"I kept my nose clean, my hands to myself, didn't join no gangs. Like you, if I remember rightly. Just biding my time, waiting for my hour. You and me, we used to hang by the fence, all alone. Just standing there, hands in our pockets, doing nothing. Didn't do much talking, either, now that I recall." He looked over Leroy's outfit. "Someone forget to tell you this is the twenty-first century?"

"I only just got paroled."

"Thought you were in for a long stretch."

"I got lucky."

"That deserves one on the house, brother."

"Then I'll have some of that," Leroy said, pointing at a bottle of Grey Goose, "in one of these with a couple of those tossed in."

"Vodka rocks, tall glass," the bartender said, and poured him a double.

Leroy sipped it and looked around. The place hadn't changed much since he was last in there. Maybe a new paint job, some new signs, stools, ashtrays. He could smell desperation, though: those who usually relied on the good stuff were nursing their habits with cheap wine and sweet cocktails.

"So, you looking to set up something?" the bartender asked.

"Always a possibility."

"Leroy's back in business, huh?"

"That's about how it shapes up." He took another sip and slapped a fifty on the bar.

"I told you, it's on the house."

"That's not for the drink," Leroy said. "It's for the bartender," he added as he headed for the door. Soon enough his name would be out there.

Half an hour later he was in the back room of the Lucky Eight noodle shop with Ping. Four other men sat at a table playing mah-jongg and drinking Tsingtao, raucous and merry when someone won a hand.

"Don't they ever go home?" Leroy asked Ping.

"They're here maybe nine, ten hours a day. They sleep, say hello to their families, come back and play."

"What's in it for you?"

"Five percent of the take."

If Ping had brokered a deal for you to sell your soul he'd take a piece of that, too, rounded off to the nearest sin. He played both ends of the law: willing to wander down any dark alley of illegality, he was just as happy being a paid informer. In fact, Leroy's paid informer.

"Well, you called me," Leroy said. "And now I expect you have something to tell me that will be of some value."

Ping stood. "Let's go someplace quiet."

The apartment above was almost too warm. The drapes had been pulled and a few small lamps cast a soft yellow glow in the corners. Yet there was nothing that made Leroy feel anything but comfortable. Perhaps it had come from living in solitude for so long. First prison, now a life without attachments. Even if he'd met a woman he'd have to lie to her, invent some story explaining how he had come to this place in his life and what he did there. This was the deal he'd cut with the police, and he often wondered if they considered how long it would be before he broke or made a run for some other idea of freedom. Sometimes he lay in bed peeling through the layers he had added to his life, waiting to feel something other than the numb protection of fiction.

Ping stood at the counter preparing tea. "My mother has had to go into the hospital once again."

"Sorry to hear that," Leroy said.

"She tries to do too much. At her age she should be doing nothing and I should be doing everything for her." He set the tray on the table. "But of course I have my work, and she would feel guilty if I neglected it. Such is the eternal conflict between parents and their children. And my sons are with their grandmother, holding my place while I sit with you, my friend." Ping took off his glasses and rubbed his eyes. "So I'll get to the point. A man came here looking for you." He sipped from the little stoneware cup. "He said he was a friend of yours."

"White man, black man?"

Ping switched on the TV, pressed a few buttons on another piece of equipment and let the security cam footage roll. Leroy glanced around until he spotted the camera mounted up in the corner. He moved closer to the TV. The time stamp raced through the seconds and the footage staggered rapidly through the fifteen minutes the man had been there. The guy was white, maybe around fifty. Thinning hair, a nervous disposition. But then again, everyone looked a little off on security film. The man meant nothing to Leroy.

"He said he was your lawyer."

It took Leroy maybe eight seconds before it came back to him. "Johnson?" Now Leroy took an even closer look. My my, what time does to people, he thought.

"He wants me to broker something between you three."

"I thought it was just him and me."

"Man has a partner."

"And?"

"It's all I know, Leroy."

"Man's an attorney."

"Yes, well, counselor wants to move some junk," Ping said with a grand smile.

Leroy reached over and turned off the TV. First Driver mentioned a couple of white men looking to dump an equal number of pounds of smack. Now this. Leroy could only sit back and take in it. "What does he know about my...current circumstances?"

Ping smiled to himself and slid another cigarette out of his pack. "Obviously nothing. All I told him was that you were out of prison. He said he'd either deal with you or have you set something up for him."

"Man seem in a hurry?"

"Without question."

"And you'll want your piece of this?"

"Well, five percent is five percent, after all. I've got to get something out of it, don't you think?"

Leroy considered it. "How do you read this? I mean, do you think he's acting on behalf of someone else? Or is this stuff his own?"

"Hard to say. It could also mean someone's trying to set you up."

Which could mean that Driver was behind this. Which meant it wasn't just another routine bust in the making but something more. Were they tempting him to break the rules?

In which case he'd be put in a van and driven straight back to Attica. Possibly Leroy had outlived his usefulness to the department; perhaps he'd been too insistent about wanting to see Meredith. Or maybe he knew too much about something and someone was afraid he might talk.

Knew too much about what, exactly?

"If I get involved in this deal," Leroy speculated, "how do you see the risks?"

"I see benefits—"

"That's the easy part, that's my job. Put 'em away, get a gold star on my record."

"Without any further reward," Ping reminded him.

"Thanks for reminding me." He set down his cup. "I've already heard something about this. There's a lot of build already, there's too much...hang time, you know?" Leroy stood. "Call me if you hear anything more on this guy, all right? Oh, and one other thing. I want you to get me a gun. Wholesale this time."

4

IT HAD BEEN A FEW YEARS SINCE FORMER CHIEF OF Narcotics Gerry Grady was this close to the city. Once he'd retired and moved to Jersey, New York became just a little less interesting for him. Armed robbery, homicide, narcotics, the nightmare real estate of newsprint, the nonstop misery of all-news radio—it all seemed to blend together into just another day gone by, something else to be forgotten, one more stake pulled from the ground. Retirement was nothing more than a state of suspended animation, where sleep and TV had taken over just when real life had begun to simmer down to a quiet sizzle. In return his dreams had grown more vivid, and though on rare occasions he relived certain events from his career, more often these became wild rides through someone else's drama, fast cars and people in hoods walking quickly toward him, reaching into their waistbands, shooting him into wakefulness and dawn and the bedroom with a mirror that reflected nothing new, the furniture he'd married into in a less sad house across the river. Another world gone by.

Lillian had died in her sleep four years earlier, though it seemed to have taken her forever to get there. "The road was long and hard," the priest said at her funeral, "her journey full of moments of true despair when she must have felt she had lost her way. But not her faith. Never that."

And that was when Gerry stopped believing in God—his wife had given up long before the cancer—Mass becoming just another habit, like watching the news at eleven or eating turkey on Thanksgiving. As she was fond of saying, "You can move your lips but it doesn't mean you're making any sense."

The man who walked up to him out of the night said nothing. Together they watched the river as it disappeared into the sea beyond.

"Still wearing that damned thing around your ankle?" Grady said.

"Which is why I can't come see you in Jersey."

The traffic below them was sparse and quick and quiet, the sky cloudless, and even here in the city you could make out a constellation or two. It seemed to Leroy that he could stand there forever. The tide as it pulled on the river, the cars passing below, the distant lights—all belonged to a life far beyond the limits of his. All he had to do was take a step in the right direction.

"So you pulled me away from my TV and my Jack Daniel's for what? A nice view and a lousy cough?"

Leroy put a hand on Grady's shoulder and gently made him turn to face him. "I want to know exactly what happened back when I was busted."

Grady cleared his throat and propelled the gob onto the Brooklyn-bound section of roadway. He shrugged. "Just like a bedtime story. Bad guys get nailed. A whole lot of coke was found in your place. Work out the moral of the tale yourself."

Leroy shook his head. "You knew I never dealt coke in my life. Never took it, never sold it, never even held it for anyone. I was strictly smack, what my customers wanted. I said it to Driver, I said it in court, and I'm saying it now. No one ever believed me."

Grady believed it as much now as he had then. "Coke, smack, what does it matter? Trafficking in that shit is still against the law. Sooner or later we would've caught up with you. You did your time, Leroy. You suffered it quietly and from all accounts cooperatively."

"And I'm still serving it."

Grady opened his arms wide. "This don't look like prison to me."

"You know what I mean. Someone set me up. You've always known this. C'mon, chief, you can be straight with me now."

Grady tilted his head a little. Years ago he'd sported a thick red mustache that went gray long before his retirement, and with his fingers he thoughtfully toyed with the memory of it. "Why now?" he asked.

Leroy knew there was no point in saying too much, not when he had begun to see a glimmer of possibility. This was just a matter of getting level with the other players. "It wasn't just to get me put away. There were bigger dealers all over this city you could've had in a minute."

"It was all about keeping our numbers up. The commissioner was getting impatient, the mayor was unhappy... All we could do was stuff the box with small-time busts, nickelbaggers and corner boys. City Hall thought we should be pulling in the big shots—the guys the small-timers were working for. They always seemed to be out of our reach. Even when things started to dry up. The department needed a success, a big one. And there you were."

"So they set me up. Just to make their numbers."

"Personally? I always thought someone in the division was playing both sides. I never said it, but I thought it. Busting dealers, bringing them to trial, making sure the evidence took a hike afterward." Grady shook his head. "Took me a while to discover it's an old story. Every big city department has been through it. One crooked cop is all you need to get that stuff back into circulation. It's the numbers that blind us to it. The more busts a detective makes, the more he's left alone. You must've figured that out by now."

"So someone was dealing," Leroy concluded. "Someone from the division."

"I suspected it for some time. He had a system: stuff in, stuff out, money in his pocket. They had to buy so they could turn around and sell the stuff. They had to keep the kitty replenished. Make it look like nothing was missing."

"And to make it work they needed someone the buyers and sellers could trust," Leroy said, seeing with sudden clarity his place in the equation. "Someone who could definitely close the deal no matter what."

Grady smiled to himself. "That's how it turned out, anyway."

"So you knew."

"I knew nothing, Leroy, because I chose not to know."

"Blind eye and all that."

"You got it."

Leroy watched a police boat make its swift, straight way downriver. "So whatever cop was running this thing basically owned the market, thanks to me."

Grady took a moment. "Customers knew who you were. You kept your head down and your distance from the school yards. Not like some of the others. You had it made. Make a sale to some rock star or movie actor and word gets around that Leroy Ives is honest and discreet and easy to do business with. I could've blown the whole damned thing wide open, demanded an investigation, cleaned out the division of all the bad apples.

And if I'd done that I'd have paid the price. Now I can live in peace and not keep looking over my shoulder."

"So right now I'm a sitting duck," Leroy said. "If people get too close to whoever's running this, if Internal Affairs starts poking around, I'm the guy set up to take the fall. I'm the front for the cop behind this."

"Afraid so, Leroy. You're the one who'll be sacrificed. Once I started to poke around thinking someone was running an inside job, they suggested I take early retirement with full pension. An offer to which I wasn't allowed to give a second thought."

"Just to get you out."

The flame from Grady's old Zippo highlighted his ruddy face, the ruts and pits of acne scars. A tracery of veins had spread outward from his nostrils and up his cheeks. Too much drink, too many memories, too much Vietnam and a shitload of years in the police: the whole map was there to be read.

"I have ten years left in my sentence," Leroy said. "Ten years'll become fifteen'll become twenty. And if someone figures out someone in the division's selling evidence, Driver will point his finger right at me. I'm the only logical guy, aren't I? The guy still doing time, still at the game."

Leroy looked at his watch. It was time to go.

"What are you thinking, Leroy?"

"You have a family?"

"A son stationed in South Korea. A daughter. Couple of grandkids."

"Would you do anything for them? Even die for them?"

"Without a second thought."

Leroy watched as Grady walked slowly toward Brooklyn. What was more dangerous, Leroy wondered, the dope or the knowledge?

5

NICK REACHED MANHATTAN A FEW MINUTES PAST NOON. He took Columbus down to Eighty-First and found a space on the street. He had no idea why that particular location had become his goal, unless it was to be as far away from Rob as possible. He turned off the engine and flipped open his cell phone. He left a brief message, and just after he clicked off the phone rang. He could tell she was on her cell phone: the soundtrack was sirens, car horns, and 1010 WINS on her radio.

"Where are you?" she asked.

"Why didn't you answer?"

"Just tell me. Because I'm probably not all that far away." He told her.

"Sit tight and I'll come and get you. Get out of your car so I can see you. Give me, oh, five minutes, tops."

He turned on the radio and put his head back on the seat. Though he'd slept heavily the night before, he was exhausted, bone tired as they say, as though simply having to think through his plans for the hours and days to come had stretched his capacity to function. Not to mention the fact that he still wanted to call Kacey's parents. He had more or less gotten over the insane notion that she'd married Jerry Bruno. OK, so it was done, it was a whim; maybe it was what she did because he was no longer available and Jerry seemed the next best thing, though on a scale of one to a hundred, Jerry came in somewhere in the low twenties, weighed down by his shady connections and uncertain past. The saving grace at this point was that Jerry was dead. The other saving grace was that she hadn't chosen Rob instead.

Which meant exactly what in the end? That Nick would leave Joanne and move in with Kacey? That presumed a number of monumental conditions: one being that he could so easily turn his back on his wife and mother of his children, which he couldn't see himself doing under any circumstances; and two being that Kacey would, down to the last dimple and personality quirk, be absolutely the same person she was back when they were in college. Which assumed that in three decades neither age nor illness had taken its toll on her. He looked up at the rearview mirror to have another glimpse of the miracle man known as Himself. How had *he* escaped it, then?

And now it started to drag its claws across that exquisite veneer he'd worked so hard to achieve over the years: all this speculative thinking based on Joanne's real or imagined infidelity. Was he in some way willing it to happen, as in a fairy tale where one says the magic words and the door to the castle creaks open? Were she to leave him, and were the legal issues finessed in such a way that Eric and Jen somehow breezed through the process undamaged, who, in the end, would get whom? He couldn't imagine living alone with Eric in that house—supposing that he got the house, which would be nothing short of miraculous. A boys' club was not quite what he'd been anticipating. In college Nick had avoided the cloistered male paradigm of Greek life with its once-pristine Victorian mansions on Fraternity Row, front yards littered with crushed Coors cans and window shutters in a state of imminent collapse. Not as though any of them wanted *him*. After all, he and those like him were freaks, and proudly considered themselves as such, "hippie" being a term more applicable to the gentle young folk who wove flowers into their tangled hair and danced in public parks and listened to Donovan before returning to their suburban families each night for meat loaf and potatoes. Nick and his ilk lurked beyond the social circles of Eden College, like tribal outcasts forming societies all their own on the edge of the forest, attracting in the meantime all the female art and English majors with their long hair and bare feet, their dark attitudes and raging promiscuity. And, as everyone knew, when it came to sex, frat boys were on a low rung of the ladder of fun.

He would much prefer to share a home with Jen, who inhabited the cave known as her room, texting friends, listening to music, trying on clothes and God knows what else, but as a bottom line demanded total privacy and distance from any parent whatsoever, which suited him perfectly. They could live parallel lives—he in his solitude, she in her cocoon waiting to burst out and take flight once she had her diploma in hand.

Fine then, he thought, just as the BMW that had nearly driven him off the FDR the other night glided past. She backed up fast, stopped dead when she was level with his car and eased down the passenger-side window. "Didn't I ask you to get out of your car and stand around so I could see you?"

"At least you recognized me."

"Don't flatter yourself. C'mon, lock it up and get in."

He climbed into her BMW and latched the seat belt. He had been in the middle of a thought when Meredith had pulled up, and now he'd lost it, a definite sign age was creeping up on him, not to mention the dreaded dementia that had taken his own father into another world altogether.

"See you left your sidekick at home."

"He doesn't know about this."

"Makes things much easier."

Already she was one giant step ahead of him.

"I thought we'd get coffee or something."

"A public place with what we're going to be discussing? You out of your mind?" She took a good look at him. "What're you, some kind of businessman or something?"

"Is it that obvious?"

More out of habit than necessity, he'd dressed as if for a pitch to a company in one of Stevens Breakstone Leary's conference rooms: Michelin or Heinz or whatever account they were wooing these days.

"I used to be in advertising," he finally admitted, as though confessing to a crime committed long ago.

"And now," she said, pulling out into the traffic that moved nimbly down Columbus Avenue, "you're a drug dealer." She turned her grand smile on him.

They were downtown in ten minutes flat. She seemed to understand the rhythm of the traffic, sensing when taxis would screech to a halt in front of her and when people with out-of-town plates would—as crazy people always behaved with utter predictability—turn without a directional. She said nothing on the way there, and when she parked she turned to him as if seeing him for the first time.

"Hi."

"Hi."

"Doing OK?"

"I think so," he said. He looked around. They weren't that far from where they'd met D'Wayne that night. He wondered if D'Wayne was in the background, keeping an eye on him, waiting for the moment when he and Rob would come out into the open with their mystery jars. It was fortunate, Nick thought, that he and Rob looked nothing like the standard-issue dope dealer. There would always be a cloud of doubt hanging over these two middle-class losers.

Her building was as anonymous as most of the others on that block, though the trim on the windows was freshly painted a nice bright red, and the French restaurant on the ground floor seemed to be doing a brisk business. It only reminded him that he'd eaten virtually nothing that morning and could happily go for a bowl of soup and some crusty bread.

When the elevator stopped at the third floor, Meredith unlocked her door with two keys. She reached inside and when she flipped on a switch, lights throughout the loft came on in sequence—first in one zone, then another—all at different levels of intensity, until the entire floor was bathed in a soft glow that made the sunlight outside seem harsh and artificial.

"I know what's going through your mind," she said. "Black woman, money..."

"I don't think that way."

"Then maybe you're thinking I'm like my father."

"Never crossed my mind."

She stepped into the kitchen area. "Your choice. Coffee or something on the rocks?"

"What're you having?"

"Tea, actually."

"Sounds about right for me."

Now he had a good look at her. Though he was an even six feet, she was maybe only an inch or two less: tall, slender as a stalk of grass, with skin the color of good chocolate milk. As she measured out the leaves, he walked slowly around the place, taking in the books and CDs on the shelves, and especially what was hanging on the walls. He stopped before a Picasso sketch from the early sixties, a portrait of a woman's head. The artist had probably whipped it up in all of seven minutes, and in a good market it could probably fetch a cool couple of million. She said, "Yes, it's the real thing."

"My mother had something like it. Except he'd taken the time to paint it."

"Yeah, well, he was turning them out pretty quickly, I guess. Still, it's worth a lot more now than when I'd bought it."

"You're a collector?"

"I'm an investor. I mean, don't get me wrong, I love art, I love looking at these. It's a lot prettier than sticking a whole lot of hundred-dollar bills behind glass. And in fifty years a hundred-dollar bill is still only going to be worth a hundred, though it'll buy you a hell of a lot less. That one will fetch a whole lot more than what I paid for it." With a tilt of her head she indicated another wall with two more, a small Lucian Freud nude and a similarly proportioned Basquiat. "Know who painted those?"

"Just because I wear a tie and once had an office doesn't mean I'm not interested in art."

"I'm impressed."

"The second college I went to required a minor. So I figured art history would be a snap. I came to like it a lot. Learned a lot, too."

Fletcher College in Hartville, Vermont, defunct since 1974, its campus now home to an Amway distribution center: discovered by Nick in an underground guidebook to colleges ("Thought of by alums as hipper than Windham and cooler than Franconia, Fletcher easily earns its four-toke rating") and chosen by him because he knew he could get in (admissions policy: please send $200 deposit), and because the campus looked like a place you went to for extended rest and recuperation, not for lectures and exams. They would still have taken him had he burned down half of Eden's buildings, murdered the faculty, and cut the brake lines on Ma Jones's Buick. So desperate for students were they that three-quarters of those attending had already been expelled from at least one school of higher learning, politely asked to leave their original institutions, or just released from prison, mostly for drug offenses. And though he was at first loath to spend the next two years in the middle of nowhere, where the nearest town with anything more than three stores was forty minutes away, he found that everyone there was more or less like himself—chemically enlightened, easy to get along with—and when it came to the faculty, well, they were pretty much indistinguishable from the students. For six months he carried on an intermittent affair with his art history professor, a recently divorced woman ten years his elder who bore a striking resemblance to Carly Simon and lived in a funky little cabin built by her ex, an angry unpublished novelist now living furiously in the Pacific Northwest.

"It came in handy when I went into advertising," he said. "You never know when you can borrow a Botticelli motif for the next deodorant campaign from Secret."

"Did you like your work?"

"It's not a bad way to live. You get to use your imagination, figure out how millions of people can be talked into buying something they'll believe is better than it is. It's a handy little talent to have."

She set out two little stoneware cups as he continued to stroll around the space. He turned to her. "Tell me what I'm doing here, please?"

"Helping me so I can help you."

"Your father, you mean."

"He was set up. Everyone knew it. And I need to give this man his life back. After all, he made all this possible for me." The warmth of the lighting in her loft cast a glow on the expensive furniture, shelves full of books, top-of-the-line stereo equipment, and a wall-mounted flat-screen TV.

"When did you last see him?"

"I was just a little girl. He had his pride. He didn't want me to remember him locked up like that. He told my mother never to bring me up there again. I never even got to kiss him good-bye."

The shadows faded as the autumn sky grew dark. It would rain soon, and if it were cold enough it would arrive as snow, the first of the season.

"After my mother died my aunt Macey found an envelope with my name on it. She was supposed to keep it till I was older."

She upended a small vase on a nearby table. A safe-deposit key on a length of red ribbon fell into her hand.

"The Hunters—the people who adopted me—gave it to me on my twenty-first birthday. Macey must have turned over all the personal stuff to them when they took me in. Most drug dealers spend their profits on cars and bling or more dope. My father stashed them away, just in case. Like he knew what might happen to him."

"How did you know what bank it's for?"

She dropped the key into his palm. "There's a little code on the key—see?"

He slipped on his reading glasses.

"There are these numbers and a letter just over here."

Her face was close to his. He could smell the freshness of her hair and whatever scent she was wearing: a hint of vanilla, a little lemon, maybe a dash of cayenne. The sweet, the bitter, the mysterious.

"The first bank I went to looked at it, told me where to go."

"How much was there?"

She just smiled. "More than you might think."

"Drug money. Dirty money."

She nodded toward the paintings. "I hired a consultant and put it into those. And those. And a few more I've got stashed away. Any of that look dirty to you?"

"Jesus. He must have left you a small fortune. And the loft?"

"All paid for."

"With his money?"

"Uh-uh. It's all mine."

That smile couldn't be entirely trusted. "What do you do to be so successful?"

"I'm an art broker. There's good money in that. That consultant I just mentioned? He's my business partner. He works out of an office in Amsterdam. I take care of the business here."

He nodded at the Picasso. "So you probably have more stashed away."

"Here and there."

"Does your father know any of this?"

"How could he?"

While she went off to the bathroom, he strayed into her bedroom area, with its expensive Swedish mattress on the floor, stacks of books and a glimpse of the Brooklyn Bridge that goosed the value of the place a few thousand, whereas he and Joanne had settled for Scarsdale, with a view of nothing but the end of Chuck Foster's driveway and the Lexus he obsessively washed every Sunday. When had everything gone wrong? When had this man who had seen the Clear White Light one Friday in Eden decided that, yes, he'd love to settle in the suburbs and make small talk with his neighbors, while all along he had touched the very thing that had turned other men into visionaries and prophets and members of the Beatles?

Meredith came up alongside him.

"Why didn't you invest in the market, like most people?"

"People ask too many questions," she said. "And there's too much of a paper trail. I get on the phone to Sotheby's, I win a bid, I transfer the cash through an offshore account and take home my painting. Or I sell a client's painting to a collector in Tokyo and my commission finds its way to my account four thousand miles from here. End of story times two."

"It's still a paper trail."

"Not when the cash is drawn from a company that doesn't exist, and the main account is in a Swiss bank."

Nick glanced around once again. "I'd say you've done all right."

Wrong: She'd done spectacularly. She didn't just game the market, she gamed life itself. This was a woman who knew exactly what she wanted and how she'd go about getting it, while he was a man who thought he knew exactly what he wanted, got it, and watched it being whipped right out from under him. For a guy who had spent the last quarter century encapsulating the appeal of Mr. Clean or the deep love that people had for Pillsbury biscuits, who wowed the men in their suits with his ability to express what they felt but could not put into word and image succinctly and with his own inimitable flair, he'd lost control of his life. He had become a walking cliché, a character in a *New Yorker* story published fifty years earlier, the gray flannel of his soul having grown threadbare and beyond laundering.

"You're a lucky lady," he said.

She turned to him. "Why, because I have stuff?"

"Because you appreciate what you have. Because you did it on your own. And you don't seem the selfish type. If I were your father I'd be very proud of you."

She threw her head back and laughed before looking him in the eye. "You got kids, right?"

"Two of them."

"They know how lucky *they* are?"

"Of course not."

She laughed again and pulled the sheet and duvet up and smoothed it all out with the flat of her hand. She found a red thong on the floor and tossed it into a wicker basket in the corner.

"Bet your missus doesn't leave her undies all over the place."

"She just keeps things to herself."

"No fun with Mrs. Nick?"

"We have fun."

"Except I bet you really get yours out of a bottle."

How well she seemed to know him already.

"Let me be straight with you, Nick. This whole thing is about my father. There's as much in this for me as there is for you. Our goals aren't the same, so I don't give a shit what you're trying to move. As long as I get to see my father. I know he's out there. He's just waiting for that door to open one day when no one's watching. You do this for me, and I'll make sure you get something out of it. You just have to trust everything I tell you to do."

"So that's the small print?"

"That's the medium print. The small print is that once this is done I'm not going to expect or ask for a cut of whatever you make out of this deal."

"Fair enough."

"And your buddy?"

"As I said, he doesn't know I'm here."

She smiled a little too knowingly. He followed her back to the table. She went to pour more tea. His, a sip less than full, had gone cold.

"You want something stronger?"

"Only if you'll join me."

She opened a cabinet to reveal an array of bottles—good single-malt scotches, Grey Goose vodka, Gran Patrón Platinum. She handed him a neat finger of Ardbeg and took down a thick photo album from one of the shelves, all fake leather and cheap gold lettering that probably wore off a week after she got it. On the first page, in a young girl's overly meticulous handwriting, was, FOTO ALBUM MEREDITH JANE IVES. Beneath it, in a different ink, had been added the name HUNTER.

She paused for a moment and looked in his eyes. "Once I turn the page there's no going back," she said.

He reached across and turned it for her.

6

DRIVER WAS THE FIRST TO NOTICE THE SUNSET, LIKE A hot splash of blood against the sky—a memory of summer with winter only a month away. He rose from his chair and passed Leroy's desk on his way to take in the view.

"You see this?"

"I've seen sunsets before."

"And I always thought you were something of a poet."

"The beautiful things in life don't need me to point them out."

Leroy tapped out another word, then hit return to start a new paragraph, another angle on the Rick Burns bust and, more importantly, the accidental shooting of Jessica Milo. He sat back with a sigh. "I'll finish this in the morning."

The office they occupied belonged to them alone. Their desks faced each other, as though they were business partners. Along the pale yellow walls were locked file cabinets and whiteboards on which names and data had been jotted in either red or black, according to the status of the case. In the end it was always only about numbers. After all, he was one himself: five digits in the New York State penal system.

The office was at the end of the hall on the twenty-first floor. There were other offices there—some with names on the doors, others not identified in any way—and the only time Leroy ran into anyone else the transaction involved a simple nod and nothing more. To get coffee they had to go through the lobby and across the street to the Starbucks. Sometimes Leroy felt like he was in the witness protection program, a man with nothing to show for himself stuck in the middle of nowhere.

He took the subway back up to the Bronx, bought a box of muesli and a quart of milk at the grocery on Aqueduct Avenue, stopped to chat with a guy he knew from the neighborhood having a smoke outside the Four-Leaf Clover, then showered and changed. He flipped on the stereo and carefully laid a McCoy Tyner LP onto the turntable. He made himself a cup of green tea and sat by the window watching the sky go dark as he thought again of Meredith. He'd never known who had adopted her or where she lived. But seeing her outside Sonny and Macey's place—more importantly, knowing that she had seen *him*—gave him hope. At least now, wherever she was in this world, she knew he was alive and out of prison. He looked at his phone. He could call information, get her number, and he went so far as to pick up the receiver and then drop it back down again. He didn't know her last name: if she was still Ives or had been renamed by her new parents.

He finished his tea, switched off the stereo, and, checking the street for anything out of the ordinary, headed back downtown. Driver wouldn't have the patience to stake him out for all this time. But he could, if he wished, track him down to the nearest square foot of the city. As far as he knew, Driver was playing poker with some of his detective pals. Same night week after week the cards came out, the chips were stacked, the bottle of bourbon was put on the table. But someone, whether man or machine, was always tracking Leroy's steps, the shadow that followed him everywhere.

By the time he rounded the corner to enter Lucky Eight, a cadre of cooks in their parkas and windbreakers was exiting the restaurant and piling into the waiting van that would take them back to Yonkers. Leroy checked his watch: Ping was closing early that night. When the van had gone, he peered in through the glass door. Lights went out, one after another, until only a banker's lamp remained on by the cash register. He could see Ping moving about in the rear of the place, and when he looked up and saw Leroy, he came and unlocked the door for him.

"Counting receipts," he said. "Only be a minute or two."

"Take your time," Leroy said. He sat at a table, and without being asked Ping brought him a bowl of noodle soup and a spoon. "*Shi-shi*," Leroy said, raising a smile from the restaurateur.

"Where'd you learn to say that? In prison?"

Leroy shrugged. "Business any good?"

Ping looked up with a smile. "Depends which business we're talking about."

"I'm not picky."

Leroy finished his soup just as Ping locked the empty register for the day. He put the cash in a metal box and held it under his arm as they walked through the deserted kitchen and up the stairs to his apartment.

Ping's mother had evidently recovered from her hospital stay, for the old woman was sitting in her housedress, smoking and reading a Chinese newspaper through a magnifying glass, ignoring them both when they walked in, even though Leroy inclined his head and said, "*Ni hao*."

"Don't trouble yourself," Ping said. "She refuses to wear her hearing aid. Otherwise she'd be my number-one hostile witness."

"Any more news?" Leroy asked.

"From the lawyer? Nothing."

Which meant exactly what? That they wanted him to come to them? Which could mean there was more risk than he'd been counting on. It was one thing knowing his old attorney was involved; it was the man's partner who really worried him, the unknown in the whole equation.

"Perhaps buying a gun isn't such a bad idea after all, Leroy."

He followed Ping to his room at the back. On the desk was an embroidered silk cloth that, pulled away, revealed a selection of pistols, all with little price tags attached.

"I have only three hundred on me."

Ping tossed the cloth back over them. "I can't help you, Leroy."

"What's your cheapest?"

"Four-fifty."

"You willing to go the distance for an old friend?"

"You're not a friend. You're someone I do business with."

"Doesn't that fit everyone in your life?" He glanced over at the man's mother. "You probably charge her rent, too."

"Tell you what," Ping said, whipping off the silk once again. "This Beretta 9000, this Taurus PT 111, and the Zastava M88—these you can walk away with tonight."

"For three."

"Plus fifty."

Leroy hefted the Zastava. "What is this? Russian?"

"Serbian," Ping said. "Nice little thing, isn't it? Smallest I have."

Leroy held it at arm's length and peered along the barrel until his eye caught the photo of Ping and his missus. He lowered it.

"Three-fifty?"

"Including a full magazine."

"Hollow point?"

"Only the best."

Leroy hefted the pistol in his palm. "Who are you kidding, Ping? I can buy this in a gun shop for two and half."

"But *you* can't walk into a gun shop, can you, Leroy? Let's call this a surcharge. Just like you ask for more if someone doesn't buy everything you're selling."

Leroy tossed a roll of twenties onto the table, then peeled a fifty off another medium-sized roll of bills.

"I thought you only had three bills?"

"So I'll do without dinner. What's in here now?"

"Eight plus one already in the chamber."

"That's all I'll need."

Ping laughed. "You intend to use that thing?"

Leroy pointed it at the man's head. "Only if you don't get that lawyer on the phone right now."

"You're joking, right?"

Leroy pressed the barrel against Ping's head. "I promise I will kill you and your mother won't even hear it happen."

Part Six

1

"**Y**OUR BUDDY CALLED," JOANNE SAID BEFORE HE'D EVEN closed the door. She was sitting on the staircase, sipping scotch. "Three times," she added. "He said you weren't answering."

"I had it on mute. Kids home?"

"For hours. He sounded like you'd stood him up. I won't bother asking if you're about to leave me for another man."

He smiled at her. "Rob? Not really my type."

"Neither am I, obviously. You stood me up, as well. Dinner, remember? *Happy birthday to you, happy birthday to you, happy birthday dear shithead, you fucking asshole.*"

He actually smacked his forehead, as though he were Inspector Clouseau. "Christ. I forgot."

"Your own birthday. If this were a movie I'd throw my drink in your face."

He glanced at his watch. It was almost seven thirty.

"And you think this is normal?"

Hands up. "Hey, I'm trying to scare up some money for us, remember?"

"Have you thought about robbing a bank? It'd be a lot quicker, and you might even make it home in time for a meal now and then."

For once he truly was sorry. Had he shrunk so low in his own estimation that his existence on earth was of no matter to him?

"So if you weren't with your chum, then where were you?" Joanne asked.

"Out." It was all he could think of.

"What're you, twelve years old?"

"Look." He put his hands on her arms. "We're almost there. It's just a matter of days. Just a question of—"

"What, another bullshit excuse?"

He could smell the scotch on her breath. Clearly his birthday party in absentia was closer to something out of Eugene O'Neill, all liquor and discord.

"Look," he said again. "When you're dealing with people it's all a matter of timing. It's a question of lining everything up in just the right way. We don't do that, Jo, we lose the whole opportunity."

The look in her eyes softened. "OK. I know that. It's just that I'm really getting scared."

He held her in his arms as the images from Meredith's photo album came to mind. Once you got past the usual school photos of a smiling girl, her hair in braids or, as she got older, in cornrows; once you flipped beyond the Christmas shots of Meredith and her adoptive parents, Meredith in purple ballet costume, Meredith in high school—all attitude and flashing eyes—you came upon a photo of some men sitting on the front steps of a Harlem tenement in the harsh summer light of 1968 or '69. It was then that Nick began to understand where all this was going. The haircuts, the bell-bottoms and chunky shoes harkened back to his own youthful days of risk and fun. A few of the guys held bottles of Rheingold; most had cigarettes. It had been taken long before she was born, and the photo had faded a little over time. The once-vivid colors had yielded to the blandness of age.

"This one on the right?" she said, and put her finger right under him. The young man was lanky and long-legged, wearing a short-sleeved, striped shirt halfway unbuttoned. A medallion hung from a chain around his neck. He was looking at something across the street, his mouth slightly open, a cigarette dangling from its corner. It's a hot summer day and everyone is just in the moment.

"My dad. With his Ray Charles shades. Later on he had an afro."

"When was this taken?"

"The summer after they shot King."

"I remember that."

"Not as well as Dad does, I'm sure."

Somehow Nick couldn't make the psychic connection between this cool black guy and a very uncool Rob Johnson. But then again, how many lawyers really did look cool? He had to say something: "Good-looking man."

"Yes he was."

"And these guys?"

"That's his brother Sonny," she said, pointing to a man who looked no more than seventeen, a more carefree version of Leroy. "These others—they're either dead or locked up. That's what Uncle Sonny told me."

There was one other, older than the others, gray-haired and thin, his suit hanging off his frame, his bow tie askew, looking more like a street-corner preacher than a member of this group. Meredith turned the page and there was another photo—just Leroy and this man—from their clothes and the setting clearly taken on the same day. This time the man stood close to Leroy, and in fact Leroy had a hand resting on the man's shoulder.

"He's Jean-Pierre Noël. From Haiti, but he was in Brooklyn a lot. Over in the Haitian neighborhood around Nostrand Avenue. Everyone called him Father Christmas. Sonny told me he treated my father like his own son, taught him how to deal clean and keep a low profile. Made sure he never sold to kids or anyone who didn't know what they were doing. After my father was sent up, he'd sometimes come and visit me at my foster home when he was in Philly. He used to carry silver dollars around in his pocket. I'd never seen them before in my life, these big heavy coins. He'd always give me one when he saw me." She shut the book and set it back on the shelf, then slid open a drawer and took out a stack of coins. "That made seven times. Jean-Pierre is the man my father relied on more than anyone before he went to prison. If you connect with my father, you'll see Jean-Pierre." She held one of the dollars out to him. "Show him this. Then he'll know he can trust you."

Nick took the coin from her and felt the weight of it in his palm.

"What did your foster parents think of him?"

She shrugged. "As far as they knew he was my godfather. Father Christmas? Nothing about him that even remotely smells of drugs."

"Why haven't you tried to contact this guy before?"

"I get involved in this, the police start nosing around, and then they bring my aunt Macey into this. That leaves my little cousin Terrell just a little dirtier."

Because of Nick and Rob, Terrell's father had been gunned down. Would the boy harbor a resentment that might turn to revenge? Would he spend his days looking for the person who'd put those bullets in his father?

"So you're setting me up," Nick said.

"For what? A bust? You don't have a record and you don't look the type." She looked him over once again. "No one would ever think you're a dope dealer. So like I said, there's something in this for both of us."

"Meaning what?"

"I'm going to say it once. You follow this exactly as I lay it out and we both end up winners."

Later, as he drove home, he took a detour and found himself in the neighborhood where Terrell lived. It was the hour when schools were letting out, the streets busy with yellow buses halting and starting and kids taking their time crossing. He cruised slowly around the block and parked at the entrance to Macey's building. Schoolkids walked by, eyeing him suspiciously. He felt like a murderer visiting the scene of his crime.

Standing in her kitchen four flights up, Macey held the curtain aside and watched the guy from the day of the funeral, one of the two white men who'd come to talk to Sonny. What the hell did he want now?

"Mama?"

"Keep your voice down. Your grandma's taking a nap."

Terrell came up alongside her. "You looking at that man?" he said.

"How about you? Recognize him?"

"Yeah," the boy said.

"He comes here once, he comes here twice, he's got something on his mind. Go out there and see what this is all about. Keep your distance, though, OK? Don't go anywhere near that car. I'll be watching."

The boy put on his jacket and for added measure buttoned the pockets on his cargo pants. He ran as fast as he could down the stairs and when he pushed the heavy front door open the cold air hit him hard. He held his jacket tightly against his chest as he stood in front of his building, waiting for the man to notice him.

Nick slid down his window. "Terrell! Hey! Remember me? Downtown man?"

"My mama wants to know what you're doing here."

"I just wanted to see how you and your mom were doing. That's all." His eyes shifted up to Macey in the open window. He nodded and attempted a smile.

The kid glanced nervously up and down the street and turned to look up at his mother. He took a step closer to the car and this time he lowered his voice. "She cries a lot. My grandma's staying with us for a while. But don't tell her I said that. The stuff about the crying, OK?"

"That's good that your grandma's with you." For some reason his eyes started to well up, a novelty in the life of Nick Copeland.

"She's old."

"Yeah. They usually are."

"Old like you."

Nick laughed. He even got the kid to crack a smile.

"Anything else, 'cause I—"

"No, that's OK. Just…take care, OK? Look after your mother. Take care of her, too." He lifted a hand in farewell, but by then Terrell was already inside the building.

"Just one question," Joanne said, extricating herself from his arms. "This meeting or whatever you just had—was it with Mitsouko, or was it Shalimar? Because frankly, Nick, you don't smell like some guy who was out on business."

For a moment he wondered if she were accusing him of having some Asian woman tucked away in his life, someone who gave him body shampoos and hand jobs, and afterward served tea and almond biscuits before discreetly tucking his hard-earned money into the sleeve of her kimono. Then he remembered that he was probably carrying the scent of Meredith Hunter, picked up as they sat leafing through her photo album. At that moment he couldn't find the fiction that would save his ass.

Joanne looked as if the wind had been knocked out of her. "I know I haven't been as…responsive as you might like. Not as loving or nurturing or whatever. And I don't blame you if you're…doing whatever you might be doing. As long as you do it safely."

"Joanne—" he started, though he'd just been handed a free pass to the Wide World of Adultery.

"But you could at least—"

"Jo—"

"At the very least—"

"Please stop—"

"You could maybe just *shower* afterward?"

He wrapped his arms around her. "Baby. I'm not having an affair."

She looked at him with something close to horror. What had he said now?

"My God, you have a family, you have children. I'm talking about some…call girl. Or getting a lap dance or something."

"Jo," he said softly. "Do you really think a half-naked woman with implants hovering over me in a public bar is really all that satisfying?"

"So it is an affair."

"Oh Christ. No, it's not an affair. I was going over some papers with"—he seized a name right out of the air—"Bobby Wagner," pulling the name of the late mayor's late son straight off the esplanade in the upper reaches of the FDR Drive.

"Bobby Wagner. And who the hell is that? And why does he wear Guerlain?"

"It's Barbara, actually. Everyone calls her Bobby."

"Everyone meaning you."

"You remember Sam Harriman?"

"The bald accounts guy from your office?"

"Bobby's his sister-in-law. She's a certified financial adviser. Sam set it up so I could get a free consultation with her. Just a favor he owed me. And you know how it is; you're looking over papers together and you…start to smell like the other person. Or whatever. She's probably home right now, getting blamed for smelling like an out-of-work adman."

"Barbara Wagner."

"Bobby."

"Why do I know this name?"

"You met her," he lied brightly. "At the holiday party, oh, three years ago, I think. Sam brought her. You remember her partner, right? Cynthia Greenspan? You said she looked like Bette Midler? She was also at the party."

He had heard the lugubrious chairman of the Federal Reserve interviewed on the way home on NPR, and Nick silently thanked the man for lending him his name, presumably at 18 percent interest, compounded annually.

She was buying it. "OK," she said. "And?"

"Well, nothing new, really. We're definitely going through a rough patch, as we know, but if we can put this Jerry Bruno thing together we should be OK. Especially if his company can retain us for further work. So Bobby suggested that I make myself into a consultant. Reach out to other clients."

He mentally patted himself on the back: she wasn't only buying it, she was tearing up the receipt so she wouldn't be able to return it. Yet the idea hadn't ever been that far from his mind. He'd been a successful creative director, after all, and working for himself would mean that he wouldn't have to deal with assholes with the power to fire him.

"OK, Nick. Sorry. Sorry. It's just that I'm starting to panic a little."

He took her face in his hands. "And I'm sorry I was late and didn't call. It was thoughtless of me."

"There's cake."

"Kids didn't eat it all?"

"Just half. I have a card for you." Playing coy, she toyed with a button on his shirt. "You know, I kind of missed you today."

"Even at Li'l Rascals?"

"Hm-mm."

"What were you thinking?"

"While I was cleaning up Ricky Halprin's vomit, or while I was wiping Angela Janklow's ass?" She just smiled at him. He had a birthday present waiting, and it was standing right in front of him.

After eating a plate of leftovers and devouring a large wedge of cake, he opened his cards. The one from Eric had been chosen with his usual lack of care. Walked into the CVS, grabbed the first one he saw, threw down his money, scribbled an unreadable *Later, Eric,* and sealed the envelope. The card was a Peanuts cartoon, and the entire message was directed at someone under the age of ten who played ball, meaning someone who had his whole life before him, not just the sad end game of his final decade or so.

Jen, bless her heart, had put some thought into hers. It played on the fact that he'd grown up in the sixties, so there was a Jerry Garcia type in a headband—why Jerry Garcia? Why not, say, Ray Davies? Or, just to get a little obscure, Skip Spence?—and a little pointed saying about how he was still a rebel after all these years.

She'd got that right.

Joanne's card was devoid of any stunning graphics, resorting to a soft-focus shot of an anonymous beach, the sun either rising or setting just above the horizon and the silhouette of a man and a woman holding hands. Inside was filled with enough words in large, loopy purple cursive that she didn't need to think up any of her own beyond her name, as though she suspected she might just have to leave it someplace and let him read it at his earliest opportunity. The words were sentimental crap: *To my Husband…Sometimes we don't always see eye to eye, and sometimes the words we use are harsh and hurtful, but never forget, my beloved, that through it all I'll always be in love with you.*

And yet as he stood there, drink in hand, reading it, he actually had to stifle a sob, because, well, there was something about these words probably tapped out by a sad bastard of an ex-adman that actually moved him. No, it wasn't the words. It was that Joanne had taken the time, as she always did when buying cards, to read it through and find it apt for him. He knew that in an hour or so he'd read it again and it would leave him enraged, for like an optical illusion it could be read in a wholly different way. This would not be seen as a declaration of love, but rather a stripping down of Mr. Birthday Boy to a human scumbag who swore at her and disagreed with everything she said and was so disliked by her that the best she could come up with was this double-edged sword of a card that cost—he flipped it over—three ninety-nine.

But right now it moved him. He thanked her and kissed her, and then held her in his arms for a little bit before inviting her into the basement for a drink. Of course a drink wasn't the main object, for "the basement" was an old euphemism for that special little act of sex, enjoyed at speed and remembered at leisure. They went immediately to the Castro Convertible they'd liberated from her mother's house after she'd died.

"Take off your clothes," he said. "Here. Now."

"No. The kids might come down."

She propped herself on the pool table and hoisted up her skirt. It was like a scene from a noir, he thought: the lady splayed out amongst the balls and cues; Robert Mitchum daintily spreading her thighs with his nicotine-stained fingers.

In something less than a hundred and four seconds they were done. It was remarkable: not once during that time did his mind drift to anything else—not his financial problems, not the drugs in the jars, not even the way Meredith Hunter had laid it all out for him, every step between now and the end.

2

NICK DRIFTED OFF TO SLEEP JUST AS JOANNE SWITCHED on *Charlie Rose*, only to wake up forty minutes later, long after his wife—her face turned away from him, her hair spread out on the pillow—had fallen under the influence of her nightly pill. He blinked a few times and, barely awake, brought the screen into focus.

Charlie was talking to a bearded man who looked strangely familiar, and for a moment Nick wondered why his urologist, Mitch Geigerman, was being interviewed that night. Had he published a book? Been appointed to the cabinet? But it wasn't Mitch, it was Paul Krugman, because the conversation was not focused on the prostate, but on the increasingly dire state of the economy. And that's when his cell phone began to shimmy on his nightstand, toppling off with a soft plop into his hand.

"Hang on a sec," he whispered, tiptoeing down to the basement. He sat in the dark, on a barstool.

"We're on," Rob said.

"Do you have any idea what time it is?"

"I've heard from Leroy."

Surprise turned to disbelief. "Go on."

"He was at a pay phone so we couldn't talk too long. He also sounds a little paranoid. We're meeting him the day after tomorrow."

"You're kidding."

"Actually I'm not," Rob said, and the F. Lee Bailey tone of his voice confirmed it.

"Where is this happening?"

"To be determined. He's going to buy a prepaid phone so he can keep in touch with us. He has my number."

"Well. Wow." It was all Nick could think of saying. He gazed into the darkness of the cellar, at the pool table, the low ceiling, the Castro that reeked of sex.

"OK, I have to go," Nick said. "I have to go right now."

He clicked off and hoped that whoever was standing at the bottom of the stairs was Joanne and not Jen. She clicked on the light and took him in: a nude, middle-aged man sitting on a barstool at midnight.

"OK," she said. "If this is a jerk-off call I don't want to kill the moment."

"That was Rob. We're going to finish the project in two days."

"You're naked, Nick."

"I know."

"You couldn't put anything on before you took the call? Or did you decide you might need to have access to yourself?"

"I didn't want to wake you."

"This isn't about furniture stores, is it?"

He didn't take half a second to think about it. "No."

"And we've already decided you're not seeing another woman. So what's really going on here?"

She perched on the stool beside his. She was wearing a pale blue dressing gown and a pair of furry pink slippers. She looked like she'd just walked out of one of his ads for Maxwell House. The happy housewife, the morning coffee, the content little family unit. Except that he was stark naked and trying to conclude a drug deal at ten minutes to midnight.

She asked the logical question: "Is it legal?"

He shook his head. "No."

"Jesus, Nick. Do I have to worry even more now?"

Everything about him was shriveling up to nuts and buttons on that barstool in the basement.

"Tell me about this Jerry Bruno," she sighed.

"He's dead."

"Right. OK. So. I'm guessing he wasn't a Weatherman?"

Nick shook his head.

"And this guy Rob?"

"You saw him for yourself."

"That's what worries me. This is a guy you haven't had any contact with in thirty years and suddenly together you're going to solve all our financial problems."

He unpeeled his buttocks from the stool and decided to pour himself a drink. He looked up at Joanne.

"Might as well," she said.

He handed her the glass and sat on the Castro. She tossed him a stray bar towel, a tasteful gift from her late father purchased on a tour of Ireland the old man had taken with Joanne's stepmother. Stitched into it was the phrase *Kiss My Wild Irish Ass*, and beside it a representation of a leprechaun with his head between his legs, illustrating the precise method as practiced in the Emerald Isle. Nick draped it over his genitalia. He proceeded to relate the story of the Cincinnati deal, from the bus trip to Ohio to the moment they'd dug up the jars.

"You're that desperate," she said.

"I'll do anything for you and the kids."

"Oh, Nick. It's so, I don't know, *insane.*"

"I know," he said with a grand smile.

"You're enjoying this whole thing, aren't you?"

"You can't imagine."

She took it in for a moment. "Can you trust anyone you're dealing with?"

"I mean, we know all the people involved. So we're not dealing with strangers."

"I just don't want the kids involved—"

"Even if it meant they stayed in school? And you could quit that lousy daycare job? And life could go back to what it was?"

"What? With you as a consultant or something? You'd be competing with some pretty big companies, including your old one."

"I was good."

She managed to work up a genuine smile. "Yes, you were."

"I can be better."

"Don't press your luck, baby," she said, and together they laughed. She said, "Seriously. You can do this. You really can."

"Right now we just need a quick rescue. And then we can do all the legal things we want to do."

"Is it worth it? I mean, we have a house in a nice neighborhood, two great kids. We have friends, we take vacations, we have—"

"A reputation to keep? And now you know that to maintain it people sometimes have to go beyond certain boundaries. Fund managers cheat their clients out of billions of dollars. Others take out insurance policies and murder their loved ones. We're just shifting a couple of pounds of what we hope is heroin."

"And if it isn't?"

"We're going to be upfront about it. If it's not smack, fine, at least we tried. And if it is, then it's jackpot time. We're not defrauding anyone, no one's going to lose his job or his retirement package. No one's going to end up like I did."

She poured herself another scotch and plopped down beside him on the ruined sofa. "And what's the guy who buys it going to do with it? Sell it to kids on the street?"

Oh, right.

"You hadn't thought that far, had you. You've got two of your own, Nick. What if it fell into their hands?"

"C'mon, can you imagine Jen shooting smack?"

"I'm a mother, I have nightmares all the time about my kids. So they don't get hold of it. So what? It'll just end up with some kids in the city. Is that any better? What'd you do with your conscience, put it in a pipe and smoke it away?"

She drained her glass, set it back in the bar with a decisive bang, went up the stairs and switched off the light.

3

"**Y**OU'RE LATE." NICK STOOD IN THE HALLWAY OUTSIDE Rob's apartment. He must've looked like death, because Rob just stared at him. "Jesus, what's happened?"

He could hardly get the words out. It was all about someone he hadn't seen in thirty years, and yet it had hit him with all the freshness of Right Now. Rob plucked at Nick's sleeve until he was inside his apartment.

"What? You ran over someone? Kids sick? What? Tell me, for Christ's sake already."

"I can't believe it," Nick said.

"The cops called you, your house burned down?"

"She's dead."

"Oh God. Oh Christ. Judy?"

"Joanne."

"Oh my God, no."

"My wife is fine. It was Kacey."

Waking that morning, Nick went down into the basement and scrolled through until he found the e-mail from Lori Streeter. There was Kacey's parents' telephone number. He studied the numerals on his laptop's screen for a few moments, as though trying to divine some narrative out of them, some clue as to what had become of Kacey. Even though it was only nine thirty and he hadn't even had breakfast, much less coffee, he opened the bottle of scotch and upended it in his mouth. The question was, what was he going to say once he reached Kacey's parents?

No, that wasn't the question. The question was, why was he so fucking terrified to talk to her? And the answer was because he was afraid she'd say he'd ruined her life.

Maybe this was the great lesson of life. Maybe it was that one word, one decision, one gesture or look, could affect another's life to such a degree that it would be like the proverbial beating of a butterfly's wings in Peru and the tsunami it leads to in Indonesia. Youth was no excuse; youth was simply the burden you carried on your back for the rest of your life. It was a sack full of false moves, stupid comments, thoughtless actions, and simmering regrets that you could never set down on the side of the road and leave behind. Nick's was as heavy as it had been thirty years earlier.

He tipped the bottle once again and drained it of its remaining drops. He reached behind the bar and found a bottle of some cheap scotch their neighbors the Fosters had brought them when, soon after they bought the house, they decided to throw a barbecue so they could size up the rest of the block. Chuck Foster's choice of Old Smuggler certainly clarified where he came from—i.e., Cheapskate Island—though Nick gladly unscrewed the top from the plastic jug and tossed a bit more down his throat.

He picked up the phone. His palms were actually damp from anticipation, and he punched in the numbers, swallowed hard and cleared his throat a few times just as a woman answered.

"Yes, hello, this is a friend of Kacey Christopher's from college, and I was just wondering if you knew where I might reach her?" Too brisk, he thought. Indeed the line went dead, or at least it seemed to. He could hear neither breath nor voice, and after a second or two the woman said, "You say you want Kacey *Christopher*? Who is this, please?"

"I'm an old friend of Kacey's. From Eden College. I'm just hoping you might be able to help me, Mrs. Christopher, is it?"

Her silence prodded him to mention his name.

"Nick, yes, of course. Kacey used to talk about you." Another pause. "Obviously you hadn't heard the news."

"I haven't heard from her, really, since college," he said.

"Well, she'd been Kacey Bruno for quite a few years. So I guess you also didn't hear that my daughter passed away eight months ago."

Nick's stomach flipped over as he tried to get his mind around this. Then the line went quiet.

"Mrs. Christopher?"

"She never got in touch with you, did she?"

"I haven't seen or talked to her since college."

He could hear her walking from one room into another. A chair scraped against a floor. Then she said, "So you never knew the whole story."

Now it was Nick's turn to sit. "I knew nothing," he said.

"After her husband died..."

"I heard. Yes, I'm sorry, Mrs.—"

"She was in such despair." And when that last word came out it was with such a sigh of grief that Nick was profoundly sorry he had taken this as far as he had. "Jerry suffered so with his cancer, and when he died she felt so alone, you know. So... terribly, terribly alone. Her father and I are no longer young, and she needed someone else, someone...for her to love."

He pressed the phone hard against his ear, as if to get inside the meaning of what she'd just said. "I don't underst—"

"They'd tried so hard to have a baby. All she wanted was to be a mother. For years, really, they tried."

Her voice seemed to drift away from her, as though she were talking to the air. And then it was back, stronger this time, because she needed to say it to a total stranger.

"She'd been pregnant once, before she married. I don't know who the boy was, but she told me about it a few years later. I guess this was before abortion was mercifully made legal and, whatever happened, it left her unable to bear any more children. If it had been legal everything would have been fine."

Nick couldn't find the words.

She said, "Are you there?"

"Yes, Mrs. Christopher. I just…wanted to say that I loved Kacey very, very much. A long time ago, back in college. And I was the one who got her pregnant. I just wanted to tell her what I should have said thirty years ago."

"You were young. So was Kacey. Are you married now, Nick? Do you have children?"

"Yes. I have a boy and a girl."

"Then the best thing you can do is to love your wife and children with all your heart. My daughter died because she felt she had no one to love and no one to love her. They'd found her… Her neighbor had called the police because Jerry and Kacey had a dog and the dog was barking all night long… It was a nice dog, a Labrador, a black dog. They called it Laddie. She tried to swallow too much Advil, and I guess that didn't work, so she found her husband's gun—I don't know if you knew Jerry, but he became a police officer—and she just…decided to end it. Don't let this happen to anyone you care for."

What darkness had entered her heart since that time he saw her, her head on his pillow, smiling at him? What shadow had fallen across her future? Just as something of her life had remained within him, a piece of her death now lay there, lodged like shrapnel let loose by a far-off explosion, a splinter of metal too deep inside to be extracted without causing catastrophic damage. Now the time had come for it to become part of him, to be absorbed by his heart, this thing that might one day shift a centimeter and finish him off. This was what consequence felt like, a strange undefined pain without dimension or definition that came and went with the tides of memory.

Thirty years ago he thought wonderful things would happen in his life. He'd seen the Clear White Light and for the first time ever had some genuine cachet. He *owned* his own enlightenment. *Satori* was his middle name. What had happened? You saw the Light and everything was supposed to change. Once you'd glimpsed this blinding whiteness, where there was no single truth worth mentioning, no profound utterance but only your own spiritual death, experienced and lived through, you were supposed to drift through life with a knowing smile on your face, the fool on the hill on the loose. Had he broken the rules? Had he failed to apply the lessons of that Friday afternoon to his life? Or was there some other glorious moment waiting for him that would complete his arc? Maybe this was it, what his life had been a preparation for, this standing here waiting to cut a deal, shake a hand, take some money, get lost in the night. And how would the night end?

"How did this happen?" Rob said. "Kacey killing herself?"

It was as though Nick only just became aware of him: "Put the dope inside a bag. Let's go do this thing."

Rob held up his palms. "OK, OK, forget I mentioned it." He checked his watch. "We still have forty-five minutes. Once he's looked it over and figured out what it is—if it is the real thing—once we've negotiated a price, one of us takes the money."

"Why is this again?"

"So if someone thinks he's onto us he won't know who to follow."

"And you saw this in what movie?"

"It's standard operating procedure, Nick. We did it thirty years ago in Cincinnati, right? We can do it again. I take the money, we'll go our separate ways and meet back here. Then we divide."

"Minus the extras you're paying yourself and the Chinese guy."

"I'll even write you out a receipt."

"Except *I'll* take it, we'll go somewhere else other than this shithole and then we'll divide. You held the dope, right? I'll hold the money."

"That's not fair."

"Since when are you making all the decisions?"

"I'm the one with the Leroy Ives connection."

"Uh-uh. I'm taking the dough. If you don't trust me with it, say so now."

Rob said nothing.

"Say it."

"I do trust you, Nick."

"Good. That's settled. So where are we meeting Leroy?"

"So what are you saying, that if I'm carrying the money I won't be cool about it?"

"Did I say that?"

"You were thinking it."

"Where are we meeting the guy?"

"Grand Central."

"You're fucking kidding me," Nick said. He could just about imagine this Leroy testing the smack over a half-dozen Kumamotos at the Oyster Bar.

"He said he's going to take us someplace else."

"And we trust him why?"

"Because we're the beggars who can't afford to be choosers, Nick. We either back out and pour the stuff down the toilet or we try this and maybe end up saving ourselves."

"All right. OK. We'll do it." He must have been looking at it ever since he'd walked in, but only now did it register. "What is this?" He picked the thing up off the table. It felt a lot heavier than it looked.

"Don't play around with that," Rob said.

"When did you get a gun?"

"It's not really real. They use it in track meets. Swim meets. You know. Bang, go. Just point it somewhere else, OK? It makes me nervous."

"What if someone pulled a real gun on us? You're going to, what? Blow out his eardrums with some blank pistol?"

Rob's voice grew in volume and passion. "It was an idea, Nick, that's all, just something to make the whole fucking thing safe for us. I thought it was a good idea that you'd support."

Nick aimed it at Rob's forehead. A lifelong member of the I Hate Guns Association, Nick felt pretty good doing this. For some reason he said, "Jerry Bruno became a cop, you know."

"Put the gun down."

"Ironic, isn't it? Tough guy Jerry turns legit. Kacey blew her brains out with his service pistol because she couldn't have any children after the abortion. I ruined her life. I pulled the trigger on her. Just like I'm going to do to you."

"Put the fucking thing down, Nick."

"Get on your knees, you slimy piece of shit. Get on your knees and plead for mercy. Beg for your life. C'mon, squeal like a pig."

"Please stop fucking around, OK?" Already he had his hands up to protect his precious head.

"Listen to me. I'm going to pull the trigger and I want to hear the bang. And then I want you to fall down as if I killed you. Then I'll feel as if my life was worth something."

Rob's mouth remained open for a few long seconds. "You need help, buddy, you know that?"

Nick set the gun down on the table, then raised his hand, formed a pistol out of his finger and thumb, and pressed it against Rob's head. "Badda *bing!*" he said, his hand recoiling like the real thing.

"OK, feel better? Now where are you and I going to meet, since even though I'm the one who set this up, all of a sudden you're the boss? I mean, without me you'd be—"

"Starbucks on Forty-Second and Lexington. And if you get there first, order me a grande double-shot espresso macchiato." He pulled out a fiver and handed it to the Prince of Parsimony.

"Fine. Great. Then you're driving. Because I don't feel like taking my car out of the garage."

"Why don't we just take the subway?"

"And travel back with hundreds of thousand of dollars falling out of our pockets? Are you crazy?"

Nick started to laugh. Another great ad for Bank of America, almost as good as the one with the baby in the diaper: *Why carry your life savings around with you? Leave it where those creeps on the subway can't get their hands on it.*

In fact at that moment Meredith was entering a branch of Bank of America on Lexington Avenue, not far from Grand Central. She walked straight through the main banking floor until she came to the safe-deposit department in the rear, with the little gate that only opened when someone pressed the buzzer. Back here the place seemed cleaner, more rarified, less egalitarian: a charnel house of memories lingering in metal boxes protected by a middle-aged black man with a big gun. It was the difference between the waiting area at the dermatologist for the ordinary folk with their acne and pre-cancers and the one set apart for the big-money cosmetic surgery babes, with its vases full of flowers, complimentary coffee, and no magazines older than a week. The carpeting was thick and deep blue, the walls a pale beige with enough indirect lighting here and there to bring comfort to the eyes and balm to the heart. Even the air seemed somehow strained of impurities, with all ambient sounds—canned music, the chiggering of computer keyboards—reduced to a quiet hiss. Here you were meant to feel as though you'd earned the right to be in this space, that somehow status had been granted you simply because you trusted this bank to store the things you treasured more than—no, as much as—cold, hard cash. The guard recognized her and smiled.

"You'll want a private room, as usual?"

"Yes, please, Lester."

He went down a little hallway to open it for her. "Getting chilly out there."

"Winter is surely on its way," she said brightly, taking the key on its ribbon from her pocket. Currently she kept a conservative balance of $46,567.89 in her money market account there, and around half that in her checking: amounts that no one would ever question, much less read twice. Because the boxes she rented—the largest available there—were so full she had to carry each with both hands. Once she was inside the room she prodded the door shut with her foot and took off her gloves, carefully unbuttoning them at the wrist. She shrugged off her coat and loosened her scarf and propped her sunglasses on top of her head. And when she lifted the lids she silently congratulated herself for having had the forethought to keep the bulk of Leroy's fortune here: bearer bonds and stacks of fifties and hundreds, all well traveled, clean as a whistle and totaling some $600,000. Had she put it in stocks she'd have nothing.

Her artwork had been placed in the hands of her dealer that morning, not for auction but for private sale, with instructions to transfer the proceeds electronically into a UBS account opened in her name a week earlier in Zurich. No questions had been asked of her. In the way of most Swiss banks, they treated her just as they would any other person of wealth: quietly, discreetly, and with polite gratitude for her business. She knew that once she walked out they would have her whole life laid out before them, screen upon screen on their secure computer monitors: her debts, her expenditures, the worth of her Tribeca loft. It didn't matter what they found. Money was money, after all. And there was a lot more due to be deposited there.

According to her dealer, who had three buyers lined up from Japan, the Netherlands, and Qatar, the paintings and the Picasso sketch were expected to bring in somewhere between $6.5 million and $12 million. This was the moment that had always been there, somewhere in the middle distance between hope and dream. She'd only seen her father that one time, outside Sonny's building, but for a few years she'd heard rumors that he was out and about: someone had seen him in the back of a car, or in the depths of a jazz club, or sitting in a diner. As far as she was concerned these were all ghost sightings, as one feels sensation in an amputated limb. None of it added up to anything resembling sense. Until she went to Attica and learned Leroy had died. No papers, no grave, no facts. He'd just died. Vanished. Only to be seen in a club, in a car, drinking coffee. He wasn't dead, or locked up; he was still somehow a prisoner. And she would be his means of escape, because she was the only person in this world he had left to trust. And Nick, as she explained to him the day he came to her loft, was going to be the one to make it happen. It was all a question of whom the cops would be watching.

She carefully placed half the money in a large Prada bag, stashing the remainder in her Strand tote, covering the contents with the cardigan she'd worn under her coat, folded and placed neatly on top. She walked out of the room as the door behind her latched shut.

It was ten to six, and the bank was preparing to close. Soon the doors would be locked and the tellers would sign off on their day's work. The cleaners would come and vacuum the carpeting and wash the tiled floors. Lester said, "You're our last customer."

"Maybe it'll bring me luck."

"Have a good one, now."

When she stepped out onto the sidewalk a few flakes were beginning to fall. It didn't matter if it amounted to an inch or a foot. Now time just stretched out before her like an endless highway to some better place.

4

"**L**ook. It's starting to snow." Rob turned to Nick with a disengaged smile. "It's just like the old days, isn't it."

He was right. Nick could feel that buzz inside him, the same sparkle he knew when they'd gone to Cincinnati to make the deal, when they'd stolen the machines from the business office, when he'd put together the bomb-scare letter. Just the fact of being on the edge of the legal, the admissible, the acceptable, was enough for him.

"Just think," Rob said. "If we only knew then what we know now we'd have made a fortune."

"If we knew then what we know now I'd have the sense to be at home with my family like a normal human being and you'd still be a lawyer."

Rob considered it. "And living with Janet, I guess."

No, thought Nick. That's not part of the equation. And he probably wouldn't be married to Joanne, he'd be married to Kacey, and their child would now be thirty years old, working in the world, possibly even a parent as well. Grandpa Nick; Granny Kacey.

"Regrets?" Rob said.

"You can't change what's already happened, can you."

"Well that's deep," Rob said with an ironic twist of his mouth.

"No it's not," Nick said. "It's all right in front of your eyes. You just have to remember to look."

"Hey, you saw the Big Bright Light or whatever it's called."

"Clear White Light." Nick wasn't going to allow Rob to belittle that singular achievement, not even three decades later.

He glanced over at Nick. "Was there really a light?"

Nick looked for the words. "There was, I don't know, a *clarity* all of a sudden. Just this kind of certainty that nothing mattered, that there was no purpose to anything I was doing in life." He shrugged.

"That sounds like a real bummer."

"No, it was…kind of nice, kind of refreshing, you know? It had a kind of *perfection* to it, like it was an absolute truth. Like a diamond. It made everything else that didn't matter disappear."

"Including you."

He looked over at Rob. "Well that's the point, isn't it? We sit around worrying about idiotic things and in the end they don't count for a damn thing."

"So life doesn't have any meaning; is that what you're saying?"

Nick sighed. There was no way to win this conversation. "I guess it is, Rob."

"What cured you of that?"

"When other people came into my life. Joanne. The kids." That was the bigger, more important lesson, he knew now: that enlightenment went only as far as where another person began, because other people really do care about the things the Light told him didn't matter, and what's important to them, the small things, those the Clear White Light shunned, were as critical as the truths that could be summed up in a catchphrase or a song lyric dreamed up after a particularly intense acid trip.

"Here's something to think about," Rob said, trying to pass the time as the car inched across the intersection of Fifth and Forty-Eighth. "Did it ever occur to you that maybe you never came down? And that you're still tripping and all of this is a hallucination? And you're still on your dorm room floor, and your whole life since then is taking place in something like eighteen seconds?"

"How do you fit into this, then?"

"Maybe I'm just a figment of your imagination. Maybe I never went to Eden. Maybe you just invented me in your weird drug state."

It was an absurd notion, but not altogether improbable. The acid had been pretty powerful and, having built up a tolerance from all the previous trips, he'd taken a hell of a lot of it, easily enough to turn on most of western Pennsylvania and a few bordering Ohio and West Virginia counties. If Rob were a hallucination, then Joanne and Eric and Jen, not to mention his entire career in advertising, counted for nothing. Just whims, flights of fancy. And what if he weren't tripping and had just lost his mind, and were in some boondocks hospital instead of driving to Grand Central? Still alive back then (or was it now?), he'd be visited by his not-yet-deceased parents who would try, with growing pathos, to wake him out of his catatonia. Assuming they had a vague idea of his tastes in music, they'd play all the wrong things—the Monkees, and the Peanut Butter Conspiracy, and Donovan—and all he'd be able to do was lie there in mute agony as "Mellow Yellow" queued itself up for another spin. And there would come those barely lucid moments when he'd be able to grunt out little noises, and though he'd be trying to say, "Kill me, pull the plug, stick a pillow over my face," all his parents would do is sing along with his animal noises, or check his adult diaper to see if the noises had signified, in the way they sometimes did with infants, that he'd soiled himself.

The whole idea left him queasy. "Do me a favor? Shut up."

Now they were a block away from Grand Central. Though normally he didn't mind driving in Manhattan traffic, tonight was different. He just wanted the whole ordeal over with, and anything that delayed it only raised his level of anxiety. He made a quick turn into the first parking garage he saw. He took a ticket from the attendant while Rob carefully lifted the bag from the back seat. When they stepped out it was into the same pleasant fall of snow they'd been driving through: untroubled by wind or breeze, the flakes simply drifted uncertainly about them, melting as they hit the road and pavement.

"Shit," Rob said. "I left the gun at home. That thing cost me sixty-nine ninety-five."

"You could always return it."

Rob grabbed Nick's arm. "Wait. What happens afterwards?"

"What do you mean?"

"I mean after we divide everything up. Are we going to get together again? You know, like be friends?"

"What're you, nine years old? Maybe thirty years from now we'll meet for a drink someplace. In the home for retired dope dealers."

"So you're saying what? This is the end?"

Nick just smiled. "The gang's got to split up, light out for the territories. Like Butch and Sundance. We make a run for it and they roll credits."

Rob couldn't believe his ears. "What? You fell asleep or something?"

"What are you talking about?"

"You never saw the ending, did you?"

"They get their guns and slip away."

Rob shook his head sadly. "I pity you sometimes, you know that?"

Somehow it didn't matter anymore what happened. But he sensed that spending more time with Rob would be a dicey proposition. Rob the loner could well turn Nick into Old Reliable, calling him whenever he wanted to go somewhere: a movie, say, or just to shoot the breeze over an early bird special at Olive Garden. And then there was the greater danger that some day Rob would open his big mouth and there'd be an investigation. Other people would be brought into it—Meredith, her nephew, Terrell—and he'd promised her that would never happen. No, silence was the only path forward. Silence and being as far away from Rob as was spiritually and physically possible.

Grand Central was buzzing with commuters on their way home to the suburbs, crossing the floor of the terminal, stopping to take calls, pulling along suitcases or carrying briefcases. The usual teams of cops could be seen here and there, their blue uniforms, shields, service pistols, and Mace canisters in plain view.

"He's going to call me," Rob said, pulling his phone from his pocket and glancing up at the clock on the information booth. "Five more minutes."

Standing on the mezzanine, Driver talked quietly into his walkie. "The deal comes down at six fifteen," he said, his eyes angling down to the clock on the information booth. This much Ping had told him, for though Ping may have been Leroy's informer, he was—because he was always paid more by him—first and foremost Driver's. As a member of his team, Leroy was expendable; Driver's only fear was that he knew too much and might one day have something to say to a few choice people. Which would cost Driver dearly, and not just Driver but a lot of other people up the ladder as well. He only prayed that the information Ping had given him was correct; otherwise, he'd have to make life a little less easy for the Chinaman.

"Yo, you got a description?" D'Wayne said. Driver looked across and spotted D'Wayne at the opposite mezzanine.

"Negative. Two white guys in their approximate fifties, period. I mean, you met them, right?"

"Yeah, but all those white guys down there look alike to me."

"Wait for the handoff. I'm taking Leroy personally. You, Valentine, and Lamar, you take the sellers. They're probably going to try to walk out of the place. We get them outside, cuff 'em, pull 'em in. Nice and quiet, nobody notices."

"Roger that," D'Wayne said.

Driver had it all figured out. Leroy would finish his sentence in addition to whatever else was slapped on him, and the next time he'd come out of Attica he'd be in a box, this time for good. As for the other two? Possession always carried a penalty, especially if it was for a class-A narcotic. Trying to sell the stuff? Boom, add some prison time to it. Best-case scenario? First offense, a nice long probation, maybe some community service. A big stain on their records, and a definite job killer for the foreseeable future. And if they tried to make a run for it? Hell, probable cause was Driver's oldest friend.

"OK," Rob said, "now I'm getting nervous."

"This used to be fun," Nick said. "All of a sudden it's not."

Rob smiled, but he'd gone pale with fear. "Was it ever not fun back then? I mean, even for a moment?"

"Not until Altamont, I guess. Big wake-up call. Someone gets stabbed under Mick Jagger's nose, and before you know it it's the seventies and disco's king. That was our punishment. The Bee Gees." He felt damp in his armpits and could barely stand still.

Driver put his walkie back to his mouth. He'd spotted a couple of black men coming into the station, each heading in a different direction. "Stand by..." Leaning forward, he scanned the group, one face after another. Everyone looking calm and collected. No one he knew. "Talk to me, people."

Valentine was over by the subway entrance. Lamar was on the station floor, not far from the information booth, some fifteen yards from an unrecognized Rob and Nick. D'Wayne was still on the opposite end of the mezzanine.

"Look at me," Driver was saying. "Nice and easy, just tilt your head and look my way."

He watched here, here, and here, as three faces casually turned toward him from their places. Valentine offered a great big grin. He might as well have switched on a spotlight and turned it on his boss.

"Listen up. There's a good chance Leroy's armed. I'm told he bought hisself a gun a few days ago. You see him take that thing out, you stand down. There will be no shooting, we are not going to have everyone coming down hard on us for bringing disrespect to the NYPD, you hear? Lamar, man, you listening?"

"I'm not shooting anyone," Lamar said.

"Just keep it that way. This place is full of innocent folks who aren't looking to die this evening."

5

H E FELT IT BEFORE HE HEARD IT, A LITTLE SHIVER AGAINST
his thigh. He reached into his pocket and pulled out his
cell phone just as it began to ring.

"Great timing," Rob groused in his other ear.

"Hey," Nick said brightly, because the number displayed
was Jen's. But this wasn't a "Hey" moment, because she was in
tears and her words came out as *blub glub blub.* "All right, calm
down, just tell me what's happened."

As he listened to fragments of words, bits of sentences,
gasps and huffing, he grew angrier. His hands formed fists, and
if he'd squeezed any harder the phone would have exploded into
a million tiny micro bits, sending the vowels and consonants of
her news all over Grand Central's main floor.

"They can't do that to you!"

The girl was beside herself. Tomorrow morning he would
drive to her school and kill everyone he saw. It would go down
in history as the Columbine of Scarsdale, and security footage,
if cameras there were in her upscale prep school, would show
a crazed middle-aged man running around throttling people
with his bare hands.

"All right," he said again. "Just try to calm down, OK
sweetheart?" She managed to get out the information that she'd

already called her mother at Li'l Rascals and called three dozen of her friends, including, because she was that desperate, her brother, Eric, who was officially not a friend. He noticed that all of a sudden Rob was also on his own phone. Had Jen even gone so far as to give *him* a call, as well? "I'll talk to you later," he said to her.

Rob slipped his phone in his pocket. "OK, we're good, we're in standby mode. He's on his way. What happened? You look horrible."

"My daughter has been rehearsing her role in *Hair* for something like two months. And now she's been replaced."

"Jesus, is she that bad?"

Nick's phone went tingle-tingle again, sparing Rob a flood of invective. It was Joanne. She was in the school, just outside the head's office. She must have driven ninety miles an hour to get there, and he could just see her, tires squealing, brakes screeching, as she pulled up to the entrance.

"I will stay here until that woman speaks to me. I'll make her sit in her goddamn office until I get some explanation why this has happened. I don't care if it takes all night."

"Way to go," he said, because it was what his kids would have said. He was well aware of Joanne's remarkable sense of justice and how, when she sensed an innocent wronged, she would simply not let go.

A moment after she hung up he realized he had forgotten to tell her something he'd meant to say for some time: that he loved her. He wasn't so sure she would know it otherwise. Not these days, anyway.

Rob had his eye on the subway exit, from which hundreds of passengers came out in a steady stream. It dawned on Nick: "How is he going to know us?"

"I was his lawyer, right?"

"Yeah, and back then you were young."

"The guy's a pro. He'll sniff us out a mile away."

Sitting at the bar of the Drake, Meredith glanced at the clock over the bar for the eighth time in ten minutes. The bartender eyed her martini glass. "Get you another?"

"Don't you think one's enough?" she said.

"Depends what you have planned for afterward." He held her glass by the stem. "On the house? Unless you're driving, of course. I mean, the hotel has lots of vacancies. Or so I hear."

"Are you hitting on me by any chance?"

"I'm off at nine, you know."

"And I'm off right now." She slid off her stool and walked out into the evening and the BMW, parked just around the corner. From one life into another. Plant no seeds, leave no roots.

Driver glanced over at the clock on the information booth. "Any minute," he said into his walkie.

"I got two white men in my sights," D'Wayne broke in. "Over by the information booth. They're acting nervous. They keep doing stuff with their cell phones."

Driver looked around and must've kept missing them. "What's the luggage like?"

"One of them's got a sack, a kind of briefcase. You know, like for laptops and shit. Want me to have a little talk with them?"

"Negative. Lamar, Valentine? I want you down on the floor. Back up D'Wayne. I still don't have Leroy in my sights. That's the man of the hour right now."

He didn't have Leroy in his sights because Leroy was on the adjacent mezzanine, barely thirty yards away, watching Driver.

The area around the information booth was just as crowded as it usually was this time of day. Everyone seemed to be talking on their cell phones, some of them sprinting across the station floor to catch the express back to Chappaqua or Greenwich. When he looked back at the information booth he spotted the two white guys. This was definitely them. Though he'd changed since the last time he saw him, Johnson was unmistakably himself. Same lousy posture, same nervous gestures. Leroy really didn't blame the guy for not getting him acquitted. No way the heat would have let him walk, anyway. He nudged up his sleeve to check his watch. Then he reached in his pocket and took out the cell phone he'd bought that morning. It would be used only twice, then conveniently dropped down the nearest sewer.

Instead of wearing his usual good suit and expensive coat, Leroy was in jeans, hooded sweatshirt, leather jacket, and a Yankees cap pulled way down over his eyes. Seen from a distance he looked like half the people who'd been out on the street ten minutes ago—guys in a hurry, guys on the make, guys on the run.

"Whoa, whoa, whoa," Driver was saying into his walkie. "Look up. Do you see what I see?" Two blue uniforms were walking straight toward D'Wayne. "Show 'em your shield but don't let the whole world see it, OK?"

"What do I tell them?"

"The truth. You're on a stakeout."

Now he saw them, the two white guys by the booth. They displayed all the trademarks of people with something to hide. But something distracted him: he watched as D'Wayne lifted his hands a little, an instinctive move that did the man no good. Now D'Wayne was shaking his head: *No, officer, I haven't been a bad boy.* Driver's eyes shifted back to the two white guys. Something was happening; the short one was getting off his cell phone and grabbing the other guy's sleeve. "Here we go,"

Driver said to himself, and his eyes flitted back to the commotion surrounding D'Wayne. "Show him your shield," he was saying under his breath, and what was happening to D'Wayne also caught Lamar's and Valentine's attention, so that no one was watching as Leroy, Rob, and Nick drifted in with a crowd of commuters and vanished from sight.

6

LEROY LED THEM FROM GRAND CENTRAL TO THE LOBBY OF the Grand Hyatt through a stream of people arriving and departing to and from the bank of elevators. There was only one word for how Nick was feeling: numb. But it was a numbness that toyed with the fringes of rage, which came from the news of Jen's dismissal from *Hair*. He had half a mind to turn around and grab the first train back to Scarsdale, a fast cab to the school, and unleash a display of anger so powerful and disturbing, especially from a man in an Armani suit, that Kathleen Warner, head of school graced with degrees from Bryn Mawr and Stanford, would involuntarily befoul her Spanx on the spot.

The three of them entered an elevator along with a party of four—mother, father, teenaged boy, and small girl, a tight cabal of silence. Something was simmering there, an unspoken resentment that traveled like low-level electricity between the members of this family, an afterglow of dissent and argument. Nick could sense the familiar ozone stink of discontent rising off of them, the distant overheard thunder of eventual breakup. Once again he thought of his daughter, alone and bereft in her school, and he ground his teeth with such intensity that he was sure he'd cracked a filling.

The family got off on the third floor, and when the doors slid shut and the atmosphere lightened, Leroy turned to Rob. "Been a long time." He put out his hand and Rob grasped it. "This your partner?"

Nick held out his hand. "Nick Copeland."

"You guys ready to do this?"

When they reached the twenty-third floor the doors opened and Leroy led them down the hallway to a room. He unlocked it and flipped on a light.

"Now first I've got to check you both out. Just a formality." He frisked each of them briskly, back, front, sides, thighs, ankles. It was like stepping into a movie, something grand and operatic, full of holdover gestures from long ago, tough guys and broads, Luca Brasi and Sonny Corleone. "Open that bag of yours. Show me you're not carrying anything that might hurt someone."

Rob zipped it open. It was just the two jars, wrapped in towels he'd stolen from his gym before he'd canceled his membership.

Leroy laughed a little. "And you intend to do what with that stuff?"

"What?" Rob said, the word barely voiced as anything more than an expulsion of astonishment.

"Sell it to you," Nick said. "Isn't that the plan?"

"So you're going to—"

"Jesus, Leroy—"

"So you're going to—" Leroy repeated.

"Sell you two pounds of—"

"What exactly?"

"C'mon, Leroy," Rob whined. "I thought we had an agreement. Yes, we're going to sell you a couple of pounds of dope. Heroin. At least that's what we hope it is."

It was as if the air in the room had subtly changed, or something had begun to burn; Nick sensed it immediately. "What the hell is going on?" he said.

Leroy pulled a shield from his pocket and clipped it on his belt.

"Oh my fucking God," Rob said.

"I'm arresting you on the charge of attempting to sell a controlled substance to a detective with the New York City Police Department. You have the right to remain silent. Anything you say can and will be used against you in a court of law. You have the right to talk to a lawyer and have him present with you while you're being questioned... Of course," he said, then shrugged, "you've got Counselor Johnson right here."

Nick looked around the room. The first thing that came to him was no one had any intention of spending any time here: no luggage meant no guest.

"I can't fucking believe this," Rob said. His knees buckled and he grabbed hold of the desk. On it was a menu, in some sort of faux leather binder, and when his fingers engaged it the thing went sliding off onto the floor and opened like a butterfly in a hurry to a page entitled *Appetizers*. Nick watched the proceedings with a kind of silent wonder.

"We blew it," Rob said. "We fucking blew it."

"Yes you did, gentlemen. Now I'll take that bag and its contents, thank you. And do not even think about trying anything foolish." He pulled the pistol he'd bought from Ping from the back of his trousers.

"Who turned you, Leroy?"

"Traded it for time off."

"Wish you'd called me first."

"What? You were going to cut a different deal for me?" Leroy said with a very dark kind of contempt.

"Now what?" Nick said.

"Well, if this stuff is the genuine article, you guys will be doing a solid fifteen years, minimum. And you won't be headed for some white-collar lockup in Connecticut with a miniature golf course and lamb-chop suppers. This is a substantial amount of a class-A substance." It was a lie, of course, and both Leroy and Rob knew it. They'd get a year, maybe a couple more, with something supervisory on the other end, but it never hurt to put the fear of God into guys like these, especially as any time served basically stamped the label *Dead End* on your soul.

"We don't even know that—"

"Intent is all that matters in the eyes of the law. Considering that chances are good neither of you has a record you'd probably just serve that fifteen and then walk into the light of day to enjoy your golden years. Not too bad, right? Spend a little time with the grandkids, stuff like that? Or we can make another deal altogether."

"What?" Rob said, as if he hadn't heard him.

"I have two choices. I bring you guys in, maybe I can negotiate to get a little time shaved off *my* sentence. I mean, bottom line, I'm not in the business of doing anything that won't benefit me, you understand?" He pulled up his trouser leg a few inches. "See, I'm monitored twenty-four-seven. Hell, I'm still serving. But if I take the shit and walk away, just disappear, well then think about it—you also walk away, and as free men. If I busted you it'd still end up disappearing and turning up on the streets, anyway. I hear that's how things work these days."

He flipped open his phone and keyed in a number. After a few seconds he said, "Isn't that right, Mr. Driver?"

"Where the fuck you at?" Driver said.

"I know what you've been up to, and I know how you've been using me, and, by the way, this time I win."

"You're under arrest, Leroy."

"Ow, you got me!" Leroy said and, laughing, clicked off.

"Are you out of your mind?" Rob cried.

"Shut up, Rob," Nick said. He shook his head and laughed at the elegant irony of the thing.

"And where are you going to go?" Rob asked Leroy.

"We don't need to know that," Nick said. "This story is all over for us. Right now."

"Breaks the dawn," Leroy said with a smile. He walked to the door. "Time to go, gentlemen. I don't like to be pushed up against a deadline. You'll walk out of here, ride down the elevator, and forget any of this ever happened. Consider yourself the two luckiest men in New York City."

"Wait, wait, hang on," Rob said. "Split it with me? I mean, I was your lawyer, I was the one who contacted you. Call it a, I don't know, finder's fee? I'll destroy your files, my notes, anything that has your name on it."

"And all those people I told you who'd worked for me? You'll get rid of their names?"

"Yeah. Everyone, all the documentation."

"Wipe my past, huh?"

"Everything I've got."

Rob wore his desperation in the sweat stains on his shirt, in the wide eyes of a man on the abyss. Leroy's glance intersected with Nick's and Nick detected the faintest smile there, one exactly like Meredith's.

"A third?" Rob ventured. "I'll take a third. That's all. All right, a quarter. Fuck it, five percent, OK?"

"If this stuff's any good, that could be quite a haul for you, counselor." He looked at Nick. "Well? You have anything to say to add to your friend's speech here? I mean, you *are* his partner."

"He has no stake," Rob said. "I'm the guy who set this all up."

"So you take the money and run," Nick said. "And you expect me to take this how? I'm just supposed to walk away and forget about it? If you remember, I did put up a third of this for the Cincinnati deal."

"Yeah, and I saved your fucking life, man. I saved your ass when you were freaking out on that acid."

"And this is payback time? After thirty years?"

Rob looked at Leroy. "Well?"

"I'm in."

"Then let's go." He looked at Nick. "Just switch off the lights when you leave, OK?"

"So I guess you won't need me to give you a lift uptown, huh Rob?"

He thought of one more thing to say. But by then they were already gone.

7

A WAITER PUSHING A ROOM-SERVICE CART SHIMMIED smoothly out of their way, leaving behind the scent of steak, potatoes, and coffee as Leroy and Rob swiftly made the journey around a labyrinth of corridors on the fourteenth floor. The silence in the halls was so thick that it seemed to have the texture of wool.

"Look, this whole thing is OK with you, isn't it?"

"I'd be more worried about your friend."

"No, no, he understands."

Leroy laughed a little. "Man, if I were you, I'd be watching my back breakfast, lunch, *and* dinner times for the rest of my natural life."

He stopped at a door and tapped lightly on it. Rob could hear someone just on the other side of it, probably peering through the spy hole. The door swung open and a dignified-looking black man in a blue suit and bow tie, a yellow foulard in his breast pocket, smiled a little and let them in. There was no luggage to be seen other than an overnight bag and an attaché case. The bed hadn't been slept in and the TV was off. He clearly wasn't intending on spending much time there.

"Jean-Pierre Noël," Leroy said. "Mr. Robert Johnson, my former attorney. Jean-Pierre has come all the way up from Haiti to conclude this transaction."

"I'm very pleased to meet you." His accent was Creole, his handshake and manner that of a seasoned diplomat: not too forward, not too strong, leaning to the neutral.

Rob looked at Leroy. "What's going on?" He felt as he sometimes did when watching one of his midday slasher films, that like the person on the screen he'd walked into a room from which he would never leave alive.

Leroy said, "Jean-Pierre is going to test the product. Just a formality. You can't expect me to buy something blind, can you?"

"Why don't you just taste it?"

"I never touch the stuff," Leroy said.

The older man took a glass vial from his inside pocket about two inches long, filled with a clear liquid. He carefully popped off the plastic lid.

"What is that?"

"Sulfuric acid and formaldehyde," the Haitian explained. "If what you have really is heroin, then this will indicate its strength to us. Just a few grains is all that's needed. The more purple it is, the purer it is. Very simple, you see?"

Leroy looked at Rob. "What are you waiting for? Take your stuff out and open one of the jars."

"There are more than one?" Jean-Pierre said. "Then we test them all."

"Whoa, whoa," Rob said. "Hang on a moment, OK? I mean, what's the problem?"

"This is how we do business, my friend," Jean-Pierre said. "I understand you would like us to take you at your word, but in our world one's word isn't worth very much, I'm sorry to say."

Rob offered a tentative gesture, more a bob than a nod. The Haitian took a little of the dope from one of the jars. He slowly, musingly, rubbed it between his fingers, then did likewise with a sample from the second jar, tasting it as well. He smiled and looked at Rob. "There's no need to test further. This is baking soda." He capped his vial and slipped it back in his pocket. "I'll get my coat and be on my way."

Rob stared at him. "What do you mean?"

"Someone's played an old, old trick on you."

Nobody took much notice when Driver strode up to the desk fifteen floors below, displaying his shield in the palm of his hand. The clerk swallowed whatever words were about to roll off his tongue. "What?" was all he could say. Driver wondered what this guy had done in his life that made him go so pale.

"I just need to see a list of guests who checked in today. Primarily any...men of color, you understand? Especially anyone in the last half hour."

"We don't...indicate the race of our guests when they check in. It's against the law."

"How long have you been standing back here?"

"Since nine. This morning, I mean."

"So if a black man had walked in ten minutes ago you wouldn't remember him? I find that difficult to believe. White man sees a black man coming, ten times out of twelve he crosses the street." He turned and dramatically swept the area with his eyes. "Altogether, I count seven people of color here at this moment. There's that couple there. That bellboy or whatever you call him—the porter, the bellhop, whatever—over there, and then there's me and my people here." He turned slightly to indicate his team.

"I think there were a few others."

"Like recently?"

The guy just nodded.

"Guy with a goatee?" He stroked his chin in illustration. "Kind of salt-and-pepper?" He could see it in the clerk's eyes: the fearful glint of betrayal. "Good. Now step it up and tell me where they might be spending their time."

"They're gone," the clerk said. "They left a few minutes ago."

Beyond the hotel entrance snow had given way to rain, and the colder winds of the early evening had turned almost balmy. As Nick crossed Lexington his phone went off again. He ducked into the entryway to a Chase Bank. It was Joanne. She was back in her car. He could hear something tinkly in her voice, the Champenoise sparkle of revenge.

"It's all fixed," she said. "I spoke to Kathleen Warner. I kept her in her office until I got an answer. It seems Sara Carpenter—you know Sara in Jen's class?"

The name was vaguely familiar to him.

"She's that spoiled little bitch whose father's a hedge-fund manager in the city? First of all, I hope the fucker falls into ruin."

"Get to the point, Jo."

"A week and a half ago, Sara's father made a big donation to the school. They're redoing the theater, right? The whole thing about that idiotic fund-raising auction? Well, he pledged a million-five to have the place renovated and named after him."

He waited for the second act of the tale to kick in.

"Sara was in the chorus. You know, of *Hair*. But they decided to replace Jen with her, so she could be a headliner. Padding her résumé for Yale or something."

"Fucking hell," he said.

"Ready for the best part? Jen's had it with the school. She doesn't care where she goes next semester. She'll even do public. Not because she was replaced. Because she hates hypocrites. That's just what she said to me. Isn't that great?"

"What did Kathleen say?"

"Here's the best part. I told her you'd come into the money you were expecting and had been considering making a big donation to the school."

"Oh for Christ's—"

"So she said, well, maybe we can rethink this part of Jen's in *Hair*. And that's when I said—"

"'Go fuck yourself, Kathleen.'"

"My exact words," she said with a happy laugh. "She's just terrified we're going to badmouth the place. Oh, and we're also taking Eric out of there. This is no school for great kids like ours."

A tear rolled down his cheek. His family had become a SWAT team, undercover agents in the cause of subverting injustice, battling the forces of evil and duplicity.

"I'm proud of you all," he said.

"So how did it go down there?"

"It's going to be fine. I have to go."

"Nick? I love you."

She never heard what he'd said back to her, as at that moment an ambulance sped by, its siren blaring.

When Nick reached the garage and his car was brought up the ramp—brought being an understatement, as the driver was pushing 112, tires squealing as he flew up the corkscrew drive of the place—and he was about to pull out, he wasn't surprised to find Rob standing in his way. In fact, he'd been expecting him. With a gesture Rob directed Nick to pull into a space on the street.

It had grown dark, and few pedestrians were on the sidewalk, though the city was humming with traffic. The air smelled of a pleasant memory of some other time that by now was all but forgotten. It had been a good summer, he remembered, full of contentment and sunshine in the weeks before he was fired. Nick got out of the car and leaned against it.

"Please don't tell me you really wanted me to drive you home," he said calmly.

"When did you do it?" Rob reached in his bag, pulled out a Mason jar, unscrewed the top and tossed a handful of the stuff at Nick's face, missing it by inches. It settled to the wet ground, turning gray in the puddles. "It's fucking baking soda."

"You had them the whole time, remember?"

"You switched the stuff before we buried them, right?"

"Jesus, Rob, that was thirty years ago—"

"Or when I came back to my apartment the other day and you were waiting for me. The whole thing's a setup, isn't it?"

They paused to let a cruiser take its sweet time drifting past them. Yet Nick remained calm. The news from Joanne had made his day. Not just his day but his week, his month—in fact, right now it was his whole justification for living. He and Jo were a perfect match. He almost wished she could have been in on this deal, and for a moment he flashed back to their wedding, and the little beads of sweat on her upper lip when he lifted the veil to kiss her. *I now pronounce you Bonnie and Clyde.*

"If anyone has a right to a grudge, I think I do," he told Rob. "I mean, you were the one who was going to walk with Leroy, remember? You begged him for a piece of it. Which would have cut me right out of it. Now can I at least have the baking soda? Might come in handy some rainy day. Cookies for the kids."

"Fuck you."

"I'm serious. I just want a souvenir. And I didn't exchange anything. We got burned by that guy in Pittsburgh, simple as that. We're not pros at this. We tried and failed, but it was a good idea. We had our little adventure. We were young, Rob. We thought we knew everything back then."

"Fuck you. Fuck you. Here's your shit."

"Rob, you can either keep pushing or walk away."

"Are you threatening me?"

"Yeah, I'm really scary," Nick said with a laugh. "It's over. No one got hurt. We're no richer than we were before, but at least we're alive. Do you understand? We're still *here*."

Rob tossed the bag to him and Nick laid it carefully in the back seat, covering it with Eric's Black Sabbath sweatshirt. He shut the door and the locks went clunk.

Rob's eyes grew big and his mouth fell slightly open. "What's going on?"

"Look—I've got a family. You just have you. Thanks for all your help. We're going to be fine now. And thanks for letting me know what you're really like. I really wasn't going to mention this to you, but now I just can't resist. Maybe it doesn't matter to you, but in my world loyalty counts for a hell of a lot more than money. Because when the money goes and no one's there to stick by you, the world looks pretty lousy, doesn't it?"

"You piece of shit," Rob said, his mouth twisted into a mocking smile. "You thought you were going to cheat me? That Haitian guy said this was crap. So you lose everything, too."

"Wrong," Nick said. "I still have my integrity."

He got in the car and started it up. He slid the window down, flashing Rob a two-fingered peace sign. "Keep the faith, baby."

But Rob could only summon a single finger, held up until Nick could no longer see it in his rearview mirror.

8

H E DROVE AROUND THE BLOCK A FEW TIMES AND PULLED
up to the front entrance of the Hyatt at just past seven,
three minutes later than expected. Standing under an umbrella,
an attaché case in his other hand, the man waiting there got
into Nick's car. Neither said anything until they were a few
blocks from the hotel. Nick parked the car in a loading zone and
turned to the Haitian. Seeing the silver dollar between Nick's
fingers, Jean-Pierre laughed. He said, "Ah, Meredith."

Nick caught a glance of his face in the glow of a lamp: the
man must have been nearly eighty, and yet his voice was rich
and strong and ripe as a tropical cocktail on a summer evening.

"Everything's arranged?" Nick asked.

"Oh, they're well on their way. At least for now, everyone's
too busy to pay any attention to that pair." He peered at his
watch. "I know Meredith will be pleased with you."

"And the stuff?"

"You really care?"

Nick considered it. He thought of Jen and of how she
had suddenly grown up, all in an afternoon. "I'm not so sure
anymore."

"Well. There was no need for me to test it for your friend.
It was quite clear to me what was in those jars of his. We used

to call it China Cat. Almost definitely from Afghanistan. The purest heroin available at the time you received it. Or now, for that matter. Ninety-six percent. Taken as it is, it would kill you. I haven't seen anything this good in a long time. I can cut this, distribute it, and by Sunday I can retire for the rest of my life *and* feed the population of my homeland for one year. You can thank my goddaughter for how this all turned out. It's only slightly difficult to trick a sober man. Much easier when the person is drunk with greed."

Nick unlatched his seat belt and turned. "Tell me one thing. Are you going to sell this on the streets?"

"Feeling moral all of a sudden, Mr. Copeland?"

"It comes with being a father, I guess."

"And if I were to sell it on the streets, as you put it?"

Nick considered it for a few moments. "I really hope you don't."

Jean-Pierre laughed. "Actually, it's for my usual customers. Wealthy ladies and gentlemen in Jamaica and the other islands. Retired people from here, from Britain, from France, with the habits they brought over with them and who find life tolerable only with a little help from their friend Mister Horse, courtesy of Père Noël. They're happy enough to pay top dollar, as well."

He placed his attaché case on his knees and unlatched it. "One hundred and sixty-five thousand. Heavily discounted, but still…it's a lot better than nothing, yes?" He opened it slightly and the shine off the packets of hundred-dollar bills caught Nick's eye. "Would you like to count it?"

Nick shook his head. "Meredith assured me that I could trust you."

"I have a flight to Port-au-Prince in three hours. This," he said, reaching back and taking Rob's bag, "has some distance to go. Now if you will drive me back to the hotel, I will transfer this to plastic bags, secrete them away in my luggage, and check out."

"You can get that through customs?"

Noël's smile shone in the darkness. "In Haiti *le chef des douanes* is a client of mine."

Just before he stepped out of the car, he turned to Nick and wagged a finger at him. "Take my advice. Don't be doing this again, all right?"

Jean-Pierre crossed the lobby, busy this time of night with people going out to dinner and a show, or returning from meetings. He caught an elevator just as the door was closing and rode it up to his floor. He turned and walked to the end, passing a couple heading out for the evening. He smiled at them, but they didn't seem to notice. Entering his room he felt sure he'd left the lights on when he went out, and so when he switched them back on the men waiting for him blinked a little. One of them, a big African-American man in a suit, displayed a silver shield between his fingers. The three other men, young and also black, held pistols straight out before them. Jean-Pierre gently placed the bag on the floor and brought his hands chest high.

"You," Driver said, a little weary from the long day, "have the right to remain silent…"

9

"**W**IFE KICK YOU OUT?"

Nick looked up at the waitress. Until a few minutes earlier there had been only one other customer there, a nurse on her way to her shift eating a bowl of oatmeal. It was quickly filling up with what were obviously regular customers. He smiled and shook his head.

"Guess you know you've been here most of the night."

"Are you closing?"

"Don't I wish," she said. She glanced up at the clock on the wall. "I can whip you up a little breakfast. Gotta have something to soak up all that coffee you've been drinking." She handed him a laminated menu decorated with little hand-drawn steaming cups of coffee and waffles with little arms and legs doing the shimmy down a dinner plate.

"That'd be very nice, Mrs. T."

She looked at him with slight alarm. "You know me?"

"I was here a few days ago with Meredith Ives—Meredith Hunter. She was a business associate of mine."

"And how is she doing?"

He smiled to himself. "I think she's doing amazingly well, actually."

"That girl deserves only the best," she said, readying her order pad.

He pointed to the number-two special on the menu. "Two eggs, lightly scrambled. Whole wheat toast, no butter."

"Hash browns?"

"Please. And some of that hot sauce you've got?"

"I'll toss in a few strips of bacon while I'm at it. You could probably use a little protein after sitting there like that. It takes a lot of effort to make up your mind about something, doesn't it?"

"You could tell, huh?"

"Me and just about everyone else in the world."

She started to walk away when he said, "You used to have a collection for that little boy. Next to the register?"

"You mean Terrell Ives? Merry's cousin?"

"I was just wondering."

"It got all filled up. Forty-two dollars and twenty-nine cents." She smiled.

"That's all?"

"We're not rich around here, you know. That poor woman and child. They got nothing after Sonny got himself killed. And all for what? He never could get himself any life insurance. Not with his health being what it was. Hepatitis C and all. Whole thing's a damn shame, if you ask me." She shrugged and went off to make his breakfast.

For most of the night—for as long as he'd been there—Dixie's had been relatively quiet. Cops coming off their beats walked in every few hours for coffee. Other locals stopped by, read the *Daily News*, or just stared into their coffee. At some point each of them eyeballed the white guy biding his time by the window, nursing a bottomless cup of coffee.

After leaving Jean-Pierre the night before, he'd headed back, reached Scarsdale, got off at his exit, and, pulling onto the shoulder, changed his mind. He was all of four minutes from home. A quick drive through town past Chez Félice, St. John's Episcopal, and the post office, and he was as good as there. A drink or two, maybe a sandwich, and early to bed. First thing in the morning he'd be at the bank, making a small deposit. The next day he'd make another at a competing bank. Then a week would go by and there'd be more, at other banks in other towns. No one would notice a thing. Everyone involved in this was a criminal: he, Rob, Leroy, even Father Christmas. The silence of complicity was a beautiful thing. And no one was left the victim. Except for a little boy and his mother in a fifth-floor Harlem apartment.

The money sat beside him in the attaché case. He was tempted to open it, just to sniff the ink rising off of it, the smell of freedom. Building on a spectacular résumé, he'd have the capital to set himself up as a consultant. He'd pay off his debts and work eight hours a day to start building a client base. And while he was at it he might even steal back an old account or two from Stevens Breakstone Leary.

He gave Joanne a quick call to say everything was all right and that he'd be in later, meaning first thing in the morning. "And I'm not sleeping with any other woman," he assured her.

"So what is it?"

"Just some unfinished business."

"Because we have an appointment with the principal at the high school at ten thirty, and at the middle school forty minutes later."

"Good. We'll have lunch together afterwards."

"But I have to go back to—"

"Forget it. Take the day off."

In truth, he would have liked the kids to succeed at Westchester Prep, to see them overcome their disappointments and, in Eric's case, sheer underachievement. But what was happening was something wickedly wonderful. Kathleen Warner knew he was an adman—retired, fired, let go or otherwise—and admen, as she certainly knew, especially *angry* admen, were a little too easy with words, a little too glib when the whiskey had flowed over the transom of their lower lips. This, he knew, was the revenge of the toker and acidhead. This was the goof to end all goofs. Because he wouldn't say a word about Kathleen or her school. He'd just make her sweat.

Rob was sprawled out on his bed, dressed only in a pair of boxers, his mouth slightly open, a pained look in his eyes, because at that moment he was dreaming about Janet. They were on a beach somewhere, and the waves, impossibly blue, came gently but urgently onto the sand. They rolled up, curled back, and the sand hissed each time like someone whispering forbidden words. Janet was between his legs, on her knees, her mouth forming a brilliant O when it wasn't curling into a smile at the edges. There was someone standing by the edge of the sea, his back to them, and Rob was hoping he wouldn't turn around. The pleasure was intense. The man on the beach turned his head and said, "Sorry, Rob, but—" and he woke up all in a rush, gasping for air, his body bathed in sweat. When he calmed down—when, sitting at the edge of his mattress, he had grasped his reality—he knew for certain he had nothing left to live for.

He found the gun on the table in the living room. He took it with him and lay back on the pillow. It was a scene out of a farce. Just as you couldn't stab yourself with a rubber knife you couldn't kill yourself with a blank pistol. And yet he knew that if he went through the motions, if he put the barrel into his mouth and pulled the trigger, something would fall away from him, this weight of disappointment that he seemed to have been carrying around for far too long. His career had dwindled to nothing, his marriage had been a disaster, the drug deal had ended up a travesty. Fate or luck or whatever one called it hadn't failed him; he'd failed himself. He was a fool, and the only recourse left for the fool was no longer to be a fool. He shut his eyes and pulled the trigger, and when the blank gun kicked as it fired, the two front teeth he'd had since he was a little boy snapped off and flew out of his mouth, leading to a month of reconstructive dentistry.

Meredith and Leroy hit a cold front a little south of Plattsburgh. Until then it had been the easiest thing in the world, a straight shoot up the Thruway, cloudy skies yet untroubled by raindrop or snowflake. When it did come, though, the flakes seemed as big as butterflies, as they sailed down and coated the road.

The snow held them up for only an hour or so. They'd been on the road all night, and now that dawn was breaking they could sense how close they were to the border. They had left autumn and driven into deep winter. Until then they had sat in the darkness, saying little, listening to whatever jazz they could find on distant radio stations. Now, as daylight united them, Billie Holiday was fading in and out with "They Can't Take That Away from Me."

She looked at him and smiled, and her smile was a reflection of his. "You like how she sings this, don't you?"

"Hm-mm."

"I bet you know who's playing on it, too."

"Ben Webster on tenor. Harry Edison on trumpet."

"How about the guitar?"

"Barney Kessel. All good people."

"Pops," she said, putting her hand on his. The last time they had done this she was just a toddler walking with her father down Lenox Avenue. Everyone on the street knew him. They smiled and nodded and said, "Hey, Leroy, what's cookin'?" and she was proud because everyone seemed to like him. Occasionally someone would call him Candy Man, and for years she thought it was because he always carried sweets in his pocket: rolls of Life Savers and sticks of chewing gum, all for her.

"You look like your mama, you know that?"

"Do I?"

"You don't remember, do you?" He looked away, out the window. "I loved her. I didn't want her to end up that way."

"But she did."

"Yes she did," he said.

"You crying, Pops?"

He slipped on his dark glasses and turned to look out the window. "What happens after?" he said.

"After we get to Montreal? I suppose to start with we find you a place to live."

"And how about you?"

"I'll be near enough to invite you to dinner now and again."

"Sticking around, huh?"

"I like to keep my options open."

Now the snow seemed to lessen. Lingering flakes continued to fall from a sky that was already breaking into sunlight at the edges. At first she didn't see the state police cruisers moving up fast in each lane, and the helicopter rising up behind them, all a mile or so back.

She glanced in the mirror. "Oh shit."

It was when he turned to see for himself that he realized he was still wearing his tracking bracelet. He almost had to laugh. "Damn. I should've thought of this before we left the city."

She groped around in her bag until she found a little Swiss Army knife attached to her keychain.

"Get rid of it. Cut it off. Right now!"

The cruisers were getting nearer, just as the copter was closing in. No one would know which car he was in. They could track but not discern. He sawed and cut at the thick plastic bracelet until it finally broke loose.

She looked at him. "What are you waiting for?"

He opened the window and sent it sailing down over the side of a bridge. She watched in the mirror as the cruisers and copter veered off the Thruway. Leroy, finally, had lost his shadow.

10

A FEW MINUTES LATER THAN USUAL, TERRELL LEFT FOR school, pushing the heavy door open with both hands, hefting his knapsack, and walking up the street, his head lowered, hoping not to be recognized once again as Sonny Ives's boy. He wavered between a kind of sad pride and crushing shame, as if kids who until a few weeks ago had only known him as the smallest kid on the block, or the clumsiest with a basketball, had now redefined him as the murdered man's son, as though his father's death had marked him in some indelible way for life, a dark and dismal future already plotted out for him. Although others were headed to school, unlike most he had no one to keep him company. A few oddjobs in sweatshirts and jackets stood in doorways, smoking cigarettes and mumbling to themselves from deep within their hoods. They watched each passerby for a sign of recognition or interest.

From a fifth-floor window Macey kept an eye on Terrell until he was gone. She hadn't yet noticed Nick sitting across the street in his car. At the end of the school day she would once again be there, he knew, making sure her son got home safely. Between home and school there were any number of dangers. For her, Nick thought, there was no middle way: either he'd be lost forever or somehow rise above it all, make something of himself. He got out of the Audi and went to the doorway. He ran his finger down the list of names. He pressed the button, and a second later a voice said, "Who is that?"

"It's Nick Copeland. We met at your—"

"What do you want?"

"Just want to talk to you for a moment, Mrs. Ives."

Nothing. She didn't buzz to let him in, and when he stepped back to look up at the window, she was gazing down at him, her arms crossed. One angry lady. And he didn't blame her. He put both hands over his heart, international sign either of sincerity or the deepest lie imaginable. The door buzzed until he reached it and pushed it open.

When he reached the fifth floor, her door was open and she was standing five feet back from it. "My mother's sick. I don't want her disturbed."

He opened his hands. "I promise she won't be."

She sized up his attitude for a moment more, then let him in. They ended up in the kitchen. The last time he had been there the room had been filled with those who wanted to remember Sonny and pay their respects to his family. The table had been covered with casseroles and plates stacked with cookies. Now there was just a half-finished cup of coffee and Terrell's breakfast dishes. A lone Rice Krispie floated in a thin puddle of milk. "You want coffee?" she said.

"I can't stay more than a few minutes."

"OK, then. Shoot."

He put the attaché case on the table. "This is for you. And Terrell. And your mother, if she needs it."

She stared at the case.

"Open it," he said.

"Uh-uh. *You* open it."

He unlatched it and lifted the cover.

"What is this, a joke? You rob a bank or something?" She looked again at the money, running a hand lightly over the top of the bills. "Jesus. This is serious."

"Yes it is."

"Are you crazy?"

"Not anymore."

She looked again. She picked up a packet and flipped through it, dropping it back in the case.

"I can't take this."

"You took the forty-two dollars from Dixie's."

"Forty-two twenty-nine. That's different. That's neighbors helping out in a time of need."

"This is me helping out. For the future. For your son."

When she sat down all the will seemed to run out of her. Her expression softened and when her eyes met his they were full of a kind of warmth.

"Where did you get it?"

He shrugged. "A business deal."

"Something about my Sonny, then?"

"No. This isn't about Sonny. It's not even about me. All I know is that Leroy would have wanted you to have this."

Now her look hardened once again. "Leroy?"

"And Meredith. Consider it a debt paid."

She tilted her head a little and crossed her arms tightly over her chest. "And you don't want any of it?"

He shook his head.

"Sure you're not crazy? Or on drugs or something?"

He laughed and reached out to touch her hand. "I just wanted to leave it with you. I know you'll put it to good use."

"And you don't care what I do with it? What is this, some kind of TV reality show or something?" She actually looked around for a hidden camera. "I mean, what am I supposed to say to people?"

"Nothing," he said. "Nothing at all."

"Why are you doing this for us? Don't you have a family of your own to look after?"

He smiled. "Don't worry about us. We're going to be just fine."

Twenty minutes later he was crossing the line into Westchester. It was funny. He felt not as if he'd given away his family's security and future, but had traded it for something. He wasn't sure exactly what it was, but he knew something was waiting for him in return. It was still early and traffic was light as it followed the twists and curves of the parkway: a few Connecticut plates heading north; one or two from Maine and New Hampshire; another from Maryland, chugging along and spewing black smoke from its exhaust. The snow and rain from the night before had given way to the impossible kind of clear, cold day that belonged in a television commercial selling satisfaction, recovery, peace of mind, and abundant happiness. The first frost of the season had left everything in suspension.

The fact that he'd had no sleep the night before seemed to have made little difference. He was just alert enough to go home, shower, shave, change his clothes, and go with Joanne to see Eric's and Jen's new schools. He slid open the sunroof and switched on the radio and found some music on an oldies station, a Dylan song made famous by the Band way back when he was in college and life, because he hadn't yet really lived, was still full of wonder and possibility. Until now, he'd never paid much attention to these words filled with awareness and longing. But now they made sense. Painful, wonderful sense.

The sky above him was blue and cloudless, the sunlight in its autumnal brilliance spreading the last of its warmth before winter truly arrived. All he wanted now was to go home, to say the words, to see the faces. Soon, and not a moment too late, just around the bend of the road, his trip would be over.

About the Author

J. P. Smith was born in New York City and began his writing career in London, where he lived for several years and where his first novel, *The Man from Marseille*, was published. His five previously-published novels are being brought back into print by Thomas & Mercer. He currently lives on the North Shore of Massachusetts.

SMITH   HBRAW

Smith, J. P.,
Airtight /

BRACEWELL
03/13